Bel-Air, CA

CHARLES WANG was mad at America.

Actually, Charles Wang was mad at history.

If the death-bent Japanese had never invaded China, if a million — a billion — misguided students and serfs had never idolized a balding academic who parroted Russian madmen and couldn't pay for his promises, then Charles wouldn't be standing here, staring out the window of his beloved Bel-Air home, holding an aspirin in his hand, waiting for those calculating assholes from the bank — the bank that had once gotten down on its Italianate-marble knees and kissed his ass — to come over and repossess his life.

Without history, he wouldn't be here at all.

He'd be *there,* living out his unseen birthright on his family's ancestral acres, a pampered prince in silk robes, writing naughty, brilliant poems, teasing servant girls, collecting tithes from his peasants, and making them thankful by leaving their tattered households with just enough grain to squeeze out more hungry babies.

Instead, the world that should have been his fell apart, and the great belly of Asia tumbled and roiled with a noxious foreign indigestion that spewed him out, bouncing him, hard, on the tropical joke of Taiwan and then, when he popped right back up, belching him all the way across the vast Pacific Ocean and smearing him onto *this,* this faceless green country full of grasping newcomers, right alongside his unclaimed countrymen: the poor, illiterate, ball-scratching half men from Canton and

Fujian, whose highest dreams were a cook's apron and a back-alley, back-door fuck.

Oh, he shouldn't have been vulgar.

Charles Wang shouldn't even know about the things that happen on dirt-packed floors and under stained sheets. Centuries of illustrious ancestors, scholars and statesmen and gentlemen farmers all, had bred him for fragrant teas unfurling in fresh springwater, for calligraphy brushes of white wolf hair dipped in black deer-glue ink, for lighthearted games of chance played among true friends.

Not this. No, not this. Not for him bastardized Peking duck eaten next to a tableful of wannabe rappers and their short, chubby, colored-contact-wearing Filipino girlfriends at Mr. Chow. Not for him shoulder-to-shoulder art openings where he sweated through the collar of his paper-thin cashmere sweater and stared at some sawed-in-half animal floating in formaldehyde whose guts didn't even have the courtesy to leak; not for him white women who wore silver chopsticks in their hair and smiled at him for approval. Nothing, nothing in his long lineage had prepared him for the Western worship of the Dalai Lama and pop stars wearing jade prayer beads and everyone drinking goddamn boba chai.

He shouldn't be here at all. Never should have set a single unbound foot on the New World. There was no arguing it. History had started fucking Charles Wang, and America had finished the job.

America was the worst part of it because America, that fickle bitch, used to love Charles Wang.

She had given him this house, a beautiful Georgian estate once owned by a minor MGM starlet married to a studio lawyer who made his real money running guns for Mickey Cohen. At least that's what Charles told his guests whenever he toured them around the place, pointing out the hidden crawl space in the wine cellar and the bullet hole in the living room's diamond-pane window. "Italians don't have nothing on gangster Jews!" he'd say, stroking the mezuzah that he'd left up on the doorway. "No hell in the Old Testament!"

Then he'd lead his guests outside, down the symmetrical rows of topiaries, and along the neat swirls of Madame Louis Lévêque roses until he

could arrange the group in front of a bowing lawn jockey whose grinning black face had been tactfully painted over in a shiny pink. He'd gesture towards it, one eyebrow arched, as he told them that the man who designed this, this house destined to become the Wang family estate, had been Paul Williams, the first black architect in the city. The guy had built Frank Sinatra's house, he'd built that ridiculous restaurant at LAX that looked like it came straight out of *The Jetsons* — stars and spaceships, and a castle for Charles Wang.

Martha Stewart had kvelled over this house. She'd called it a treasure and laid a pale, capable hand on the sleeve of Charles Wang's navy summer-silk blazer with the burnished brass buttons, a blazer made by his tailor who kept a suite at the Peninsula Hong Kong and whose name was also Wang, though, thank god, no relation. Martha Stewart had clutched his jacket sleeve and looked at him with such sincerity in her eyes as she'd gushed, "It's so *important*, Charles, so *essential*, that we keep the spirit of these houses whole."

It was America, really, that had given him his three children, infinitely lovable even though they'd never learned to speak an unaccented word of Mandarin and lived under their own roofs, denying him even the bare dignity of being the head of a full house. His first wife had played some part in it, but *he* was the one who had journeyed to America and claimed her, *he* was the one who had fallen to his knees at the revelation of each pregnancy, the one who had crouched by the hospital bed urging on the birth of each perfect child who walked out into the world like a warrior.

Yes, America had loved him once. She'd given him the balls to turn his father's grim little factory, a three-smokestack affair on the outskirts of Taipei that supplied urea to fertilizer manufacturers, into a cosmetics empire. Urea. His father dealt in piss! Not even real honest piss — artificial piss. Faux pee. A nitrogen-carrying ammonia substitute that could be made out of inert materials and given a public relations scrubbing and named carbamide, but that was really nothing more than the thing that made piss less terribly pissy.

The knowledge that his father, his tall, proud father with his slight scholar's squint and firmly buttoned quilted vests, had gone from quietly

presiding over acres of fertile Chinese farmland to operating a piss plant on the island of Taiwan — well, it was an indignity so large that no one could ever mention it.

Charles's father had wanted him to stay at National Taiwan University and become a statesman in the New Taiwan, a young man in a Western suit who would carry out Sun Yat Sen's legacy, but Charles dropped out because he thought he could earn his family's old life back. An army of well-wishers — none of whom he'd ever see again — had packed him onto a plane with two good-luck scrolls, a crushed orchid lei, and a list of American fertilizer manufacturers who might be in need of cheap urea.

Charles had spent half the flight locked in the onboard toilet heaving up a farewell banquet of bird's-nest soup and fatty pork stewed in a writhing mass of sea cucumber. When he couldn't stomach looking at his own colorless face for another second, he picked up a miniature bar of wax-paper-wrapped soap and read the label, practicing his English. It was a pretty little package, lily scented and printed with purple flowers. "Moisturizing," promised the front; "Skin so soft, it has to be Glow." And on the back, there was a crowded list of ingredients that surprised Charles. This was before anything in Taiwan had to be labeled, before there was any sort of unbribable municipal health department that monitored claims that a package of dried dates contained anything more than, say, "The freshest dates dried in the healthy golden sun."

Charles stood there, heaving, weaving forward and back on his polished custom-made shoes, staring cross-eyed at the bar of soap, trying to make out the tiny type. Sweet almond oil, sodium stearate, simmondsia chinensis, hydrolyzed wheat proteins, and then he saw it: UREA. Hydroxyethyl urea, right between shea butter and sodium cocoyl isethionate.

Urea!

Urea on a pretty little American package!

Charles stood up straight, splashed cold water on his face, and strode back to his seat, the miniature soap tucked in his palm. He pulled his gray

checked suit jacket down from the overhead bin, took out the list of fertilizer manufacturers, and tucked it into the seat pocket right behind the crinkly airsick bag. When Charles walked off the plane, the scrolls and the pungent lei also stayed behind. He stuck the soap in his shirt pocket, slung his jacket over his shoulder, and swallowed the last trace of bile. Charles Wang was going to come out of America smelling sweet. He was sure of it. "Shit into Shinola," he said to himself aloud, repeating one of his favorite American movie phrases.

And he'd done it.

Turned shit into two hundred million dollars' worth of Shinola. Made himself into a cosmetics king with eight factories in Los Angeles, factories that he'd gone from supplying with urea to owning outright — each one turning out a glossy rainbow-scented sea of creams and powders and lipsticks and mascaras.

In the beginning, he'd operated all eight of them separately, sending the clients of one into the disguised folds of another any time they complained about his steadily rising prices. They'd get hooked in again —"Special offer! Just for you my prices go so low!"— and find their invoices once again mysteriously padded, just a little bit, just enough to be uncomfortable. Later, as it became clear that women were willing to pay twenty, twenty-five, thirty dollars for a tube of lipstick, that sort of subterfuge became unnecessary, and there was no end to the number of hotel chains that wanted to brand their shampoos and makeup artists ready to launch their own lines.

One of them, a tiny Japanese girl who stared out at the world through anime eyes, came to him with empty pockets and a list of celebrity clients. He'd fronted her the first set of orders for KoKo, a collection of violently hued shadows that came in round white compacts with her face, framed by its perfect bob cut, embossed on the front, the fuchsia and monarch yellow and electric blue powders glaring out through two translucent holes cut through her printed irises. The line was an immediate smash hit, going from runways and editorial layouts straight to department store makeup counters and into the damp suede reaches of a million teenage purses. And Charles, somehow, got credit for being a visionary, a risk taker, an integral part of a new generation of business talents who

made their millions on mass customization, on glamorizing the role of the middleman, on merchandising someone else's talent.

Yes, America had loved him. America was honest enough with him to include chemical piss in a list of pretty ingredients; America saw that the beautiful was made up of the grotesque.

Makeup was American, and Charles understood makeup. It was artifice, and it was honesty. It was science and it was psychology and it was fashion; but more than that, it was about feeling *wealthy*. Not money — wealth. The endless possibility of it and the cozy sureness of it. The brilliant Aegean blues and slick wet reds and luscious blacks, the weighty packaging, with its satisfying smooth hinges and sound closures.

Artifice, thought Charles, *was the real honesty.* Confessing your desire to change, being willing to strive, those were things that made sense. The real fakers were the ones who denied those true impulses. The cat-loving academic who let her hair frizz and made no attempt to cover her acne scars was the most insidious kind of liar, putting on a false face of unconcern when in her heart of hearts she must, *must* want to be beautiful. Everyone must want to be beautiful. The fat girl who didn't even bother to pluck her caterpillar eyebrows? If life were a fairy tale, her upturned nose would grow as long as her unchecked middle was wide. And for a time, a long and lucrative time, the good people of America had agreed.

By the turn of the millennium, he was rich already. Rich enough, probably, to buy back all the land in China that had been lost, the land that his father had died without ever touching again. Never mind that the Communists would never have allowed it to be privately owned. The simple fact that he could afford it was enough. He wouldn't even have done anything with those fallow acres, just slipped the deed in his pocket, received the bows of his peasants, and directed his driver towards Suzhou, where the women were supposed to be so beautiful it didn't matter that they were also bold and disobedient.

But really, Charles Wang was having too much fun in America to dwell on the China that might have been his.

Just four years ago he'd had the hull of his sexy little cigarette speedboat painted with twenty-seven gallons of Suicide Blonde, his best-sell-

ing nail polish color — a perfect blue-toned red that set off the mahogany trim and bright white leather seats. As soon as the paint dried, the boat ripped from Marina del Rey to Costa Careyes with a delectable payload of models for an ad campaign shoot, four morning-to-midnight days that Charles remembered mostly as a parade of young flesh in a range of browns and pinks interrupted only by irrelevant slashes of bright neoprene.

Now the boat was gone. Some small-hearted official with a clipboard and a grudge had probably plastered notices on the entrance to his slip or routed some ugly tugboat into the dock and dragged his poor *Dragon Lady* away — how Charles had laughed when the registrar at the marina asked if he knew that term was racist — leaving her to shiver in a frigid warehouse.

He never should have fallen for America.

As soon as the happy-clappy guitar-playing Christian missionary who taught him English wrote down Charles's last name and spelled it W-A-N-G, he should have known.

He should have stayed leagues away from any country that could perpetrate such an injustice, that could spread this glottal miscegenation of a language, with its sloppy vowels and insidious *R*s, across the globe.

In Chinese, in any Chinese speaker's mouth, Wang was a family name to be proud of. It meant *king,* with a written character that was simple and strong. And it was pronounced with a languid drawn-out diphthong of an *o* sound that suggested an easy life of summer palaces and fishing for sweet river shrimp off gilded barges. But one move to America and Charles Wang's proud surname became a nasally joke of a word; one move and he went from *king* to *cock.*

No boat. No car. No house. No factories. No models. No lipstick. No KoKo. No country. No kingdom. No past. No prospects. No respect. No land. No land. No land.

Now, now that he had lost the estate in America, all Charles could think of was the land in China.

The life that should have been his.

China, where the Wangs truly belonged.

Not America. Never Taiwan.

If they were in China, his ungrateful children would not be spread out across a continent. If they were in China, his disappointed wife would respond to his every word with nothing but adoration. Angry again, Charles turned away from the window and back to his bare desk. Almost bare. In the center, dwarfed by the expanse of mahogany, was a heavy chop fashioned from a square block of prized mutton-fat jade.

Most chops underlined their authority with excess, an entire flowery honorific crowded on the carved base, but this one, once his grandfather's, had a single character slashed into its bottom.

王

Just the family name. Wang.

Over a century ago, when the seal was first made, its underside had started out a creamy white. Now it was stained red from cinnabar paste. His grandfather had used the chop in lieu of a signature on any documents he'd needed to approve, including the land deeds that were once testament to the steady expansion of Wang family holdings. Charles was thankful that his grandfather had died before all the land was lost, before China lost herself entirely to propaganda and lies. The men of the Wang family did not always live long lives, but they lived big.

The land that had anchored the Wangs and exalted them, the land that had given them a place and a purpose, that was gone. But Charles still had the seal and the deeds, everything that proved that the land was rightfully his.

And in a few fevered hours of searching the Internet, he'd uncovered stories, vague stories, of local councils far from central Party circles returning control to former owners, of descendants who, after years in reeducation camps, managed to move back into abandoned family houses that had been left to rot, entire wings taken over by wild pigs because peasants persuaded to deny their history could never appreciate the poetry and grandeur of those homes. He stored each hopeful tale away in a secret chamber of his heart, hoarding them, as he formed a plan. He would make sure that his three children were safe, that his fearsome and beloved second wife was taken care of, that his family was all under one

roof, and then, finally, Charles Wang was going to reclaim the land in China.

He popped an aspirin in his mouth, pushing back that new old feeling of a tunnel, a dark and almost inevitable tunnel, closing in on him, and crunched down on the pill as he picked up the phone.

Helios, NY

SAINA WANG smoothed out the tabloid-size *Catskills Chronicler* and paged past the op-ed column, skipping the list of new high school seniors, glancing over the photos of the mayor's Labor Day barbecue and the Pet of the Week, in search of the horoscopes. Usually she read the *New York Times* — made herself read it, a reminder of the life she could be, maybe should be, living — but that paper would never carry anything as frivolous and as *useful* as horoscopes.

There. There they were. Squeezed onto the recipe page under a photo of creamed corn succotash with crisped prosciutto.

Libra (Sept. 23–Oct. 22)
You resonate with things and people you love. The more you let yourself love, the better you feel. The better you feel, the healthier you become. Love is a healer, and so are you.

It was exactly what she'd always feared was true.

From the time Saina was very young, she worried that she would always be the lover and never the loved.

And then she grew up and it got more complicated. Now she thought that she would always be the salve to some artist's eternally wounded soul — an unwilling goddess to be worshipped and adored, but never, ever worried over or taken care of. No one thinks to make the goddess a cup of tea; they just ply her with useless perfumed oils and impotent carved fetishes.

Giant canvases that glorified her naked breasts and half smile, songs rhyming *Saina* and *wanna,* unfinished novels about an unknowable girl of dreams — none of that (and she'd had all of it) was as romantic as a boyfriend who would notice that the lightbulb in her hallway had blown out and change it without even bothering to mention the favor.

Sometimes, when you're in love with an artist, it can be hard to see that it's not about you at all. You get lost in the attention, the deep, soulful gazes and the probing regard. And then, gradually, you come to realize that you're not so much a woman as you are a statue. A statue on a pedestal that he chiseled and posed, a foreshortened figure that he sees only through a single squinted eye. When you're in love with an artist, you're no longer *you,* exactly, but a loving and generous Everywoman who will weave your life into a crafty plinth for his work.

And it doesn't even matter if you're an artist, too. You could have a whole room — a small one, but a whole room nonetheless — at the Whitney Biennial. Your gallery in Berlin could be paranoid enough about your potential defection to a rival that you'd have to fake an eccentric demand for weekly shipments of special-order, octopus-shaped Haribo gummies just so they'd stop asking you what they could do to make you happy; your dealer in New York could be fending off a waiting list filled with scores of discerning millionaires and you could be a permanent fixture on both the *Artforum* party pages *and* NewYorkSocialDiary.com, but your beautiful boyfriend with his perpetually dirty fingernails could still be so obsessed with the politics of his own creation that he would take all of that in with an absentminded kiss and ask you again and then again and then a fifteenth time if you heard the difference between nearly identical sound loops on the track accompanying his latest installation.

And then he could leave you. After making you his art object, making your love for him his symbol and subject, after presenting you with a heavy, hand-hammered gold band set on the inside with an uncut black diamond so that only the lump of it, sheathed in gold, could be seen when you wore it — a ring that got its own miniprofile in *Vogue* — after all that, he could still make your life into a Page Six blind item by leaving you for a jewelry-designing mattress heiress named Sabrina, with unattrac-

tive knees and a maddening sheaf of corn-silk hair. And yes, yes, it could be the same jewelry-designing mattress heiress who made your gorgeous, heartbreaking, stupid, human rights disaster of a ring.

None of it surprised Saina anymore. She was twenty-eight and she had turned unshockable. So when the phone rang and she picked it up and found her father in tears, her heart stayed put.

"It is over," choked her father, coughing to cover the angry wobble in his voice.

"What's over?" she asked.

"Our whole life."

Saina looked around the room. *My life was already over,* she thought. She was washed up, tossed out, ruined and ridiculed and exiled from the magic island of Manhattan. What could be more over than that?

"Baba, don't be so dramatic. What's going on?"

"We are leaving."

"What do you mean?"

"It is over. I lost it. Oh Jiejie, I lost it."

"What?" asked Saina, her heart now quickening. "What did you lose? Tell me. You have to tell me. You can't just not talk about it like . . . like everything."

Saina's father's words came out in a rush, the breaking of a giant dam.

"All. Baba lost all. *Wan le.* You understand what that mean? Everything over."

"The stores. You just mean the stores, right? That's what you lost? We talked about that already." Was he starting to forget things? He was too young for Alzheimer's.

"Everything."

"Everything?"

"Everything. Now we come to New York."

Her father's English sounded more broken than usual. Not that he'd ever bothered to perfect it in the first place — the rules of grammar were beneath him, bylaws for a silly club that he had no intention of joining. Why should he spend any energy on English, he'd explained once, when soon the whole world would be speaking Chinese? Now, though, he sounded like a sweet-'n'-sour-chicken delivery boy who'd missed out on

America and instead taken up residence in a new country called Chinatown.

"What do you mean you're coming to New York?"

"We have no home, Jiejie. We come live with you now."

"The house? But why was that tied up with everything else? I just . . . Baba, I don't understand. How could there be nothing left? What about your savings? What about your other clients?"

There was a long, humid silence. Finally, he spoke again. "Daddy make a mistake. I think that if I can just hold on for long enough, then everything is okay again. So I just throw it all in, like throwing in a hole."

"Oh. Daddy. I'm sorry."

"No point in sorry now."

"Okay." What should she do? What could she do?

"How long it take to drive across country? Maybe eight day? Ten day?" He sounded small. Wounded.

Saina looked around her house, panic creeping in. It wasn't even a house, really. Not in any way that her father would understand or approve of. Not a Bel-Air Georgian or a rehabbed modernist gem — not even a downtown New York loft. It was a Catskills farmhouse three generations away from any kind of respectability perched on the edge of a town abandoned by Lubavitchers and just beginning to be occupied by weekending gay couples and Third Wave farmers carrying blue-eyed babies in batik slings.

When Saina sold her New York apartment out from under her cheating boyfriend, all she could think of was retreat. Their entire bright white loft had been arranged around a slightly hysterical pair of Biedermeier chairs that they bought at an auction back when he still thought it was important to suggest that his family had as much ready cash as hers. The pair, scallop edged and velvet upholstered, held court in front of a twenty-two-foot-high blank wall that backdropped his confession about Sabrina. Lovely, pregnant Sabrina. He'd whispered it to Saina, *whispered* it, and then tiptoed out the door like a thief.

Her first thought was that she'd always hated those chairs. Her second thought was that all the letters of her name were contained in Sabrina's, as if Sabrina encompassed everything that she herself was and then, in all her goldness, offered up even more.

Saina couldn't do anything to Sabrina and her maybe baby, so she'd gotten rid of the chairs instead. Just picked them up and placed them on the curb, where they'd at least have the chance to become part of someone else's good-luck story. Soon, though, she couldn't even stand looking at the empty wall where they once were; she started to wish them back, to wish him back. It hadn't been enough to cast out the only piece of furniture they'd ever bought together, she had to strike the entire set on which they'd acted out their lives. So Saina had sold the whole damn thing and now here she was, manufacturing domestic bliss all by herself. Except. Well, except.

"Baba, really? All of you? What about Meimei *gen* Didi?"

"Daddy will go pick them up."

"You're going to make them drop out of school? You can't do that!"

"What are they learning in those schools anyway? Arizona State. Not even a school — party school only. And Gracie, she can go to high school in your town. They have high school there?"

"But what about their tuitions? They should be okay for at least the semester, right?"

He was quiet.

Saina had a terrible thought. "Is everyone's money lost?"

"Not you," said her father. "You are old enough to be separate."

At least there was that. But with it came an unexpected sensation: Responsibility. Saina's instinct was to abdicate it.

"I'll give the money all to you! It's not mine anyways, it's yours, you made it! Take it and buy another house."

Her father laughed.

"You old enough to be separate, but it is all Wang *jia de* already. All of ours. Family, Jiejie."

Saina pictured her father, near dead from a million tiny cuts, oozing a glistening mercury blood. She didn't want them to come, but there was no question as to whether or not she would receive them, find space for their things, buy enough food for five, and put fresh flowers in all the guest bathrooms. There were four bedrooms in this house. Exactly enough for her father, her stepmother, her brother, her sister, and herself. As if she had always known that it would be a refuge for the entire Wang family.

P9-BBO-697

The Wangs vs. the World

The future has an ancient heart.

— CARLO LEVI

To get rich is glorious.

— DENG XIAO PING

For the Changs (all three of them)!

For information about permission to reproduce selections from this
book, write to trade.permissions@hmhco.com or to Permissions,
Houghton Mifflin Harcourt Publishing Company,
3 Park Avenue, 19th Floor, New York, New York 10016.

www.hmhco.com

Library of Congress Cataloging-in-Publication Data
Names: Chang, Jade, date, author.
Title: The Wangs vs. the world / Jade Chang
Description: Boston : Houghton Mifflin Harcourt, 2016.
Identifiers: LCCN 20160055160 (print) | LCCN 2016014904 (ebook) | ISBN
9780544734098 (hardback) | ISBN 9780544734203 (ebook)
Subjects: LCSH: Chinese American families — Fiction. | Immigrant
families — Fiction. | BISAC: FICTION / Literary. | FICTION / General. |
FICTION / Family Life. | FICTION / Humorous. | FICTION / Coming of Age. |
GSAFD: Humorous fiction.
Classification: LCC PS3603.H357284 W36 2016 (print) | LCC PS3603.H357284
(ebook) | DDC 813/.6 — dc23
LC record available at http://lccn.loc.gov/2016005160

Book design by Chrissy Kurpeski
Typeset in Garamond Premier Pro

Printed in the United States of America
DOC 10 9 8 7 6 5 4 3 2 1

The Wangs vs. the World

JADE CHANG

Houghton Mifflin Harcourt

BOSTON   NEW YORK

2016

The Wangs vs. the World

≡

Santa Barbara, CA

"*SERIOUSLY*, DAD?"

"You can't talk to Baba that way, Grace."

"But they're kicking me out of school!" she hissed into the phone, embarrassed. "I *told* you you should have gotten me a car!"

"Gracie, we coming to pick you up tonight, okay?"

"Who's *we?*"

"With your *ah yi*."

"Oh her. Okay. But what happened? Dad, I'm being kicked out of school! It's like they think I'm a criminal or something."

"Grace, we certainly don't think you're a criminal," said Brownie, the headmistress, who wasn't even pretending not to eavesdrop. "In fact, I told your father that we would likely be able to work something out. Perhaps —"

"You are *not* going to make me work in the cafeteria," said Grace, horrified. "There's no way. I'd rather go to public school, Dad. Daddy!" Grace could swear that she heard her father crying on the other end of the line, but she didn't want to say anything in case it turned out to be true.

"Okay, *xiao* Meimei, don't worry, okay? It's okay. We come pick you up and then we go get Andrew, and then we go to Jiejie *jia*."

"Dad. Baba." Grace felt very reasonable now; she could see that she was going to have to be the adult here. "What are you talking about? I am not driving cross-country with you guys. Who goes on a cross-country family trip? Anyways, I have to take my SATs. I'll just stay at home, okay?"

Ugh. The headmistress would *not* stop looking at her. The last time

Grace had been in this office was two semesters ago when her art teacher had narced on her. The art teacher, who made all the students call her Julie. It was embarrassing when adults tried to act like *people*.

The problem hadn't been the dwindling supply of muscle relaxers hidden in the lining of her Louis Vuitton change purse or the bottle of Belvedere stashed under her rainbow of cashmere sweaters. No, the bitchy art teacher, who was so *nineties* with her ugly dark lipstick and riot grrrl bumper stickers, had walked into the computer lab and caught Grace uploading a photo of herself. She'd been in one of her best morning outfits ever: black lace Wolford tights, navy blue school uniform skirt (hemmed way up), Saina's beat-up old cowboy boots, a new Surface to Air buttondown topped with one of her dad's old paisley Hermès bow ties from the eighties, a pair of thick tortoiseshell glasses with fake lenses — which no one had to know about — and, holding together her deliberately messy hair, a bright yellow silk sash tied in a knot. *So* much cooler than that poseur VainJane.com's outfits — Jane lived in *Florida*. How could anything really stylish ever happen there? How did every single outfit of Jane's get so many comments, anyway? That girl thought that Louboutins were enough to make any outfit — so *boring*. Grace couldn't understand it.

Anyway, Grace was sure that this outfit would be a hit, and she was about to post it to her blog, already anticipating the responses from her followers, when Julie had crept right up behind her, trying to be quiet. The teacher wasn't even smart enough to realize that you couldn't sneak up on someone who was using one of those computers because they'd be able to see the reflection of your stupid face on the screen.

As she'd reached out to tap Grace with one burgundy polished nail, Grace had turned and smiled.

And that was what she'd gotten a demerit for: Insubordination.

The ethics committee had decided that Grace's blog was fashion focused and not about "exploiting herself and undermining her power as a young woman" — in other words, not about sex — but that she'd shown an unwillingness to accept guidance. It was a totally ridiculous thing to get in trouble for, but whatever. It didn't matter anymore.

"Gracie, you pack your things up — but just the important things, okay? We be there in a few hours," said her father

The headmistress cut in. "Grace, if you'd like someone to help you clear out your room, just ask. You shouldn't be afraid to ask for help, alright, darling?"

Grace pressed the off button on her cell.

"Don't call me *darling*," she said. At least no one could give her demerits anymore. *Ugh*.

Sometimes she hated talking to her father. Was it possible to love someone and hate them at the same time? Or to love someone even if you didn't actually like them? If her mother were alive, things would be different. Everyone she knew got along with their mothers and hated their fathers, but she didn't have the luxury of a spare parent.

"So . . . we're poor now."

Grace's roommate stared at her.

"It's true, Rachel. We don't have any money left. Nothing. I have to drop out of school, and my dad and stepmom are coming to pick me up, and we have to drive all the way to my sister's house in some weird little country town in New York. Drive! I don't know if we even have any stuff left. Don't they take all of that when you're bankrupt?"

"You're bankrupt? Like, completely?"

"Well, my dad said he was, so I guess that means that I am, too."

"Um, are you okay?"

"Do I *seem* okay?"

"I guess so . . . I mean, no one's dead, right?"

"Except for my *house*. I was practically born in that house, and I didn't even get to live there for long—I had to come live *here*. And now I'll never even *see* it again."

Rachel had heard about Grace's family's house even though she'd never once been invited over for break. There were secret passageways, and modern art, and once Johnny Delahari had taken a weird combo of E and H (everyone at school called it the Canadian Special, but no one else was crazy enough to actually do it) and passed out in Grace's stepmother's walk-in closet for hours with a silk camisole wrapped around his face.

"It smelled like lady pussy," he'd told Rachel.

"But you said it was a camisole," she'd said. "That's like a tank top."

"Okay, it smelled like lady *boobs*," he'd replied, grinning, and then tried to reach up her shirt.

Now she wished that she had let him, because with Grace gone, he'd probably never come around to her room again.

Grace wheeled a desk chair over to the closet and balanced on it, pulling her luggage down from the top shelf. She jumped off the chair, launching it backwards towards Rachel, who stopped it with her purple ballet flat.

"Maybe you'll get to have your own room," said Grace.

"I think your roommate has to kill herself before they let you room alone."

"Do you think it counts if it happens after they transfer?"

"Shut up, Grace. You're not going to kill yourself."

"You never know," said Grace, pulling all her jeans off their hangers. Maybe they'd all commit suicide together. Or maybe her dad would drive them off a cliff. God, maybe she should just leave everything. If they were going to be poor, or dead, what was the point of having the same exact deconstructed rabbit-fur vest that Kate Moss was wearing in last month's *Elle*? On the other hand, maybe being poor could be kind of glamorous, with holey old T-shirts and guys who had to work as bartenders and whole meals of just french fries, in which case, maybe it would also be kind of glamorous to have her clothes. She'd be like a Romanov or something, deposed and in hiding from all the worlds that mattered.

Her father had said, "Just the important things." What was that supposed to mean? Grace looked at the pile of denim on the floor, then kicked it towards Rachel.

"Here," she said. "Take it. I'm sick of them all anyways."

"Seriously?"

Grace didn't answer, just kicked the pile again as she turned to pull down the cork bulletin board, layered with clippings, over her desk. She laid it across her bed and started picking out the tacks, cupping them in her left hand. As she worked, she thought about Parents' Weekend last year, when she'd walked up to their room and seen Rachel lying on the bed, her head in her mother's lap. The door to their room had been ajar, and Grace had stood there for a long moment, watching as Rachel's mother smoothed her daughter's hair away from her face and gazed down at her, half smiling, full of love. She'd never felt jealous of Rachel for even a second until that day.

"Are you really bringing everything on that board? All those pictures and things?" asked Rachel.

"Of course."

"Isn't it kind of . . . kind of *morbid?*"

"What's morbid about it?"

"Well, they're all pictures of dead people."

"People die. Deal with it."

"Yeah, people die, but that doesn't mean that you have to plaster them all over our walls."

"They're your walls now, aren't they."

"I'm just saying, I know why you put them up and I think it's creepy. You can give up pretending that's not the reason." Rachel took everything so seriously. That's what happened when you were a total drama nerd.

"Why don't *you* give it up, Rachel? Rachie Pie? Oh wait, I forgot. You're saving yourself for, like, Andrew Lloyd Webber or something. You're too good to just have s-e-x."

"That's not what this is about! Why does everything have to be about sex with you?"

"I thought that everything was about death with me."

They faced off for a moment, then Rachel spoke. "I'm . . . I'm sorry for you. Do you need anything? Is there anything I can do? Like, do you want to borrow some money or something? Or, um, we could . . . steal you some food from the cafeteria? That you could take with you?"

Grace stared at her roommate, who was kneeling on the ground, greedily feeling up a pair of her jeans. She could kick Rachel in the face right now and never even have to deal with it. A satisfying crunch in her annoying, curly-haired face. She'd aim straight at the zits that always piled onto Rachel's forehead, a bubbly constellation of them, and Rachel's head would snap back and she'd have to shut up and Grace wouldn't even get in trouble. Or maybe she'd have to go to jail, but what would it matter?

She turned back to the board.

"Isabella Blow," said Grace, untacking a photograph of a thin woman quivering in profile, a crazy confection of a hat perched on her dark chignon.

"Elliot Smith." She untacked another torn-out photograph, the singer's Frankenstein face staring straight at the camera, pockmarks unretouched, holding his fist over his heart.

"Theresa Duncan and Jeremy Blake." Two photo-booth shots side by side, the woman with half-moon eyes and the man with his sweet, sad mouth, both raising their chins and looking down their noses like rebel bank robbers.

She looked at Rachel again. "They're all brilliant."

Rachel walked over to the board bowlegged, struggling to button up a pair of Grace's jeans. "The cover of *The Bell Jar*. Kurt Cobain and Courtney Love on *Sassy*. And this? *Teenage Couple on Hudson Street, N.Y.C. 1963*," she said, tearing the Diane Arbus photograph off of its tack and reading the caption. "Dead, dead, dead. How? Oh yeah, that's right, suicide, suicide, suicide."

Grace shrugged. "God, Rachel, you're boring."

Grace reached over and plucked a faded pair of jeans out of the pile — they were '70s-style and high waisted, with a rope of braided denim looped through the belt holes. "You can't have these."

Grace pulled them on, along with an old T-shirt that she'd cut into a tank top and shoved her feet into a pair of lace-up prairie boots with just a little bit of a heel. And the vest. Her rabbit-fur vest.

Grace was raised to know that appearances mattered. If you put your Xanax in a Tylenol PM bottle, no one would care if you took four of them, and no one would judge you if, a little bit later on, you fell asleep with your head on your boyfriend's shoulder after just two vodka Red Bulls. Not that she'd ever commit suicide like that.

Pills were a coward's way out. You weren't really *doing* anything; there was nothing *decisive* about them; one call from a dorm monitor and you'd be halfway to the hospital with a tube down your throat, getting your stomach pumped out.

Slitting your wrists was a good method, along the vein instead of across it, the steely knife following the blue-purple terrain of your upturned arm. If Grace slit her wrists, she'd use a long, thin blade, freshly sharpened, and trace a delicate V on her left wrist — but that would only work at home because there were no bathtubs at school. Bleeding out on a dorm room bed was way too depressing. She'd rather be in a milky bath with a flickering candle and a pile of books. The blooms of blood would turn the water pink, and she'd drape herself across the edge so she looked like that painting they'd just learned about, *The Death of Marat.*

Hanging was ugly. By the time anyone found you, your face would be a purple bloat and your eyes would be bulging out of their sockets. A gunshot depended too much on aim, jumping in front of a train would make the conductor feel guilty, and self-disembowelment was just medieval. Swimming out to sea sounded nice if your brain would let you give in instead of fighting the ocean for air; freezing to death would be even better, you could just close your eyes and succumb to a sleep where everything felt warm. And your corpse would be perfectly preserved even if no one would ever find it because you'd have to be all the way out in the Arctic or something for it to be cold enough to kill you.

She'd run through all the different methods to Rachel when they'd first met. Rachel had still seemed cool then, like she might be someone to stay up late and get in some good trouble with, but Grace had figured out pretty quickly that first impressions were always a lie.

"You might look gorgeous if you froze to death, but you'd still end up in the guts of a beggar," Rachel had said, staring up at Grace with round little eyes like an awestruck rabbit. An awestruck rabbit who wanted desperately to prove that it was faster and smarter than the tiger that was about to eat it, kind of like a girl version of the white rabbit in *Alice in Wonderland.* Maybe with the same waistcoat. God, Rachel wore such stupid things.

"Guts of a beggar?"

"Shakespeare. 'A man may fish with the worm that hath eat of a king, and eat of the fish that hath fed of that worm.'"

"The worms would all be frozen, too," said Grace. And then she realized that she'd forgotten about poison. Maybe OD'ing on heroin or something would be the best way of all. Then at least she would have gotten to try it out before she died.

As wrong as Rachel proved to be about boys and music and understanding anything beyond how to kiss Mr. Taylor's ass so that she was cast in every single play, she was right about the suicide thing.

It's not that Grace actually wanted to flail around and lose control of her bowels and lie there with her eyes cranked open until she was carted away and incinerated — actually, that was exactly what she *didn't* want to do. She wanted to die young and beautiful, not all messed-up looking. It's just that, well, with suicide you got to *choose* — what you were wearing, what kind of note you left, how the whole thing actually went down when you slept that sleep of death. If life was all about making choices and taking responsibility for them, like adults were always saying, then why did death get to be something that just *happened* to you?

四

Bel-Air, CA

YEARS AGO, Barbra had picked Charles out as the one among all the young men in his class who would make the most of himself. That was before she'd picked out her English name, before she'd learned to pluck her eyebrows and smooth her hair, before she'd yanked herself out of Taiwan and set out for America.

They were still Wang Da Qian and Hu Yue Ling then, just two on a campus of two thousand. Half of Charles's classmates had been born in China, sons and daughters of tea merchants from Guangdong and government officials from Beijing. And the other half? Mostly children of mainlanders, too, but deposited headfirst, scrunch faced, and squalling, covered in a sticky film of blood and viscera, into the waiting arms of Taiwanese midwives who cooed over them all the same.

Not Barbra. There was no China in her blood. Her mother came from Taiwanese hill people who rode to town on an ox-drawn wagon loaded down with the daikon radishes that the Japanese occupiers pickled and grated and boiled in nearly every dish. She met Barbra's father when he was a delivery boy, picking up produce and freshly plucked chickens for the kitchens of National Taiwan University. He went from pedaling around the markets on a rickety bicycle to keeping watch at the foot of a perpetually bubbling stockpot to presiding over the students' communal lunches, which eventually underwent their own change, going from noxious oden stews to hearty rice porridges when the Japanese were defeated and a new Republic of China government took over.

Barbra had grown up in the college's employee quarters, a too-smart girl with a too-round face, who cursed under her breath in her parents' native Hokkien but still learned to trill out the smooth hills and valleys of Mandarin as easily as she'd mastered driving the university's old Datsun and smiling at the college boys with just enough intention to keep them guessing despite her funny little nose. She could critique Marxism and mock Teresa Teng's overwrought love songs and do most of Audrey Hepburn's beatnik dance and ride a bicycle without touching the handlebars and take a puff of a cigarette without coughing — everything that was important for a poor but ambitious high school girl to do in Taipei in 1973. The only thing she hadn't managed to do was turn the head of Charles Wang.

Barbra had spent the summer working as a secretary at the cannery in Tamsui where her uncle was a supervisor, a summer in which she'd managed to keep her skin pale and lovely by walking to work swathed in a cotton overshirt and hidden under a straw visor. Not once did she venture onto the beach in the bright hot afternoon, even though she'd learned to swim there, where the sands were always crowded with young people. She'd refused any rice at dinner, even though her uncle's wife urged fluffy spoonfuls of it upon her. Instead, she'd restricted herself to a single egg beaten into a cup of boiling water for breakfast and a tin of the cannery's sardines for lunch, and she'd worked all summer for enough money to order the sleeveless qipao that she was finally slim enough to slip into.

When the graduate students returned to campus that fall, she walked into the library off of Zhoushan Road, hair a cap of neat waves, proud of her legs in new flared trousers — the qipao was much too formal for someone else's first day of class — heart pounding at the thought of seeing Wang Da Qian again. Except that she didn't see him. Not through the window of the economics class that he should have been taking as part of his master's degree, not in the cafeteria where her father was shouting at his assistants as they rushed to wipe up a pot of sweet mung bean soup that someone had knocked over when she walked in. Nowhere.

Everyone said he'd gone to America — not to study but to work. It made Barbra love him even more, a love that lasted even though he never responded to her too-carefully worded letters, sent care of his mother, that wished him ten thousand years of luck and praised him for his courage while wondering if he'd be back to honor the new year with his revered parents. Not so much as a Golden Gate Bridge postcard.

She heard nothing more about him at all, despite the fact that she dated one of his former best friends for weeks, discreetly probing for news about Wang *gege* and receiving, instead, long disquisitions on the possibilities of praxis in a democratic society and endless replays of *A Hard Day's Night* as they sat side by side on a brown plaid comforter that was all stiff from being dried in the sun.

It wasn't until the last week of the semester that Barbra's detested boyfriend showed up one morning holding a light blue airmail envelope plastered with American stamps engraved with a portrait of Einstein. Philately was popular at the time and several of the boys Barbra was sitting with tried to lay claim to the stamps, but he'd shushed them all by unfolding the letter and showing off a photo of a girl ripped out of a magazine. The captions were in English, but the girl was unmistakably Chinese. She was smiling straight out at Barbra, her head turned towards the camera and her hands holding up the collar of her paisley-patterned shirt as her legs splayed out in a leap.

"Wang Da Qian says that he is getting married to her. She's a *model. Wah,* just look at her — I should have moved to America, too!"

"I thought you had better taste," Barbra had said, shoving the page back at him.

"It's true," said bookish little Tuan, who later surprised them all by becoming the mayor of Taichung, as he leaned over to pick the page up. "Those long, slanted eyes and those tiny little lips, she's the kind of girl *lao wai* likes."

"Maybe Ming-Ming is like a foreigner now. Milk in his tea and socks to bed."

"Wouldn't *you* like to be the one who knows what he wears to bed," said Xiao Jong, waggling his eyebrows at her. Jong always had been too stupid with his own intelligence. Just a few months after those boys had all graduated, he was picked up in one of the Kuomintang sweeps of student leaders with suspected Communist sympathies, and not even his meek little wife ever heard from him again. Served him right.

· · ·

Barbra flipped the light switch outside her closet door and stepped in, letting out her breath as her bare feet, toes freshly painted, sank into the smoke-blue silk rug.

This, this was her favorite room in the house.

Let Charles talk endlessly about the hidden wine cellar that he'd retrofitted for whiskey. Let their friends marvel over Ai Wei Wei smashing a Han dynasty urn in a triptych of photos that hung on the wall behind a considerably less valuable Ming dynasty vase. Let the other rooms of the house be photographed for that new California magazine with its condescending editor who described Charles as a "small but gracious man." This closet was the only corner that mattered to her.

Having this romantic inner sanctum in a house full of polished glamour gave Barbra the same sensation — something halfway between lust and power — as wearing a red silk peignoir under an austere dress by one of those Japanese minimalists that Charles hated so much.

She was supposed to be packing — "Quickly!" Charles had said, clapping his stubby hands together. "Quickly!" — but she didn't feel like it. Barbra pulled out the little upholstered stool she'd always loved for its brass claw feet and sat down in front of the mirror. She closed her eyes and let the crisp 68° air settle into her skin, then raised her eyelids and held her own gaze for a long moment.

First, the forehead.

Good, still good. One thin line just barely etched across, just enough to show that she wasn't using Botox.

The eyes. They'd always been too round, but now she skipped over that thought. The eyelids were beginning to look loose, but not so much that eye shadow disappeared in the folds. A few wrinkles on the edges and one curved line under her right eye because, though she had been trying for years, Barbra simply could not fall asleep unless she was lying on her right side. Cheekbones still high. Nose, same as always. Small and upturned. All those white women a generation older who went and got nose jobs that ended up looking like her own lamented-over nose made her laugh. How had that become their chosen shape? Her tiny little skull nose?

Her lips were undeniably starting to thin, and lipstick had started bleeding into the fine wrinkles that edged out from them on all sides like tiny tributaries of age, sapping her of the best semblance of youth.

And those naso-labial lines that dropped down either side of her nose and skipped a beat before continuing along the sides of her mouth, dragging it down into a disapproving bulldog frown. "What are you doing on my face?" she whispered at them.

Barbra placed her fingers gently on her hairline, encircling her forehead, and tugged up. Then she reached her thumbs down onto either side of her cheeks, softly, slowly, and pulled the skin back, stopping just before her nose began to splay out. There. This was the face she should be looking at. Like this, she looked better than young — she looked ageless.

"*Ah bao!* Are you almost done?" Charles called from the bedroom door. Barbra dropped her hands and the years came rushing back — five, ten, fifteen, twenty, until here she was again, a fifty-year-old woman married to a ruined man, sitting in a world that she had built up only to toss away again. Seeing her rumpled jawline reemerge, losing the image of her real, ageless self, was almost worse than knowing that she was going to lose the world she had put together so carefully. The venal optimism that had enabled her to immigrate to America and scoop up Charles and his almost empire as soon as she heard about the helicopter crash that killed his first wife was limited to desperate island girls with no fear or knowledge of the world.

Stupid. How could Charles be so stupid? How could a man who'd made himself so wealthy be so stupid about finances? That was the one thing she'd never suspected of him. Everything else, but not that. She'd known for years that he was unfaithful, but as long as she never betrayed him with her knowledge, that was nothing they'd have to lose a house and a marriage over. She suspected that his factories were not as scrupulously safe as he claimed, but that wasn't something that concerned her. She knew about his prejudices and knew that they probably extended rather further than he let on — especially about the native Taiwanese, especially about her own parents — but those were easy to indulge. Money made everything easy to indulge.

"*Wang tai-tai, kuai yi dian la! Ni je me hai mei you kai shi shou yi fu? Mei shi jien le!*" Ama shout-whispered as she appeared over Barbra's shoulder in the mirror, a slash of coral lipstick under her beauty parlor perm.

"Yes, I know," Barbra replied, staring back. "I'll be ready in a moment."

Ama, who had been Charles's own wet nurse when he was a child, claimed that Barbra's perfect Mandarin was too tainted with low-country squawk to understand, so in retaliation, Barbra spoke to her only in English, a language that the older woman barely spoke at all. It worked out perfectly well because Ama never wanted to hear Barbra's replies to her faux-polite comments and commands anyway.

"*Ah bao.*" It was Charles. Talking to her in that vaguely disappointed tone that he'd used ever since he first came home and told her what had happened. As if she had been the one to let him down.

"I don't need both of you here telling me what to do. I know, I know, only the important things."

"*Ah bao,* we leaving soon."

"*Wo nu er zai deng wo men.*"

Barbra burned inside. She didn't care if Ama's daughter was waiting for them. Her last moments in her dressing room and they refused to let her have a moment's peace. She picked up a photo of herself and Charles at the dinner that Hermès sponsored for Saina's last show in New York, the one with all those refugee women and scarves that had gotten Saina in so much trouble. They were turned towards each other, smiling, Charles's eyes half hidden behind the giant Porsche Carrera frames that he'd insisted on getting when he started developing cataracts — how unfair that every middle-aged Asian man in glasses now gave the impression of looking vaguely like Kim Jong-il — her own eyes opened wide, still looking at him flirtatiously after all these years. Well. Maybe she'd feel that way again, but she doubted it would happen packed in an aging car with Ama, Grace, and dunce-headed Andrew.

五

Bel-Air, CA

CHARLES'S CONVERSATION with Ama had been humiliating.
In the Mandarin that they shared:

"Rong-rong," she said, calling him by the pet name she'd given him when he was a downy little baby wrapped in a fur blanket, "it is good that we have daughters and that they have homes. I am going to go to my daughter's house."

"Oh, Ama, it's nothing. We'll be fine. But perhaps it would be best if you did go stay with Kathy for a little while. Until things blow over."

"But I am an old woman, and I cannot get there on my own. I have the car you gave me, but I don't drive it anymore."

"Maybe Kathy can —"

"No, no, Kathy has too much work. You drive me, and then you are already on your way to your daughter's house, too."

And that was how she gave him the car, the powder-blue Mercedes station wagon he'd bought for his first wife when she'd gotten pregnant with Saina. It was the only car that hadn't been repossessed because he'd sold it to Ama for a dollar sixteen years ago; she drove it once a fortnight to a mah-jongg game in the San Gabriel Valley.

And that was how she told him that she knew he'd lost everything and would be running into his own daughter's reluctant arms. The worst part is that he'd known that she would turn over the old Merc, counted on it.

Charles couldn't have been more embarrassed if he'd woken up to find that he'd regressed half a century and was sucking on her nipple again, a grown man in Armani trying to draw milk out of her wizened breast.

六

Bel-Air, CA

SO HERE THEY WERE, the three of them. Barbra, Charles, and his Ama. No longer so young.

And here was the car, a 1980 model, both bumpers intact, gleaming still from the weekly wash and wax that Jeffie, the gardener's son, gave all the Wang family cars.

Cleaned more than she was ever driven, this car was a lady. Her cream-colored seats and sky-blue carpeting made her impractical for anything beyond a polite spin around the block or a tootle over to a neighborhood association meeting four estates down. She might, *might* consent to a weekend spree down the coast, provided an air-conditioned garage at a La Jolla villa was waiting on the other end. Even after nearly thirty years, her perforated leather interiors remained uncracked and the wood burl along her dash still shone. Her only blemish, really, was one little carpet stain, a resolute Angelyne pink, where Charles's first wife, May Lee, had once let an open tube of lipstick melt in the bright white L.A. sun.

Never, not once, had the gears of her clockwork German engine been asked to cogitate on the notion of driving all the way across the country, rear end sagging with baggage, oil lines choked with cheap Valvoline. But, like the family, she suited herself to her circumstances.

Barbra lugged her own bags down the steps and waited for Charles to come open the back. He was behind her, grunting as he tried to lift the last of Ama's suitcases — a matched pair of classic Vuitton wheelies that had also once belonged to May Lee — over the threshold. Barbra didn't want to help. Let him do it. Ama shouldn't even be here with them. *How much was she still being paid,* Barbra wondered, *and for what?*

It was early still. Seven thirty. The quiet time after the dawn joggers had put in their miles and just before the housekeepers started their long walk from the Sunset and Beverly Glen bus stop. A weathered white pickup full of gardeners and lawnmowers sputtered up the street, spewing exhaust onto the same topiaries that they watered and trimmed daily.

Housekeepers and gardeners, dog walkers and pool men, they were the front lines, the foot soldiers. Later would come the private Pilates instructors and the personal chefs, the assistants sent from the office to pick up a forgotten cuff link or script. A home theater consultant, a wine cellar specialist, a saltwater fish tank curator — necessities all.

Charles and Barbra had never understood their neighbors' obsession with bringing services into the home. Why have some masseuse carry in a table when you could just go to the Four Seasons? Why open your life up to more strangers than you had to? Now, of course, there was no need to think about any of that. Luisa and Big Pano and Gordon and Rainie had all been let go, fired, weeks ago. Barbra hadn't told them why. Let them think that she had finally turned into a crazy, demanding Westside wife, unsatisfied with Luisa's immaculately ironed sheets and Gordon's bright, abundant blooms, maybe even pathetically sure that her husband was eyeing Rainie's swinging breasts. She was positive that they'd be rehired immediately, even in these unhappy times. She was equally certain that her former household help had already jointly developed some theory of the Wangs' downfall, something scandalous and unflattering that would doubtless be pried out of them by each of their new employers.

The worst moment for Barbra and Charles was the reveal. The Reveal. That's how she thought about it in the days after — like they were on one of those makeover shows, but instead of finding that their house was beautifully revamped, the hosts had removed their blindfolds and made their whole charmed life disappear.

"Why?" Barbra had asked.
  "What why?"
  "All our everything?"

At that moment the word *our* rankled. Charles had never had a problem with generosity — he'd cultivated a casual way of picking up the check before he'd even made his first million — but just then the way that his wife said *our* brought out something small and sour that he forced himself to swallow, along with the true word: *Mine.* Barbra had given nothing but her bullish charm to this family — she hadn't made the money or borne the children or even decorated the house or cooked the food. He'd done the first, his dead first wife had done the second, and they'd hired people to do the rest. Nothing was *our.*

"Yes," he'd said. "All."

"But how? How could you? Don't we have anything saved? We had so —"

"So much. And now, not so much."

He'd said that, and then he'd spread his arms out in a leaden swoop, like an aging showgirl. It had severed something between them, that gesture. Charles had never done anything awkward or unsure in his life. Not in front of her. Not in her eyes. But now her broken heart saw every wrong-footed step he'd ever taken.

"How could it happen?"

"It happened!"

"But *how* did it?"

"How, how, how! You never ask how it get good, how I make so much money, how I know what everybody want, only how now that it go away! No how!"

Had they always sounded so stilted and childish? After sixteen years in America, speaking English to the children and her American friends — whose company and mah-jongg rules she preferred to those of the mainlander wives of Charles's friends — her own speech had attained a smooth perfection, but when she spoke to Charles, she found herself picking up his broken grammar, and the two of them gradually dropped the private Chinese they had once shared.

"Okay," she'd said. "No more how."

And for then, and for now, that was it. No more how. No more how, and no more house.

·   ·   ·

Charles couldn't. He couldn't tell Barbra what had happened, how their personal assets — their home! — had gotten wrapped up in the bankruptcy. It was something a true businessman never would have done. That was the worst of it. And now here they were, creeping out of the driveway under cover of dawn with their meager belongings stashed in the back, a troupe of Chinese Okies fleeing a New Age Dust Bowl. He'd always respected this home, kept it sacrosanct. He may have betrayed his wives in body, but he never did so under their shared roof.

Now Charles wanted to curse the land somehow, to cry bitter salt tears that would curdle the earth and kill the thick wall of bougainvillea that shielded the lawn. Any child conceived in these rooms would be an insult to his children; any love found on these grounds would make his own loves into a lie. When some other family moved in, some family whose dollars flowed greenly from their hands, dark thorny vines should spew out of the ground, twisting through the iron gate and out across the grass, choking the magnolia tree, with its generous branches and sweet-smelling blossoms, snaking around the house until all the windows were blinded and all the doors taken prisoner. Gallons of overturquoised water would roil and churn and splash over the charcoal slate that framed the pool, rotting the impenetrable stone until it crumbled and sank, pulling the foundations right out from under the house.

Charles closed his eyes and mentally erased the house from top to bottom, scrubbing the whole thing out in wild strokes, leaving a white patch between the Leventhals' five-bedroom-plus-six-car-garage Spanish Mission and the Okafurs' seven-bedroom-plus-tennis-court Cape Cod. And in that blank space he pictured instead the mountainside estate in China that he had heard so much about as a child.

He could feel Barbra sitting next to him in the passenger seat and knew without looking that she was pulling her cashmere wrap tight around her shoulders though the morning was warm even for September in Los Angeles. A door slammed shut and that was Ama, settling into the backseat with a grunt.

Keeping his eyes closed so the estate stayed in place, Charles turned the key in the ignition and shifted into drive. At the edge of the darkness behind his lids, there was the cliff that had been waiting ever since his doc-

tor warned him about the possibility of his ministrokes presaging something bigger and more devastating. But Charles wasn't afraid. He could
negotiate the driveway by feel — the lazy 180-degree curve around the
front lawn, then 900 feet of concrete and a pause at the automatic gates
before the tires hit asphalt.

Lately, the gate had been slow to open. The crank mechanism groaned
and he could hear it sticking, bit by bit. Charles sat, eyes still closed, and
thought about a time when he might have noticed that and gone for a
can of WD-40 himself, made a Sunday project of it instead of waiting for
Pano to figure it out.

   Barbra and Ama were both silent. After another moment, Charles lifted
his foot off the brake and let the car roll forward. Forty more feet and he'd
hit sidewalk, but Charles squeezed his eyelids tighter together. No one
ever walked at this time of day. Most of the houses on their block didn't
even have sidewalks in front of them, just dipped from lawn straight into
street. The station wagon surged on, lowering itself out of the driveway
and wheeling into the road. If he kept his eyes closed for long enough,
Charles wouldn't have to look at the assessor's hearse of a black car parked
hastily at the curb. Maybe he'd even be lucky enough to hit it. At the last
minute, though, self-preservation kicked in and his eyes snapped open
in time to catch Ama and Barbra looking at each other in the rearview
mirror.

七

Santa Barbara, CA

·

FINALLY, SHE WAS ALONE. Rachel had folded up six pairs of Grace's jeans and skipped down to lunch, where she'd probably tell everybody that the Wangs were headed to the poorhouse and were going to start collecting food stamps and stuff. It didn't make any sense. Half the girls at school probably had at least one KoKo lip gloss or eye shadow — some of the guys probably even had the special-edition guyliner that they'd put out. *Emo fucks.* And now they'd all be talking about her as they chewed their disgusting giant mouthfuls of disgusting chicken fingers.

Grace flipped open her phone and hit the call button. This was the fifth time she'd called Saina today, and her sister still wasn't picking up.

"Hey, this is Saina. I miss you, too. Leave a message."

Beep.

"Jiejie! Where *are* you? Do you realize that we're coming to your house, like, today? God, I wish that you were still living in New York. I mean, I know you're still living in New York, but I'm talking about the city. Listen, you have to call me back, okay? I need, need, need to talk to you before Dad and Babs get here. Okay, bye."

God. How could Saina ignore her calls like that? Especially today?

It was Tuesday, so Andrew was probably still in his Bio lab. Grace texted him.

Have u talked to Dad yet? Call me asap after Bio.

Okay. Fine. She'd pack. But she was just going to bring the stuff she actually wanted to bring. Forget about being practical — they couldn't be so poor that they didn't have money to buy underwear, right? She could sell ads on her blog or something.

Grace's phone started buzzing as soon as she set it down, inching its way across her bedspread.

"Andrew!"

"Hey, Gracie." Oh Andrew. He didn't even sound upset. Grace wasn't sure whether that should make her more or less worried.

"Did you talk to Dad?"

"Nah, I was in class, but he left a message. Sucks, huh?"

"Sucks? Uh, yeah, it does. Andrew, the *house*."

"I know. Hey, Gracie, I can't talk right now, okay?"

"What? Why not? But you called me! How can you not talk to me right now?"

"I just, I wanted to make sure you were okay, but I've got to finish something right now. But you guys are getting here tomorrow, right? So I'll see you soon, okay?"

八

Phoenix, AZ

ANDREW PRESSED the end call button on his iPhone and looked at it again to make sure that he wasn't somehow still connected. He dropped the phone on top of his jeans, which were puddled on the floor of his dorm room, then picked it up and placed it on his desk, where no one could step on it accidentally. A second later he reached over and checked again, just in case he'd pocket-dialed someone when the phone landed on the floor.

He had to do all of that with just one arm because the other arm was trapped under Emma Lerner's breasts. They were great breasts. "A great rack," Howard Stern would have called it. Yes, Howard would definitely think that Emma had a great rack, and he'd be even more impressed because they were 100 percent real. Why was Howard always talking about boobs on the radio where no one could see them? He should have gotten himself a TV show instead of that satellite gig, although he probably wouldn't have been able to show naked racks on TV either. Unless he was on cable.

Emma wiggled in place next to him, face hidden in the pillow, and pretended to snore, then raised herself up slightly and brushed her nipples along his arm. Phone forgotten, Andrew flung his free arm and leg over her and pulled her in tight, burrowing through a mess of blonde hair to kiss her perfect pink cheeks.

"Hair in my mouth again!" he teased.

"Better than a hair up your butt."

"You're going to get something else up your butt!"

Emma flipped over to face him, grinning. "Really? And what's that, *hmm?* Look at you, you're blushing already!"

Andrew rolled his eyes at her. Sex talk plus beers before noon equaled red cheeks for him and Emma knew it. She loved teasing him about his Asian flush even though he tried to make it clear to her that his family was actually descended from ancient Manchurians who rode wild horses and were nothing like the engineering geeks on campus. Unable to think of a comeback, he pounced on her instead, catching her wrists in his hands and attacking her neck with half bites.

Hot. If only she wasn't so freaking hot. With those plush lips and the little freckles on her nose and that beach volleyball body. And now her red-and-pink-striped panties — *panties!* Andrew loved that word! — and his black boxer briefs were the only barriers keeping him from everything he'd ever wanted. Sliding his hands down her upstretched arms and slipping his tongue between her lips, Andrew tried to stop himself from pressing into her too much. But just a little. And a little more, and more, and, oh, another torturous bit. Just enough to feel exactly how they'd fit together, so easily.

"Andrew," she whispered, breathing out on the first syllable. "C'mon. Let's." She tugged at the waistband of his underwear and then slid her hand inside, reaching for him.

"Emma." One warm hand around his penis.

"Oh Andrew. Come on. You're leaving. Let's just . . . let's."

He felt the rest of his body tighten and his erection loosen a bit in response.

"Em, you *know.* We talked about this."

"I have condoms in my bag over there."

"Look, I think you're amazing, and you're so, so hot. And not just hot, you're beautiful, too."

"But you don't love me."

"I'm sorry, I —"

"Dude, I don't care! Who cares! I've had sex with tons of guys I don't love! I mean, not tons, but a few. A couple."

"And that's okay!"

"Is it because you think I'm a slut?"

"No! No, no, no. I don't even like that word."

"Stop being such a feminist, Andrew, it's gay."

"I'm not gay!"

Emma laughed. "I didn't say you were. I know you're not gay. Would this happen if you were?" She gripped him again, tugging him towards her, and he immediately sprang to attention. "See? Your body knows what you want. Aren't you tired of being a virgin?"

Andrew turned away from her and put a hand over his penis, willing it to quiet down. He *was* tired of being a virgin, but that didn't mean that he was just going to have sex with Emma without being in love with her first. Andrew just wished that love wasn't so difficult to figure out. It had been simple with his first girlfriend, Eunice, whose Groucho Marx eyebrows had just made her even more beautiful. For the last two years of high school and the first year of college, they'd been in love — he'd felt buoyed by her very existence and fascinated by the smallest detail of her being — but they'd never once had sex because Eunice's father was a minister and she loved Jesus just a little bit more than she loved Andrew. They'd done everything but —"But not everything butt," he'd joked to his high school friends — and in a way he'd relished his relatively chaste devotion to her. It meant that he was nothing like his father, who didn't even bother to hide his affairs from Andrew, though it seemed like Barbra and his sisters didn't know about them.

"Em, have you ever been in love?"

"We're in *college.* We have plenty of time to fall in love. And that's got nothing to do with sex anyways."

"But shouldn't it?"

Emma was quiet for a moment. She sat and hugged her knees to her chest, not seeming to care that she was still nearly naked. Just as Andrew started to think that she might tell him she actually was in love with him, Emma made a gazelle leap over him, out of bed, and yanked her sundress off the closet door.

"Hey! No! Stop! Are you mad? Why are you getting dressed?"

"You have to pack. Don't let me stop you."

"It'll take me twenty minutes. They're just leaving L.A. now — we still have —"

"You know, I know where Bel-Air is. You could say that they're leaving Bel-Air."

"Well, but Bel-Air is in L.A."

"Ha ha. Funny. You're so funny. You should be a comedian."

"Why are you doing this?"

"No, I mean it. It'll be awesome. You can hang out with Long Duk Dong and Harold and Kumar. Have a good time. Make tiny-dick jokes. Oh, and Margaret Cho. Good thing she's a lesbian. You won't have to have sex with her."

"Actually, I think she's bisexual. She went out with Quentin Tarantino."

"Are you fucking kidding me?" Emma shrieked, hurling one of her lethal heels at him. It skidded against the stucco wall like a nail on a chalkboard and landed, innocent, on his pillow. *What was wrong with her?* Emma was usually so uncomplicated, so easy to be with. She didn't confuse him like most girls. Why was she being so mean? And why did she care if Margaret Cho was bisexual?

"Whatever, Andrew," said Emma, quiet again. "I'm not going to beg you to fuck me. And you are the last hot guy I'm dating. My mom was right." And then she turned and walked out, shoeless, slamming the dorm room door so hard that his Lenny Bruce mug shot poster slipped off its nail.

Andrew let himself fall back on the bed, his elbow narrowly missing Emma's spike heel. Well, that was that then. Another breakup. At least Emma thought he was hot, too. But already this year there had been Jocelyn, and then the end of Jocelyn, a rekindled fling with Soo-Jin, and then the end of Soo-Jin, and now Emma and, very soon after, the end of Emma. And fall semester had just started.

It was really hard to fall in love when everyone kept breaking up with him. Eunice had broken up with him, too, because she'd met someone on a mission trip who was as devoted to purity as she. "It'll be better this way," she'd said over video chat, as he'd stared at his own face in the corner of the screen, willing himself not to cry as she enumerated all the reasons he should forget about her. Andrew thought that he'd spend his newfound singlehood on finally having sex already, but when the opportunity presented itself after a drunken make-out session with a cute nursing major at some fraternity's '70s party, it had all felt sordid and desperate and coercive in a way that it never would have with Eunice, and he'd left before either of them could fully disrobe, deciding then that he'd rather wait until he had something closer to love. Who knew it would take so long to find?

Andrew was just reaching for his phone to call Grace back — she'd sounded so wounded that he couldn't talk — when Saina's name flashed on the screen.

"Hey."

"Angie, did you talk to Dad?"

"*Saina!* You can stop calling me that already."

"Drewly?"

"This is serious."

"Seriously serious."

"It is."

"God, I know. Did you ever think —"

"Let's call Gracie."

"Wait, Andrew, before we do. How do you think Dad is?"

"Oh, you know. How is Dad always?"

"He almost cried when I talked to him."

"What do you mean?"

"Cried. Like actual sadness tears."

"What did you say?"

"Nothing! I couldn't. I felt weird even hearing it." They were quiet for a minute. Andrew picked up Emma's heel and tapped it lightly on the wall. How could girls walk in those things?

"Andrew."

"Huh?"

"Why aren't you saying anything?"

"I guess it just doesn't feel real. Out of nowhere Dad just tells us that everything's gone and he wants to go back to China to reclaim our ancestral lands or some bullshit? That he doesn't have enough money left for ASU tuition? How does any of that happen? I know we're not billionaires, but he always said, you know —"

"'Be happy that Daddy is rich man.'"

"Yep. So what the hell now?"

"Wait, he didn't tell me that he wanted to go to China. That's insane. He's never even *been* to China," said Saina, sounding surprised.

"Well, you know, he always said he wouldn't go back until he could do it properly. But, yeah, it was on the message he left — I haven't actually talked to him yet —"

"I have a whole conversation with him and he doesn't tell me, but he leaves you his master plan on a voicemail?"

"Maybe he's getting real Chinese in the face of adversity. I *am* the first-born son."

"But not the first*born*."

"XY trumps XX." Saina laughed and he felt that old relief. Before he could make another joke, something to keep her from sounding tense and worried, she spoke.

"Hey, Andrew, do you want me to pay your tuition? Look, I have my whole trust, everything that's vested so far anyways, it's not tied up with the bankruptcy as far as I know. And I still have money. I mean, you know, I made a good amount of money. So I could if you wanted."

Stay at college. Let Saina deal with Dad. Pay her back when he could get at his money, if it still existed. It probably didn't exist anymore. What-ever, pay Saina back when he earned some money. Make up with Emma. Do some more open mic nights. Decide to be in love with her. Maybe even try an open mic in L.A. some weekend. Fall in love with her. Write more material. Who knows, he could already be in love with her, and he wouldn't know unless he stayed. And then *sex,* sex with Emma.

"Oh wait, here's Grace calling again. She's going to go crazy if we don't talk to her already," said Saina. "Hold on, let me merge calls."

Andrew heard a beep and quickly shut down his Emma fantasy.

"Saina!" It was Grace, at her Gracie-est. "I'm *so* annoyed. Why haven't you been picking up? Where have you been all day?"

Before Saina could respond, Andrew leapt in. "Did the king of the Wa-tusis drive a car?"

"Andrew! How come you guys are talking to each other already? How long have you been on the phone without me?" demanded Grace.

"Barely at all," said Saina. "Like, two minutes."

"Well, why did you call each other first?"

"Gracie," said Andrew. "Aren't you going to answer?"

"No! I'm mad."

"Then how do we know it's you?" he teased.

"Fuck you, Andrew." She really was mad. Grace always jumped to the angriest place without warning. She was capable of conjuring up a fury that felt like a living beast — a palpable, pulsating thing that crouched next to her — and the only way to stop it from appearing was to head it off with lightness.

"Language, language," he said. "Now: Did the king of the Watusis drive a car?"

"No," pouted Grace. "He was a savage. A noble savage."

"*Bzzzt!* I'm sorry, that is not the correct answer. You may not enter."

"Okay! Fine! Yes. He drives a specially built 1954 Pontiac."

"Thank you very much, Bunny Watson."

This was how he wanted them to remain, the careless, carefree brother and sisters that they had always been, that they had made themselves be. As long as they could do that, maybe nothing was different, maybe everything wasn't ruined.

"Poor Gracie. Andrew, stop torturing her," said Saina.

"This is brotherly love in action, yo. No torture."

"Guys," said Grace. "They're on their way to pick me up. What should I do?"

"Stall!" said Andrew and Saina together, jaunty. It was their old routine, born of a hundred, a thousand, summer afternoons spent piled on the slipcovered couches in the media room, shivering in the air-conditioned house, hypnotized by the whirr of the film projector. That's what L.A. kids do on sunny days: shut the doors, crank the air, pull the shades, dim the lights, and pop in the movies. For the three of them, it was a pile of old Katharine Hepburn movies in metal film canisters that Andrew found the year their mother died. All three of them could reenact the licorice gun scene in *Adam's Rib,* knew every insult in *Woman of the Year,* and used the research questions in *Desk Set* as passwords. The films had been stacked in the dusty crawl space under the stairs and were marked PROPERTY OF BREEZY MANOR. Andrew pictured Breezy as a sexy sixties dollybird sort of lady until Saina told him that a manor was a house and that it was probably what the last owners had called their house.

"What is *wrong* with everybody? Saina! Andrew! Why aren't you guys upset? Do you just totally not care about this? We're. Poor. Now."

"Well, not exactly," said Andrew. "Saina's still rich."

"What? What do you mean?"

"She hasn't had the Talk," said Saina.

"Dudes, I'm sixteen. I know how babies are made."

"Not that one, the money one," said Andrew.

"Wait, did any of you actually get a birds-and-bees talk?" asked Saina.

"I think that's what moms do," said Grace. "Babs isn't ever going to give us the Talk."

"I don't know, girls, maybe she's just dying to be asked. Maybe all she's ever wanted to do is explain the wonders of menstruation to you both."

"Gross, Andrew. Stop," said Grace. "Will you both just be adults for a minute? What talk? And what money? Saina, why do you have money? Do you mean, like, besides from your art and stuff?"

"It's the seventeenth-birthday talk. Dad takes you to the Polo Lounge and tells you about your trust, and then you sign something that says you won't get to touch it until you're twenty-five," said Saina.

"Actually, Dad took me to the Palm," said Andrew. "You know, steaks. And he let me drink a martini."

"If he's going to wait, why not wait until we're eighteen?" asked Grace.

"I guess he figured seventeen was old enough. You have to sign before you actually turn eigh —"

"Wait," interrupted Grace. "How *much* money?"

Andrew waited for Saina to answer. She took a moment, and then said: "Two million at twenty-five. And then it was going to be another five million when we turned thirty-five."

Suddenly, Andrew felt sick. Hearing Saina say the number out loud made it crunch in his head.

Seven. Million. Dollars.

Holy fuck.

Somehow, he had kept himself from thinking about that number. In the abstract, he'd actually found it a little embarrassing, to be due seven million dollars just for being the product of his father's sperm. "I'll earn my own way," he might have said, knowing that the money would still be there and everyone would just think he was even cooler and more honorable for turning it down at first. But now, to lose seven million dollars without having done anything wrong — one day to have it and the next day not — it just wasn't *fair.*

He could have been rich. And so what if he hadn't earned any of it? He was *going* to be rich. He *was* going to be rich. No more.

Grace wasn't saying anything. Neither was Saina.

"Guys," said Andrew. "We'll be cool, yeah? Gracie?"

"That was a lot of money," she said. "And I didn't even know I had it."

九

Helios, NY

"BABY, YOU OKAY OUT THERE?"

Oh. Right. Grayson.

"Are you coming back to bed?"

She'd have to get him out before the family got there.

"Saina, baby — I'm cold here without you! Come in and get snuggly."

Now. It would be easier if she did it now. They would feel the stink of him if she waited too long, and her siblings would look at her in that new way they had, like they couldn't understand why her life had stopped being amazing but didn't want her to know it. They hated Grayson now. Andrew — sweet, peacekeeping Andrew — had responded to Grayson's betrayal by asking her: "Am I supposed to come to New York and beat him up now? Because I will if you want me to. I really will." And Gracie had offered to bomb his Facebook fan page with mean comments, offered it so seriously, like a battle tactic, that Saina had laughed and incurred further Gracie wrath on Grayson's behalf.

Would he go? Saina was half afraid that he wouldn't. Half hoped it, too. He'd shown up on her doorstep a week ago carrying a rucksack stuffed with rumpled T-shirts, offering up a fistful of wildflowers that he'd picked off her front lawn. Even before she heard the knock, Saina knew it was him. She'd felt it: a quickening, a shimmering, a pitched battle between her red and white blood cells and then *boom boom boom* — his closed-fisted pounding. Her wineglass squeaked against itself as she set it down, its molecules crowded tight, the liquid inside turning to blood, then vinegar, then back to an organic local blend. That glass had held together, but she'd fallen, fallen out of her carefully molded resistance and — hair down, bra off, legs splayed — into him.

It was over fast. Afterwards, Saina had half slumped against the leather chesterfield, looking up at the raftered ceiling, blinking as Grayson buried his face in her neck. "You still smell the same," he'd said, lips against skin. She'd blinked again. The ceiling needed work, but it was hard to find someone willing to leave the beams undisturbed.

Grayson had let himself go slack against her, taking the weight off his own knees. His arms tightened around her shoulders and he'd fallen damply against her leg.

There was a place in sex that emotion didn't quite reach. No matter how great the betrayal, how intense and inflamed the anger, how long the separation, there was a place that was just bodies fitting into each other — unquestioning, uncomplicated. Easy. It felt so easy to lie here, joint and groove. Maybe they should do this. Make a new life in the Catskills. It would be far enough from the people they'd messed up being. Grayson could share the little barn that was going to be her studio, or maybe he could have it and she'd take the attic, with all that good light.

Easy.

Easy?

Is that what Grayson thought?

Did he come here thinking that it would be this easy? His head felt greasy against her clean skin and his three-day beard pricked her neck. He hadn't even bothered to clean himself up for her, probably came straight from Sabrina's bed. What kind of beds do mattress heiresses sleep in? Saina had pictured Sabrina lying atop an impossibly high pile of satiny mattresses, her golden hair fanned out across a mound of pillows, Grayson leaping off the top and landing at Saina's door. And he'd known that all he had to do was knock.

"Is this what you thought?" she'd asked, furious. "That you'd show up at my door and I'd just welcome you with open legs? Do you really think you're that irresistible?"

He'd stared at her a minute before replying, "Saina, what the hell." Just like that. Flat. No affect.

She pushed him off of her and then reached over to tug his jeans up.

"Get dressed," she said. "I don't want to see you like this. God, you haven't even *said* anything to me yet!"

And then Leo, her Leo, had walked in through the still-open door with another bunch of flowers — picked from his *own* front lawn — walked in, seen them, and turned right back around. Saina jumped up, thanking god that she was wearing a skirt and not a pair of pants that would probably be swamped around her ankles, and grabbed his arm before he could get through the doorway.

"Nothing happened," she said.

"I think that is probably false."

"It's not just anybody, Leo. It's Grayson."

"That's even worse. Underwear."

"What?"

"You don't have any underwear on."

Saina felt nauseous. "That's ridiculous."

"I can see it on the ottoman thing."

Defeat, lacy and pink. "Okay."

Grayson broke in. "Saina, baby, who is this? You're dating someone else already?"

She turned to him. "*Dating* someone else already? How long did you expect me to wait, Grayson? Until you guys had another baby? You got someone *pregnant* already, and you didn't even wait until we'd broken up!"

Her former fiancé was already lounging on the rug, as comfortable as if he'd built the place himself, leaning back on one elbow, pants kicked aside, indigo eyes staring straight up at her, unfazed.

"I'm not going to be part of this," said Leo. He opened his hand and dropped the flowers. Fragrant, obedient, they beheaded themselves on Saina's salvaged-wood floors.

"That's it?" said Saina, not sure if she was in despair or not. "That's how you leave? No him or me, no fight, nothing?"

"You're not wearing any underwear. How could this possibly turn out well?"

Saina swallowed the very slight urge to make a threesome joke and took a step towards Leo. Battered wool shirt, mended and torn work pants, old leather lace-up boots, faded leather belt with a worn brass buckle that could have brought in a few hundred at her friend Dahlia's boutique on Ludlow, fingernails scrubbed scrupulously clean the way, she'd learned, that farmers' always are.

And then she looked over at Grayson. Paint under his nails, always. Even if he hadn't touched a canvas in weeks. Hair cut by a Lower East Side stylist who required a password to make an appointment (last she'd heard, it was "seventies bush"). Striped boxers from Paul Smith, which even she thought was a needless expense. Yes, Grayson was an asshole. But he'd left Sabrina on a stupid pile of mattresses in the city and come back for her, for Saina. He had.

She felt that sick tug that leads us down paths we know are doomed.

"Leo," she said, sad. "I'm sorry."

"You're sorry *sorry* or you're sorry *goodbye?*"

"Don't make me say it."

"Be a grown-up, Saina. You make me stand here and talk to you while he smirks at us, you can say goodbye to me."

And so she'd done it. Closed the door on Leo and turned around to Grayson's triumphant hug. Later that night, after the tears and the confessions, after Grayson said that Sabrina had miscarried and he'd stayed out of guilt because she'd seemed so sad — an explanation that Saina had known was suspect but still couldn't stop herself from believing — after they'd explained and apologized and finally crawled into bed feeling like they'd earned it, Grayson had turned to her with a grin and asked: "Is it true, then?"

Knowing exactly what he meant, she asked, "What?"

"What they say about black guys?"

"What's that, Grayson?"

"You know, big feet, big hands . . ."

"Are you really asking me about Leo's penis size?"

He'd shrugged and grinned at her again, and somehow she'd fallen for it. She'd shrugged back, and said, "Yep, all true." And then she'd winked, *winked.* As much as she'd hated herself for it, she wanted to keep on being that person: loose and funny and lovable. The girl who can joke about her lovers and their dicks, and didn't get hung up on little things like cheating fiancés who knock up their mistresses.

And for seven days that was who she'd been. Playful and light, blissed out on a permanent sex buzz that didn't let up even when she'd come down with a urinary tract infection. For seven days it had been spaghetti out of a pot at midnight and long drives to estate sales in the middle of nowhere and ignored phone calls from her friends and family. Only the farmers market was off-limits, because Leo would have been there and how could she parade Grayson in front of him? Or worse, put him in a position where he might have to *serve* Grayson? Bag up his vegetables and count out his change? She couldn't, and so the tomatoes in the sauce on their midnight spaghetti remained distressingly unheirloom, the off-season apples they ate while lying, legs entwined, in the backyard were dug out of a plastic bin at the local A&P.

Really, though, it wasn't some sort of noble consideration for Leo's feelings. It was more that she wasn't ready to deny Grayson's gravitational pull, to be knocked out of his orbit. A satellite, after all, can still look like a star.

But one phone call with her brother and sister was all it took to send Saina hurtling back down to earth. She couldn't let them come here, battered and bruised, to find Grayson in her bed.

And her father.

She wasn't even sure if he knew why they'd called the wedding off.

"Why you need to get marry already?" he'd asked, when she first told him about the engagement. "You still young. Is there a baby in there?"

And when the end had come, her father ranted about how he'd never liked Grayson, sent her peonies and a whole salted caramel chocolate cake, emailed Grayson's parents and told them that he'd cover the lost deposits — how much did he now regret that oversize gesture? — told her to keep the ring and throw it out the window. But he'd never asked why. For all Saina knew, one of his friends had seen the Page Six item and told him about it. Maybe he thought that he was saving face for her by not mentioning the betrayal, just like he'd never mentioned the backlash to her last installation even though he and her stepmother had flown out for the opening and held court at the Hermès party, going drink for drink with her old sculpture professor and telling her gallery owner that she should be selling Saina's work for more. He'd been a charming embarrassment and Saina had been glad when he'd packed up and flown back to Bel-Air after an obligatory Peking duck dinner.

That was it, then. She started up the stairs. Grayson had to leave. It wasn't going to last anyway. She couldn't keep him in hiding forever.

Just say it, she told herself. *Just do it.* It would be worse if she waited until the last minute, until right before her family got here.

"Hey, baby, we have to talk about something," she said, pushing open the door to her bedroom.

Grayson sat naked and cross-legged on top of her comforter. He held his cell phone up to his left ear with his right hand and held out his left hand, index finger up, to shush her.

"Oh my little darling," he said to the phone, "and I wasn't there for you." A pause. "Yes. Yes, yes, yes."

Saina went cold.

"Grayson."

He looked up, annoyed, and shook his head wildly, waving his finger. "Wait, how big? Nine pounds? Nine? Wow."

And then something happened: Grayson got beatific.

She had heard of people looking like they were lit up from within, but this was the first time she'd seen it. With that "wow," all his edges and wrinkles smoothed out and the air around him thrummed, like he'd found a note on some universal chord that she still couldn't even hear, much less play.

"I'll be there," he said to the phone. "A few hours. Don't do anything else yet, okay? Just wait for me, I'll be there. Yes. You're amazing." And then whispering it again. "So amazing."

He dropped the phone and looked at her.

"Saina, I know I'm an asshole and I bolted and then I lied to you and she never had a miscarriage, but I'm a dad! I have a son! And I know you're going to hate me, and I'm going to have to fix that at some point, and we can probably never be together again, but I . . . I have to go. And that's all I can say right now. Okay?"

She was choking on something. Or she would be choking if she were breathing. Was that right? Maybe it was the other way around.

"Not okay. No! I can't believe you're doing this to me again. How could you say that she'd lost the baby? Is that what you wanted to happen?"

"I thought I wanted you."

"And now?"

"I'm a father." He glowed again, just thinking about it. "I have a child. Can't you see? This changes everything! I can't wait to see him. Maybe you'll understand when you have kids."

"Fuck off. You don't have kids, you had a phone call. So you're transformed just like that? In a minute? That's all it takes? And Sabrina?" Just saying the name made her feel seasick, made the world shift and sway for a minute.

Grayson kneeled up on the bed and grabbed both of her arms. "She just had my *baby*." Again, the glow. Like a firefly. Like a glowworm. A lying little glowworm.

In a minute Saina was going to hate herself, but she said it anyway. "And that makes you not love me anymore."

He shook his head. "It's bigger than that, hon. I mean, procreation, that's the whole point of being a man, of being *human*. This is like the best piece of work I've ever made, or better than that. You'll see, you'll see. You're going to be an amazing mother someday, too."

That was it. Saina did the only thing she could think of. She reached out and stroked him, taking some satisfaction in his stiffening, and then tried to smile as she tightened her grip and shoved him as hard as she could back onto the bed. His head clunked against the wall.

"I was going to break up with you anyways," she shouted. "I was just about to, and then you had to do this! Why couldn't you just let me break up with you? You couldn't just give me that?" Wild, disbelieving, she ran to the bathroom, locking the door and leaning against the vintage clawfoot tub. A minute passed in silence, and then she heard Grayson start to pack up his bag. When he knocked on the bathroom door, she opened it and threw his leather Dopp kit at him and then slammed it shut again.

"So, no chance of a ride to the train station, then?" She stayed silent, no longer even surprised at what he could say. "Okay, I know, of course not. And you probably don't want to lend me your car, right?" Or maybe his advanced degree of fuckery could still surprise her. "I'm kidding, Saina. A little levity. You always like that, don't you?" She sat on her fingers, smashing them against the penny tiles, examined a crack in the grouting between the basin sink and the wall, looked at her toenails, still pink. "Saina, please don't hate me forever. Please try to be a little happy for us, for me and the baby. I think we might name him James. Good name, right? Solid." He rattled the doorknob. She stayed very still. "Okay, I'm leaving now. You'll understand someday." He rapped on the door. Another moment. "I'm not sorry that I came up."

And then he was gone.

+

Santa Barbara, CA

84 Miles

NOBODY CAME UP to say goodbye to Grace. Maybe no one knew. Her best friends, Cassie and Lo, were out of school at the moment — in Athens with their Greek class — and the thought of telling anyone else felt exhausting. Later, other students would drop out, their families bankrupted by Bernie Madoff and bad real estate, but right now there was only Grace, and she stood in the front vestibule alone, a pile of bags at her feet.

She wasn't really used to being alone. That's what happens when you're the youngest child and every space you occupy already belongs to someone else: your sister's clothes, your brother's old kindergarten teacher, you as the tagalong, like a Girl Scout cookie, waiting to see if you'll be included in their games. And then you're the only one to be sent off to boarding school, where every moment is communal: breakfast, lunch, and dinner with the same 125 people who know exactly how you butter your toast and how high you roll up your uniform skirt.

Now this. Everything bad was happening to her before anything *interesting* happened. She sighed. Wasn't that just the way life was.

"Hello, dear." It was Dr. Brown, the headmistress.

"Hi, Brownie."

Brownie raised an eyebrow. "You know we're very sorry to see you go, dear."

Shrug.

"But I'm sure that everything will be alright. Your family will find a way through this."

Grace turned away. The school was built on a hill that sloped up gently from rows of red-roofed houses. A long driveway wound towards the front arch where they stood; over the suburbs and the cypress trees Grace could see a glimmer of ocean and town, and the highway that led south to home. Except it wasn't home anymore. She wondered which car they'd be driving to Saina's and how there'd be enough space for all of their things.

Or maybe all the cars were gone, too. Her dad tended towards small, fast vehicles — he was dismissive about the SUVs that crowded the parking lot on Parents' Weekend: *"Gei bai pang zi,"* he'd whispered to her stepmother, and then said loudly, for Grace, "Fat white man, fat white ladies, only they need such big cars. Ha!" Never mind that she'd understood the Chinese — he always doubted her ability to understand the simplest words and then expected her to get allusions to old Chinese poems and pointless ancient sayings — or that everyone would hear him. Grace couldn't care less if other people's fat parents heard themselves get called fat. No, what completely annoyed her was that "Ha!" Any time her father said something that he thought was funny in English, he had to add that "Ha!" at the end. Totally irritating.

Brownie tapped her on the shoulder, trying to get her attention.

"What?" Was she expecting a hug? Grace hoped not, fake hugs were so gross.

"Grace, dear, I'm afraid I'm going to have to take your laptop, you know that it's school property."

Grace stared at her. "It's not! We paid for this!" It was supposed to be part of the tuition package — a new laptop for each student, each year, with last year's donated to the teen center. Except, oh god, now *she* was a poor at-risk youth. Maybe she could go to the center and find her laptop from last year.

"I'm sorry, dear, but unfortunately it's the property of the school."

"Brownie, you *can't* take it away. My *life* is on there! And my dad *paid* for it, it's not the school's!"

"Well, Grace, unfortunately you have not paid for it. You actually began the year without any tuition being paid. We had no reason to doubt your family's ability to do so, and we know that some accountants are not as vigilant with regards to tuition as they might be, so we chose not to press the matter, which clearly turned out to be a mistake." She placed a hand on Grace's laptop case. "It's too bad that you have to be affected by these adult matters, but I do hope you understand."

Oh god. This must be what a heart attack felt like. Something seizing her inside, pinching off her veins. Blood kept flowing out but no oxygen could get pumped in; it would keep on happening like that until her heart shriveled into a tiny thing and rattled right out of her chest.

"Fine," said Grace, shoving her whole laptop case at Brownie. No crying. No. Crying.

The headmistress pulled out the laptop then held the case — really Saina's old Marc Jacobs satchel — out towards her. Grace shook her head. Brownie sighed.

"Please, Grace. Your attitude won't make this any better. You know we don't want your bag" — they stared at each other for a moment, Grace refusing to move —"but we will need the power cord."

"I know. Fine. It's in here." Grace dropped to the floor in lotus position and pulled her checkered rollie down so that its outstretched handle clanged into the brick floor. Jamming her hand into the side of the bag, she felt her way past the soft layers of her tank tops and dresses and jeans, searching for the white cord. "Wait, it's not here. No, I know it is." She looked up. "I'm not lying, okay?" Tears prickled against the back of her nose, crowded towards her eyes, threatened to pool over and spill. It took three more tries before her hand connected with hard plastic and she pulled out the cord.

Grace looked at Brownie again. The headmistress was staring at her cryptically. It wasn't pity on her face. She wasn't looking at Grace the way that Rachel had, with that totally cloying combo of pity and guilt. This was something different.

"Are you going to let me download my stuff, or does that belong to the school, too?"

"Of course you can download any personal information. I know you probably have quite a lot of photographs of, well, of yourself."

"Yeah. So?"

Brownie sighed. "Grace, just go ahead and do whatever you need to do."

Weird. She was acting weird, like *she* was the one who deserved to be upset or something. Maybe she just didn't understand style blogs.

Grace powered the laptop on and plugged in her backup drive.

Finder > Grace Home > Photos > Morning > September.
Select All.
3,212 photos.

She dragged the folder over to the icon for her drive and dropped it in. A progress bar popped up. Two percent. Three.

Grace looked up at Brownie, who was tapping at her phone, probably trying to figure out text messaging or something. "You don't have to wait out here. I'll bring it over to the office when I'm done."

Brownie hesitated. "It's alright. I'm sure you'd rather not be on your own at the moment."

Ha. "Um, I don't mind being on my own. And it might take half an hour to copy everything over."

"Then that's what it takes."

"Hi, Gracie, Daddy here now!"

A car door slammed, and Grace looked up from the screen to see her father climbing the brick steps towards her, arms outstretched, shouting loud enough for the whole school to hear.

No! She wasn't done yet. There were still five more folders of self-portraits, plus a bunch of street style shots that she took of kids at school. Maybe it would go faster if she copied a few batches at a time. Quickly, before her dad could get all the way up the steps, Grace dragged two more of the folders in the Morning file over and tensed as she waited for another progress bar to pop up.

"*Xiao bao!* What's wrong, heh?" Charles put a hand on Grace's head and then slowly crouched down next to her, using her shoulder for balance. He was out of breath from the sprint up the stairs but, Grace knew, he didn't want to get his linen pants dirty. "Hey, don't sit like that, Mei-mei," said Charles, pointing at her outstretched legs. "Always cross knees, okay?"

Suddenly, Grace felt deeply embarrassed. She didn't want her father to know what she was doing, didn't want him to know that he hadn't paid for the computer. He must know, of course, but he didn't have to know that *she* knew that he knew.

"Welcome, Mr. Wang." Brownie rose from the bench across the entryway, where she'd been sitting for the past twenty minutes. Grace felt her father wobble and kept her head down, willing the computer to go faster. Half a moment later, he had sprung up and was heading towards Brownie, hands outstretched.

"Ah! Headmistress Brown! It is lovely to see you again, though the circumstances are quite unfortunate! Is Grace giving you any trouble?"

"Dad! How is any of this my fault?"

"No, not your fault," said her father quickly.

"Oh no, Mr. Wang, Grace has been handling herself in a way that befits her name."

Still spinning. The little Mac wheel of death. The files were never going to finish copying over and her father probably wouldn't wait. She could see Babs in the station wagon — why the station wagon? — staring straight ahead.

"*That's* the car that you kept? Why, Dad?"

Her father shrugged. "Ama gave back to us."

"Are we going to switch to Andrew's car?" It was a Range Rover. That probably made more sense.

"No, no. Ama give this back, we give that back."

"Dad, what do you mean? Give it back to who? Isn't it his?"

"Gracie. *Bu yao zai shuo le,* okay? We talk later."

Rebellion burned in Grace's chest. Her father wanted her to be on his side, to smile and wave and skip in front of Brownie so it would look like nothing was wrong, but he was the one who sold her out first with his "Is Grace giving you any trouble?" Of course she wasn't. He was the one who was giving them all trouble, all the trouble was always about him. He was the one who'd freaked out and packed her off to boarding school two years ago just because she'd fallen for a boy. Diva Daddy, Saina sometimes called him — she and Andrew had a whole song about it, complete with jazz hands. Babs should have been the diva, but instead it was her father.

The laptop burned through her jeans, making her legs feel itchy and constrained. Both of the adults looked at her, not talking to each other.

"Gracie, what are you doing? Time to go now, okay?" Again, accusing. *Fine.*

Then she wasn't on his side at all; everything was his fault.

"Dad, is it true that we didn't pay for this?" She jutted her chin towards the computer. "They're making me give it back to them, but I have so much stuff on here, it's going to take forever to copy it all over and I didn't know that I couldn't keep it."

"What you need to copy?"

"Stuff for my blog, my photos, important stuff."

Expansive, proud, her father beamed. "Gracie! You have the blog? Why you don't tell Daddy? Good, good, now you can be Internet millionaire! No problem!"

Nice try, Daddy. "Well, maybe, but it's a style blog. I didn't invent Facebook or anything. But it does get a lot of hits, and people link to my stuff a lot."

"That's okay, you become Internet star! So you need this computer?" Charles turned to the headmistress. "Dr. Brown, we can pay you for this now and then take it with us? How much does this cost?"

"Well, I don't know if that will work, Mr. Wang. It really remains the property of the school and —"

"This Apple Mac Pro laptop, right? You buy in the summer, I think it probably $1,100 new?" As he spoke, her father turned towards her and gave her just the slightest smile, really more a wrinkle of the eye and a tug of the lip. Grace felt her heart leap and swell so that it stopped being a tiny heart-attack heart and filled up to its proper size. Brownie was the enemy, after all! Grace rushed to cancel the file transfer and started to shut down her computer. "But you get school discount, about 10 percent, so that make it $990 —"

"I suppose $1,000 would be an acceptable compromise, Mr. Wang. We will, of course, still have to send you a bill for the time that Grace has boarded so far this year —"

He cut in. "But this not possible to sell for $1,000, and there are no other students who need one, right? You can't give old one to a new student even if someone transfer. All you do with this is donate to the shelter, which give school tax write-off of $990, which mean you pay a little bit less taxes. Maybe $75 less? So this computer now worth almost nothing to you — just \$75. Maybe not even." He hauled up Grace's suitcase, then pulled a roll of cash out of his pocket. "Here, I give you \$300, it almost like the school make money." He peeled off three bills and thrust them towards Brownie, who took them hesitantly. They were old, Grace noticed, like they'd come from the '80s. Grace jumped up, laptop and backup drive already shoved back into their satchel home, and grabbed the rest of her bags.

"Bye, Brownie! Thanks for everything!" In a giddy rush, Grace ran down the steps, waving a hand backwards as her father bumped along behind her, the suitcase wheels banging against each step. She looked back and he was grinning wildly, the sun glinting off his reflective lenses, knees akimbo as he charged forward. She wanted to say something else, something that would just make the headmistress fall over with fury, something that the other kids would hear and repeat to one another until it became legendary, but she was almost at the bottom of the steps and her mind was a pure, pulsating blank. Leaping off the last two steps and onto the driveway, she turned and shouted: "Tell Rachel I killed myself!"

Laughing at her own stupid bravado, Grace raced herself to the car and stopped by the back, not even out of breath. Half a minute later, her father slammed into her with a hug and pulled open the back door.

"Back full," he said, tossing her bags in as Ama shook her head and arranged them on the floor in front of her. "Say hi to your auntie, Grace." She leaned in the open window of the front passenger seat and gave Barbra their usual quick, no-pucker kiss on the cheek and then stood on her knees in the backseat so she could reach Ama over the pile of luggage.

"*Eh, wo men ba* Andrew *fang zai na li ya?*" asked Ama.

Charles started up the car.

Uh-oh. Brownie was heading down the stairs towards them, clipping along in her pointy brown boots. If Grace's last name was Brown, she would never, ever wear the color; same with Green or Gold, though it would be hard never to wear Black. Grace leaned over the front seat, the wheel of her suitcase jamming into her hip as she pointed up at Brownie, and urged, "Daddy, go, go, go!"

"Daddy pretty good, right Gracie?"

"*Ah bao,* what did you do?" asked Babs.

"Oh, he did good. Really good." Feeling daring, Grace patted her father on the head. "Who needs money! Right, Daddy?" She giggled, and said, quick, "He stole a computer!"

"No, no, no," protested Charles, putting a hand on Babs's arm, "I buy it! Just for very good price."

"Dad, you have to go! Faster!" He shifted his hand back on the wheel and swerved towards the gates.

Grace turned as her father sped out of the lot so that she could see Brownie out of the rear window. She almost expected the headmistress to wave her fist in the air like a vanquished supervillain, then drop to her knees and raise both arms to the sky as balled-up hundred-dollar bills tumbled from her hands.

Well, three of them, anyway.

Really, this was all starting to feel like a movie or something, like a scenario that Saina and Andrew would come up with and make her act out under their direction until it all ended in tears. Hers, mostly, but sometimes Andrew's, too. Like it could all be some elaborate practical joke. The possibility spun itself together in Grace's mind, a cotton candy cloud that sweetened the embarrassment of the past day.

Maybe! She turned around and sat down with a bounce, feeling encouraged as she fastened her seat belt. Maybe this was why her siblings had been reluctant to tell her about the inheritance, why she didn't even know that there was a Talk and a Lunch. And, after all, didn't this make so much more sense than the cover story? That her father had lost everything?

Ridiculous. Impossible.

Maybe Brownie was actually in on it. Actually, Brownie probably resented her. No one who had money would ever be stuck working at some boarding school in Santa Barbara, not even teaching, just . . . *administrating.* If Brownie knew, then that meant she'd been keeping the secret during the whole computer exchange; it all just made Grace feel more conspiratorial glee at the way her father had come out on top.

They were flying down the hill now, speeding past middle-aged cyclists in ridiculous spandex outfits, and Grace knew, just knew, that Andrew and Saina were both headed back to L.A. for some sort of party at the house. That was probably why they'd kept not calling her back, and why they didn't even seem all that upset about everything. They'd never been very good actors.

Or maybe everyone was going to keep up the charade for a few days. In fact, maybe it wasn't so much a joke as a test, something to teach Grace the value of money by making her think that it was all being taken away from her. Like that movie with Michael Douglas — was it called *The Game*? — where his whole life is ruined and then he ends up jumping off a building but there's a net at the bottom for him and then a whole party. Her birthday wasn't for a few more months, but she was a New Year's Eve baby so it probably would have been too complicated to pull off the whole thing over the holidays.

Seven million dollars!

Well, she'd be good and earn it all. There would probably be tasks, like on *The Amazing Race,* challenges to solve, places to prove that she wasn't a snob, even if her dad totally was. She wouldn't complain, she wouldn't whine, she'd just play along. What if someone was actually filming the whole thing? Though her dad probably wouldn't let that happen — he hated reality TV.

"*Xiao bao, ni you zhang da le,*" said Ama, reaching over to squeeze Grace's hand.

Maybe this was all Ama's idea. Grace was pretty sure that she was Ama's favorite, and she couldn't remember anything like this happening when Saina or Andrew turned seventeen. Of course, she had only been a kid when Saina was seventeen, so it might have all been hidden from her — since everyone was so good at keeping secrets from her — but this definitely hadn't happened back when Andrew turned seventeen and sprouted eleven proud hairs on his chest. It was kind of gross, but they'd counted them.

"Hi, Ama," said Grace, bringing their clasped hands up to her cheek. The older woman's hand was soft, like the underbelly of some baby animal, and Grace rubbed it absentmindedly against her face. "Oh, I haven't really grown up all that much, I'm not even seventeen yet." *Was that a smile from Ama? A conspiratorial wink?*

Ama took her hand back and settled it in her lap. "*Da yie shi* big, *bu zhi shi* old."

"Oh, I know. I grew another inch." She marked the distance with her fingers and Ama nodded, satisfied.

Grace slouched down, driving her knees into the back of Barbra's seat. This had been her mother's car when she was still alive. Her mother, who Grace didn't have any actual memories of because she'd died just eight weeks after Grace was born. All she had were borrowed ones, taken from Andrew's own barely there memories and Saina's infrequent stories. Or made-up ones that she thought up herself as she flipped through albums of old photographs and scrapbooks of her mother's modeling shots.

Their mother, cutting open oranges and feeding them into the industrial-looking juicer that still lived in the kitchen, hidden deep in some closet or cabinet. Their mother, scooping out the seeds from a maw of pulp and teaching Saina and even Andrew to spit them using some sort of tongue-funnel technique that they'd never been able to successfully explain to her. Their mother, dressed to go out for the evening in a scarlet-pink gown with flowing skirts — probably Oscar de la Renta, Saina had added — whispering stories to baby Andrew while Daddy shouted for her downstairs.

Their mother laughing. Their mother braiding hair. Their mother telling stories about *her* mother, who was in a nursing home now, but had owned a Chinese restaurant downtown. Their mother getting mad at Daddy and throwing a bowl of salad against the wall, a clang and then a shower of green.

Their mother stepping into a helicopter.

That last one was the story Grace told herself over and over again. It was based on a photograph she had tacked up in her dorm room, the final image of their mother, the one Rachel had skipped over in her death catalog. The story had only two lines.

"She had me. She got into a helicopter."

Sometimes there were variations, but it was still always just two lines.

"I was a little baby. She got into a helicopter."

And: "She had me. They went to the Grand Canyon."

And once, just once: "She died. Daddy didn't."

Grace opened her bag and flipped through the manila folder of images she'd pulled off her wall and slipped out the photo, laying it on her lap so her father wouldn't be able to see it in the rearview mirror. There was still a little Blu-Tack left on the back of it, just enough to make it stick. Bending down slowly and shaking her hair over her left shoulder so that it made a sort of shield, Grace reached over and stuck the picture onto the bottom edge of the car door. Its '80s colors faded now, the canyon a sepia wash behind her mother's buoyant perm and snakeskin cowboy boots, her father behind the camera, clicking her mother into place, making her always thirty-two years old, the pregnant fullness forever just fading from her cheeks.

A hand reached out to tuck Grace's hair behind her ear. Startled, she moved her leg to hide the photo and glanced up, but it was just Ama, old Ama, who smoothed Grace's hair down and looked at her with watery eyes, irises faded and pupils yellowed.

$$+ -$$

Grand Canyon National Park, AZ

MOST PEOPLE THOUGHT May Lee died on a mule. That was the worst part of it. Once they heard that it happened at the Grand Canyon, half of them just assumed that a mule was involved.

Charles Wang hated mules. Ugly, whimpering, misbegotten creatures; infertile beasts of burden. The only people who still used mules for anything other than entertainment were the mujahideen and the Amish, both lost tribes fighting for the useless past. Still, Charles let the misconception stand. After all, he could hardly go around reminding people that the mother of his children had ended her days in a fiery helicopter crash and not stumbling off the edge of a cliff on the back of a dusty gray excuse for a steed.

In truth, May Lee never stumbled. She was light and graceful and sweet, and by the time she died, Charles was thoroughly tired of spending his life with her.

Before that trip to the Grand Canyon, right after little Gracie was born, Charles had visited his lawyer to discuss initiating a divorce, but he hadn't gone through with it.

He and May Lee had been married for a little more than ten years, without a prenup.

When Charles bundled May Lee off to city hall just three months after they'd met, in a rush of lust and tenderness that he'd mistaken for true love, the word *prenup* wasn't even in his lexicon. And California, in its infinite wisdom, was a community-property state, which meant that he would lose half of everything he'd made in the years they'd been together because he'd been misled by a lopsided dimple and a well-applied swoop of eyeliner.

Mischief.

That's what he'd been promised, but instead he received a dim bulb of goodness and passivity; it was a trade that a lesser man might have seen as a victory, but Charles Wang knew that he didn't want to live out his life with goodness.

But the babies! Oh, the babies!

Charles was a man who loved children. His were small and soft and beautiful — God help the ugly babies! — with chubby little arms that always reached out to him. They were encased in sweet rosy skin that looked so perfect, so smooth and unblemished, that he wanted to roll them up in bales of cotton fluff and stuff them down his shirt like a kangaroo. He wished they could stay hidden away, with their damp, trusting little mouths, until they developed some sort of hard shell impenetrable to drugs or sex or disappointment or any of the thousand poison-tipped arrows the world might aim in their direction.

He could never trust May Lee to take care of them half the time. Or more. Those shortsighted judges would likely have awarded her and her dimple more custody of the children, more money of his, even though she had remained as resolutely empty-headed as she was the day they'd met.

The mother of his children was a beautiful woman who took her beauty for granted, who modeled only because a photographer had walked into Joy Loy, her parents' Little Tokyo chop suey joint, and seen her standing there behind the counter, ready.

And why did she marry him?

Because he'd walked up to her at a party full of surfer-blond waiters in tuxedo shirts and stonewashed jeans passing trays of Wolfgang Puck's first attempt at smoked salmon pizza to beturbaned Grace Jones wannabes and held his hand out to her, May Lee Lu.

May Lee. It meant *beautiful* in Chinese, though most immigrants would spell her name Meili. But May's parents were third-generation Chinatown babies who tried to give their daughter a name that would go both ways, and it did. It spoke to Charles, who was lost in a sea of Jennys and Donnas, and it rolled off the tongues of the photographers and agents who kissed her cheeks and tried to ply her with champagne cocktails.

Charles had looked at her, the only other Chinese person in the room, and thought he recognized something fundamental in her. A deep kinship. An abiding drive that had landed them both in this strange room, at this strange moment. A willingness to dive into the whole wide world.

And May Lee looked at him, the only other Chinese person in the room, and thought about how much easier life would be if she was married.

Charles and May Lee Wang went to the Grand Canyon eight short weeks after the birth of their third child in order to do all the things that white people do with their marriages.

> Try to reconnect! *(Hint: Eyes are the windows to the soul — have a sexy staring contest!)*
> Have romantic dinners! *(Hint: Oysters are aphrodisiacs!)*
> Talk about your feelings! *(Hint: Men love to solve problems — let them!)*

It was all from a list May Lee kept folded in her purse, torn out of the February 1990 issue of *Mademoiselle.* Sixteen years later, he could still remember the photo of the laughing blond couple in matching denim shirts at the top of that list, and the careful way she unfolded the tearsheet and smoothed it out every time she referenced one of the hints.

Item four on the list: Share new experiences! *(Hint: Fear is bonding! Why not try a roller coaster?)*

May Lee was scared of heights. Charles was scared of dying in a helicopter crash. So they booked the Lover's Special, a seventy-five-minute aerial tour of the Grand Canyon departing from Las Vegas that promised majesty, grandeur, and two glasses of champagne apiece. As May Lee stepped into the helicopter, Charles took a picture and then bounded across the tarmac to settle into the bucket seat beside her. In a determined show of affection, he adjusted the straps of his wife's seat belt and leaned in close to buckle it, but left his own undone so that his shirt wouldn't rumple. As they flew over the South Rim and caught their first glimpse of the canyon out of the fishbowl windows, Charles took hold of May Lee's small hand.

"Wow, it's so pretty! It's huge!" she said, squeezing his hand.

Charles didn't answer. Instead, he felt the helicopter sway from side to side like an old-fashioned cradle and wondered if this was one of those daredevil pilots who was going to try to get a rise out of them by pretending he was about to crash. Charles felt the sweat prickle under the rough linen of his Rive Gauche safari shirt and was just about to tap their pilot on the shoulder when the man's voice broke into their prerecorded tour narration.

"Folks, we seem to be having a problem —"

And then a wild, sick lurch and a screech from the front seat as the pilot — a former Coast Guard sergeant who completely lost hold of his military demeanor — gave up control of the craft. Their helicopter slammed into one of the 270-million-year-old Kaibab Limestone formations, bounced, once, on a ridge, and exploded as it dropped five thousand feet to the floor of the canyon.

Still on the ridge: Charles, saved by his sartoriphilia.

The bounce threw an un-seat-belted Charles against the improperly latched door, flinging him out while slowing his trajectory just enough that he landed with no more force than, say, a fall off a bicycle. Charles experienced the entire event as a flash of heat and steel and noise, accompanied by a gunpowder-and-roses smell so unexpectedly sweet that he was sure he'd open his eyes to find himself in the testing room of one of his factories, a broken vial of rose oil at his feet. Instead, he stood at the edge of death, choking on dust and surprise, wiping mule shit from his shirt, and was instantly flooded with a shameful relief. He wasn't *happy* that May Lee was almost certainly gone, but as he looked down on the fireball at the bottom of the grand and glorious canyon, he knew that luck had once again smiled upon Charles Wang.

Vernon, CA

186 Miles

DRIVING SOUTHEAST on two and a half hours of freeways, plus an hour at a U-Haul rental place on Western and Venice, landed the Wangs behind a building in Vernon close to sunset. Covered with a faded mural of giant Aztec women grinding maize under gargantuan stalks of corn, the former tortilla plant was now — or was until last week, at least — one of the three buildings that warehoused the output of Charles's factories.

He still had the key. In fact, he still had all of his keys, encircling a wide brass ring, each bearing a piece of dark green label tape embossed with a number and a letter. This was the fifth property that he had acquired, after the vast mixing plant in Garden Grove and before the former aircraft hangar next to a thread manufacturer downtown, so he located key 5a (the front door) and 5d (the back door). 5b was for the bathroom and 5c opened the small office inside the warehouse. The letters were assigned depending on Charles's own migratory patterns: whichever door he opened first received an *a*, and then onwards through the alphabet, so that each time he revisited a place it also meant retracing that first heady rush of acquisition.

"Dad, what are we doing here?"

"Daddy just getting some things to put in the U-Haul. No problem."

Charles slammed the car door shut. Let them puzzle over what he was doing; better that than to explain or ask permission. Anything stealthy was always best done out in the open; confidence was the truest disguise. Not that there would be anyone else watching in this strange little city where only factories and warehouses lived. He and KoKo had once explored their way through Vernon after her first big order went into production — she in a violet-and-canary-patterned kimono minidress and platform sneakers, he in a crisp, banded straw fedora, walking arm in arm through the dusty streets littered with salsa-smeared balls of foil and other taco-truck detritus. Now KoKo wouldn't even speak to him and that fedora was still hanging on a peg in his closet, waiting to be sold off.

Charles rounded the corner. When the bank took possession of his properties, he'd been required to sign a stack of contracts, one of which ensured that he would no longer approach or access any of them. The surveillance cams weren't mentioned in the endless triplicates that he signed, each with a flourish bigger than the last, so Charles had asked Manny, the manager — so satisfying that match between name and occupation! — to switch them all off. He'd never bothered to contract with an outside security firm; pricey as it was, there wasn't much of a black market in argan oil.

This should be simple. Go in the front door, grab a dolly from the office, locate the fifteen boxes that were marked for Ellie and Trip Yates in Opelika, Alabama, go out through the back door, load up the U-Haul, maybe slip the dolly in with the boxes, and speed back onto the 10 freeway.

And then he saw it. Glinting betrayal in the form of a new doorknob, gaudy gilt where the old brass one, worn smooth by years of maize-powdered hands, had once been.

Now the sun felt almost unbearably hot and Charles backtracked around the corner only to spot the same Home Depot special on the rear door. Alright. There was one more solution left.

"Gracie . . . ," said Charles, leaning in through the driver's side window. "You want to help Daddy?"

She looked up, frowning at him. "With what?"

Charles paused. It was hard to predict what would launch Grace into a wounded fury. She never used to be like that, his Gracie. It was his fault. He never should have sent her away. Charles could feel himself sagging with middle-aged defeat, a loser who lacked the hot-blooded need to wrestle America to the ground and take her milk money, who never had the balls to flip his father's shame into a triumphant empire, who marched obediently towards death and hid from life and always chose the wrong path. *No. Not yet.* He was still Charles Fucking Wang and he would lead the way out of the wilderness. Straightening to his full five feet eight inches and sucking in his stomach so that his shirt rode smoothly into the waistband of his trousers, Charles cocked his head at Grace and gestured for her to get out of the car.

"Sorry, Daddy, yes — I'll help you. What do you want me to do?"

Charles looked down the alley. It was past sunset and all the workers at the factories on either side of his had long since gone home.

"Daddy's key not working. You just climb in the open window up there and open door from inside, okay?"

One long look from Grace, and then a smile that he wasn't expecting. "Good one, Dad."

"Not a joke, okay? Daddy too old to climb things, right?"

"Oh, no, I know, I don't think it's a joke. Just a good one," she said, winking.

Teenagers were such a mystery. Parts of Saina and Andrew had turned unknowable in those years, too. There was a time when he thought that Saina might be someone else forever, back when she was entangled with that fiancé of hers. Grayson.

Charles shook his head. A terrible name. Cold and limp, followed by a diminutive. The son of something boring and colorless could only be even more boring and colorless, yet somehow his brilliant daughter had been taken in by him. It was true that the boy had been good-looking. Charles suspected sex was the lure, though he didn't quite want to admit that to himself.

"Okay, I'm ready." Grace had taken off her ridiculous fur vest and little boots, and slipped on a pair of those fabric shoes that Charles had noticed on the feet of more and more of his friends' children recently. Ugly shoes, like the ones that poor people in China wore. "What if we pull the car over and I stand on the hood? I think I can boost myself up from there."

She could, and now her head poked out the back door.

He'd never seen the warehouse so empty before. It was infuriating that someone would take hold of his business and sell it off in pieces instead of letting Charles turn it back around. Because he could. Even though

Lehman Brothers filed Chapter 11 yesterday and interest rates were down
to 2 percent, he could have turned it all back around because America still
needed makeup. He knew, with the certitude of someone who had grown
up calling this land across the Pacific *Mei Guo* — Beautiful Country —
that, more than any other country, this was one that would never reject
improvement. Even those signs along the freeway said it: KEEP AMER-
ICA BEAUTIFUL. But the bank with its unimaginative managers had refused to see things his way. They'd rather pull down the entire country
than believe in Charles Wang.

Shafts of streetlight filtered into the building through the dusty windows, giving off just enough of a glow for Charles to find the pile of boxes
destined for Opelika.

"So why do we need these?"

"We make personal delivery."

"Okay, but why these?"

Why these? Because it was one of the few orders he'd personally sold
since his business had grown. Ellie and Trip were a glowing young couple
that he'd met on a flight to New York. They'd been bumped up to business class and refused his offer to switch seats, instead including him in
their enthusiasm over the warm mixed nuts and free mimosas. The pair
were en route from one friend's wedding in Malibu to another's on Cape
Cod. Afterwards, they were moving back to her Alabama hometown to
open a new-school take on a traditional general store. Handmade clothes,
vintage hoes, and whole grains. Enchanted by their entrepreneurial drive
and soft southern accents, Charles found himself recounting his first
flight to America — the nausea, the revelation in the bathroom, all of it.

"I come to America to get rich, and now I am!" he'd finished.

"So you came here for the American Dream!" said Ellie, pleased.

Charles had laughed. "Not only American Dream! Everybody, every
country, have same dream! Al Gore think he invent Internet, America
think they invent American Dream!" And then he found himself convincing them to develop a line of magnolia-scented lotions and candles.
"Magnolia oil you get local, send to me, I do everything else, you sell and
say 'local magnolia' and everybody will buy!" he'd enthused, imagining it
as the beginning of a southern beauty empire for them, a surefire meld-
ing of gracious tradition and modern style. Pooh-poohing their lack of

capital, Charles waived his minimums and promised that they could spread out their payments, that their orders could grow as their business grew.

He did it for that bubbling, champagne-in-the-veins high, that desire to be part of someone else's new life, someone else's realized potential.

Vampires must feel like that.

"Because I sell to them personally, and I make them spend all their money, so Daddy feel bad if they lose. Besides, we never go to Alabama before."

"But couldn't you just mail it?"

"Business is all about the personal."

She looked at him, considering. "Okay, that's a good lesson. I'll remember it. Business is all about the personal."

Love surged in Charles. Gracie wasn't lost. Living away from home those two years hadn't ruined her. Family was still family. "Good girl, *xiao bao*," he said, reaching out to pat her on the head as she loaded the dolly with boxes.

Grace straightened up and smiled at him, then skipped ahead. She was taller, and she'd loosened up the prim, baby-doll manner she'd had as a girl, all quiet voice and shy eyes. It had been such a shock when Grace, at fourteen, ran away with a boy who flattered her into thinking he was in love with her, who tricked himself into thinking the same thing. A Japanese boy, no less, a fact that Charles felt was a betrayal of the entire nation of China and everything she had suffered at the hands of the Japanese soldiers. He would have expected that kind of treachery from Saina, maybe, but not of his youngest, a girl who had never so much as ordered a pizza on her own and still liked to be tucked in bed each night by Ama. She was fourteen and the boy was fifteen, so they didn't get far; Saina had come home and tracked the wayward lovers to a family friend's empty beach house in La Jolla. A new Gracie had ranted and raved and called it a Shakespearean tragedy; Saina had insisted that she was being more like silly Lydia Bennet, the runaway youngest daughter in *Pride and Prejudice*, than a Bel-Air Juliet; and Charles had privately lamented and rejoiced at the irresistible beauty of his daughters. But when Grace responded to his order that she never speak to the boy again by wailing at the dinner table every night and trying, again, to run away with him, Charles had packed her off to Cate, which, besides being the only boarding school he'd heard of in California, also used its feminine name to make him think at first that it was an all-girls school. A week into the semester, he missed Grace terribly and was increasingly upset that the school was coed, but by then it was too late to go back on his declarations.

But now here they all were again. Almost all. Charles pushed the last of the magnolia-scented lotion out through the back door and slammed it shut, testing the knob to make sure that the warehouse was locked against any other interlopers.

十三

I-10 East

EVERYBODY BUT BARBRA was on the phone. She alone had no one to notify, no one with whom to plot or commiserate. Her everyone was in the seat right next to her, driving with both hands on the wheel and a phone wedged to his ear, edging his shoulder away from her as if that would be enough to keep her from overhearing. Grace chattered to Andrew. Even Ama talked — shouted, actually, voice sharp, face animated — to a someone.

Barbra nudged her husband. "How are all the phones still on?"

He took a hand off the wheel to cover the mouthpiece, and whispered to her, "Not end of month yet."

And once it was, what then? Would they just be cut off from civilization, left to languish in Saina's house, relegated to the role of poor relations? Barbra closed her eyes and leaned her head against the cool pane of the window, letting the family's conversations wash together. They alternately spoke and were quiet, listening to the people on the other end of their lines with an intensity that exhausted her, ratcheting up their voices with each response.

CHARLES: That is all the names I have. What did they say?

AMA: *Yi ding yao zuo fan la!*

GRACE: Yeah, I thought tonight too, but they think it'll be too late —

AMA: *Shei ne me xiao qi? Qian, wo gei qian!*

GRACE: Something Palms? Thirty-four Palms? Ninety-nine Palms?

CHARLES: Of course. Everything good also is difficult. No, no matter —

GRACE: Oh yeah, that's it, Twenty-nine. So just tonight.

AMA: *Hao le la, bu yao zai chao . . .*

CHARLES: The money, don't worry about.

GRACE: Seriously? Who, like a bounty hunter?

CHARLES: Enough for this.

GRACE: And they just showed up?

CHARLES: Okay, okay, I wait.

GRACE: Oh my god, Andrew, really? They just took it?

AMA: *Hao, wo men bu jiou jiou dao le. Xiao Danzi zen yang ah?*

CHARLES: Yes, I wait. You call me again when you have anything.
   Thank you.

GRACE: Are you okay? Did they do anything to you?

AMA: *Ne jiou hao le. Hao,* bye-bye.

GRACE: What did you do?

GRACE: (Laughing.)

GRACE: But seriously, I can't believe it happened like that. Dad said
   something about giving it back, but I thought it would be
   something . . . civilized, at least.

GRACE: Yeah, okay. So we'll see you tomorrow. God, lock your doors!
   Do you think they're going to try to repossess your iPod or
   something?

GRACE: (Laughing.)

GRACE: Okay. Bye.

Barbra heard her stepdaughter sigh and, despite herself, felt a prick of
worry for Andrew. "Grace? What happen to your brother? What are you
talking about?"

Grace was quiet for a moment, then she searched out her father in the
rearview mirror.

"Dad, Andrew said that a repo man came and took his car."

Charles kept his eyes on the road.

"Did you know that was going to happen?"

Barbra watched her husband's grip on the wheel tighten as he stared
straight ahead. Then he shrugged, small.

"I don't know, exactly."

"But you knew that he had to give the car back. You *said.*"

Silence.

"What happened to the other cars? Babs, what happened?"

Barbra hadn't taken her eyes off of Charles, but he didn't seem to react to Grace's question. Well, there was no reason she should be spared the truth. It could hardly have escaped her notice that she'd been pulled out of school, and soon they'd be bunking down in dingy motel rooms across America. She turned to face Grace.

"They were all repossessed last week. Your father didn't want to ask Andrew to drive back home, so his was repossessed at school."

"Daddy?"

Charles shrank into his collar. He really wasn't going to reply. Nothing. In all the years of their marriage, in all the years since they'd met, really, Barbra's admiration of Charles had never wavered. She respected the fact that he wasn't an academic, someone with extant family money and a nearsighted squint; that he'd wrested a cosmetics empire out of the wilds of this foreign land. There had been a time, in the sex-soaked half decade that began their relationship, when the sight of him snapping a shirt straight before putting it on had been enough to send a weakening shot between her legs. But now, in the silence that sank into the pinpoints of the perforated leather upholstery, Barbra looked at Charles and felt curiously maternal. She had never even held a newborn before, but it must feel something like this, this urge to soften the world around him while simultaneously finding herself bewildered by the creature to whom she had once been so intimately connected.

Touching his arm, she pointed at a rapidly approaching In-N-Out sign, and said, low, "We should eat before we get there — we can't ask her daughter to feed us all." Charles turned towards her, grateful, and flicked on the right turn signal.

"Eh?" Ama called out. *"Ni yao jia you ah?"*

"Wo men qu chi In-N-Out, *hao ma?"* replied Charles.

"Bu bu bu, wo nu er yi jing zai zuo wan fan le."

Oh, dinner at Ama's daughter's house. Barbra couldn't bear the thought. A casserole. A can of soup hastily heated in a dinged pot. An iceberg salad. Or, even worse, something that had been labored over and was still nearly inedible.

Chicken à la king. Beef stroganoff.

Any one of those horrid American cookbook concoctions that Ama's daughter probably tried to solder together out of supermarket ingredients in her desert shack.

But Charles, dutiful to his Ama if nothing else, kept the car on the highway and didn't even glance at the cluster of fast food joints as they zoomed past.

"Do we have to stay there?" asked Grace. "Like, for the night?"

Charles peered at her over his shoulder, trying to gauge his daughter's tone. "Maybe we stay. Rest and leave early in the morning. Ama invited us, so it not so polite to refuse."

Oh dear. Barbra hadn't even considered that possibility. Scratchy Kmart sheets and thin bars of soap. It would be a preview of every motel they were due to check into on this journey, probably with a desperately chugging swamp cooler dampening the hard carpet and sun-faded patches on the vulgar sofas. Back to a life she thought she'd left behind.

Grace said nothing, but Barbra could hear the girl shift in the backseat, and a moment later, she felt a pair of teenage knees jam themselves into her spine. May Lee's daughter. That's how Barbra thought of her sometimes. The last productive thing May Lee ever did. Saina felt like Charles's daughter, and Andrew was a sort of free agent, sunny even in the aftermath of his mother's death and strangely impervious to parenting. Grace was the one she had known from infancy and probably the one who came closest to her practical outlook on the world, but a polite distance always remained between the two of them.

Even in close proximity like this, there was a barrier. Barbra felt her seat jostle and sat up slightly, turning her attention to the dusty world outside the car. She had never really seen the point of the desert. It was a useless landscape, more a failure of evolution than a valid ecosystem. Scorpions and cacti, leftovers from Mother Nature's rebellious phase; shouldn't She have gotten past all that by now?

十四

Twentynine Palms, CA

328 Miles

THE HOUSE was way tinier than Grace had been expecting. Of course, she'd *seen* bad neighborhoods before, but they were always places that you passed through on your way to somewhere else. First of all, the walls on the outside were *metal.* And not a cool metal, like titanium, which would have made it look maybe like a giant MacBook. No, instead they were something flimsy and dinged, probably tin or even aluminum. A foil-wrap house. Second, there was a bouncy castle out front. Like the kind people rented for little kids' birthday parties. Except that Ama hadn't said anything about it being one of her grandkids' birthdays, and the half-deflated castle was covered with a layer of grime, as if it had been sitting on that same patch of dying grass for months, years maybe.

To be fair, this didn't even really seem like a bad neighborhood. Just weird. If you thought about it, this combination of spaceship house and dusty lawn and bouncy castle wouldn't ever exist anywhere else but out here in the desert. Or maybe Vegas — though Grace had never been there before — it's just that whenever ugly things happened people usually said that it looked like Vegas or Florida.

What if the money really was all gone and they ended up having to live somewhere like this? God, suicide really would be better than that.

Ama had gone quiet. Grace tapped her on the shoulder.

"I haven't seen Kathy in a long time."

Ama didn't turn. Just said, *"Mmm,"* in response.

"Maybe almost ten years, right?"

"Kathy *hen meng.*"

"Busy? With the little ones?"

Because Kathy didn't just have kids, she had grandkids, too. Already. That was like her dad having grandkids. Which meant that it was like her having kids.

Wait, that didn't quite make sense — Ama had been her father's wet nurse, she was older than Grace's father. But really not by much. Ama had only been eighteen when she came to take care of him, cast out by her landowning-class family because she was a wayward daughter who had a baby — stillborn, discarded — out of wedlock. She'd been taken in by the neighboring Wang household because they'd had the misfortune of birthing a child who had thrived in the aftermath of a world war. Almost forty years after that, Ama had arrived in America with a teenage Kathy, whose father was an American GI stationed in Taiwan, though no one ever spoke of it.

Ama's daughter followed in that unfortunate military tradition by finding herself married to a Latino man who discarded a promising beginning as a line cook at Michael's in Santa Monica to become an army chef. Kathy was pretty much a single mother even though she was technically still with her husband; in reality, he spent all his time with hot broilers in Bahrain and giant saucepans in Mosul and none of it at their house near the Marine Corps base in Twentynine Palms.

And then Kathy's own daughter had gone and wasted her perfectly lovely face — a face that, Ama always said with a sigh of relief, was still Chinese despite her diluted blood — by actually joining the military herself. When she went and married a fellow soldier whose family happened to be from the Dominican Republic and popped out two coffee-colored babies in quick succession, Ama didn't even try to contain her dismay.

It was a misfortune that had been amply conveyed to the Wangs.

Before Ama had even managed to shuffle her stockinged legs towards the yard, the house door flew open and two *adorable* little kids came running out. Grace didn't even like kids — they were always so *sticky* — but these kids were like baby cocker spaniels or something, all light-up sneakers and squeals with their hair in two miniature Afros. They ran towards the bouncy castle and clambered in, but it sagged so much under their weight that Grace was pretty sure they'd bounce all the way down through the dirt.

"Ama! Are these them? *Look* at them!" Grace hated girls who squealed over teacup Chihuahuas, but she finally understood the impulse. Now the two little ones were tumbled together in the middle of the castle, the half-inflated floor sandwiching them as they giggled and waved coquettishly at the strangers. Grace waved back and grinned at them. Maybe the next test would be babysitting these kids or saving them from kidnappers or something — that wouldn't be too bad.

Before Grace could walk over to the little duo, the door opened wider and Kathy came out. Dressed in an oversize gray fleece zip-up and anonymous sneakers, she looked almost Ama's age. For just a minute, everyone was quiet, and then Grace's dad bounded forward and threw an arm around Kathy's shoulders.

"Ah, it is good to see you again! So many years!"

Why was he always bouncing? If Grace didn't know her dad, she'd probably think he was gay. Kathy didn't seem that into him either. Instead of returning the hug, she shrank back, pulling her reading glasses off her head and putting them on.

"Alright," she said. "Okay." Turning towards the castle, she shouted, "Nico! Naia!" and a second later the kids were at her side. "Say hi to uncle and auntie," she instructed them, as Barbra leaned over and patted each of their cheeks for a moment.

"So cute," said Barbra, and then, cocking her head towards Charles, she said, *"Hwen de hao."* That was another one that Grace knew.

Hwen de hao. Well mixed.

Once, in front of one of her mixed friends, Grace's dad had told Barbra that it was too bad that the girl was *hwen de chou.* Mixed ugly. "Like maybe she have the Down syndrome." The girl had cried, Grace had flamed with embarrassment, Charles had sworn that he forgot he was speaking English and got his secretary to send the girl an enormous box of cosmetics the next day, which made her totally stop talking to Grace at all. But it was what Barbra said that Grace remembered most. In the midst of the commotion, she'd just shrugged, and said, in an effort to stop Grace's pro-testing, "Daddy was only telling the truth. There's nothing wrong with being ugly if that's what you are."

And now Ama and Kathy understood her, too, of course, but they didn't say anything, just held on to each other's hands for a minute and headed into the spaceship house.

Conversation savers. That was another good reason to have kids around. Whenever there was a pause in the grown-ups' talk, before it got unbear-able, one of the adults would look over at Nico or Naia, who were setting up a store with stray personal items charmed from their visitors, and make some comment about their cuteness. Everyone enthusiastically agreed, and then the conversation could resume again. *Phew*. After a while, Grace slid off the scratchy plaid couch and scooched across the linoleum floor.

"Want me to be your customer?" she asked.

Nico, the older one, beamed at Grace and nodded, holding out a leather key fob unhooked from Barbra's purse.

"You could have it," he said. "Except that you have to put it in your pocket."

She tucked it into her jeans as Naia crouched close to the ground and examined Grace's shoes.

"Why do you have holes in your shoes?" she asked.

How do you explain fashion to a little kid?

"Don't you think they're cool-looking?"

Naia looked up, all serious, and shook her head. "Is it because you couldn't buy the other parts?" Grace cocked her head and locked eyes with Naia. This couldn't be part of it. These kids were too . . . kidlike to be a test.

Nico turned to Grace. "Guess what we're having for dinner? Guess!" Grace shrugged and pretended to look very mystified. "Hot dogs! Hot dogs! Hot dogs!"

Hot dogs? Cow lips and tails and ears and vaginas, probably. Or ud-ders. Mushed udders. In a tube. Tube steak. Gross.

"Ai-ya, ni je me xing zuo hot dog *ne? Shei yao chi zhe gou? Jen shi de!"* Ama hissed disapproval at her daughter while Grace tried to avoid her fa-ther's and Barbra's looks.

Kathy shrugged. "What's wrong with hot dogs? Did you think I was going to make a banquet?" Shouldering the kids, she headed into the kitchen, leaving Ama to splutter after her, *"Shei shuo bi yao ge* banquet? *Nu er tai chou la!"*

Ten minutes later, Kathy came out with a platter of boiled hot dogs nestled in soft white buns and then brought out an armful of brand-new condiments: A big forty-ounce Heinz ketchup bottle, a bright yellow bottle of French's mustard that was half as big, and a tiny squeeze bottle of Vlasic sweet relish.

Bleh. Hot dogs were just as gross as Grace remembered. It was like they were all gathered around the living room eating skinny penises on buns — seriously, hot dogs were basically the same thing.

Barbra had drawn two thin lines on hers, one of ketchup and one of mustard, and was now taking neat bites of it, not smudging the lines. Her dad's was piled with relish and he opened his mouth for a giant bite. Kathy was cutting Nico's into pieces and popping them in his mouth while Naia had hers gripped in both hands and inserted halfway in her mouth. She slipped it out again and grinned at Grace. "It's like a ketchup lollipop!" she said.

Ama's plain hot dog rested in her lap, her hands folded on top of it. She watched Kathy for a long moment before she turned to Grace's dad, and said, quietly, bowing her head, *"Jen shi dwei bu qi."*

"Hmm?" he asked, focusing on the last, mustard-streaked bite of his hot dog.

"Wang jia dwei wo ne me hao, wo xian zai je me xing zhi gei ni men hot dogs *lai chi?"*

Grace watched the bulge of chewed-up hot dog go down his throat as he swallowed before answering. "Ama, *qing ni bu yao ne yang zi xiang la."* He turned to Grace. "Gracie, you like hot dog, right? Say to Ama that there is nothing to apologize." Grace wanted to leave, to get up and run out on this moment, on huffy Kathy who must feel completely betrayed by her mom, on this test that was feeling less and less like a game, even on the kids who were getting sticky with ketchup.

"They're great," she said. "It's like we're at a carnival! There's the kids, and the bouncy castle, and the hot dogs!"

"She me boun-cee cah-sul *de?"*

As soon as Ama started talking, Barbra leaned back. *She always did that,* thought Grace, *just took herself out of the family whenever she wanted to.* Of course, when Saina had a big gallery opening or something, Barbra was always ready to get dressed up and be part of the Wangs, but she never stayed on the team for the whole game. So unfair.

"Oh nothing, Ama. It's just — hot dogs are fine, really," said Grace.

"See!" said Charles, waving the last hot dog at Kathy. "All good! No worries!"

"*Ah bao,* I think that's Kathy's," said Barbra. "Kathy, have you had one yet?"

"You want it, you take it," said Kathy, shrugging again. Her salt-and-pepper hair was all bristled up; with her gray fleece and un-made-up face, she looked like she was all one color.

"Well," said Barbra, "we should probably be going soon."

"Ni men bu shi yao zhu yi wan ma?"

"Oh," said Kathy, in a strange, high voice, "did you drive two cars? Did I miss the other one? Did you drive another car besides my ma's?"

Grace looked at the three of them. Getting old was horrible.

She watched her father shuffle uncomfortably on the sofa. Grace hadn't even thought about it, but it was true. This car was supposed to be Ama's. Were they just going to steal it from her now? Sure, her dad had been the one to give it to Ama, but a gift was a gift, wasn't it?

"Ama is very kind, too kind," said Grace's dad. "She will let us drive the car to Saina's house. We hope we can give it back soon."

"Too kind," said Kathy. "Too kind, too, too kind."

十五

THE WANGS had fallen so far, so fast.

As a child, Charles never entirely believed his own family's tales of grandeur: The five-story estate carved into the side of a stone mountain, with a legion of porters ready to carry the mistress of the house up and down on a palanquin. The koi ponds and amusing lap dogs and gold-edged dishes brought out for endless banquets of freshly slain suckling pigs. The hall of treasures, where hunks of amber that contained prehistoric creatures lined the rosewood shelves along with polished nautilus shells and a Fabergé ostrich egg. All of it surrounded by acres upon acres, all green.

He could never parse that mythic life with the spare rooms and quiet meals of his childhood. Over the years, his aunties' remembrances of their familial past had taken on a faded fairy-tale air, mixing in his young mind with thumbed-through stories of the archer who saved the world from seven suns and the goddess who was exiled to the moon, where her only friend was a rabbit.

And now Charles had managed to lose an entire gilded existence twice as quickly, without the assistance of a world war or a murderous demagogue. Maybe failure was encoded in the DNA, like sickle-cell anemia or Tay-Sachs disease, revisiting generation after generation until some quirk of crossbreeding finally managed to eradicate those traitorous chromosomes. Maybe May Lee's blithe stupidity would bubble up and lift the stain of failure from his children. Not that it was working yet. Saina was hiding out in the forgotten countryside, Grace was still a child, and Andrew, well, Andrew wanted to be a stand-up comedian, a career choice that might as well be a deliberate rebellion against success.

He'd tainted them all with his own fatal misstep. Charles had always thought of himself as a businessman's businessman. He was in the makeup game because he had landed on a way to produce popular products cheaply, but it could just as easily have been gourmet peanut butter or building insulation or shoelaces — wherever the opportunity presented itself. He'd trained himself to love the mythos of makeup because of the money to be made, but if he'd come to America with a list of algae-farm contacts, he might even now be extolling the virtues of green juice and branching out into bee pollen.

Everything he did, he did with passion; emotion didn't enter into it. Women were ruled by emotion; men by passion. That was the truth of it. Forget Mars and Venus, the real secret of the difference between the sexes was right there.

Men: conquerors of lands, seekers of beauty, upholders of truth.
Women: bearers of the children, keepers of the homes, mourners
    of the slain.

It was something that Charles had always known. Look at magazines. Women's magazines were all about feeling something. There was advice on how to feel pretty, how to feel love, how to feel happy, all sold to you by making you feel like you were none of those things. Men's magazines, on the other hand, were about making money, going places, having sex with beautiful women, and eating rare or bloody things. Passions, not emotions.

He had pleased himself with that thought whenever he looked over the piles of glossy business magazines commingling with the fashion books in the waiting room of his office: *Fortune* pairing with *Vogue, Elle* and *Marie Claire* splayed across *Fast Company,* staid *Inc.* and *Money* getting their kicks with *V, SmartMoney* sticking it to *Glamour.* Those magazines had always made him feel vaguely sorry for women, as much as he admired them and lusted after them.

Charles remembered reading something in one of the magazines —

Fortune, he thought it was — back in the early days of the millennium, when it had seemed like nothing he did could possibly go wrong. "Companies fail the way Ernest Hemingway wrote about going broke," the writer had said. "Gradually, and then suddenly." That was exactly what it had been like for Charles, though even the gradual part had been very, very sudden.

Emotion was the culprit.

Really, Charles's mistake had been as dumb as keeping all his cash in a box under the bed and then getting drunk and chatty with a thieving locksmith.

For years he'd expanded judiciously, buying factories only when demand raged or prices dropped, but suddenly, simultaneously, sales of three of the brands that he manufactured had skyrocketed, bringing a jump in orders and an influx of cash. The money needed to be reinvested in order to avoid a big tax hit, and Charles's competitive streak was stoked. Why stay in the background, churning out goods for small-time makeup artists, when, in fact, *he* was the visionary? If it was all about the verticals, then *he* should be getting right in front of the consumer with his *own* product. Why let these amateurs earn the giant markup? Charles Wang knew what the world wanted, and he was going to give it to them.

But to do it right, he needed more cash.

In certain dark moments, Charles allowed the conversation to replay in his mind. Each time the turning point loomed larger, each time his own failings stood out more harshly.

Really, it was a series of strikes.

ONE:
Marco Perozzi, the banker he was accustomed to dealing with, was gone.
In his place, J. Marshall "Call me Marsh" Weymouth.
Charles was not a man who believed in the false familiarity of nicknames.

TWO:

It was 2006.

The Fed had just raised interest rates to 5.25 percent and
    threatened to go higher.

Charles was a man who knew that when governments made threats
    they tended to keep their word.

THREE:

The luxury cosmetics market was worth $6 billion.

The largely untapped ethnic cosmetics market was worth a
    potential $3 billion.

Charles was a man who believed in potential.

Right, wrong, wrong.

"Marsh," Charles had said, wielding the nickname like a hundred prep-
school roommates and fellow eating-club members had done before him,
"no one is doing this right now. We can make fortunes!"

Marsh twisted his signet ring. He looked at the line of products that
Charles had arranged on the long obsidian tabletop and fiddled with the
trackpad of the laptop that Charles used for his presentation.

"What are your intentions in creating this line, Mr. Wang?"

"Intention? To make money."

The banker shifted again. "Is that it?"

Charles was confused. He had already talked about his growth strat-
egy, about the buying power of nonwhite women, about the success of
other targeted makeup lines, about his stellar supply chain and his plans
for distribution.

"What else is there?" asked Charles.

Marsh leaned back dispassionately, dismissively.

"Business is no place for politics," he said.

"Politics?"

"The fight for inclusion is a worthy fight," said Marsh, "but it's not one
that traditionally yields high financial returns."

Who did this wan, overbred man think Charles Wang was? Some sort
of brown-people revolutionary with a tube of red lipstick in his raised fist
and an ammo belt strung with eyelash curlers?

"This is not some NAACP for eye shadow, Marsh. Do you know what the markup is on cosmetics even when label is buying straight from manufacturer? Seventy-eight percent! Do you know how much I can make, since I make it all myself? Ninety-five percent markup! The research is there. The market is open. I know how to sell. I have mucho skin in the game. I only need more capital; not so much money for very substantial return."

"No one is questioning your business sense, Mr. Wang. You've clearly been very successful so far. It's my experience, though, that businesses created to do some perceived good rarely achieve that goal."

That asshole. Worse than the Communists, with words that confirmed their meaning by denying it.

"We simply like to be certain that our money is being used to make more of it."

Charles thought longingly of Perozzi, his former point man at the bank. They had enjoyed a nearly perfect borrower-banker relationship. Charles requested; Marco assented. Charles prospered; Marco collected. What more was there?

And then it came. The fatal flaw. Emotion slunk into the picture.

J. Marshall Weymouth made Charles feel small, like he hadn't made his first million by the time he was thirty-three years old, like he didn't have a flaming redhead named Saoirse on call, like he hadn't blown out of Taiwan with nothing but a urea pipeline and lucked himself into the most ideal wife-and-children combo possible. Made Charles feel like five thousand years of Chinese culture didn't stand up to a few generations of penitent nobodies who thought a single act of tea-soaked rebellion was enough to crown a nation. Nobodies who took pride in being nicknamed for a winged parasitic bug. Fucking WASPs.

"Fine," said Charles. "Personal guarantee. This is not some sort of multi-culti show, this is a strong and serious business investment. Here —"

Charles reached for the loan papers and uncapped a black Sharpie. Across the section that began LOAN AND DELIVERY OF COLLATERAL PURSUANT TO PROMISSORY NOTES, he penned *836 Glover Circle*.

"My home," he said, shoving the papers back across the table. "You wonder how much money I expect to make for you? Enough that I stake my family house on it. Personal guarantee. This tell you enough?"

Hot. Charles remembered being burning hot, the tiny points on his scalp jumping and prickling.

Weymouth had simply raised an eyebrow, and said, "Alright, Mr. Wang. I'll choose to believe in the numbers."

And then, to add insult to stupidity, Charles had said — oh, how he hated himself now! — "Right, then. I believe in the numbers, too," and opted for a fixed-rate loan.

And then interest rates dropped step by step as surely as they had climbed in the twenty-two months before he locked in his loan. Every day Charles watched them fall as he bit his knuckles and told himself that he was about to be so successful that none of this would matter. Nothing would matter. The point of making so much money was so that money itself would no longer matter. He'd pay off the whole loan at once and beat the rates at their own game.

He was, of course, wrong.

All of it mattered; mattered so much that it wiped out everything else that had ever mattered before.

All it took was two years. Charles secured that loan and opened two ten-thousand-square-foot, no-expense-spared flagship stores in San Francisco and Chicago — cities that, he thought, were underserved by beauty — and filled them both with a flotilla of makeup-artists-slash-salesgirls who ranged in hue from champagne gold to glistening obsidian, each possessed of the ability to transform a customer's face with a few sure strokes, raising cheekbones and defining jawlines using creams and ointments that melted smoothly into the clientele's variegated complexions.

It should have been a success. Charles knew it was brilliant. And necessary. At its core, good makeup involved nothing more than a technical knowledge of skin tone and facial structure — it had as much in common with taxidermy as it did with art — and no one else was bringing that knowledge to the millions of nonwhite women who were walking around with chalky faces.

But from the start, it was a mess. His factories were focused on supplying the new stores, which made them late on shipments to a few long-standing clients. Some of them were understanding, and some were ungrateful pricks who forgot that Charles was the one who had believed in them when they'd first walked in with lint in their pockets and a meager little dream in their hearts.

And the stores weren't drawing in customers the way they should have been. Charles himself had masterminded the ads for the Failure and, just as he'd predicted, they had created a sensation: five beauties, glistening and nude, covered only in images inspired by their cultures. The black woman, a regal Ethiopian model who had grown up in a tiny brick row house in Astoria, had a tribal pattern that ran from knee to hip; that leg was slung across the lap of the Asian woman, a fiery Tibetan girl whose favorite word was *balls* and whose breasts were painted with a fire-breathing dragon; it panted flames towards the Latina model, actually an Italian who took care never to let her tan fade, who faced away from the camera, her back entirely covered in an Aztec sun; the rays of which were obscured only by the smooth brown head of the Indian model, a well-behaved Orange County girl who had never been seen entirely naked by a man until the makeup artist disrobed her and whose arms were intricately patterned with mehndi; wrapped in those arms was the final model, a mixed-race girl so beautiful that Charles almost, almost, began to feel a bit more sanguine about the prospect of grandchildren that were not 100 percent Chinese. Her name was Opal and she was the face of the store, an exclusive contract that took a not-insignificant bite out of the Failure's generous ad budget. Thanks, in part, to that very, very generous ad budget, the beauty press was quick to lend Charles their support, but their readers didn't follow suit.

They were self-haters, all of them, slavishly buying makeup formulated for other faces.

By the first quarter of 2008, it was clear that the Failure was failing or, at the very least, proving to be spectacularly unsuccessful. But Charles knew, with a kind of sureness that came from years of landing in shit and getting out clean, that he'd be able to turn things around between Thanksgiving and Christmas. Almost half of all cosmetics sales were made during the holiday season, and if they could just stay open until then, they could ride the rebound through 2009, when things were sure to change.

"A bridge loan," said Charles. "That all I need. Enough just to keep both locations open through late fall."

There were three bankers this time. Three dry white men stacked like dominos along one side of a mahogany table, their dry white lips speaking dry white lies about their inability to extend any more credit, no matter how soon the Failure might turn into a Success.

"In this climate," said Banker #1, "it's just too difficult to get approval for a loan of this sort."

"Of course, we're taking your admirable track record into consideration," said Banker #2, "but in this climate, past success is no guarantee."

"Makeup," said Banker #3, "may not be the wisest investment. Not in this climate."

And then, in unison, the three had lifted their small glasses of water up to their pointed noses and taken a chorus of quick, polite sips. Charles burned, but he kept it down, a flat palm inside his chest pressing down his heart before it exploded in a splatting fury. Instead, he ran through the numbers again, wondering if they'd somehow missed his explanation of the holiday season. It seemed impossible — these men were all supposed to be retail specialists; they should be familiar with the insatiable American need to end each calendar year with a frenzy of purchases — but how else to account for their stubborn reluctance to understand that recovery was just a blush-happy gaggle of teens away?

"The lipstick index," said Charles. "Leonard Lauder. 2001. Right after 9/11, America was in a recession that was more than just recession, right? The whole country depressed. Everyone sad. Nothing the same ever again."

He had paused there and looked at the three faces before him. Their pupils had widened a bit at the mention of 9/11, and they'd all assumed an appropriate air of seriousness and concern. *Oh yes,* he'd thought, *Charles Wang for the save!*

"Nobody was buying anything, except for lipstick. That's right! Lipstick sales go up 11 percent after 9/11."

Charles waited for a moment. None of the three had batted an eye.

"So maybe we start another recession now, but even if we do, lipstick go up!"

Banker #1, Charles's old nemesis, Marsh, shook his head. "Lipstick sales have been steadily declining since 2007."

These literal-minded motherfuckers were ruining America.

"Lipstick do not just mean lipstick!" shouted Charles. "Lipstick mean all makeup! Anything that make a woman feel good, feel rich, feel like she is taking care of herself but not cost too much, that mean lipstick! We think it going to be nail polish this time around! Everybody get creative! A canvas on your pinky! Small luxuries! Manageable delights!"

"Please, Mr. Wang," said Banker #2, reaching out one bony hand and placing it on Charles's shoulder. "There's no need to get so riled up. Let's just carry on this discussion peacefully."

Charles stood up.

"No more discussion."

He slammed together his notes and pushed away his small glass of water.

"Your no is only a no, is that correct?"

Banker #3 had a bit more fight to him. "Mr. Wang, it is a no. It's your decision now whether you want to look for another investor or whether you want to cut your losses and fold the business immediately before things get worse. Because it's going to get worse."

Pessimistic fools, Charles had thought.

"I come to you as a courtesy," he said. "If you are not interested in getting for yourselves a larger stake, then I go elsewhere."

"Our recommendation would be to restructure your existing loan and then fold the business. If you do that, you'll still be able to retain your personal assets. But if you decide to take your chances, then we sincerely hope that you have better luck elsewhere," soothed Banker #2, before shutting the door behind Charles.

But he didn't. There was no better luck.

Other loan institutions, entrepreneurial investors, larger beauty companies, current manufacturing clients, old friends — not a one wanted to invest in the Failure.

Another payment due date came and went. Two months of payroll came out of Charles's personal accounts, a loan to himself that demanded a bitter interest. A third. A fourth. The ads, the international fashion week sponsorships, they were cut, bits of ballast flung out into a stormy financial sea. In the end not one of them weighed enough to make any real impact.

And then, against all reason, the bank called the entire loan — factories and house included. A phone call, a notarized letter, and that was it. Back to nothing.

Even in failure, Charles Wang was a success. Looked at from one level up, from a perspective devoid of good or bad, where action trumped stasis, this was a perfect failure. Swift and complete. None of the usual built-in fail-safes managed to float him — instead, Charles had somehow tricked himself into erecting a needless financial deck of cards that went up only to be toppled by a historically anomalous financial tornado.

I couldn't rescue the Wangs, Charles had thought then. *The Wangs will never win. Our failures will ever be epic and our sorrows will ever be great.*

十六

ALL ACROSS THE COUNTRY, one by one, foreclosed house by shuttered business, in cold bedrooms and empty boardrooms and cars turned into homes, people had the same thoughts.

I couldn't rescue myself.

I will never win.

My failure will always be epic and my sorrow will always be great.

I alone among all people am most uniquely cursed.

In the intervening weeks, as they slowly began to poke their heads out of their own private failures, each would come to find that the curse was, in fact, not theirs alone. Instead, it was spread across the country: a club, a collective, a movement, a great populist *uprising* of failure in the face of years of shared national success.

十七

Phoenix, AZ

THE LAST THING Andrew had done the night before was to slip his top five pairs of sneakers — original issue Infrared Air Max 90s, Maison Martin Margiela Replica 22s, Common Projects Achilles Mids, beat-up checkerboard Vans, and a pair of never worn Air Jordan 4 Undefeateds — into felt dust bags and roll those in T-shirts before laying each mummified pair heel to toe in his duffel. Everything in his minifridge went into a big Postal Service bin that he'd left out in the lounge area. It would all be demolished by now. He'd sold his flat screen to poor Mac McSpaley, who was always trying to hang out with Andrew and his friends. He knew that Mac would buy the TV even if it was with tips that the skinny double-E major earned working at the sandwich stand on the quad. A job where he had to wear an apron. Poor, poor Mac McSpaley. Now Andrew had a soft wad of small bills stuffed in his back pocket and a vaguely guilty feeling that he expected would dissipate once he left campus.

His collection of vintage comedy albums — Richard Pryor, George Carlin, Lenny Bruce — and extra clothes were neatly packed into a cardboard box taped and labeled with Saina's address in upstate New York. Grace said that she'd just given away all of her other clothes, but that seemed like the worst decision if they were going to be poor now. It would only cost something like forty dollars to mail everything, otherwise he'd have to buy new clothes; he couldn't just wear the few things that fit in his duffel forever. Andrew wondered what had happened to his snowboard and gear, to everything in his room at home. Probably nothing. Probably it was just sitting there, locked up, and if he could just climb through a window and break it out, it could all be his again.

He was sitting on his naked mattress, holding Emma's spiky heels in his hands, looking at his bare walls, when his alarm went off.

9:15.

Fifteen minutes before Econ 201. Most Monday, Wednesday, and Friday mornings he hit snooze at least once, which made it 9:22 by the time he rolled out of bed. Another five minutes to brush his teeth and take a piss, one to choose a pair of sneakers, eight minutes to walk to class, four for an egg-sandwich stop, another five to say hi to people along the way. By the time he got to class, it was usually 9:45.

But not this morning. He pressed snooze, put down the heels, picked up his backpack, and walked straight to class, not even pausing to talk to that cute Pi Phi girl who'd smiled and said, "Good morning."

It was weird being there so much earlier. Who knew that so many people got anywhere on time? A solid five minutes before class started, the hall was already three-quarters full of fed, caffeinated students with laptops at the ready. From his unaccustomed vantage point in the back — usually he had to slip into one of the last open seats right in front of the lectern — Andrew could see that almost everyone was on Facebook, clicking through photos from last night.

The professor finally walked in at 9:40, carrying a cardboard box. Andrew knew it. You really didn't need to get to things on time. Not only had he not missed anything with all those added seven minutes of sleep, he'd probably tacked an extra year onto his life because he was more well rested than everyone else. Mental note: Stop wasting time worrying about being late.

"Make no mistake, we are in a recession," said Professor Kalchefsky slowly, holding up a copy of the *Wall Street Journal*. He read the headline: "'U.S. to Take Over AIG in $85 Billion Bailout.' You heard it here first. No one is willing to admit it, but we are smack-dab in the midst of a giant, ball-breaking recession, and every one of you ought to be furious because you are the unfortunate generation who will be graduating and trying to obtain jobs in a busted economy that we might as well pack up and sell to the Chinese."

Andrew opened up his laptop. He wasn't sure why he was even there, but if he was in class, he might as well take some notes. People liked jokes about the economy, right?

Kalchefsky 201, he typed.
Recession.
W. T. F.

Oh shit. He was going to have to work! Actually *work.* At some uninspired, uninspiring job. Maybe with an apron on. For money. Money that he would need to pay for things like rent and phone bills and air-conditioning — or maybe air-conditioning was free? It seemed like one of those things that should be a basic human right for people living in the Southwest.

Forget it. He wasn't going to leave. After class, he'd call Saina and ask her to pay his tuition, then he'd call and tell his dad not to come, tell him that they could stop by for a visit if they wanted, but maybe suggest that they just drive past Arizona altogether. Andrew wanted to skip out on Econ and call everyone immediately, but if he was going to finish school and then get a job, it was probably time he started doing better in his classes.

And Emma. He'd bring her shoes back tonight and tell her that actually he loved her. He did. He must. Definitely. Why was he always trying to be such a good guy all the time, anyway? Nothing stayed perfect forever. Being a good person hadn't kept his mom from dying. Being some kind of business star hadn't kept his dad from messing it all up after all. He'd make himself love Emma, and then he'd finally get to have sex.

Kalchefsky was writing on the board now.

Our first big mistake — we believed that money was rational.

Andrew sat up. Kalchefsky was a mess. Stubble and dark circles. Some sort of yolky residue on the corner of his mouth. Cuffs undone. He looked like an older person, a tired adult. Like he'd gone from being somewhere around Saina's age to Andrew's dad's age overnight. More than that, though, he looked wired — pissed off and strangely awake, his slight Eastern European accent suddenly strong.

"The market doesn't lie. How many times have you heard people say that? The market doesn't lie. People who have no business knowing what the market is capable of are nonetheless convinced that it is somehow bound to the truth. That things will always cost exactly what they should because of some sort of free-market fairy dust. Why did shares in the East India Company trade for £284 in 1769? Why did a single streaky tulip bulb fetch the equivalent of more than £25,000 at auction in 1637? I'll tell you what — it's not because people used to be dumber."

With that, he picked up the cardboard box by his feet, held it over his head, and gave it a desperate shake, releasing a shower of purple stuffed animals. The class burst out laughing. Beanie Babies! Andrew had one when he was a kid — a tie-dyed bear from some client of his father's. Kalchefsky picked up one of them and held it out to the class, squeezing its soft plush body.

"A Princess Di Beanie Baby, $2.50 plus $.99 shipping and handling on eBay. But go on there right now and you'll find an auction where one of these guys is listed for $45,000. Forty-five thousand dollars! For a little purple toy bear with a white rose sewn on its chest, mass manufactured in a Chinese factory." Kalchefsky shook his head violently, his shaggy hair flying, as the class laughed.

"I bought all twenty of these on the same day, which was enough to set off a rumor that Beanie Baby prices were back on the rise. Here's what one Beanie Baby message board reported." He looked out at the class and slowly raised an eyebrow. "Oh yes, they still exist. For a furry few, the dream lives on."

Kalchefsky picked up a piece of paper and peered through his glasses. "And I quote, 'OMG. What up, doubters. Looks like a new wave of collecting has been unleashed — eBay trackers say that Princess Di Beanie sales are up 1,100 percent. Time to buy, bitches.'"

Andrew let out a laugh.

"Throughout history we have believed that markets determine worth and that bubbles are eternal, despite ample evidence to the contrary. In the midst of each bubble, we believe that this time it will last forever. We have all been complicit in our own deluding."

The professor paused.

"It's all bullcrap. There is no market. The market is people, and people are dolts. Even the smartest people are moronic. You're all a little too young to remember that there were people — educated people, people with serious careers — who chased down 'rare' Beanie Babies. Who bought heart-shaped plastic-tag protectors. Who told themselves that their massive collections of *plush toys* would pay for their children's college tuitions.

"In fact, you *were* those children, and I'll wager that none of you are being floated in this fine institution with proceeds from Beanie Baby auctions. We all mocked those assholes, but their only mistake was that they chose to believe, as we all have, that money is rational. That price is truth. That the market doesn't lie. But it does. It lies. Or, at least, it will stretch the truth for a very, very long time.

"Real estate. That's our present-day delusion. More than that: Mortgages. Because a mortgage is never just a mortgage, is it? It's a promise. A promise that your life can change. A promise that you can be the sort of person who should live in that house no matter how far it is from your real price range. And let's be truthful, shall we? What is a promise like that but your world-famous American Dream?"

Kalchefsky looked out at the class, breathing hard, jaw clenched, like a wolf in some sort of intellectual standoff over a carcass. "You can grow up to be anything you want. Isn't that what they told you? Your mommies and daddies in the front seat of their SUVs while they were driving you, their special snowflake, to soccer practice? Except that you got it mixed up and thought that it meant 'You can grow up to *own* anything you want.' Not the same thing, America. Nowhere near the same thing."

Maybe Saina was right.

Maybe people from other countries really did hate Americans.

Why was Kalchefsky being such an asshole? How surprised would he be if he knew about Andrew's SUV, how it had just been towed by a shiny black truck with gold fangs painted on the grill, the keys pocketed by a wiry repo man Andrew hadn't even bothered to argue with? If he knew that Andrew *had* owned everything he wanted and that now maybe he was going to grow up to own nothing at all?

Crack! Kalchefsky slammed a palm down on the lectern. "And what people want to own, of course, is real estate. So a dental hygienist with bad credit making forty thousand dollars a year felt that she *deserved* to park her ass in a million-dollar home. With a little creative financing, and as long as housing prices continued to rise, she believed that she could *afford* a million-dollar home. And as long as the dental hygienist continued to pay interest on the mortgage for the million-dollar home, as long as housing prices continued to rise, as long as more loan officers approved more loans for more dental hygienists with bad credit who could continue to pay the interest on their overblown mortgages, housing prices would indeed stay stratospheric, and banks could print money based on that certainty. And, like your nursery rhyme, that was the house that Jack built."

Kalchefsky picked up a marker and slashed at the whiteboard, then moved aside so that the class could see what he wrote.

Our second big mistake — we thought that risk could be quantified.
Our third big mistake — Alan Greenspan.

The class giggled. "Oh no," he said, shaking his head at them menacingly. "It's not funny. It's not something that any of you should be laughing about unless you're so rich you don't have to care. Alan Greenspan is going to go down in history as a social-climbing, self-hating, Ayn Rand–loving, Zionist fraud. You just don't know it yet. But I do.

"But before we break down Greenspan, let's look at our second big mistake," he said. "Does anyone know the name David X. Li?"

Andrew looked up. Kalchefsky was writing it on the board: *David X. Li,* which meant that he was probably Chinese. If it was Lee, with two *e*'s, then it could have been a white guy instead.

"Learn it. Remember it. He's going to go down in the history books as the accountant who took down America."

Kalchefsky's losing it, Andrew typed.

Character? Crazy prof vs. whole world is against him? Recurring. Goes downhill through set, thinks club is lecture hall. Meta, meta, meta.

"Ole David X-marks-the-spot Li. A Chinese swashbuckler who rode into town and duped the entire American financial system into believing that he could lasso risk." Kalchefsky turned and wrote on the board:

$$\Pr[T_A<1, T_B<1] = \varphi_2(\varphi^{-1}(F_A(1)), \varphi^{-1}(F_B(1)), \gamma)$$

Whoa. How did he just reel that off? Impressive.

"You know why the dental hygienist got the mortgage for her million-dollar home? Because of this formula. You know why AIG needed a bailout? Because of the ways that Wall Street tried to profit off of that mortgage. You know why Wall Street thought that they could make millions off of the millions of people across the country with bad million-dollar mortgages? Because of this formula.

"The thing is, no one on Wall Street can make sense of this thing. *I* can't make any real sense of it, and I grew up in a country that took math seriously, unlike America, where you just study the Top 40 pop hits of math. All you know is the Pythagorean theorem. Avogadro's number. Eureka and apples on the head. So how can any of your finance guys possibly be expected to understand something even slightly more complex than $A^2+B^2=C^2$?" He turned around again and skewered the formula on the board with arrows. "This is the Gaussian copula. Named after Carl Friedrich Gauss, one of the greatest mathematicians ever to live. What this particular formula does, as I'm sure none of you know, is correlate variables that seem unrelated, predicting a connection between them. Li didn't invent the copula, but he did bring it into the finance game, and he was the one who made the crucial second mistake, which we all get to pay for: He made us think that risk could be quantified. And he thought that corporations were like people. Like people! Because before David X. Li rode into the canyons of Wall Street, way back in 1997, he worked on the broken-heart syndrome, which is a very real phenomenon that none of you have the experience to comprehend. True, dedicated love. Love beyond the grave. Take a couple: Whitehairs, oldsters, married for fifty years. One of them dies and odds are the other one is not far behind. They die because their heart is broken and they're alone, and glorified accountants like David X. Li had to go in and meddle with the beauty of that because they wanted to figure out a better way to price life insurance policies. The antithesis of beauty, no? Those accountants developed a method whereby they could plug in various pieces of information and churn out one number: A likely date of death. David X. Li took one look at this and decided that with a few modifications he could use it to churn out another number entirely: An entity's likelihood of default.

"If you've been paying any attention at all this semester, you know what is at the center of all studies of economics: Risk. Harness the risk and you're minting money. Let the risk run you and you're sunk. So, naturally, when David X. Li came along and said that he'd found a way to quantify risk, every hedge funder and bond trader out there was ready to hop aboard the Orient Express. He created a formula that he claimed could solve Wall Street's biggest problem, without any complications, and set it loose in a field of greedy, shortsighted bastards."

Andrew's hand shot up. It was a surprise even to him.

He was all the way in the back of the room, so he shouted. "Professor Kalchefsky!"

The professor paused. Looked up at Andrew. A poisonous, tired look.

Andrew stood up. "Why is it David X. Li's fault? I mean, I don't think it's his fault. He didn't force anyone to use it, right? The . . . what's it called? That formula? He just wrote it. He didn't say that everyone had to use it." Andrew paused, waiting for the professor to agree with him. He was right, he knew he was right.

"Force? No, he didn't *force* anyone to use it. And no one *forces* children to pester their parents for the sugared cereal that's packed with their favorite action figures; no one *forces* young women to starve themselves anorexic so they can look like a billboard. No, Li just created a formula he claimed could solve Wall Street's biggest problem. But he's perfectly innocent, perfectly. You know what else he's innocent of? Besmirching Carl Friedrich Gauss's good name. Gauss deserves to be remembered as the prince of mathematicians — his work impacted the fields of astronomy, optics, differential geometry, all the ways in which we observe and understand the physical world — but in democratic America, his name will forevermore be associated with financial ruin. And that's not the inscrutable David X. Li's fault either, is it?"

Andrew rolled his eyes. He couldn't help it. Inscrutable was such a lame dig, it was barely worth protesting. "Are you getting scared yet? Are you finally sitting up and thinking about something besides keg parties and sexting? You know that Li was trained in China's most respected university, the Harvard of Tianjin, and that the Communist government encouraged him to set sail for North America? How do we know that he wasn't working for them from the start? Right now China owns 8 percent of America's debt. How do we know that this wasn't all a plot hatched in the honorable Deng Xiao Ping's official opium den?"

"Oh come *on!*" The voice came from somewhere on the edge of the room. Andrew turned, along with everyone else in the class. As Professor Kalchefsky got more and more riled up, the guy next to Andrew had taken out his cell phone and started recording surreptitiously — now he held it up, tracking the room like a periscope, trying to figure out who was talking.

The voice kept on going. "Okay, let's just say that it was a plot, right? Doesn't the West deserve it? Maybe this is just payback. Fact! In the year five hundred something, Christian missionaries stole China's silkworms and used them to prop up the Byzantine Empire for a thousand years. Fact! In the late thirteenth century, Marco Polo went to China and learned about pasta, and now everyone thinks the Italians are the last word on spaghetti."

It was Mark Foo. He was a militant Asian kid, not the kind of guy Andrew usually hung out with. Foo Man Chu was always organizing protests and group dumpling dinners; he was the kind of guy who made up names for those Asian girls who always dated black guys (the current frontrunner seemed to be "chocolate banana") or white guys ("lemonhead"); he was president of the Asian American Student Association.

"Payback for ancient crimes. Alright, let's call it that. A karmic kung fu kick to the balls. But you know who's getting kicked in the balls? Is it the descendants of those missionaries? The Anglo-Saxons who profited from that original theft? No, they remain in their Martha's Vineyard mansions, eating lobster and fighting over who gets to give Bill Clinton handjobs. And who really gets jacked off? *ME!*"

The professor grabbed at the newspaper that he'd held up at the beginning of class, crumpling it in his fist. "Do you know that I make as much each month tutoring rich junior high schoolers in calculus as I do as an adjunct professor? The whole economic mindset of America is warped. Your parents are willing to pay five hundred dollars per credit hour to get you through a good college — if this can be considered a good college, which it isn't, which means that your particular parents probably didn't open their wallets wide enough — and the actual professors you came to learn from are barely being given a living wage. In fact, there are so many people who want to go into academia that they could just as reasonably not pay us at all, yet here I am, training my replacements. Academia begets academia. Yet, despite my paltry pay, I managed to accrue a plump little nest egg and now, without warning, it is *gone*. Wiped out."

Andrew leaned over to his neighbor. "Isn't this dude, like, thirty or something? How much could he have saved?" A quiver of anger ran through him. Would Kalchefsky still be such an asshole about their parents if he knew what was going on with the Wangs? "And on a freaking *professor's* salary."

Kalchefsky stopped talking and stared up at Andrew. "Is there something you'd like to share with the class? Did you, maybe, have a funny comment about my retirement savings? You're the comedian, aren't you? I remember you from the freshman show last year."

Glee. That was how Andrew felt whenever someone mentioned the finest seven and a half minutes of his life. A rush of pure sensate pleasure that brought him back to standing onstage and receiving that first laugh, and then a slightly guilty glow of "This is what it's like to be famous!"

It took a moment to pull himself out of that greedy joy and remember that Kalchefsky had actually called him out.

Andrew shook his head. "No," he said, "nothing."

"That's about as much as I would have expected from that performance."

Wounded, Andrew felt his mouth gape open. He stood up, knowing that he had to say something, *something,* but not sure what would come out. It turned out to be this: "You've been so insane this whole class, and that's why? Because you lost a little bit of money? You said your salary is almost nothing, so how much could you have saved? I mean, I thought that those Beanie Babies were like little minigrenades or something and you were about to Columbine this whole place! You're supposed to be a professor! It's not our fault you lost the money! Why are you getting mad at us?"

"You seem to be very concerned about attributions of blame, Mr. Wang."

Everyone was looking at him now. Again.

"Because you're throwing blame around all over the place! And it doesn't need to be! You're acting like it's everyone else's fault and no one else lost anything. But you — I mean, I don't know how big AIG is, or how many people had accounts with them — but you said the bailout was, like, $85 billion, so I'm sure it's a lot, and they all lost something, too. It wasn't just you!"

Andrew stopped, even though he could have kept going, because Kalchefsky's eyebrows raised up and together like a guilty dog's.

"In a sense, you're right and I'm sorry. None of you can really know what it's like to lose the result of years of effort because you haven't had years to put in. I can't blame you for failing to grasp a concept that is beyond your scope."

Condescension. That's all it was. As if everything mattered more just because he was a few years older.

Andrew wasn't planning on telling anybody about what was happening, he hadn't even really said goodbye to anyone besides Emma, but now, without warning, it all upended out of him.

"*You* don't know what it's like! *You* don't know anything that's going on!" No crying. There's no crying in econ class. "*I know* that it's a recession because my family's pretty much totally bankrupt now. I have no house to go back to and I'm dropping out. Some guy out of, like, a Spike TV show repossessed my *car!*"

Kalchefsky's eyebrows went up even more. The girl on his right reached out and touched his arm, her eyes wide. The class was a wall of sympathetic faces. Andrew's heart slammed against his insides, and he looked down at his phone to make sure that he hadn't accidentally dialed his father sometime in the middle of that speech. He had to go. That was all he could do. He had to leave class right now, and then he had to leave the state of Arizona altogether. Things started to move again. More hands reached out to him. Professor Kalchefsky started to put his face back in order.

That was it. Andrew couldn't stay. He picked up his bag in one hand and his laptop in the other, and ran for the door.

十八

THREE BIG MISTAKES.

But, of course, it's never that simple.

Before we even got to the third one, we were down and done.

As much as our willingness to believe in the constant rise felled us, as much as our eagerness to conquer risk opened us up to more risk, as much as Greenspan stood by as Wall Street turned itself into Las Vegas, there was also Greece, and Iceland, and Nick Leeson, who took down Barings, and Brian Hunter, who tanked Amaranth, and Jérôme Kerviel and every other rogue trader who thought he — and it was always a he — could reverse his gut-churning, self-induced free fall with one swift, lucky strike; it was rising oil prices, global inflation, easy credit, the cowardice of Moody's, the growing chasm of income inequality, the dot com boom and bust, the Fed's rejection of regulation, the acceptance of "too big to fail," the repeal of the Glass-Steagall Act, the feast of subprime debt; it was Clinton and Bush the second and senators vacationing with banking industry lobbyists, the Kobe earthquake, an infatuation with financial innovation, the forgettable Hank Paulson, the delicious hubris of ten, twenty, thirty times leverage, and, at the bottom of it, our own vicious, lingering self-doubt. Or was it our own willful, unbridled self-delusion? Doubt vs. delusion. The flip sides of our last lucky coin. We toss it in the fountain and pray.

十九

Helios, NY

SAINA SAT BEHIND the wheel of her parked car, a hand-me-down Saab that the house's previous owner — a widowed theater director who couldn't take the upstate winters anymore — had left behind along with an attic full of ancient furniture and a shed piled with buckets of un-applied weather sealant. Two cloth bags were balled up on her lap. She peered across the dirt lot, willing Leo not to materialize. Some weeks it was Gabriel, his assistant, who hauled the cartons of hydroponic lettuces to the market and explained to the aging dads with Mohawked toddlers riding on their shoulders that Fatboy Farm's only crops were in the Aster-aceae family, not the Cannabaceae.

What if Leo's farm wasn't there at all? Would that be because of her? She'd emailed, once, an apology that apologized for its own pointlessness, and texted, twice, with smaller, sadder apologies, but in the end, she'd al-lowed herself to be Graysoned into selfishness, reasoning that it was bet-ter, really, that Leo had seen things for himself. Better to rip off the ban-dage than let it grow into the wound.

But they were in the Catskills, and this was the only farmers market within twenty miles, and her father was coming. If she couldn't gather up his lost world, then she had to at least welcome him with all the bounty this one could provide. Waxy Red Delicious apples trucked to the A&P from Mexico might have been okay for Grayson, but the Wangs deserved crisp, fragrant local Macouns, all rosy veins and bright white flesh.

. . .

The market itself was laid out like a cross, with a bluegrass band and tres-
tle tables set up in the center. Children with faces painted like pandas
and cows ran through the crowd, half of them barefoot. Saina hoisted
one bag over her shoulder. It was full now, a spray of turnip greens spilling over the top, and she remembered, too late, that it had started life as
a gift bag from Gucci's UNICEF fundraiser, one of the endless rounde-
lay of events that made up her New York life. The fashion label's logo was
printed on both sides, so she couldn't even turn it around to hide the giant interlocked *G*s.

Saina was examining a bunch of multicolored carrots when she saw a
movement, a series of movements — an arm, a twist, a shoulder, a lift —
and froze, swallowed her breath, dropped the carrots. Not Gabriel. Leo.
He was smiling now; she could see just the edge of his face, but she knew
the folds and bumps of it so well that she could read them even through
this scrim of carbon dioxide and chlorophyll. He was smiling and holding
a bag of salad out to a white-haired woman in a draped sweater and red-
framed glasses who faced Saina straight on. This is the person Grayson
should have seen, this tall, sure man.

How good it made them feel, these well-meaning Upper West Side
transplants, buying organic produce they didn't even have to wash from a
handsome black man who would greet them with an exotic fist bump! An
attractive, articulate chap, not unlike the young senator from Illinois they
had just congratulated themselves for nominating, who would show the
world that slavery was behind us and that we could appreciate hip-hop.
Yes! So many pretty boxes to check all at once!

Saina stopped herself. She and Leo used to do this together sometimes — half jokingly turn everyone around them into the worst kind of
self-congratulatory liberal, using that familiar colored-person shorthand
to align themselves with each other. But it was unfair. It was just a step
down, really, from her father telling her that Indians were nice to look at,
and held beautiful festivals, but were not to be trusted under any circumstances.

For a minute, Saina let herself picture her father meeting Leo. His reac-
tions to people were completely unpredictable — with Leo he'd either be
moved to embarrassing displays of emotion or an ugly patrician prudery

would rear up and he'd declare Leo and all he represented to be irrepara-
bly beneath the glorious Wangs.

No matter what, Leo would be a puzzle. His full name was Lio-
nel Grossman. The Grossmans had a long Catskills lineage of Borscht
Belt comedians, big band leaders, and the occasional heroin addict, men
whose love of romance was equal only to their love of the road, result-
ing in a peripatetic lust that produced generations of illegitimate — but
adored! — children and an ever-shifting backdrop of spouses. Leo was
adopted into that family at age seven, brave and small, a ward of the state
since he was two, already resigned to being unwanted. "It was the early
'80s," he told her once. "We knew that nobody took little black boys. Ce-
lebrities weren't scooping up bushels of chocolate babies from Malawi.
It was a different time." And then he joked that the big-living Grossmans thought they were lifting a pickaninny out of the ghetto, but really
they were bringing him into a family of shiftless musicians. If they'd been
black, they would have been trouble; as Jews, they were just bohemian.

Saina lifted her bag of produce over her head, shimmied past the folding tables, and ducked out the back of the booth, her eyes on Leo. He was
still smiling.

She felt light-headed.

It seemed unfair to walk up behind him, to surprise him like that, but
she couldn't, didn't want to, approach from the customer side, where flats
of lettuces would be wedged between them. As she crunched across the
gravel towards an unsuspecting Leo, a tiny piece of rock wedged itself between her toenails, red now. She leaned down to pick it out and felt the
strap of her mint-colored silk dress, just a summer dress, nothing special,
slip an inch off her shoulder. *Good.* Heart beating, she pulled her hair
over to the opposite side, leaving her neck bare. Not that she was expecting Leo to even look at her, really, but it didn't hurt to be worth looking at.

And then, before she was ready, there he was. Close enough to touch.
Close enough to smell. Shoulder blades pulling on the fabric of his faded
black T-shirt.

Saina meant to tap him lightly, but instead her hand laid itself on his
warm back and felt its way down to the curve of his waist. He turned. She
dropped her hand. Stepped back.

"Oh. Hi. Leo. Hi."

He looked down at her, neutral.

She lifted up her bag. "I'm buying things. Vegetables. I got river trout from the fish guys. And cheese. Taleggio."

A nod. His eyes flicked to the oversize logo.

"It's from an event. I didn't buy it. I wouldn't do that — I wouldn't buy a Gucci farmers market bag." Saina remembered that Leo didn't know about her father and his fall.

"You might."

Now. Say it now.

"Grayson's gone."

Leo froze, looking at her.

"He's . . . I didn't want him here anymore."

He considered this for a moment. "Did he still want to be here?"

Hesitate and all is lost.

"Yes," said Saina, immediately.

And then Leo's eyes got soft in that terrible, amazing way that only men who are supposed to be invulnerable can soften. He looked at her, full of hope, and Saina felt herself die a little bit inside.

Saina knew that twenty-eight was still young. In New York she had friends in their early forties, holding on easily to beauty, who met talented men ten years their junior or rich men twenty years their senior — all the ones who were their age seemed to be too preoccupied getting divorced to fall into marriage — met them, married them, and made families with them as if their lives weren't decades out of step. But up here in Helios, anyone in their late twenties was obstinately coupled. It was as if they'd all stepped out of some home ec manual left over from the 1930s, the women with their vintage flowered aprons and pots of small-batch preserves, the men with their beekeeping ventures and T-shirt-design companies. It wasn't that Saina didn't like the idea of growing her own heirloom tomatoes, it was just, well, it was lonely to make a fetish of domesticity on her own.

Back at home, she opened the door of her new Smeg refrigerator, specially powder coated in a bright yellow, and pushed aside containers of truffled Israeli couscous and goat's milk yogurt to make room for a farmers market bounty of summer fruit, knobby cucumbers, ears of white

corn, fresh mozzarella wrapped in asphodel leaves, and two overflowing
bags of Fatboy Farm greens that Leo had handed her before they parted.

Outside, a car door slammed shut.
  Her first thought: *Grayson came back!*
  Her next: *Leo really forgives me!*

Who was this girl, yo-yoing between boyfriends, heart expanding and
contracting based on how well she was loved? Not Saina. Certainly not.
She was an artist; she was autonomous. Could someone's base impulses
usurp their better nature, making them forever into someone they didn't
recognize?
  Footsteps sounded down the slate path and headed towards the side
door. In a second the person would pass by the open kitchen window.
Now was the time to duck down and slip out to the unfinished studio,
where she should have been working all along, trying to recast the double-
barreled disgrace of her betrayal and fall.

Curiosity kept her upright.
  She watched as an asymmetrical haircut strode purposefully past her
window, perched on top of a gangly body dressed in a hipster riot of neon-
pink skinny jeans and a loose V-neck so deep that a nipple threatened to
peek through. Billy Al-Alani. He spotted her through the window.
  "The queen in exile!"
  Saina sighed. "Friend or foe?"
  "Knight-in-waiting and biggest fan." He spread out his arms and
dropped out of sight. Reluctantly, she stepped outside where he grabbed
her up in a sweaty hug and kissed at her cheek. She pushed away from
him, forcing a smile.
  "What are you *doing* here? How did you even know where I live?"
  "How can you *live* all the way up here? Don't you miss Manhattan?
Here, I brought you something." He thrust a paper sack at her.
  Saina opened it and looked inside. "There are bagels in the Catskills,
Billy."
  "New York water, baby, there's nothing like it!" He looked past her

into the open door. "This place is pretty rad, though. I bet you're really getting shit done here, right?"

Instinctively, she blocked his view. "If by shit you mean going to every estate sale on the Hudson, then totally."

"Aren't you going to invite me in?"

The hostess in her reared its well-bred head and she swept Billy into her refuge, putting a white wine spritzer on the weathered handcart turned coffee table in front of him — "My love of wine spritzers is fully un-ironic," he declared — and settling herself on a Moroccan pouf underneath a pair of Marilyn Minter lips. He was the first visitor she'd had besides Grayson. All of her New York friends seemed to be locked in some perpetual work/party circuit that ran from Sundance to TED to Spring Fashion Week to Fire Island weekends to Burning Man to Fall Fashion Week to Art Basel Miami, with interludes of detox in Tulum or Marrakesh. When she first arrived in Helios, she'd been too wounded to speak to anyone, then she'd been too wrapped up in Leo, and after that, she had to hide Grayson's return from all those loyal friends who had vowed to excommunicate him but, Saina suspected, continued to put out their faces to be kissed whenever they happened to meet.

"Okay, Billy, seriously, what are you doing here?"

"Can't I just come visit an old friend?"

She tilted her head and took him in. He played with the piece of bone that hung from a leather cord looped around his neck and tipped one canvas shoe against the coffee table.

"Am I an old friend?"

"Of course. Absolutely. You're actually one of the first people I met in New York."

"I remember. At that group show I was in. You were, like, brand-new. Straight out of —"

"Compton, yo. Yup. And you were doing those tiny sculptures. And then in Miami, remember?"

She did. The first time they'd met, almost five years ago, he'd been a sweet-faced, small-town boy in a dead man's suit, hanging on the edges of conversations, downing flute after courage-building flute of Taittinger. Six months later, when she'd seen him again, he was manning a booth in the publications ghetto at one of the ancillary fairs at Art Basel—NADA, maybe, or SCOPE—and looked so like a disaffected ex–prep schooler that she'd doubted her own memory of him. That is until he'd pumped her awkwardly for invites to all of the week's parties and recounted the art world luminaries he'd seen: Robert Rauschenberg in a wheelchair having a caipirinha! Jeffrey Deitch rocking to the Scissor Sisters! Tobey Maguire watching Terry Richardson watch Amanda Lepore!

"When you started writing for the party pages. What are you up to now? Are you still the Army Archerd of the art world?"

"I wrote about you then, remember?"

Saina had gone to Basel that year without a gallery, but with a plan. The group show where she'd met Billy was her last. She'd been in New York for six years at that point—four at Columbia, two after—and she was making sculptures that were, she saw later, very derivative of her idol, Lee Bontecou, but intricate and tiny where Bontecou's could dominate whole rooms. They weren't attracting much attention. That might have been alright—*Ars longa, vita brevis,* she lied to herself—but Saina didn't want to be one of those girls who lived on her parents' money and called herself an artist in a way that slowly devolved into paid vanity shows, duty sales to those parents' friends, and membership on museum boards in lieu of any real artistic creation. When the only sale she made was to strange, miniature KoKo, the makeup artist whose line her father manufactured, Saina could see the sad, gilded path that stretched out before her.

Disheartened, she volunteered for one of Cai Guo-Qiang's gunpowder pieces. His suspended car-crash sculpture had just gone up at MASS MoCA, and this was a way to get close to an artist of his stature without signing on for unsung months as a studio assistant. Too, she was curious about his main assistant, a girl her age whose father happened to be the president of Taiwan and who Saina's own father rather baldly hoped she would befriend.

It was three cold fall days of kneeling on concrete floors in a cavernous warehouse near Cai's New York studio, X-Acto knifing stencils out of a playing-field-size sheet of cardboard. The show, titled *Sky Ladder,* was a compendium of failed flying machines rendered in exploded gunpowder. Once the stencils were carved, each employee had a very specific job. One person followed behind him and lifted the stencils off the cardboard, another carried a stack of reference images that he matched to each awkward carving, a third pushed around a little cart stacked with bowl upon bowl of different gunpowders that he sprinkled as casually as you would salt on an icy road. Once the powder was ignited — a satisfying explosion of sparks and smoke — a fourth and fifth ran in and pounded out the embers with little pom-poms made of T-shirt scraps. It was like a factory where all the robots were imbued with ambition and anxiety instead of intelligence. Cai, on the other hand, was unwavering as the calm and cool center of everyone's gaze, a gaze he seemed simultaneously not to notice and to be electrically aware of.

As they waited and watched, one of the other volunteers, a China studies professor who treated the artist like a god, told them that during the summer Dragon Boat Festival, when all of the bugs and monsters awaken, it was traditional to make a mixture of sulfur and liquor, and write the word *wang* — 王 — on children's foreheads. *King,* like her own surname. *King,* like the tiger's stripes, because the tiger was the king of the forest and the yellow of sulfur is a tiger yellow. The professor relished the telling of his tale, and a few feet away from them, small worlds exploded.

Saina hated herself for thinking it, but the whole thing struck her as immediately, resolutely, male. The immensity of scale, the use of gunpowder, the corralling of volunteers to do the artist's bidding. Women, she realized, were scared to be assholes. And what is any artist, really, but someone who doesn't mind being an asshole?

That was when she birthed her plan: *Be an Asshole.*

So she went to Basel without a gallery, but waiting for her in her ocean-facing room at the Delano were three giant cardboard boxes that contained a thousand lightweight Tyvek jackets, as thin as tissues, special ordered for $4.85 apiece from a factory in Guangzhou.

On the back of each jacket, from neck to waist, was a giant, pixilated image of her face in a rainbow of acid brights.

On the front, sprawled across the chest, her signature: *Saina.*

By eight o'clock on the morning of the vernissage, nine of the ten young club promoters she'd hired via a DJ friend had shown up, all wearing sunglasses and toting Starbucks, all unexpectedly enthusiastic once she outlined the plan of attack. She loaded each of them down with a hundred factory-fresh jackets, three hundred dollars in dollar bills — paper clipped into bundles of five — and a map of Miami with their territory highlighted in yellow. She took the last hundred, slinging the nearly thirty pounds of Tyvek in a bag over her shoulder, and set out with her nine warriors.

The first man she'd approached was sitting on a crate outside a Starbucks, holding up a cardboard sign that he'd markered with, $$$ OR ☺. He'd locked eyes with her as she'd begun to explain, cutting her off and yelling, "I don't see a smile! Smiles or dollars!" So Saina had plastered a grin on her face as she held out the jacket, but still he'd spat at her, full of anger. "You think I can't make my own fashion styles? You think you can buy my body? My body? You can't buy my body! I wouldn't sell you my mind and now you come swinging for my body!" She'd backed away, frightened, worried that the whole project was going to end with this. Behind her, there was wild, threatening laughter and Saina had felt a moment of genuine fear. Did the man have friends coming to his defense, ready to jump the clueless rich girl who'd thought that she could exploit them all so easily? Turning, she'd faced three teenagers, Mohawks atop their baby faces, band patches safety pinned to their ripped denim vests. One of them held a gray pit bull puppy on a length of soiled rope.

"Sorry, sorry, um, cute dog," she'd said, trying to retreat before they got mad at her, too.

"Hey, lady, I'll do it."

"What?"

"Yeah, you said it was for art, right?"

"Yeah! It is. I'm an artist." Saina had scrambled in her bag, pulling out three jackets. "Yeah, if you could just wear them for today, that's it."

The one with the pit bull looked at her, skeptical, not making a move to take it. "I'm an artist, too," he said.

"Cool."

"So we support your art, what are you going to do to support mine?"

Saina felt in her pocket and reached for three paper-clipped sets of bills. "How's this? For each of you."

His friends had snatched the cash and pulled on their jackets in one easy motion, her face swallowing up their punk posturing, but he'd taken the money from her fingers slowly, deliberately, curling his lip as he pocketed the bills. "Makes things pretty easy, huh?" he'd snarled, before moving on with his friends, her jacket, nonetheless, on his back.

The rest of the day was easier. Saina hadn't counted on the number of homeless people who would be passed out — drunk or asleep — that early in the morning, but she'd ended up overcoming her guilt and just draping a jacket over each prone form, holding her breath against the urine smell of neglect that wafted up at her every time. When she'd texted the others and suggested they do the same, the responses had come back fast — *Yep DUN! Duh, doing it. Thought that wuz the plan?* Hustlers all. Saina mentally filed junior club promoters alongside talent agency assistants and nail salon owners as reliable sources of creative aggression.

And three hours later, there it was: Saina's face and name on the body of every single homeless person in the city of Miami.

When eleven o'clock approached, Saina inserted herself in the teeming press of people outside the convention center; well-preserved Miami women in furs and flimsy dresses jostled against global nomads in bespoke suits and art students in carefully constructed personas. Then the glass doors were flung open and the crowd surged in, hot and eager, and within minutes, an epidemic of little red stickers bloomed like measles across the hall. Those who weren't buying were talking, and one of the main topics was the rash of Saina's face across the city. Some thought it was brilliant; some thought it was disgusting. Everyone who mattered thought it was both.

By the end of the vernissage, her voicemail box was full of frantic calls from journalists, gallerists, and collectors. That evening a breathless post by Billy hit the web, confirming that she was the artist in question and spilling details about her parentage that she hadn't realized were common currency. Reports surfaced of homeless men being offered five hundred, seven hundred, a thousand dollars for their jackets — stains, stench, and all — and before she even landed back in New York, Saina received a dinner invitation from a soft-spoken gallerist whose artists often found themselves being asked to take over the Turbine Hall at the Tate or the Guggenheim ramp.

And then for four years that should have lasted forever, everything was perfect. Her first show, *Made in China,* opened on June 4, 2004, the fifteenth anniversary of the Tiananmen Square Massacre. The opening was a fashion show with a tightly edited line of ten different looks that Saina culled from thousands of photographs of protesters on the streets of Beijing. Each one was re-created with painstaking precision by a collective of seamstresses in China. The last look, titled "Wedding Gown," was a copy of the white button-down shirt and black trousers worn by Tank Man, the famous lone protester who faced down a column of tanks armed with only a plastic shopping bag in his right hand and a satchel in his left.

Anyone who stopped by the gallery after opening night found a replica of a high-end boutique, where the pieces were hung in editions of three: S, M, L. In one corner was a dressing room where patrons could try on the art as long as they didn't mind being watched via video feed by a group of tittering Chinese seamstresses taking tea breaks. Within ten days, a scandalized local government official shut down the China-side link — word was that he barged into the break room with two local toughs while a well-known fashion editor was on-screen clad in nothing more than her signature bob — but by that time, the show had sold out and Saina's reputation was assured.

See Me/Say You opened the next fall. Each day for ninety days she had gone out into the city with an old leather mah-jongg case emptied of its game pieces and filled instead with pastels, watercolors, pens, and markers; sandwiched under one arm were a pair of clipboards, each with a sheet of rough Arches paper. Each day for ninety days she'd searched out one unsuspecting New Yorker and asked that person to draw her, Saina, the artist. As they did, she drew them, picking up the materials that her portraitist laid down, making the two of them into twins of a sort. When the show opened, all of the pieces were suspended face-to-face, forming a long, narrow corridor that placed the viewer in between Saina and her subject/creator.

After the public opening, Louis Vuitton threw an intimate, late-night dinner for seventy-five and issued a very limited-edition case with neat little compartments for an impractical rainbow of art supplies. She spent that whole evening smiling and smiling, suddenly used to the fact that everyone in the room wanted to get close to her.

That was where she met Grayson.

She already knew who he was. He'd exploded out of Cooper Union with his clubscapes — chaotic, room-size installations composed of trash scavenged from the Dumpsters of the Soho House, the Norwood, the Colony, cobbled into replicas of the exclusive interiors of those same private clubs. The openings were eerie bacchanals, dark and heavy with pumped-in scent meant to underscore the sweet stink of rotting trash, thumping with the sound mixes that Grayson put together from surreptitious recordings made of conversations between club members. Collectors and critics alike blew rails beneath grotesque reproductions of the Core Club's art collection, starlets waded topless into the roiling muck that mimicked the sulfur baths at the Colony.

The two of them were instantly besotted, and it was all Saina could do to pull away for long enough to put together her Whitney project: *Power Drum Song.* Manhattan's tourist spots were full of street-corner artists straight from China's Central Academy of Fine Arts who could produce a picture-perfect rendering of anyone who sat in front of them. Saina trolled South Street Seaport and Central Park for her favorites, then employed her stunted Chinese to gauge their experience with more traditional Song dynasty scroll paintings. In the end, she hired fourteen of the artists, all men, and matched each of them with a young couple. She and Grayson also sat for one of the pieces, painted in classical style with inksticks and calligraphy brushes, then mounted on long vertical hanging scrolls.

At the opening, each artist was posed uncomfortably by the scroll he'd painted, limbs arranged to mimic one of the subjects in the piece. Most of the men treated the whole thing as a lark — if the crazy American girl was going to pay them one thousand dollars apiece to paint her friends like Chinese people and then be examined and exclaimed over by peacocks holding wineglasses, then, by god, they'd do it! — but one of them, the one who spoke the most serviceable English, held out for an exorbitant raise. "You think we don't know art world?" he demanded. "Not for wall at home! Gallery! Museum! You pay five thousand dollars!" And, in the end, she had.

It was all worth it when Peter Schjeldahl's review — a full column! — had come out in *The New Yorker,* saying that she was brave and brilliant for "exposing the uncomfortable tête-à-tête betwixt the viewer and the viewed by turning the artist's twenty-first-century position of power back to a position of servitude — the brush only strokes at the command of its paymaster, the hand that holds the brush has no more agency than the bristles themselves."

A hat trick. A trifecta. A father, son, and holy ghost of growing critical and commercial success that, of course, had to be gunned down by unlucky number four. Saina remembered her mother telling her, when she was very young, never to choose the number four. *Sz.* It sounded like the word for death and was so unlucky that people avoided phone numbers and addresses with the number, which was why her undemanding mother always insisted on a room change whenever they were assigned to the fourth floor of a hotel. Her fourth solo show, which had opened this spring, the one that had taken the most work, the most thought, the most time, was torn down by the same people who had praised her every previous effort. And then, on top of that, the lady reporters went crazy. Jezebel came out with an early post trashing her show — their commenters called it "emotionally rapey." The day after, the *Huffington Post, Slate*'s Double XX blog, and *Ms.* magazine joined in. Soon, in a mind-boggling show of solidarity, the American Task Force on Palestine, Amnesty International, and the American Jewish Committee had banded together and issued a statement condemning Saina, her privileged ignorance, her gallery, American intervention in foreign wars, and the general callousness of the art world. For two weeks, protesters had picketed the show until her gallerist finally shuttered it a week early, claiming that the space had been cited for code violations and needed to make emergency renovations. The next day Hermès issued a statement apologizing for their involvement and pledging that all proceeds from the sale of the scarves they'd special issued for her show would be donated to refugee charities.

Saina still couldn't see what was so offensive about this show when none of her others had raised any eyebrows. There had been no *Big Issue* screeds about the exploitation of the homeless in response to her Basel project, no Chinese groups hounded her with photos of dead Tiananmen Square protesters. And yet, even as she'd been supervising the hanging of this fourth show, one of the handlers had turned to her and said, "Oh boy, they're gonna get good and pissed about this one." He'd been holding the bottom of a 48 x 72 canvas with a blowup of a stunning young Palestinian refugee in a flower-print headscarf whom Saina had removed from a *Time* photo that also included armed Israeli soldiers and, with the assistance of Photoshop, placed on a seat in a beautifully lit studio. The catalog for the show was printed like a fashion lookbook, with sans serif text in the bottom right corner: "Soraya is wearing the *Conqueror* scarf in *Beit Hanoun.* Cotton-rayon, 4′ x 4′. $1,200. Delivery 7/08."

"So, what do you think?" asked Billy. "They're talking cover story!"

"I don't know. I don't know if I'm ready for that. Or if it would really make sense for me right now. I don't know if I want to be memorialized as a cautionary tale. Anyways, I've already been a cover story."

"The *Village Voice,*" he said, dismissively.

"It was horrible."

Just remembering it gave Saina a cold feeling. The tabloid used a photo of her from that first opening for *Made in China,* where she was dressed in a ridiculous confection of a dress and laughing, mouth wide, eyes squeezed shut. The headline type was giant — EMPEROR'S NEW CLOTHES? — and the entire piece pilloried Saina, saying she was an insensitive, opportunistic rich girl who preyed on the public's feelings and insulted the fine tradition of conceptual art that was born in glory with the Dadaist movement and died an ignoble death at her hands. She had already sold her apartment by then, but even if she hadn't, just seeing her once-happy face screaming out from every battered red kiosk and strewn across coffee-shop floors would have been enough to send her slinking out of the city, a starving alley cat running from a gang of murderous children.

"Garbage. Anyways, anyways, I wrote that *first* story." He leaned forward, urgent. "*That* was the one."

It felt like a million years ago. Another world. Another life. Saina looked at him. "Are you trying to say that you made me, Billy?" This was one thing she'd always been able to do — say the things that might have been better left unsaid.

He was still for a moment, caught. "'Made you' is a little strong, but, yeah, that story helped. You know it did. And I think this one will be good for you, too — don't you want to speak up for yourself?"

Billy had grown up. Everyone did. He wasn't the same ambitious innocent who revered the esoteric, who thought that names like Deleuze and Guattari were passwords to a different life, spells that could glamour away a drab past. When she met him, he had read all of Foucault but had never cracked Shakespeare; he knew about *Minotaure* magazine but couldn't name the countries involved in World War II. He'd entered her world thinking that it was a magical place, and somewhere along the way he'd become a fixture.

Saina knew exactly the kind of article that he was planning to write. It would contain a shocked series of references to her barely controversial past, an ironic look at her current state of singular domesticity, a supposedly neutral summary of the protests, a sidebar on what Grayson was doing now, with maybe a tiny inset of his chaotic canvas of her in chola mufti, rendered in splashy, '80s-style primary colors.

But Saina was still too raw to put herself back into the public eye like that, naked, without a new body of work to back her up. The whole time she had been up here, she hadn't made a thing. Somehow, in all the attendant commotion and loss, the thing itself, the eternal, singular piece of art, had gotten away from her. What she didn't want to say to herself was this: Saina couldn't create art without spectacle, and spectacle, by its very nature, had to be witnessed. Not for the first time she wished that she had never sold her Manhattan apartment, never fled to Helios.

"You know, I could always do a write-around."

"What's that?"

"It's when you don't interview the person. I mean, I could describe this, where you are, what we talked about, even if you don't participate in the story."

Was Billy threatening her?

"Speaking of, how did you find out where I was?"

He ignored the question and pressed on. "I could do it, but I don't want to. I want you to be on board. Saina, this is a *cover* for *New York* mag — it's huge! Look, I could set up a sort of summit, you could meet with some of the protesters, and people are going to look at you differently now, with everything going on with your family and stuff."

"Billy, you're freaking me out. How did you know about that?"

"I ran into your ex. He was wasted."

Saina felt a flash of cold. Even if Grayson didn't care about her heart, she thought he'd at least want to protect her privacy. Or, failing that, her physical safety.

"And he just *told* you? What, did he program the directions into your phone and give you a ride to the train station, too?"

"Hey." Billy sprang up and gripped her arms, a liquid look of concern in his eyes. *Fake,* Saina reminded herself. It was probably fake. Billy was like those serpent-tongued eunuchs who slunk around royal courts, trading on scraps of gossip. "I just want to help you. I know I'm a reporter, not a critic, but I am really just a fan. I mean it. I think you're going to be up there with, like, Marina Abramović someday. Those protesters are crazy."

"You'd think I was creating false images of Mohammed and putting *him* in a flowery headscarf," she said, glad even for this scrap of sympathy.

"That's what America likes to do to its successes, right? Eat them up and spit them out?"

Saina laughed. "Exactly. I'm definitely in the being spit out phase."

"But it means that you're someone to be taken seriously. Why else would they want to give you a cover?"

"Because my life is an art world soap opera." They stared at each other for a moment. "Did you . . . did you pay him or something?"

"Would that have worked?"

"Well, apparently he was willing to sell me out for nothing, so cash could only have sped up the process."

"Does he need it?"

Saina stopped herself. Of course. Billy was just trying to get his story. In a way, she didn't even fault him — she was a commodity in his eyes, their connection a stock that had yielded excellent dividends in the past and now promised to pay off even more if he could persuade it to split.

"Billy, I'm tired. And you have to catch the seven-thirty train. I'll call a cab. There are only two in town, so it'll probably take a while for one of them to get here."

"Hey, no, no, no. I thought we were having a good talk, right?"

She wanted to wound him. Who was he to insinuate himself into her life, to ambush her here where she should be safe, to suggest that he'd had anything to do with the life that she'd made?

"I never thought you'd end up just being a paparazzo, Billy."

She said it with as much nonchalance as she could muster. It worked. She could tell. He froze and raised one eyebrow as high as it would go. He was a lot bigger than she was, Saina realized. He was skinny, and he always slouched, but he was at least six feet tall with broad shoulders and big, veined hands. His face was thicker now — too much happy-hour beer and midnight melted cheese. He didn't feel like a boy anymore. Saina wondered if she should be scared. *Would Billy hurt her?*

"Did your former fiancé tell you that he's getting married?"

No. Billy wouldn't hurt her. He'd destroy her.

Or try to. Once she'd gritted out her bravest smile and boldest lie, assuring him that she knew everything, once he'd left, disappointed, and she'd locked the door and prepared to crumble, to let herself just wash away, Saina found, instead, that she felt blank. A lightness. A widening space inside that was neither positive nor negative. She remembered the weeks after Grayson had first left her, when she sat straight up in bed every morning at four, heart racing, knowing only that something bad, bad, unutterably bad had happened. This already felt different.

Her only thought was embarrassing. It was this: *But . . . Sabrina's not an artist!*

Because how could Grayson have loved her, Saina, for all the reasons he said he did if he could just turn around and love Sabrina instead? She pictured him calling his new wife's jewelry *art* and felt sick at the lie of it all.

Wife.

Saina focused back on that space. Dark, quiet, internal. It expanded and buoyed her heart up so that it could not sink again, like it had done once before. She made herself remember, instead, a road trip they took to a friend's wedding, not far from where she was now. The radio played a cheerful little tune and then the host announced that futures were looking good. Grayson cocked his head and looked at her, cute, saying, "Futures? I thought there was only one." So she'd explained it to him again, trying to remember the way her father had untangled the world of options and futures and puts and shares for her, and for the third time, he'd nodded and said that he understood. Finally, though, she realized that he just liked to hear himself voice confusion, liked to think of himself as an artist who couldn't be expected to understand base financial matters. Her suspicion was confirmed when she heard him again at the wedding itself, saying to a group of friends who were talking about an upcoming IPO, "How can people buy something that doesn't exist?" and shaking his head sagely at the wonder of it all.

Your *clubscapes* don't really exist, she had wanted to say. They're a bunch of things that are supposed to make a statement about another thing. Your collectors are buying a series of symbols because critics have conferred meaning upon them. It's the same damn thing as buying a piece of paper that the banks say represent a group of homeowners' individual promises to pay back their mortgages. Wasn't that abstraction the beautiful thing about what they did? Wasn't that what made it different from painting a house or welding a car? Different from staging a kid's birthday party or serving a meal in a restaurant? From making a fucking ring?

The things we agree to call art are the shamanic totems of our time. We value them beyond all reason because we can't really understand them. They can mean everything or nothing, depending on what the people who look at them decide. Everything or nothing. Saina knew it was nothing, and yet she kept on doing it. Grayson thought it was everything, and somehow that made him . . . what? Better? More successful? Worse? Stupider? More self-delusional?

In a way, finance was even better than art. It was nothing but an expression of potential, of power, of our present moment in time, and existed only because a group of people collectively agreed that it should exist. Out of nothing but a shared conviction was born a system that could run the world. It was beautiful and terrible. Saina thought that she and her father would probably see eye to eye on this, if they were ever able to have a conversation like it without arguing.

Saina had decided that she was going to be an artist when she was in junior high. It was because of a story that Morley Safer did. In Saina's mind, he was a sort of cross between Peter Falk's Columbo and Walter Cronkite, and the story had a hint of murder mystery to it. She even remembered the title: "Yes . . . But Is It Art?" Portentous, like it should be followed by an ominous chord progression. Safer had focused his skeptical eye on Jeff Koons. The trio of floating basketballs, the vacuum cleaner, they had all felt like revelations to her. *I can make anything art,* she'd thought then, not realizing that Safer was producing a takedown of the contemporary art world.

Fifteen years later, she'd still felt the same way. Until now.

A week ago, lost in a Grayson Google loop, Saina found a brief mention in *Art in America* saying that his last piece had sold for half a million dollars — it was an entire order of magnitude greater than any of his past sales. *He's doing better without me,* she'd thought. In a sort of daze, Saina had rewatched the old *60 Minutes* piece, which looked hopelessly outdated — the early '90s might as well have been the '70s — and tried to comfort herself with an interviewee's observation about collectors: "The act of spending that money on an object makes them feel like they are collaborating on the creation of the art history of their time." That was why. Grayson gave good artist. He was tortured and handsome and unpredictable, willing to hold forth for hours on the nature of beauty and creation.

Koons, it turned out, had been a commodities trader before he became an artist. It all seemed so appropriate somehow. Maybe all modern art was the strike of beauty against wealth, the artists mocking the collectors for their vain attempt to purchase the inimitable spirit of the artist. But what if you were cursed with both?

Saina wondered why she'd ever stopped watching *60 Minutes.* Would her life make more sense now if she'd continued to see the world through Morley Safer's eyes, if every week still ended and began again with that ticking stopwatch?

All I wanted, Saina thought, *was to make someone feel something.* Money can't do that. Just looking at a dollar bill did nothing to the emotions — you have to make money or lose money for it to make you feel anything. You can earn it, win it, lose it, save it, spend it, find it, but you can't sell it because you never really own it. On the other hand, you didn't have to possess a song or a sculpture for it to make you feel something — you only had to experience it. So why did collectors want to collect? What feeling were they pursuing? Or was a portfolio just a portfolio no matter whether the investments it held were financial or artistic?

Other artists cared about their place in the canon, about color and brushwork, about pushing forward the lines of inquiry that obsessed and impressed their peers. Sometimes Saina pretended to care about all of those things, too, but really all she wanted to do, all she'd ever wanted to do, was to look very closely at the world in a way that resonated. And her show, her last, best show, had done that. She was sure of it. Saina kept the catalog from *Look/Look* on her desk, a punishment and a reminder, and too often she found herself rereading parts of the introduction that her gallerist had written.

> *In 2007, while war raged on in Iraq, Wang began to notice something about the photos of civilians and refugees published in mainstream news-papers. They were often composed so that the frame centered on a single, striking young woman. While researching this observation, Wang remembered a photo of the war in Bosnia that she first encountered as a child living in Los Angeles. "I'd been flipping through my mother's back issues of* Vogue," *she recalls, "and then I opened up the* L.A. Times *and was instantly struck by a beautiful girl in a really chic headscarf. It wasn't until a moment later that I realized that she was on the back of a truck with a dozen other refugees." Wang tracked down that older photo, and then spent months poring over published images of America's wars, going back to Vietnam.*
>
> *Then, in a daring move, she selected the loveliest of the women — women who might have already perished in the conflicts they were used to illustrate — and, with the aid of Photoshop, excised them from their place in history, transported them to a moody warehouse, and looked at them again through the Vaseline blur of desire. There, the women became all beauty, taking on new roles as the models they might have been, had they the fortune of being born in another place and time.*
>
> *— New York City, February 2008*

What was so bad about that? Her gallerist had issued an apology on her behalf of the "I'm sorry if anyone was offended" sort, but she still couldn't understand how her show had become the flash point of so much anger. Lately, the only professional interest she'd received was from people who had heard of her fall: A gallerist in Germany who wanted to curate a show of modern-day failures, a filmmaker whose documentary on anti-Semitic fashion designer Jean Lugano's bid to remake his career had just premiered to some success. The only offer that wasn't outright insulting came from Xio, the persistent curator of the new Beijing Biennial, who wanted to include Chinese artists living abroad. She'd had a conversation or two with him and been dismayed to learn that gossip of her disgrace had spread all the way to China, though it didn't seem to change his enthusiasm for her work.

In the end, though, none of it appealed to her. It would never work to try to make something mannered and safe. Pandering to your detractors was even worse than pandering to your collectors.

Saina closed her eyes. It was too much. For the first time in her life, she felt old, tired, like the effort that it took to fight for recognition was no longer worthwhile. It was true what they said — leaving New York made you soft.

二十

Phoenix, AZ

605 Miles

THERE WAS NOTHING grosser than a naked mattress, the quilted, satin surface of it all pilled and stained from more generations of Arizona State students than Andrew wanted to think about. He rubbed the palm of his hand against the rough little bumps raised all over the flowered beige surface and shivered. It tickled like riding a bike over a bumpy gravel road, but something about the sensation turned his body's attention inward and he felt himself press up against the ridge of his pants. *Damn skinny jeans.* Andrew pulled down his zipper and wriggled them halfway down his legs as he looked around the room for a forgotten bottle of lotion, anything viscous, *anything,* but it had all been packed or given away.

He hated spit. The smell of his own saliva was never a turn-on. Why couldn't he smell it when he was making out with someone?

He could feel himself getting hard and straining at the cotton confines of his briefs and put aside the unwanted urge to pee. Andrew reached a hand into his backpack. Laptop, cell phone, beanie, a few wrinkled envelopes, and the crumpled bag from yesterday's egg sandwich.

Oh. That could work.

He thought of Emma, gorgeous Emma, who wanted nothing more than for him to let her have sex with him, Emma squirting ketchup on his dick like a hot dog and swallowing it down. He held that image in his mind as he rooted in the bag with one hand and tugged his briefs down with the other, closing his eyes and flicking over again to Emma, now jumping up on the volleyball court and arching her body back, back, back, one arm up, throat exposed, breasts pushed high, then pounding the ball across the net in an explosion of sweat and heat. With his teeth, he tore open a ketchup packet and emptied it into his palm, flicking again to Emma on her knees in front of him, reaching out for him as he reached down with his ketchup palm, sliding his hand around and up. He was lying down now and Emma was gone, replaced by a girl he saw once, Rollerblading across the Venice boardwalk, her dress billowing up with a gust of wind so that he caught just a glimpse of her naked bottom and the neat little strip of hair between her legs. He pushed himself into his hand, and for just a second, a half second, Professor Kalchefsky crept in, making him wonder whether *copula* and *copulate* had the same root, but Andrew banished him and brought in his most timeworn and reliable image, a flash of Cinemax he somehow saw as a kid, a few stolen minutes of a man and a woman spread out on the hood of a car, hips thrusting, boobs jiggling, the man angry with a bush of a mustache, the woman pleading for more, pleading for him to stop when, like a flicker on the screen, he saw his doorknob turn.

"Stop!" He choked on the word, tried shouting it again. "STOP!"

"Andrew?"

It was his dad. No, no, no, no, no. His heart stuttered and his lungs froze.

"Andrew?"

And his sister. And probably Barbra, too. Andrew stood up and staggered towards the door, throwing his weight against it.

"Just hold on," he said. "Give me a minute." He could hear them on the other side of the door, his dad asking what he'd said, Grace shushing him, Barbra saying nothing. He looked down. His right hand was a ketchupy mess. He closed his eyes, thinking of vomit, shit, his dead mother, until he hung limp, dark smears of condiment caught in the wrinkles of his shrunken penis. Still pressing his back to the door, Andrew pulled up his underwear and pants. Zip. Button. *Oh god.*

He wiped his hand on his jeans and opened the door, pretending to swallow.

"I was just . . . eating. But, I . . . I had to get dressed."

"Why you don't want us to see you eating? You were eating naked? You have girlfriend hiding in closet?" His father sounded hopeful.

Andrew half turned towards his closet, wishing that Emma really was in there, disheveled, beautiful. That would have been way less embarrassing. He'd always wanted the kind of father who would shoot hoops with him, but his dad was way more likely to introduce him to a couple of models than to buy him a baseball glove or attend a soccer match. He hated the wink that his father would give him whenever a woman's name popped up on his cell phone. Once, late at night, he'd even seen his father waiting at a valet stand in downtown L.A., his arm around a surprisingly beautiful redhead who looked not much older than Saina. It was gross to think of the women who made themselves available, grosser to think of Barbra caring about sex at all, and grossest to know that if his dad cheated on Barbra, then it meant that he had probably done the same to Andrew's beautiful mother. Maybe that was why Andrew was holding out for true love. *Who knew rebellion would be so boring?*

"No, Dad, no one else is here."

Oh. He couldn't hug them like this, hand still slick with ketchup and sweat, dick barely tucked back into his jeans.

"I have to go to the bathroom — it'll just take a second." He put a hand over his stomach. "Bad food."

Backing into the hallway, he narrowly avoided bumping into the RA, spun around, and ran to the coed bathroom, praying that no one would be in there.

Coast clear. Andrew splashed water on a stack of brown paper towels and ducked into a stall. The ketchup was starting to burn. Nervous, quick, he scrubbed at himself roughly until the damp wodge of barky smelling towel started to shred down his pants. He plunked it in the toilet and flushed, but the mass wouldn't go down. *Whatever.* He was leaving. He'd never use this toilet again. Let it be someone else's problem.

Slam. Soap. A blast of hot water, a blast of hot air, and he was back out the door, ready to be a son, a brother, a stepson, a middle child.

. . .

"Andrew!" Grace barreled down the hallway and threw her arms around him, squeezing him so tight that he felt sharply aware of how much he was loved. It was enough to make tears pool in his eyes, which he tried to flick away by picking her up and whirling her around.

"Gracie! How's the road trip been going?"

"Terrible. Terrible! We dropped Ama off at her daughter's weird place in the desert and the kids were cute but she fed us *hot dogs,* Andrew, and the whole place was so weird and creepy and I know you're going to say that I have no sense of adventure but that's just not the kind of adventure I want to have and I don't care. Stop laughing at me!"

Andrew tugged on her ponytail. "It'll be better now. I'll be with you guys."

Grace smirked at him. "So, what were you doing when we got here?"

"I told you! I was just eating! Anyways, listen. I have an idea — this is going to be my first comedy tour!"

"What do you mean?"

"I have a set. We're going on the road. So I figured I could, you know, take my act on the road!"

"Did you book things?"

"No, I'm thinking open mics. I talked to Dad about the route that we were taking —"

"What? When?"

"A couple days ago."

"But I didn't even know that we were leaving until a couple of days ago! No one tells me anything."

"It was all one conversation — we're leaving, your car is being repossessed, I'm not paying your tuition, I'm going to get back all the land the Communists took, oh, and by the way, what's the best way to get out of Tempe?"

"Well, I don't understand why he tells you everything."

Andrew's father stepped out of the dorm room just then, carrying Andrew's giant duffel bag.

"Okay, we ready? You say hello to auntie?"

Andrew leaned over and gave Babs a kiss, and then, at the last minute, he reached his arms around her in an embrace. It would have been nice to have a mom right now, if they were going to go somewhere as a whole family. But he didn't. He had a dad and an auntie, a Baba and a Babs, and that was better than nothing.

The last time Andrew had ridden in this station wagon he'd been strapped to a car seat and his mom had been behind the steering wheel, wearing a giant pair of sunglasses, hands encased in white gloves. She'd hated the sun. She would have hated Tempe, where every sun-bleached building was the same dusty pueblo color and the city felt bright even after dark. Andrew had spent most of his college career in sunglasses, terra-cotta roofs and palm trees mirrored across his shielded eyes.

He had them on now, hiding another well of wholly unexpected tears. Andrew opened his lids wide, trying to will the tears back inside their ducts, but that just made his eyes sting so that he had to blink, sending a tiny salt waterfall spilling down his cheeks. He didn't even really know why he was crying. He didn't think that he felt all that sad to be leaving school. Maybe he was just a pussy. They were driving by Grady Gammage Auditorium now, its weird circle of curtained arches reflecting in the pond. *See ya later, Tempe.* Was there a GED for college that he could take? Or maybe it wouldn't matter once he was on the road.

"Baba," called Andrew up to the front.

"Hmm?"

"So, you know how I want to be a comedian?"

Andrew's father glanced back at him in the rearview mirror and didn't say anything. Sometimes Andrew felt like his father didn't understand anything he said, like Charles Wang wished that he had a different son altogether.

Maybe if he said it in Chinese. *"Shuo xiao hua?"*

His father nodded.

"So, I have to practice. A lot. With, like, different audiences." Andrew pulled out his phone. "So we're going to be in some cities with open mic nights. I thought I could sign up and, you know, do my set."

"Are you funny?" asked Grace.

"You know I am! Remember I told you about the thing at school? We put on that show? People loved it."

Charles shrugged. "You go to party school. They think everything funny funny, everything party party."

"I'm not saying I'm like Steve Martin or, uh, Bob Newhart or anything yet," said Andrew, trying to think of a comedian his father might respect, "but I can be good. You come watch me, you'll see. So, can we do it? We can get to Austin by Sunday. I called a club there already, and they said that they'd let amateurs go on if I came in and signed up early enough. Okay?"

Andrew could see his father's reflection pursing its mouth and glancing towards Barbra. She would never say anything. He tried again.

"I mean, if I'm not going to go to college, I have to do *something*, right?"

His father's head jerked back. *"Ben dan ya? Ni yi ding yao huei xue."*

"I know, I will, but I'm not right now, right? So what's wrong with comedy? You're proud that Saina's an artist, aren't you?"

But that was different, Andrew knew. More right, somehow. Less embarrassing. The sort of thing a girl could do. Also, she was crazy successful pretty much immediately, so that made a difference, too. Well, he'd let it drop for now, but when they were near a club, he'd just go. They couldn't stop him. Grace would help create a diversion, and they'd leave the parents at the hotel or motel or wherever they were going to start sleeping now that they were on the road.

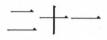

El Paso, TX

1,038 Miles

GRACE POINTED her foot and dipped a toe in the acid-green pool. The water was hot. The night air smelled like gasoline and burnt sagebrush. All around them the flat desert streets lay still; just out of reach, a cicada spun itself in circles, drowning.

"We should rescue it," said Andrew, not moving.

"It'll just die later."

"Still."

"'Someone has to die in order that the rest of us should value life more.'"

"What?"

"It's Virginia Woolf." She tipped the little airplane bottle of Jack Daniel's to her lips, waiting for the last drops to drain out as she stared at the striped roof of the Whataburger across the street. The layered *W*s of the sign looked like a Missoni-ish chevron pattern. Maybe she could start a website that found fashion influences in fast food places. She'd name it Couture Road Trip. Or Couture by Car. And then some designer would call her his muse and make a pattern out of Whataburger signs and then she'd be famous and could do a shoe collaboration and wouldn't need to inherit any money anyway.

Because she probably wasn't going to. Somewhere between driving away from Kathy's house in Ama's car like a family of thieves — her stolen laptop banging against her knees in the backseat, the U-Haul filled with lifted merchandise rumbling along behind them — and walking in on Andrew playing with himself, Grace had admitted that she was lying to herself. There was no show, no party. Instead, this was the end. It couldn't be, but maybe it was.

Checking into this crappy Texas motel had somehow clinched it. They had gone up to the room, the four of them, standing still as the hollow door creaked shut. Barbra had taken out a handkerchief and used it to pull aside the plastic-backed drapes and then their father had looked at the two queen beds, and said, "One for boys, one for girls?" She and Andrew had been horrified. What did he think would happen if they shared a bed? Grace had looked at Andrew, who nodded at her, and said, "You guys take your own bed. We're going to go out to the pool." Andrew grabbed his backpack and one of the key cards, and they ran out, leaving the grown-ups to figure it out for themselves. A narrow escape.

"Gracie, do you think they're asleep yet?"

"What if they're having sex?"

"Oh god, why would you say that? Brain! Burning!"

"Does it really gross you out that much? It's just sex."

"Yeah, but it's *Dad* and *Babs!* I don't want to picture them all naked and saggy on a motel bed!"

"I don't know . . . it kind of doesn't gross me out. I can picture pretty much anyone doing it without getting grossed out."

"But your own father!"

"I know! Logically, it's gross, but when I picture it, it's like picturing someone eating or something. You know, just like a normal, everyday thing."

"That you do with someone else. Naked."

"Yeah . . ."

"And sweaty."

"Eew! Okay, now it's gross!"

"Thank god, I was starting to think you were some kind of perv."

Grace waggled her eyebrows at him. "I could picture you and some lovely young coed."

"Grace, stop it! Seriously! Maybe I'm too innocent to share a bed with you after all!"

"Oh, I blur out all the private parts in my mind."

"God, *I* can't even picture me having sex."

"What do you mean?"

"I just can't. I mean I can, I do picture it, but then I kind of can't, you know?"

"Wait, have you not?"

"You have?"

"Well, yeah. But what about you and Eunice? I just thought for sure..."

"You know how religious she was."

Grace shrugged. "I haven't seen that matter much with other people."

"Wait, you're kind of skipping over the more important revelation here."

"Andrew, I'm sixteen! It's not a big deal. You just think it's a big deal because I'm your little sister."

Andrew looked at her for a second the way some other guy might. She was pretty, of course. When she was a kid, she'd looked like a doll, with her pink cheeks and rosy little lips. But now, though Andrew hated to even think it, little Gracie was kind of sexy. *Oh god. She was.* He knew that guys liked Saina, but that was different. She was his older sister, which meant that she was always part of a vague, adult world that swirled just slightly above his head, alluring and unreachable. Even when he'd hit sixteen, and then eighteen, and now twenty-one, all the ages that had seemed so wise and *fun* when Saina occupied them, it felt as if he were failing to tap into all the adventure those years promised. Road trips! Cigarettes! Drunken adventures! Saina had done all that with abandon, and now Grace seemed to be following her easy lead in a way he'd somehow talked himself out of doing.

"Hey, big brother," Grace singsonged, "are you ruined forever? Have I blown your mind by admitting that I've blown other things?"

"Oh my god, Grace! Stop it!"

"Okay, okay! I'm sorry, that was too much — I just kind of couldn't resist. C'mon, it was a good joke, right? Like, from a professional standpoint?"

"It was a terrible, terrible thing to say from any standpoint."

Grace kicked at his submerged leg, splashing the chemically charged water up onto the tile, which was still hot even though the sun had been down for hours. "Do you think I'm a slut now?"

"No! Why does everyone keep asking me that?"

"If I'm a slut?"

"Oh no, no. It's just this girl that I was involved with. I really liked her but she —" Andrew paused and looked at his sister. *Well, why not?* "She wanted to sleep with me, but I just wasn't sure."

"Was she hot?"

"Grace, is that really all you think it's about? Was she *hot?* Is that what you do? Just fuck anyone you think is *hot?*"

She looked up from braiding a strand of hair, shocked. Behind her winged eyeliner and baby hipster layers of necklaces and bracelets, his little sister was still so young. A pinprick of anger broke through his heat-heavy torpor.

"Have you fucked a lot of guys?"

"I'm not telling you!"

Okay. Andrew would have to change tack. The important thing now was to save her from becoming one of those girls that everyone wanted to sleep with and no one wanted to take out to dinner. "Grace, look, I'm not trying to shame you. It's your choice, right? I mean, it should always be your choice. But you don't have to choose . . . to, uh, do it with a lot of people."

"You are so condescending."

"You don't know what guys are like —"

"No, *you* don't know what guys are like because you're deciding that you have to be a *virgin* for some reason. Dude, why is it such a big deal? Are you a Republican or something?"

"I don't care what other people do, I just . . . I just think that things like sex matter. It's your connection with another person. It should mean something." He looked at her, underlit by the glow of the pool. Should he tell her about their father and his unfaithfulness? He hesitated. "Just . . . just don't be stupid, Grace."

Grace scraped back on the concrete and jumped up, kicking a spray of pool water in his face. She stood, looming above him, furious now. "Why are you being like this, Andrew?"

"Like what?"

"All judgy, like you're my dad or something. Are you going to try to send me off to boarding school, too?"

Contrite, Andrew leaned over and grabbed at her ankle. "No! Hey. No. Look, I'm sorry, I didn't mean to make you feel bad."

"Well, you did."

"Don't be Gracie mad! Be my friend again." He held up the empty minibottle of Jack. "Say hello to my little friend?"

"It's not going to work, Andrew. Guys can just quote things from movies and everything's cool, but it's not going to work with me."

It was always like that, thought Andrew. Any time Grace felt like someone was disapproving of her, even the slightest bit, it became an all-out battle. Youngest child syndrome. That had made so much sense when he first read about it. He was always in the middle, bringing Grace and Saina together, giving in to their dad, being nice to Barbra. He felt like Rodney King sometimes, arms outstretched, asking for everybody to just get along.

"So is this all real?" asked Grace.

"You being mad at me for no reason? I hope not."

God. Andrew. He should be a stupid comedian — he always tried to make everything a joke. Grace briefly considered the possibility of both of her siblings being famous. If that happened, then she'd have to be famous, too, which she was planning on anyway. It wouldn't be fair if she was the only one who wasn't.

"No, asshole. All of this. Us staying in this piece of shit place, Dad not having money for our tuitions, our house being gone. Is that all real?"

For a minute, Grace still expected the answer to be no. She looked for a flicker in Andrew's face, a hidden smile, a creased eye, something that would congratulate her for stumbling on the secret. And then a hail of balloons would fall out of nowhere and all her friends would run out from behind the Dumpsters and the whole place would erupt like an episode of *My Super Sweet 16,* but instead of giving her a car, her father would give her a giant check and tell her that no one ever expected her to pass all the tests as quickly as she did.

"Grace —"

"It is, isn't it?"

"Well, yeah," he said, gently. "What did you think it was?"

She curled up her toes, scratching them against the concrete, breathing in the throat-searing chlorine, closing her eyes to the harsh fluorescents that cut through the hazy moonlight. She licked her lips. They were salty with sweat. How could she have been so completely, utterly, nonsensically, next-level idiotic? Of course it wasn't like *The Game.* Her father would never have gone to so much trouble for something that wouldn't make money. Her stepmother would never have agreed to drive with all of them to Saina's house just to teach her some sort of lesson. Grace looked down at her brother's face. Open. Concerned. Andrew was so fucking sweet. He would have done it. He would always do anything for her.

"What did you think it was?" he asked again. So worried.

"Nothing," she said, dully. And then she kicked him in the chest, hard, her bare foot leaving a wet imprint in the middle of his T-shirt, and took off, running back towards the room.

Behind her, she could hear his *oof* and then a scrabble on the concrete as he struggled up after her.

He reached the door a step behind her and waved the beige key card in her face.

"Tell me what's going on," he said. "Are you just upset about things?"

"Don't talk to me." She snatched at the key. He pulled it away. She reached again and he did the same thing. This dance. She hated it. "Don't make me do this now, Andrew. Please."

Andrew relented and slid the card into the door. The adults lay huddled in one bed, two soft lumps, breathing too lightly to really be asleep. He headed towards the empty bed, tired now, and slipped in without bothering to change clothes or brush his teeth.

Andrew closed his eyes. He could hear Grace unzipping her suitcase, banging the lid against wall, storming into the bathroom and turning up the water. It was freezing in the room, the air conditioner anchored next to the door fanned gusts of cold air back and forth. Andrew burrowed himself into the pillows and pulled the scratchy coverlet up to his neck.

He was just starting to drift off into sleep when Grace swiped a pillow out from the pile and tossed it onto the foot of the bed. She yanked the sheets out from under the mattress and got in, kicking her feet towards Andrew's face.

He was disappointed. Andrew realized that he'd been looking forward to the familiar comfort of sharing physical space with someone who wasn't going to drive him crazy with repressed desire, but Grace made it into a war instead. Her dirty feet were tucked under his pillow now, one grimy heel, blackened by running up to the room barefoot, inches away from his nose. He could smell them. They didn't smell bad, really, just like a sweaty T-shirt left too long in the backseat of a car. Sharing a bed should have been like watching movies with his sisters when they were kids, before Saina left, before Grace was sent away, when they would all just pile together like puppies, Grace's legs kicked across his lap, his head resting on Saina's shoulder, Saina doling out snacks from their father's stash: roasted melon seeds, walnut-studded date cakes wrapped in edible rice paper, little rolls of coin-shaped haw flakes, sticks of dried squid sandwiching a thin layer of black sesame. Andrew reached over and squeezed one of Grace's toes, trying to be friendly. She thrashed out at the touch. *Fine then.* Andrew turned and pushed himself all the way to the very edge of the bed, pulling the sheets with him, making an empty tent between their two bodies.

二十二

I-10 East

JUST THREE DAYS on the road and already her powder-blue exterior was covered in a thin veil of drab dust that made her look grimy and uncared for. Across her windshield, a smattering of bugs. Squished into the tread of her tires: gravel, garbage, gum. On her roof, an avian bomb site with white splatters ringing shrapnel turds. And hitched to her lovely chrome bumper, a horrible box on wheels, so heavy that it pulled at her screws, loosening them thread by thread.

Gone were the days of May Lee and her neat, gloved hands steering the two of them through the palm-lined streets of Beverly Hills. Gone, even, were the days of conveying Ama, who drove as if she were in a wrestling match, all the way to the San Gabriel Valley via an interminable series of surface streets. Gone was the gardener's son, who had washed and polished her along with all the other cars, and never mind that she wasn't used nearly as often.

Inside, things were even worse.

Charles, knees akimbo, farting constantly into the upholstery, was always in her driver's seat. He had stuffed her door pocket full of ancient maps that must trace their way across some forgotten America and was constantly jamming his giant sunglasses into her visor, where they'd fall and hit him on the head over and over again.

Behind him was Andrew, so much bigger now than when he'd last been in that same seat. He scrubbed at her lovely carpet with his dirty sneakered feet and scattered bits of paper inked all over with nonsensical notes. And every time, as soon as he got inside, he placed his metal-cased phone directly on her seat, not caring that the little devil box got hotter and hotter as he continued to use it.

Next to Andrew, in her right rear seat, was the worst of all—his little sister, Grace. The girl was the one who started the abuse, using some sort of tacky blue substance to stick torn magazine pages onto her pristine doors and mashing the glue right into the holes in her perforated leather upholstery. It would probably never come out, even if by some miracle Jeffie reappeared and took a needle to it, as he once had when a baby Andrew spilled his bottle of formula across her entire rear flank.

She supposed that they had to make a home out of her somehow. That they—

Wait. She had almost forgotten what was in the front passenger seat clouding her air with some sort of cloying scent: the interloper, the carpetbagger, the stepmother. The one self-named Barbra, who had covered her window with a scarf, though a bit of darkening in the sun could only have improved that ugly face.

This was her lot now. Disgrace, meted out in asphalt miles. Her engine shuddered once, twice, but, ever loyal, she continued eastward, onward, always forward, with Charles's heavy foot depressing her gas pedal and draining her insides.

二十三

I-10 East

"*KAI CHE bu yao ting dian hua,*" said Barbra.

Charles ignored her and stabbed at the voicemail button on his phone. He wasn't a child. He could hold a phone and drive at the same time. He could eat and drive, read the paper and drive, shave and drive. He could even pat his head and rub his belly at the same time, something that used to send Andrew and Grace into shrieks of laughter when they were little, though he wasn't sure why the activity was in such high demand.

The first message: "Hello, Charles, hello." (Pause.) "It's Lydia. Grant spoke to me, I'm very sorry to hear about your company's (pause) difficulties. I do hope it hasn't been too (pause) *difficult* for the family. And I hope that we'll see you and your wife next week at our fall dinner." (Pause.) "And I'd like to thank you for your generous support of the Gardens over the years, and your continued generous support. It's very kind." (Pause.) "OkaywellIhopethewholefamily'sdoingwellgoodbyenowgoodbye."

Oh, the anxious, aging wives of his white business associates, fingers weighted down with diamonds, constantly tittering on about how busy they were with this committee meeting and that school event, all the while shedding pretty tears for dark-skinned children in distant countries. Charles loved being around them. They flattered him like concubines, wheedling checks for orphans in Burma or wells in Namibia, angling for ever-larger donations of cosmetics to put on the block at one of the endless silent auctions for their children's private schools. Nothing made him feel better than tossing off a check that elicited a breathy gasp of pleasure from one of the wives. Charles remembered the one he'd written for Liddy's dinner. $5,000 a plate. $10,000 for Barbra and him. Well, someone else was going to eat his share of ahi poke or steak roulade or summer trifle or whatever the absurdly fashionable food of the moment happened to be.

Having money made things so *easy*. Ease. That's what he was born for. By rights, Charles Wang never should have had to doubt the state of his accounts, not for a single moment of his life. By rights, he should have had an ancient kingdom at his feet — if the tide had not been turned by history, who knew how vast his family's holdings would now be?

Second message. "Wang Gege! You don't call, you don't email!" *My email got impounded,* thought Charles, *along with everything else.* "Are you switching sides on me, hmm? I'm still counting on your support this November, Wang, don't forget it. You promised to show up with those models on your arm, Gege. I'm waiting for them. That'll spring some wallets open, eh?" Little Mark Shen. The bastard had squirmed his way into Charles Wang's life by wielding a city council seat in Vernon, that tiny municipal fiefdom where Charles's largest warehouse and factory was located. Except that it wasn't his anymore. Someone else could war with that joke of a city, that gutter-and-ash city, about taxes and permissions and inane regulations that were really just bald attempts to rout more cash out of the pockets of honest businessmen. All the campaign contributions that he had given bowlegged Mark Shen were pointless now.

Charles tried not to think about it, but there was a relentless adding machine in his mind that refused to stop its guilty tally of all his unnecessary expenses: the campaign contributions — not just to Shen but also to California's governor and anyone who looked like they might have a chance of becoming mayor of Los Angeles; the donations to charities that meant more to the people running them than to the people they were supposed to help; the tables that he'd taken at dinners; the membership to a country club when he didn't even want to strike a ball across artificial lawns with a stick; the bottles of wine and whiskey ordered to show that $500, $1,000, $10,000 meant nothing to him. Wasn't money supposed to beget money? So how did all of his mighty dollars shrink up and cross their legs and refuse to breed anymore? If only he could claw it all back.

Rewind to that moment before some fireball of greed and ambition and catastrophic self-confidence made him stray from the sure path that he'd been on for so many years.

Safe and sure.

Bravery was for fools.

Third message. "Hey, Mr. Wang. Just calling to say that we got your email and that's cool, if you're fixing to come visit us, we'll be here. Uh, we definitely weren't expecting it, but it would be an honor, sir, to have you come in person. We'll see you all in a few days. Oh, this is Trip. BTW. You know, by the way. Yeah. Okay. Have a good drive." At least there was that. The cases of product in the bread box of a trailer that bumped along behind them, occasionally threatening to fishtail the car. Maybe they would be the start of something, a huge lifestyle brand that would overtake Martha and magnolia scent the world. And it would all be because he'd rescued their dreams from the detritus of his Failure — it would be the perfect comeback story.

Charles focused on the road in front of him. At some point the landscape had started to shift from the red dirt of New Mexico to the scrub flats of West Texas. Benighted lands, both of them.

His phone rang; his lawyer's name flashed across the screen. With a sneaky glance at Barbra, who wrinkled her forehead and turned away, he picked it up.

"Hello, I am driving. Is there anything?"

"How's the road trip?"

This lawyer was always bombarding Charles with pleasantries when he should have been figuring out how to reinstate the Wangs' lost acres. They continued in Mandarin.

"I pay you six hundred dollars an hour. It would cost me too much to tell you about it. Do you have any news?"

A laugh. "Well, we're not sure what this means yet, but it looks like you never left."

"What? Where?"

"Home. China."

"I don't understand."

"Neither do I, really, but we have obtained a copy of your identification record. Wang Da Qian, age fifty-six, born at 7:35 a.m. on March 14, 1952, parents Wang Wen Xi and Chong Jie — you're still there."

"Impossible!"

"You're a Communist Party member —"

"How can that be?"

"You have three children. And a wife named Mei Li."

"But I do have those. That is me. Who else could it be?"

"Don't lose heart; we'll figure it out. I have a colleague in Beijing looking into it; we'll surely be able to know if this is just some sort of paperwork issue."

"But the land?"

"You must have patience, Mr. Wang. China's not like America. Things take time."

"It's been weeks!"

"And we are edging forward. You don't clap your hands and make things happen over there. We have colleagues who help us, but it —"

"Alright, alright. Enough. I expect more next time we connect. You know, my colleague, he had only good words to say about you."

"Mr. Wang, this could turn into a long journey. The government won't be handing land out. There is no set reclamation process. There are no guarantees of any sort. Even with last year's new property law that you're so hopeful about, nothing is straightforward. I cannot say what will happen if you insist on going to China."

"I know all of that. I don't expect you to be able to figure out how to proceed — I'll take care of that. Your job is to give me all of the information I need to formulate a plan. Be sure that you know more than I do the next time we talk."

When Charles hung up the phone, Barbra was staring at him.

"The *land?*"

He kept his eyes on the road.

All his life, the land in China had been a promise. Starting back before he could even remember, his father's friends had gathered nightly around the mah-jongg table, cracking melon seeds, drinking tumblers of *gao liang,* and talking about the land in China. Later, through all the long, humid evenings in Taipei, as he did homework in the next room, their big words had floated in and settled all around him: "We'll get back the land in China," they reassured each other. "We'll go back and demand it." *Qu ba di yao huei lai.* That's what they told themselves, those displaced men who had once ruled a continent and were now exiled to an island — *the landinChina, the landinChina, the landinChina,* until it became a promise that seeped into little Wang Da Qian's very bones.

Could they have been wrong?

Or were they so right that he was there already, living out another temblor of his fault-lined life?

"*Ah bao,* what is 'the land'?"

He didn't want to tell her. Barbra knew, of course. He'd talked about it before often enough, but he didn't want to tell her now that the last of their money, his money, had gone to hire this lawyer who might prove, somehow, that the land was still part of the Wangs. The Nazis had to return looted artworks — why shouldn't the Communist Party return looted birthrights?

"Is this about your such-a-big-deal family, hmm? I tell you before, there is no way you get anything back from the government!"

His wife was never easy to ignore, but Charles kept his lips pressed shut and his eyes on the road. Barbra couldn't understand because she had never had anything. Not really. She grew up in school housing — a single shared room with bedrolls spread every night, showering next to the janitor's kids — and had barely left that meager house before she slipped right into his bed.

If you never have anything, you can never lose anything.

Charles tried to think of an analogy Barbra would understand. What if, he imagined telling her, what if all the Persian kids in Beverly Hills torched their Ferraris and smashed their bottles of Dior Homme before joining the Taliban? What if they marched through the city and snatched up properties, pulling you onto the street and calling you a godless capitalist pig, kicking you with feet still clad in the tasseled Prada loafers they couldn't bear to relinquish? Wasn't your house still rightfully yours? Wouldn't you want it back after they were inevitably vanquished by some makeshift Arizona militia? And wouldn't you just burn with anger at the thought of the state taking ownership of your property after the rebels had been routed? At a ragtag bunch of false politicians trying to build a new America on your hard-won acres?

Of course. And you would be right to feel that way. Everyone would think so. Your wife would support your every effort to regain that home instead of insulting your family and turning up an unappreciative little nose at your goals.

"Big deal, small deal. You would not know the difference," he said, defiant.

"What do you mean?"

Charles shrugged his lip.

He wanted to say it.

He didn't want to say it.

He said it: "You can't understand this! I give you everything you have! You never have to worry about anything!"

Barbra stared at him, eyes big. Her nostrils widened as she breathed in.

Now he couldn't stop, didn't even want to. "You think all I want is the land, the land, *the land?* No! The land is important because it is Wang *jia de!* Part of the family —"

"And because my family is poor we —"

"You don't know what it is like."

They stared at each other until Charles had to turn his eyes back to the road. It wasn't just the Wangs' land that mattered, it was all of China, every road he'd never trod, every mountain he'd never climbed, every monument he'd never beheld, every bush he'd never pissed behind — it all should have been his.

His parents and their friends had created an island within an island, a mini-China in Taiwan, but that wasn't enough. They were a colony of escaped mainlanders who never accepted their lives among the people who had no choice but to give them refuge; they spoke their home dialects and taught their children the geography of an unseen motherland, taught it so well that Charles knew he could have driven from the wilds of Xinjiang to the docks of Shanghai without so much as glancing at a map.

In the rearview mirror, both of his children sat staring at the windows, pretending not to listen.

· · ·

Outside, the alien desert unfurled itself in all directions. Punctuating the endless interstate were fading billboards for strip clubs and churches. As they passed the city limits of Van Horn, Texas, a brand-new billboard lit by a row of spotlights that managed to shine even in the midday sun screamed PATRIOTS UNITE! SECURE OUR BORDERS!, black block letters on a billowing flag.

America was a great deceptor. Land of Opportunity. Golden Mountain. Life, Liberty, and the Pursuit of Happiness. But inside those pretty words, between the pretty coasts, was this: Miles and miles of narrow-minded know-nothings who wanted no more out of life than an excuse to cock their AK-47s and take arms against a sea of troubles. A Great Wall? Ha! This country could never build itself anything as epic as that. America wanted to think of itself as a creator, but all it could do was destroy — fortunes, families, lives. Even the railroads needed the Chinese to come and build them.

America celebrated Christopher Columbus, a thief and a liar, a man who called himself a great sailor but couldn't even navigate his way past an entire continent. A man who discovered nothing, who explored nothing, yet was made into a hero all the same. Charles was reasonably generous with holidays for his employees: Veterans Day, the day after Thanksgiving, New Year's Day, his factories were shuttered. But Columbus Day would never be a day of rest for him, for any of the hundreds of employees he'd once had. There was nothing patriotic about honoring a man who made a mockery of true pioneers, a man who proved that America couldn't even take charge of its own discovery myth!

He couldn't let himself get too excited. That's what Dr. Kaplan had said. Excitement and exhaustion, any kind of stress, could trigger another tiny stroke like the one he'd had the day he signed the papers turning everything over to the bank. His doctor had wanted him to get an MRI and an entire battery of tests to rule out something more serious, but Charles didn't want anything to stand in the way of this journey. Now that he'd relinquished everything he'd built in America, all that remained, the only thing that he could focus on, was reuniting the Wangs under his oldest child's roof and then turning all of his attention to reclaiming China.

When Charles's father had his first stroke, he'd made it sound like nothing. *"Mei shi, mei shi. Bu yao dan xing,"* he'd insisted on their brief call, and Charles had allowed himself to believe it. After all, there was so much happening in America! The sales numbers had just begun to come in from KoKo's line, higher than they'd imagined in their margarita-fueled meetings, and, of course, he needed to be on hand in case the production run had to be increased. And then there was another big deal about to close, but it would be bad business to leave the country before all the papers had been signed. Not to mention a new house that he'd just put in an offer on, a house he would buy and his father would never see.

Charles wished his father had held on for longer. Made it to the peak of the success and then had his last stroke right before the Failure. Instead, he'd dropped to the ground in the entryway of a fish market and died with his head propped up on a burlap sack of geoduck clams just as Charles was postponing his trip to Taiwan for a fourth time.

Another billboard loomed up ahead, an image of a giant plate of BBQ ribs. Lunchtime had come and gone. His family must be hungry.

Charles leaned his head back. "Gege, Meimei, are your stomachs hungry?" Barbra twisted awkwardly in her seat and turned her back to him, facing her scarf-covered window. He remembered buying that scarf for her at the Hermès store on Fifth Avenue — a 56 x 56 silk square that he'd blithely plunked down $820 to acquire — right before Saina's disastrous show. Was it supposed to be a provocation, that scarf? Some sort of message about the Wangs and their failures?

He looked over his shoulder at Andrew and Grace. They hadn't responded to his question. "We have lunch at that restaurant?" he pointed up, as that billboard flew by. "Texas B-B-Q!"

"Oh Dad, let's just get something to go, okay? If we stay on track, we should get to Austin in four hours and twenty-three minutes," said Andrew, looking down at his phone.

"Why you so rush? You have girlfriend in Austin?"

"Baba! You know why! I want to get there in time to sign up for the open mic. It says on their website that sign-ups start at seven, and we'll probably go to the hotel first, and then I'll still have to find it, and maybe I can take the car or something?"

Barbra chose that moment to break her angry silence. "It won't ever happen! You lose the business, okay. Okay. I understand. Sometimes businesses get lost! But now how much do you spend on that lawyer? Maybe he speaks *zhong wen,* but he is not in *zhong guo*! What will he be able to do? Is it so hard for you not to be a big man? You can't just get that land and be a big man again — it won't happen. Communist Party never let it happen. Why they want to give it up?"

"Well," Charles heard Grace say to Andrew, "that might be the most words I've ever heard come out of Babs's mouth."

Charles bit down gently on his tongue and worried it between his wolf teeth. His wife didn't deserve a response. She deserved to be put out on the side of the road, left to fend for herself in the desolate fields of West Texas. The scarf could go, too.

"Andrew," he said instead. "Okay, yes. You take car, go to stand up."

"*I'm* hungry," said Grace. "Can we at least get french fries?"

Charles swerved to the right, just making it onto the off-ramp before it, too, flashed by, lost forever. As he coasted down towards the golden arches, he stretched a hand out towards his wife, reaching for something to pat, to reassure. Her hand, a delicate little bag of bones, found its way into his. Her body still faced the window, but she let him take her hand in his and squeeze it, tight.

二十四

Austin, TX

1,612 Miles

MAY LEE and Barbra had the same birthday, and it was today.

Barbra hadn't even known that they shared a birthday until six months into her marriage, when Charles came home and told her to get dressed for a special dinner. Pleased, thinking that he'd forgotten, she hurried into her closet and was happily laying out jewelry when she heard him down the hall telling Saina and Andrew that they would all be celebrating tonight. She remembered feeling a pang of disappointment at the thought of sharing the evening with the children, but that was nothing compared to Saina's wail when she saw Barbra descending the stairs in a new dress.

"Why is *she* coming?" Saina cried, pointing up at Barbra as if she were a murderess. There had been very few such accusatory moments. From the start, Barbra had kept her interactions with Charles and May Lee's children cordial but distant, always allowing them their way, rarely displaying any sort of softness, never encouraging any kind of reliance. It was a very satisfactory arrangement. She did not trouble herself over her relationship with her husband's children and they, in turn, barely paid any attention to her. This, though, had seemed beyond the pale, and Barbra let the anger show in her voice when she'd responded, "Well, it's *my* birthday."

"Daddy! She can't take Mommy's birthday! That's not fair!"

Ama stood in the doorway with baby Gracie in her arms, smiling, pleased, no doubt, that Barbra was being embarrassed. And Charles?

Charles was trapped in the middle of the foyer, the enormous chandelier casting a prism of shadows over his face as he looked at each of the women left in his life, utterly bewildered.

It had felt like a nightmare, but now Barbra thought that it was more like a fairy tale. One of those American Disney stories where malevolent spirits switch two babies born on the same day — in those tales, one child is always beautiful and good, and the other, the Barbra, is ugly and wicked. She was the Evil Queen, usurping Snow White's place next to the prince.

Except that these days, Charles was more like the frog. When had he become this scared and secretive man, hunched down in some swampy deep? Barbra leaned her head against the lush silk of her scarf, bumping against the hot glass that it covered, and let the moment he first told her replay in her mind.

There it was, over and over again — that awkward swoop of his arm, like a magician whose cape had gone missing.

And now here was the man left behind, still holding her hand. Her husband, who shrank a bit each day in the ceaseless desert sun, diminished by his lack of surety and, more than anything else, by his strange new secrecy. Barbra had loved Charles for his brashness; she loved him for the forthrightness of his desires, the way he took what he wanted and never lied about wanting it. What right did he have to change those things? Fortunes might shift, but character, at least, was supposed to be constant.

She took her hand back and folded it neatly in her lap. With any luck, Charles would forget this birthday. Barbra couldn't bear the thought of a makeshift celebration, cheeseburgers and a bottle of cheap champagne. The children probably remembered, but neither of them had said a word; it was unlikely that they would do any more than whisper about it to each other. Besides, tonight there was witless Andrew's comedy performance. Barbra wondered if she could claim a headache and stay in the hotel room, which would, at the very least, be air-conditioned. And quiet.

"How come 'You Don't Bring Me Flowers,'" she heard Andrew say to Grace in the backseat, quiet.

Barbra suppressed a sigh.

After a moment, Grace gave in, and replied, "Because 'A House Is Not a Home.'"

"Oh! You know what we're heading towards? A 'New York State of Mind.'"

A pause from Grace. "But what about 'The Way We Were'?"

"'Send in the Clowns,'" whispered Andrew, hushing Grace when she giggled.

This juvenile game. They thought she didn't understand it, that after all this time she was still too fresh off the boat to know that they were mocking her, but they were wrong. Saina, of course, had been the one to start it.

"You spell it B-A-R-B-R-A?" she'd asked, surprised. "Like Barbra Streisand?"

"Yes, from Strei-sand-u," Barbra had replied, hoping that Saina wouldn't ask any other questions. In truth, it was the first American name that had sprung to mind when she'd purchased her one-way ticket to Los Angeles from a uniformed girl her own age at the China Airlines office jammed between the noodle shops on Zhongshan Road in Taipei. The night before, when she was still Hu Yue Ling, she'd attended a university showing of *The Way We Were* and dreamed of Charles as Barbra Streisand and Robert Redford fell in and out of love on-screen. As she shuffled out with the crowd, crumpling up her package of shrimp chips, the boy in front of her said to his friend, "Well, Strei-sand-u is definitely ugly enough." It had surprised her. Somehow you didn't notice that she was ugly unless it was pointed out to you, ugly and determined, which Barbra herself found infinitely reassuring. Ugly, determined, and rich. A worthy namesake.

But Saina, of course, hadn't seen it that way. "You named yourself after *Barbra Streisand?*" she'd asked, incredulous. "But can you sing? Or are you just a total fan or something? I mean, *Barbra Streisand?* That is so weird." Barbra had watched the words come out of her stepdaughter's perfectly glossed young lips, which rested underneath an aquiline nose that gave her a faintly Native American air, as if Saina were descended from some noble, nearly extinct tribe rather than two crooked branches of a billion-person Chinese tree. It would have been unthinkable to tell that hateful little beauty that she had chosen the name because she admired the singer's apparent disregard of her own odd looks, so in the end, Barbra had merely shrugged, and said, "Good English practice." Except at the time it had probably sounded more like "Good-u Eng-u-reesh pu-lac-u-tis-u." And now it seemed like the sum of her sixteen years in America was her hard-won ability to say that sentence flawlessly. Nothing more. And sometimes not even that.

For a minute, Barbra was deaf to Andrew and Grace's backseat mockery as her own anger pulsed and swelled, threatening to blow out the windows of the ancient car.

One must do something with one's life, so she had done this, and now, even though it was all falling apart, it could not be undone. Charles. She couldn't take another minute of Charles. Barbra sat like this, in a private stew of rage and regret, frozen in place by blasts of air-conditioning and her own lying face until they pulled up to a W hotel.

"What are we doing here?" asked Grace. "Aren't we supposed to be poor?"

Charles laughed, uncomfortable. "I figure out that I still have some hotel point left that not part of credit card, so we come here for special occasion." He said all of this towards Barbra, voice hopeful, but didn't have the courage to look into her eyes or touch her shoulder.

"Guys! Can we get a move on? Um, does anyone want to come with me?" said Andrew.

"I'm coming!"

"Oh, Grace. I'm sorry, I just checked, it's twenty-one and over. You can't come."

"That's so unfair! What if you were headlining? You wouldn't be able to bring your kids?"

"I don't know," said Andrew, who never knew anything. "I guess not. But I really have to go, like right now."

Barbra finally turned to Charles. *"Wo qu. Ni ying gai pei* Grace *zai lu guan."*

Not what he was expecting, she thought triumphantly. He tried to look mischievous as he said, *"Ke shi wo shi xiang wo men ke yi . . ."*

Barbra shook her head, an emphatic no. As if she would even consider having sex with him at this moment. It would have been pathetic, sprawled on the coverlet of this midrange hotel, clothes tossed atop the children's luggage, groping at each other's flaccid bodies as some sort of nod to her birthday. Absolutely not.

"I will go with Andrew," she said again, this time for the children's benefit. "You stay, keep Grace company."

"I don't need a *babysitter*," said Grace, as Barbra had known she would.

"I'm not babysitter; I am Daddy!" said Charles, as Barbra had known he would.

And Andrew, of course, had no choice but to acquiesce and they drove off, leaving Charles and Grace in the lobby on either side of a giant white chair.

The comedy club smelled like all bars did — cold and sticky. Andrew was likely embarrassed to have her here with him, a silent mother figure hovering as he worshipped the black-and-white headshots that lined the hallway. Barbra recognized some of them, the lumpy ha-ha faces staring out of ugly oak frames.

"Steven Wright," whispered Andrew, touching the scarred glass as if it were a reliquary. He was wishing himself onto the wall, it was clear. Barbra had never seen her stepson look at anything like that before. The Wang children were so used to getting things that it rarely occurred to them to want anything. But was this what Andrew really wanted? A life of lonely motel rooms, performing for white people who probably wouldn't think that he was funny?

Andrew walked on ahead of her and found them a tiny round table, its black top cracked from years of damp drinks and once-upon-a-time cigarette burns, then dutifully fetched a gin and tonic cluttered with chunks of lemon. His own beer sat sweating and untouched as they suffered through a vaguely amusing comic who talked about mistaking himself for a bear on a hunting trip, a rather boring one who spent his entire seven minutes affecting an unconvincing lisp, and a succession of indistinguishable men in ill-fitting plaid shirts who all seemed to have been blessed with crazy girlfriends. And then it was time.

"Alright, dickheads," shouted the chubby emcee, his mouth hidden behind a bushy beard that was inexplicably dyed blue. "We've got a virgin here tonight! Let's help pop his open-mic cherry with a warm Austin welcome. Come on up, Andrew Wang! Hey dude, here's a comedy tip. Don't suck. Unless you're gay."

Without looking at her, Andrew squeaked his seat back and ran towards the stage, managing not to trip as he bounded up the stairs. Once the emcee was done making a lewd gesture with the microphone, Andrew grabbed it and turned towards the audience.

"What's up, Austin! Yeah, it's true. It's my first time here. So, uh, yeah, why do girls always want guys to take them out to a romantic dinner? Dude. Dinner is the least romantic thing ever. There's nothing romantic about eating. When you buy someone dinner, you're just, uh, buying things for their . . . you know, for their, uh, for their ass. Right?"

Barbra cringed. What was wrong with Andrew? He'd bragged about how much laughter he'd gotten from doing stand-up at his school, but if this was any indication of his abilities, those classmates must have laughed out of pity or embarrassment.

"I mean, it's either going to turn into shit and come out their ass, or it's going to turn into fat and stick to their ass!"

Probably the latter.

"The next time a chick asks me to take her out to dinner, I'm just going to tell her to *sit* on her ass and listen to this poem — I mean, what's not romantic about poetry? — Roses are red, violets are blue, let's go to bed, because I want to fuck you! Yeah!"

Andrew paused, waiting as the trickle of polite laughs failed to become a roar. Barbra considered being offended, but found that really she was rather amused. At least the excruciating awkwardness had resulted in something unexpected.

Someone near the front of the stage called out: "He said, 'Don't suck'!" She craned to see who it was, but the heckler was hidden by his friends. Andrew flinched and continued.

"So . . . I've totally disappointed my dad. I know what you're thinking — I'm Asian, so this must be some joke about how he's disappointed that I'm not a brain surgeon or not a lawyer or how I took a whole month to learn how to play Vivaldi or something. But, no, no, my dad is cool about that kind of shit. He actually wants me to play the guitar and get laid. No, honestly, he does." This apt description of Charles did make Barbra laugh, a sudden yelp of it, but she was embarrassed to be the only one.

"So, the thing is, my dad, the immigrant, is really, *really* disappointed that I have an allergy. A peanut allergy. Because immigrants do not believe in allergies. I swear to God, ask any brown person with an accent that you see and they'll tell you that allergies are some New World shit." *Well, that was true,* thought Barbra, remembering her own surprise when the mother of one of Grace's young friends refused to allow her daughter to play at the Wangs' because their housekeeper didn't use nonallergenic cleaning products.

And then, without warning, Andrew launched into a cross-eyed accent that made her cringe. "My dad was, like, 'I sail here under cover of night! I fight pirates! I hide out in American sewage system and work as busboy for twenty year, and you cannot defend yourself against *peanut?* One peanut? Peanut that so teeny tiny and de-ricious?'"

Across the room, maybe even from the heckler, there was a single shout of laughter. Besides that, silence. The tables around her fidgeted with their cell phones and drinks, waiting for Andrew's turn to be over. Not for the first time, Barbra was glad that she'd never wanted to be a performer.

"By the way," continued Andrew, valiantly, "I know that the only thing that white people love more than jokes *about* white people is when *black* people make jokes about white people. Right, guys, right? But you know what white people really, really, *really* love? When Asian comedians make fun of their parents. Yep, because you guys just want an excuse to laugh at Asian accents. Black people, no offense, but in this joke you basically count as white people. Admit it, as soon as I came up, you thought to yourselves, 'Oh man, I hope he says lots of *r* words, just tons of them, I hope this whole night is brought to you by the letter *r*.'"

All that scribbling in the backseat and *this* was what he came up with? It wasn't going very well — Barbra saw a black girl roll her eyes at her friend. Andrew must have rehearsed his pauses, because he again stared out into the audience, expectant, uncertain, waiting for the laughs she knew were never going to come. Finally, he went on.

"Here's what I don't understand: British people do not say the letter *h*. They just drop it entirely. Like, don't even try it, but we don't laugh at that. French people are not on speaking terms with zee *th*s, isn't zat true? But none of that turns y'all on like an Asian person messing up the letter *r*. The only thing that comes vaguely close is a Canadian *oo:* aboot, hoose. Just close your eyes for a minute and imagine an Asian immigrant who learned to speak English in Canada saying the word *roustabout*— oh, what does that mean? It's an unskilled laborer, you roustabouts! Seriously, though, what does that even sound like? Here, let's try it, let's say it out loud. You know you want to. It's okay. I'm telling you, on behalf of Asians everywhere, it's okay. Here, I'll say it with you, we can do it together, okay? On three. One, two, three — *loostaboot!*"

Only a couple of game audience members played along, dutiful. Someone else said something that sounded like "Loser dude," and several people headed towards the bathroom, but Andrew went on, his good cheer starting to sound a little desperate.

"You racist motherfuckers! No, no, I'm just kidding. Really, I'm kidding, I know all of your best friends are colored. Ha! Aw, I feel kinda guilty. I tricked you into it, and now you feel like douchebags." Andrew flapped his hands in a gesture that would have been meant to quiet down the crowd if they'd been making any noise at all. "Okay, okay, to make up for it I'll give you what you really want, okay?" He stood up straight and looked off into the distance. Raising an arm, he said, in a Laurence Olivier voice, "An elderly Chinese man, perhaps my father, perhaps not, just saying words. Words with the letter *r*." And then, again, that embarrassing accent. "*L*obots. *L*ogaine. *L*ome. *L*ota*l*y *C*rub — good one, right? *C*or*r*abo*l*ate. *C*o*ll*obo*l*ate — that was two different words, by the way. Well, thanks for helping me undo the last fifty years of the Civil Rights Movement. Y'all are assholes. Good night!"

Barbra realized that she'd managed to drink the entire gin and tonic, and was now clenching the small red straw between her teeth. She let it drop, the plastic shredded and wet, onto her lap.

In Chinese, the word for ugly was *chou* — it was the same as the word for shameful. Ugly and shameful, both *chou*. And the slang for shameful was *diou lian*, which was usually translated to English as "lose face" but more literally meant "throw face." As if the bereft had willfully tossed away anything worth finding and keeping. Thrown away the pretty face on top, leaving only the ugly, embarrassed face underneath.

Andrew stood in front of her, dripping sweat.

"Can we go?" he asked. She looked up, trying to pull together some words of congratulation or encouragement, but she had none.

"Now?" he added.

Andrew was too soft, thought Barbra. It made sense that you had to *make* people laugh. Comedy was an act of aggression, and Andrew was not a fighter.

"Please?"

For a brief moment, Barbra felt the urge to refuse, to make him stay and watch the other comedians, to point out the moments where he'd fallen short. She could coach him into being a better comedian. Force him into it.

But Andrew continued to stand, not taking his hurt eyes off her, and Barbra realized that it was a decade or two too late to be a mother, so instead she gathered her things and led Andrew out of the bar.

二十五

Helios, NY

IT WAS STRANGE that nothing calamitous happened when Saina and Grayson first broke up.

She'd expected the Los Angeles basin to split apart like a giant glacier, calving pink stucco islands studded with palm trees that would float off across the Pacific. She'd expected an epic fire in New York City. A cross-town conflagration that would swallow entire neighborhoods, leaving behind a crisped and broken Manhattan. An earthquake, a tsunami, another flood or terrorist attack — something, anything, to commemorate their cleaving. But instead, nothing. Just a mild winter and a glorious spring and fewer murders in the five boroughs.

It wasn't vanity.

Everyone thought that their breakups should cause time to stop and birds to drop out of the sky. It's just that with Saina's, it actually happened.

In first grade she'd spent an entire art period building a papier-mâché rocketship for Adam Garcia, who told Kelly Park that he liked Saina. But when she tried to present her handiwork to him, he laughed and said that it was a joke. As her heart broke, the Challenger exploded right in front of them on the classroom television screen.

Three months later, Adam saw a corner of her notebook where she'd written SW + AG. He said he thought she was gross. She cried.

Then Chernobyl.

Saina had sworn off boys after that, avoiding the potential nuclear disaster of spin the bottle and ignoring the famine that was sure to come if she confessed her crush on her best friend's older brother. In tenth grade she'd developed a giant, embarrassing crush on her art teacher, who had praised her teenage insights and given her his favorite art books and stared a beat too long at her cutoffs. She imagined a bohemian life for the two of them that was interrupted by heartbreak when she saw him kissing the Spanish teacher in the school parking lot. That night, as she lay awake into morning, the walls of the house jumped up and slammed down into the earth with a crack and roar. It was heartbreak that measured 6.7 on the Richter scale and felled an entire apartment building in the San Fernando Valley. She limited herself to a string of amusing dalliances for the rest of high school, but after the first breakup with a college boyfriend who went on to launch an empire of pinup porn stars, September 11. After the second, with a sweet and lovely Canadian who studied the structure of snowflakes, Hurricane Katrina.

Saina knew it was gross. She felt guilty for ever having made that first connection, for thinking that her minuscule personal heartbreak had anything to do with the Challenger or Chernobyl. But we can only ever see the world through our own half-blind eyes, set in our own stupid heads, backed by our own self-obsessed brains, and from that vantage point, it just didn't make any *sense* that nothing fell apart after Grayson left. If Saina was being completely honest with herself, half the motivation for her retreat to the country was a fear of some calamitous terror strike that was sure to follow that first, worst breakup with the man she thought she was going to marry.

Instead, she'd walked into the Catskills and met Leo.

It was the first warm day of spring. She had headed towards town aimlessly, looking for the kind of escape that could be found only in a solitary walk through a crowd. Except that there were no crowds in Helios. At four o'clock its only street was nearly deserted and the shopkeepers were occupying themselves by sweeping sidewalks and gossiping in doorways. Neither of the street's restaurants was scheduled to open for another couple of hours, but the door of one swung open on a lazy hinge. Taking a chance, Saina pushed in, tiptoeing through the wood-paneled vestibule. All of the chairs were stacked on top of the tables, and a mop and bucket sat abandoned in the middle of the ceramic-tile floor. The lamps were switched off, but the late afternoon sun sent a hazy, dust-filled shaft of light across the men on either side of the copper bar, making the two of them look like a Caravaggio.

Behind the bar, a dirty blond with a red beard held a glass up to her. "Afternoon drinking. Nothing like it." His voice echoed across the empty room.

She grinned. "Morning drinking. Even better."

And then the other guy, the one who would turn out to be Leo, leaned back and laughed, parting his pink lips, showing every single one of his pretty teeth, leaving his smooth throat open and vulnerable.

That, she thought, *looks like a healthy diversion.*

Saina had chosen a house on the outskirts of Helios because the town was small (population: 1,214) and isolated (three miles off of County Road 19) and she thought that she didn't want to see or talk to anyone ever again.

Actually, that wasn't quite right.

It was more like she'd seen it all as bucolic set dressing for her inevitable comeback. This was the magazine story she really wanted — not some exegesis on failure penned by Billy, but a tribute to her rebirth.

> *Depressed and disgraced, artist Saina Wang traded her Meatpacking District loft for a ramshackle Catskills farmhouse only to undergo a creative and personal renaissance.*
>
> *"I'm thrilled," says the stunning twenty-eight-year-old, grinning as she holds an Araucana — the artisanal hens lay bright blue eggs that match the shutters on the eighteenth-century barn she converted to a studio. Wang talks to us about chickens and eggs, the birds and the bees (wink, wink!), and doing her best work yet.*

Some parts of it were true. She was twenty-eight, and she had painted the shutters on the barn bright blue, but she'd never know for sure if they matched the tufted bird's eggs because it turned out that baby chicks, no matter how heritage, can freeze to death even in sixty-degree weather. It also turned out that chopping wood was impossibly hard. On the first attempt the ax slipped from her hands and went flying, the second time she kept a vise grip on the ax and it was the wood that flipped off the stump.

Convinced that the third try would cost her a toe, Saina draped a tarp back over the woodpile and hid the ax in the broom closet.

It wasn't just the buried chicks and the pile of unchopped wood. It was the vegetable garden that wouldn't grow despite the manure she heaped over the soil, the flowers that budded but never blossomed, the neighbor who inched his fence over her property line, the gang of neighboring goats that made a daily escape from their enclosure and pillaged her stunted garden. The countryside was refusing to live up to her pastoral fantasy, just like the rest of her life. Inside the house, where money could reliably fix most problems, things were nearly perfect, but outside, butch nature trampled all over wimpy nurture.

When she interrupted them, Leo and his friend Graham, the owner-bartender-chef-occasional-butcher, were putting together a new cocktail menu for G Street, Graham's restaurant-bar-occasional-town-hall.

Herbs from Leo's farm were piled all around them, spilling out of torn-open paper bags with the Fatboy Farms logo. Leo was pounding sprigs of rosemary in an oversize mortar and pestle. Graham was sifting freshly ground nutmeg together with turbinado sugar and white pepper. The smells came at her like Christmas and Thanksgiving over the chemical lemon of the floor cleaner. The men had invited her to join in — "We need to temper the testosterone a little" — and the three of them spent the next hour infusing simple syrups over a portable burner and trying to put together the most herb-intensive cocktails they could think of.

"I want something *burly*. Bitter. Pungent. A gut punch. But, you know, suave," said Graham.

"A *man's* drink," said Saina.

"Mixology: The New Bespoke Tailoring." Leo, it turned out, sometimes spoke in pronouncements.

As the sunlight faded, Leo edged closer to Saina, balancing a foot against her stool, placing his lips precisely over the spot where she'd sipped from a glass of basil-cucumber-cayenne-gin-and-ginger. Soon it was just the two of them sitting and drinking in the half dark. The restaurant was officially open, but no one had ventured in. Graham was in the kitchen, drunkenly calling out instructions to his prep-cook-waiter-accountant and Leo leaned towards her, conspiratorial.

"Let's surprise Graham."

"By raiding his cash register?"

"I have a better idea." He stepped off the stool and picked up the discarded mop. "Do you know how to do a three-corner fold?"

Saina shook her head. "But I can make it up."

He tossed her the package of freshly laundered napkins. She tore open the plastic and pulled out a bright white cloth. As she folded, she watched him swab the tiles until they were shiny, and then they put the chairs in place and ripped long sheets of butcher paper to drape over the tabletops.

Leo held up a napkin, inspecting the fold. "Very impressive. Precision and beauty."

Saina felt her cheeks get hot. *Who was this guy?* This greens-growing, Catskills-living, yeshiva-named black man whose first drunken instinct was to do sweet favors for his friends? Who wielded a mop with balletic swoops and wore his T-shirt tight and loose in all the right places?

The kitchen door swung open to reveal Graham, a chef's hat on his head and a giant zucchini in his hand. "Dudes! You're my magic mice! Cinderelly! Cinder — ouch!" Before the second "elly," the door swung back and smacked him in the nose, then opened again. "Where's *my* prince?"

Saina and Leo smiled at each other. They smiled and smiled and didn't stop until a couple walked in and asked to be seated. As Leo settled them at a table and brought over glasses of water, she stayed in place, watching him.

Her just-wounded heart might have been on hiatus, but it turned out that the rest of her was still alert, ready to bloom in the direction of any new sun.

That was six months ago. Enough time to fall halfway in love, once. To betray someone, once. To be betrayed, once. And, maybe, to win someone back, once.

二十六

I-10 East

BY THE TIME they crossed the border into Louisiana, Andrew started to feel like they'd live out the rest of their lives in the backseat of this car. There was no way to really get comfortable. He and Grace tried opening the windows and sticking their feet out in the open air, tried taking turns lying down, but no matter what, every position felt awkward.

Thanks to some unspoken mutual agreement, they didn't talk about the pictures Grace had taped up around her seat — especially not the picture of their mother that Andrew didn't remember ever having seen before. Instead, he let Grace lay her head in his lap and told her what was going on outside the window.

"This is so weird. There's a guy on a skateboard pushing a guy in a wheelchair right now, and they're, like, *flying* down the street."

"Mmm . . . what's the guy in the wheelchair like?"

"White guy, scraggly beard, Hawaiian shirt."

Ama had been in a wheelchair once, back when she'd sprained her ankle chasing their dog Lady down the stairs. Would he ever see her again?

Andrew turned to Grace. "What's Ama's name?"

"Isn't it Ama?"

"No, that's what she *is,* an *ama.* It's like a nanny."

"What?"

"Yeah. You've basically been calling her 'caretaker' all your life."

"Well, you have, too!"

"I know. It's terrible. We're terrible people. Dad — what's Ama's name?"

Their father looked at them in the rearview mirror. "Why do you wonder?"

"Because she's a *person,* Dad!"

"Okay, Gracie, okay . . ." Charles thought hard. What was Ama's name? It was lost somewhere in the past, when Ama was pretty and young and she carried him everywhere on her back. "I think she was from Lu family, and then she have to come live with us, come take care of your baba. Maybe she tell Jiejie?"

Grace was doubtful. "Why would Saina know if we don't?"

"Let's call," said Andrew.

"I want to call."

"We'll conference. If she picks up."

Ring. Ring. Ring. Ring.

"I was just about to call you guys," said Saina.

"We have a family dispute to resolve."

Grace kicked him and waved her cell phone in his face. "Wait, I'm being abused. What are you supposed to do when you're in an abusive relationship?"

"Rehabilitate them with love."

"Kill them with kindness?"

"Kill's a little extreme. Maybe just maim."

"Hold on." Andrew dialed Grace's number.

"Finally! Saina, this is important. Do you know Ama's name?" She kicked against Barbra's seat, dislodging the Diane Arbus photograph.

"Doesn't Dad know it?"

"No." Grace glared at her father, but his eyes were on the road. "All he knows is her last name even though he's known her all his life."

"You've known her all your life, too," said Saina.

"Yeah, but I've known her for the shortest amount of time compared to everyone else, so you guys have been assholes for longer."

"What made you think of it?" Saina asked.

"Andrew did. I don't know."

He felt silly, suddenly, for insisting on this piece of knowledge. Of course they'd be able to find her. "Dad! Do you know Ama's daughter's phone number? Kathy's number?"

Charles, busy unfolding a map, shook his head.

"But then how do we call Ama if we need to? I didn't say goodbye to her!" said Andrew.

"You mean we won't see her again?" Grace thought back to their escape from Kathy's house. It had been a hurried, uncomfortable exit, and she'd only given Ama a quick hug. They'd abandoned Ama as if she were a puppy, an off-season sweater, this woman who had changed their shitty diapers and bandaged their skinned knees and spooned porridge into their baby-bird mouths. She would never have done it if she'd known. Never. This was her father's fault, and Barbra's. Grace kicked Barbra's seat again, but still her stepmother did nothing. *Nothing.* What did she ever do besides get her nails done and organize her closet and buy sunglasses? Babs had *so many* pairs of sunglasses. The only worthwhile thing she'd ever taught Grace was how to apply lipstick without looking in a mirror.

"Hold on, I'm checking Facebook," said Saina over the phone. "Where are you guys stopping next?"

"Remember Uncle Nash? We're going to stay with him in New Orleans."

"That guy? He always had such a crush on Mom. Oh wait, here, Kathy's on Facebook!"

Andrew reached over and touched his little sister's leg. "See, we found her. It's okay."

Suddenly, finding Ama didn't matter as much to Grace. "Hold up, Uncle Nash had a crush on Mom? How did you know?" Worried, she looked at her father in the rearview mirror, and whispered, "Does Dad know?"

Saina laughed. "I don't think it was that big of a deal. He just used to always compliment her and open doors for her and stuff."

"I guess it makes sense," said Grace. "She was so beautiful."

"Do you want me to message Kathy?" asked Saina.

"I don't know," said Grace. "What do we write? 'Dear Kathy, sorry we kept your mom for so long. But at least we gave her back. Love, the Wangs. PS. Um, BTW, what's her name?' You guys didn't see how mad Kathy was. She's never going to talk to us unless maybe we tell her that we're coming to give the car back."

"What do you mean?"

Andrew and Grace rolled their eyes at each other. "Saina, what car do you think we're driving?" he asked.

For a long minute, she was quiet. Andrew pictured her sitting in one of the weird invisible plastic chairs that were in the pictures she'd emailed of her new house. Once she moved out to the Catskills, the house was pretty much all she talked about anymore. Wood flooring and contractors and something called subway tiles — for a while it had seemed cool and grown-up, like everything that Saina did, like she was some sort of New Age pioneer, but now it all sounded pointless to him. She'd isolated herself in a lonely outpost, and now they were all going to live there, too. It was as if she'd been building a prison for them. A pretty, pretty prison.

"I didn't think about it," said Saina. "Yours? Wait, is Dad driving the whole way? You guys should split it up."

"Yeah, like he's going to let anyone else take the wheel — we tried. And nope. Not mine. Ama's."

Grace looked at him as she replied. "You know, *our mother's.*"

"Across country?"

They both nodded, and then Grace said, "Yeah, if we make it."

They were driving her mother's old car? What else had she missed? Saina picked up her bottle of beer and took a long swig. Leo was in the kitchen, rendering duck fat that they would later stir into a vat of rice, making each of the grains glisten. "But it's ancient! I didn't know that we still had it, even."

"You'd remember if you came home last Christmas."

She glanced towards the kitchen, not wanting Leo to overhear. "Gracie, you know why I didn't come home."

"Yeah. Because sitting in a room and crying was more important than seeing your family."

Yoga breath. Yoga breath. "I couldn't even brush my teeth. There was no way I could have gotten on a plane and flown to L.A." Yoga breath.

"We would have still loved you with gunky teeth," said Andrew.

"And smelly feet," added Grace.

"And greasy hair."

"And hairy legs."

Saina laughed. Grace and Andrew, bumping around in the backseat of the old station wagon, probably hurtling down the highway at ninety miles an hour — her dad had always been a fast driver — drinking Slurpees and eating Cheetos, falling asleep leaning against each other.

Leo called out from the stove: "Hey, which bottle do you want to open? The red or the white?" Before she could even respond, Grace pounced.

"Saina! That was a boy! Who is that? Do you have a new boyfriend?"

Leo was in the doorway now, holding the wooden spoon between his teeth and waving both bottles in the air. She smiled at him. "Leo, my sister wants to know who you are."

"Who's Leo?"

He raised an eyebrow and spoke with the spoon still clenched. "She doesn't know?"

"Who's Leo?"

"I wasn't sure if you were ready to meet the kids."

"Saina! Who's Leo?"

"And now?"

"Saina! C'mon!"

"Guys," she said into the phone, her eyes locked with his. "There's something I haven't told you. I like a boy." Saina wanted to hook a finger through one of his belt loops and pull him towards her. She winked at Leo and nodded towards the bottle of red.

Her boyfriend turned back to the kitchen with the Malbec held aloft as Grace whispered something Saina couldn't quite hear.

"What?"

"I said, can we tell Dad? He just asked who Leo was."

"Yeah, because you kept screaming it!"

"Well, you were ignoring me."

"It's oka —"

Before Saina finished, Grace was saying, "Daddy, Saina has a new *boy*friend! Leo's the new *boy*friend."

"Is it serious?" asked Andrew.

"I think so. You guys will meet him. You'll like him — he has a farm."

"Like, a real one?"

"Crop rotations, fertilizer, harvests, the whole shebang. He even has a tractor. But it's organic."

"The tractor?"

"Yeah. It runs on daisies."

Grace broke in. "I think Daddy's happy."

Faintly, she heard their father call back, "Daddy happy if Jiejie is happy."

"Did you hear that?"

"Yeah, that was nice. Thanks, Gracie."

"So, are we going to meet him?"

"Of course. Yes. He's . . . yes."

A boyfriend, thought Andrew. *Already.* Saina clearly didn't have any problems with love. Maybe people just decided they were in love and then — *bam!* — they were. Everyone always said that there was nothing like first love — maybe he just had to stop looking for someone who made him feel the same way that Eunice had. Why hadn't he stayed at school? Other people went to college without their parents' money. Other people's parents didn't even *have* any money. Why hadn't he just gotten a job and a loan?

Andrew stared out the window, half listening to Grace quiz Saina on how she and her boyfriend had met. They were winding down the greenest road Andrew had ever seen, verdant swamp on either side of them. Occasionally a sign would appear at the head of a narrow path snaking into the wild: ATASKA GUN CLUB/KEEP OUT. OLD BOGS GUN AND FISH SOCIETY. He imagined those secret societies, blood oaths and racist jokes over some delicious barbecue. There were so many worlds he'd never even considered — which one would be his?

二十七

New Orleans, LA

2,123 Miles

THE SOUTH wasn't how Charles remembered it. Where were all the biscuits and black people? In the twenty-four hours that the Wangs had been on the outskirts of New Orleans with Nash, all they'd seen were various incarnations of exhausted southern gentry, old friends of Nash's who rotated in and out of his family's ancient estate as if it were some sort of *Gone with the Wind* commune. All around the edges of his acreage, brand-new "plantation-style" condos crowded in. The last time Charles had been here, some twenty years ago, they'd sat on the porch drinking bourbon doctored with sugar cubes and gazing out at the lazy rows of willows; now a gaudy funfair of banners flapped at the tree line: THE ORSINI, THE VAN HELM. IF YOU LIVED HERE, YOU'D BE HOME.

Tonight, all those cousins and aunties had reassembled in an odd little bayou shack with a corrugated tin roof and rough wooden picnic tables covered with newspaper. When Nash insisted that the Wangs come along to his second cousin's wedding, Charles had expected white-gloved waiters and polite dancing under moss-draped trees, not the honky-tonk bacchanal unfolding around them.

"Watch yourselves!"

A slick-haired man with arms covered in snake tattoos muscled a steaming colander to their table and spilled out a crimson tide of crawfish, mixed with halved pieces of potatoes, onions, and lemons. The night outside was humid. As a briny fog rose from the piles of boiled shellfish, the windows steamed up and the air inside immediately turned dense and heated. Through that mist, two women followed, one with a pot of melted butter balanced atop a ceramic bowl of steamed corn, the other carrying a tin platter piled high with blackened link sausages that still sizzled from the grill, spitting out their juices in spicy rivulets. The first woman, white-girl dreads held back by a kerchief, plunked down the corn and went around the table ladling a rich splash of butter into the little bowl at each place setting. The second set down the sausages just an inch farther away than Charles would have liked.

He unrolled the plastic lobster bib and tied it around his neck, taking care to cover as much of his shirt as he could. He reached for a pile of thin white paper napkins and unfolded four of the squares, overlapping them on his lap until his pants were completely protected.

Ready.

Barbra had stayed behind at Nash's house, claiming that she had a headache. Sitting in the roomful of strangers, his back aching from seven straight hours of driving, feeling a creeping numbness that made him grasp at the aspirin folded in a napkin inside his pocket, Charles half wished that he had begged off, too. But Grace was next to him and Andrew sat across the table, a too-skinny Nash cousin on either side.

One of them elbowed his son. "Ever eaten a crawdaddy?"

Andrew looked at him for help, and Charles felt a familiar mix of pride and annoyance. Why was Andrew always so tentative and half formed? It made no sense the way he scuttled sideways through life. Proud! Any child in the Wang family should always be proud, instead of well mannered and unsure.

"Hello? Um, hello?" Someone tapped on a microphone. It was the bride, a pale, creamy little thing with a sweet, limp face who had been squeezed into a lace shift. Her cheeks could have benefited from some blush stick — the Failure might not have made any money, but Charles had manufactured some very effective makeup. "Glenn and I just want to thank everyone for coming tonight, for helping us celebrate our wedding. Um, that's it, I think. Honey?" She cradled the microphone like an offering and passed it to her brand-new husband, who had short legs and too much muscle, like one of those ugly dogs that gay men were always leading around on studded leashes. Weren't gay men supposed to like beautiful things? It pained Charles to imagine their matrimonial bed; the groom would probably squeeze his bride into a doughy, complicit ball and just gnaw at her, grunting and drooling all the while.

"Family and friends, we welcome you to our blissful evening." The dog-groom had worked hard to memorize his human speech. "It means the world to me and Merrily that you were able to travel from near and far to join us in our joy. As you may know, it is a blessing upon your union if strangers are made welcome at your wedding, so we'd like to welcome Uncle Nash's friend Charles Wang, as well as his wife and children, who are here all the way from California. Thank you, Wangs."

Charles quickly tucked his cell phone back in his coat pocket — still no call from the bastard lawyer — and raised the frosty glass of champagne that had appeared at his place. Maybe this wedding wasn't quite as hopeless as it seemed. He stood and bowed slightly, which unleashed a wave of delighted bows from the rest of the guests.

The young bride swigged at her champagne, then surprised everyone by grabbing the microphone again and shouting into it: "Now dig in, y'all!"

Finally. Charles zeroed in on a fat little creature hiding under a bay leaf and plucked it up, cracking the shell in half and sucking out its delicious swill of rich yellow brain mixed with the smoky boiling liquid. Already the red juice from the shell dripped down his hands, but it was worth it — he'd just have to find someone to bleach it out of his cuffs later.

Food should be like this — elemental, honest, a little cruel. It should make no apologies for what it was, and it shouldn't allow the eater to lie to himself about what he was doing. Charles would rather bite into a pig trotter than a ground-up, unrecognizable hamburger any day. Shellfish were the best. With crabs, you could break off the pointed tips of their tiny legs and use them as tools to dig out the stubborn white meat in the other half of the appendage. Oysters provided their own serving platter. Snails, too. Tiny lamb chops, which had enjoyed a brief vogue at cocktail parties, came with a built-in handle. And terrines, which the Chinese made and ate as enthusiastically as the French, were always satisfying — the meat gelled and held in place by the essence of its own traitorous marrow. In Chinese, there were no separate words for animal meat and human flesh. It was all just *rou.* Muscle was *ji rou,* fat was *fei rou.* Beef and

pork? *Niou rou* and *ju rou*. Forget about special words like *poultry*, designed to coddle and protect. Chicken was chicken, and it was all meant
to be eaten.

Bodie, one of the skeletal Nash cousins, leaned across the table and gestured in Charles's face with a sweating bottle of beer. "I can't believe it —
y'all know how to eat crawfish?"

Midsuck, Charles grinned at him. He removed the creature from his
mouth and waved it in the air, arms flailing, to make his point. "The only
thing with legs Chinese people don't eat is table and chair!"

That sent Bodie into the sort of belly laugh that would have been more
believable on a fat man. "That's good, man, that's good. I like it. I like it.
Table and chair." He straightened up. "But I meant West Coasters, man,
I'm not a racist."

"Wait a minute," said Artie, the one who wasn't Bodie. "Here's what I
want to know. What about man's best friend, then?"

"True!" shouted Charles, gleeful. It was one of his favorite topics.
Americans and their endless capacity for offense had always perplexed
him. "Some Chinese do eat dog! So what? American all eat pig, and pig
just as smart as dog! If something is good to eat, why not eat it?" He
turned back to Bodie. "Anyways, my kids always say I am racist when I am
surprised American people so good at chopsticks, but you say you are surprised I am good at crawdads. You see, Meimei, Didi, Daddy not racist!"

Grace glared at him. "He meant the opposite of that, Dad."

She had a growing pile of crawdads in front her, his little girl. Andrew,
meanwhile, was poking through the pile in search of more potatoes. He
watched his son spear a white, mealy chunk of tuber and eat it daintily.

What if Andrew was gay? That was impossible. He was too handsome.
Girls had always liked Andrew — even when he was a teenager with
braces and a pimple or two, they had called the house at all hours and
gathered in eager bunches around the pool during the kids' birthday parties, their smooth young bodies in bikinis that would have been unthinkable thirty years ago in Taiwan. But there were men like that, Charles
knew, gay men whose friends were all beautiful women who were half in
love with them.

"Andrew," said Charles, "did you have girlfriend at school?"

He caught Grace smirking up at her brother. What did that mean? Was his son going to tell him here, over this stinking pile of mudbugs, that he was a gay?

The boy blushed. "Um, sort of . . ."

"How could this kid not have a girlfriend?" asked Bodie. "Look at him! He's a stud! I bet the ladies are throwing themselves at his feet!"

Charles ignored him. "What do you mean, 'sort of'? You have *boy-friend*?"

"No! Dad, no! What do you mean?" Andrew dropped his voice to a whisper. "Do you think I'm gay or something?"

"You might as well be," said Grace.

On either side of him, the southern goons mirrored Grace's smirk. *What was this?*

"Well?" Charles asked.

"No!" Andrew repeated. "Why are we talking about this here?"

"Hey, hey," Artie interrupted. "There's nothing wrong with that if that's the way you are. Nothing to be ashamed of, right, Dad?"

Charles didn't reply, just kept his eyes on Andrew.

"I had a girlfriend, her name is Emma, she's really pretty."

Okay. Charles relaxed. *Okay.* Andrew didn't know how to lie to him.

"Why did you say that, Gracie?" Charles asked.

"Yeah, *Gracie?*" asked Andrew.

She opened her eyes wide. "Oh, I don't know. I just meant that Andrew was very . . . gentlemanly."

Ah. Charles had never set out to be secretive about sex with his children, but over the years, that was what happened. It always seemed like something that should have been the mother's job, but he couldn't expect Barbra to bear the responsibility for explaining things, so it somehow became the subject that wasn't raised. They had never come to him with any questions, so he had never given them any answers.

Maybe he had failed his son. Charles himself had never needed any instruction on that front — even without movie-star looks, even before he had any real money, Charles had wanted things, and women had responded to that — but maybe, put in vulgar American terms, Andrew simply didn't know how to close the deal.

He looked at his son. "Andrew. Girls very easy. Listen. You always tell smart girls that they pretty and pretty girls that they smart."

"Dad. I don't . . . it's not . . ."

"Hey, Mr. Wang, what do you do if a girl's pretty *and* smart?"

Charles smiled at Bodie. That skeletal southerner probably needed all the lady advice he could get. "Easy. You just tell them you think they are a *very good person.*"

Andrew laughed at that, at least. "I don't have a problem with girls, it's just, I want to find the right one, you know?"

"You don't have a problem with girls not want to go out with you because you are Chinese?" he asked.

"God, no! Dad, it's not like that anymore. Or it is, but it's not like that for me."

Charles nodded, proud. Of course it wasn't like that for his son, his handsome son. Sometimes it was hard to understand this generation of boys — they had so little to rebel against that it made them soft. No wonder they had sold out of the special-edition guyliner that Andrew had convinced him to market.

Bodie nudged him. "The boy is holding out for *love!* Your son ain't gay, Mr. Wang. It's worse — he's a *romantic.*" Bodie and Artie caught each other's eyes over Andrew's head. "And probably a virgin."

Andrew blushed immediately. "Why is it such a big deal to everyone? I don't see why this is even something to discuss! And, anyways, what's wrong with wanting to fall in love? Don't you all want that?"

Charles shrugged. "Love is easy. Daddy in love with every woman!"

"Dad! Why do you always have to say that? Why can't you just love one woman? You're married!"

"I say love any that'll have you, right, Mr. Wang?" Charles laughed along with Bodie as he watched Andrew cringe.

"Okay, I'm going to go to the bathroom. And when I come back, maybe we'll talk about something else." Andrew twisted his way out of the bench.

Always so sensitive, his son.

Andrew stayed away. Hours later, when even his little Gracie was probably drunk, Charles and Nash ended up side by side with a bottle of whiskey between them, their feet kicked up on the edge of the table. He spotted Andrew across the room talking to a woman, thank god, though probably not one the boy would ever fall in love with. Tall and dead pale, like the deracinated endgame of generations of milk drinkers, with a battlefield of frizzy red hair stuck out all around her, she was at least a decade older than Andrew.

Nash followed Charles's gaze. "Dorrie Van Sleyd. She's still living in her family's old plantation house as well, though half of hers is open to snap-happy tourists at the weekend. Maybe that's what I should be considering."

Charles turned his attention back to Nash. His friend. His compatriot. Proud member of a dwindling southern aristocracy made up of Anglophiles and drunks. If the world had continued the way it should have, if Charles had stayed in the China he was meant for, he never would have met Nash almost thirty years ago, when this brother in arms was one of the only white men living on a tree-lined block of Monterey Park in L.A.'s San Gabriel Valley.

Charles and May Lee had moved to the San Gabriel Valley because, to Charles's great surprise, they were about to have a baby. No question, that baby had to speak Chinese as well as she ever spoke the bastard English, so the Wangs, back when there were just three of them, made their first home in a sunburned suburb that had the advantage of being close to both Charles's first factory and an ever-growing spread of dim sum emporiums and noodle houses brought in by a new influx of immigrants.

As for Nash, Nash was a budding China scholar in the midst of his PhD slog at USC, hoping to pick up the language by immersion and looking forward to the day that he would get a China studies professorship and a lovely Asian wife — he wasn't picky about nationality, any part of East Asia would do. Charles knew that his friend was half in love with May Lee, and sometimes on those crisp California nights, when they were down to the last inch of liquor and it was so late that even the mosquitoes had gone to bed, he wished that the two of them could just swap houses. Baby Saina would sleep at the foot of his bed in one — he could stow her in the closet whenever a girlfriend stopped by — and May Lee could perch on Nash's lap in the other, giggling and feeding him delicacies with chopsticks instead of getting into a helicopter with Charles Wang.

When that convenient vision failed to manifest — May Lee didn't have enough imagination to leave an increasingly wealthy manufacturer for a poor scholar, even if that scholar had been raised on five thousand acres of cotton; she didn't have enough second sight to know that it might have saved her life — all parties moved west instead. The Wangs took up residence in Bel-Air, and Nash landed first in a Marina del Rey bachelor pad of the wet-bar-and-whirlpool-tub variety, then, as his professorial duties increased, in an unlikely Victorian on the outskirts of L.A.'s depressed downtown, and finally here, scrambling to hold on to his family's ancestral home. When they first met, all their talk had been about the glorious futures that surely awaited them; with age, and distance, and a widening and calcifying of their own worldviews, these discussions became more and more like jousts where they lanced at each other with their shifting opinions and left bloody and sated.

In the end, he and Nash agreed on only two things: History had failed them both, and the only solace left was that China, their China, remained the greatest civilization in the world.

"Wang xian shen!" Nash, at least, pronounced Charles's last name the way it was meant to be said, long and rounded, not flat and nasal. "You've been fingering that phone all night."

"Sorry, sorry." He slipped the cell phone back into his jacket pocket, embarrassed. The lawyer wasn't going to call now; he'd probably been out of the office since lunch, spending Charles's six hundred dollars an hour on golf course fees and showy watches. Charles looked at Nash and hoped his friend wouldn't ask. Anything.

Another hour. More whiskey. The night was almost over. Drink made the world thrum with possibility. When sober morning came, Charles always realized that he'd spent the previous evening talking too loudly and with too much conviction about things that he would never do and could never change, but in the moment, it all seemed endlessly possible.

Sometimes Charles thought that conversation must be the truest art form. In a good back-and-forth, you're continually creating something new, something that only exists in a single present moment. Whole universes were built and destroyed in the course of a good conversation.

"Some of my students haven't even read Plato. They barely deserve to be enrolled in a university!" said Nash.

"Aha! You say all should be love and equality, but now you want exclude people depending on what they read. What if someone grow up in house with no books? Not everyone have grand library like you!"

"No, that's precisely what I do not want to do! Books are the simplest gateways through which to pass. There are public libraries! Anyone can pick up a book! There are compendiums of the classics that a lazy person can read through in a week!"

Charles tried to edge in with an excellent point, but Nash talked right over him.

"Look, I don't expect everyone to be well versed in Sino-American relations or the history of the Great Leap Forward. I recognize that those are specialized areas of interest, but whatever happened to our shared references and understandings? How can we be a polis when 95 percent of us would rather watch aging housewives bicker on TV than express a well-formed opinion of our own? When I go to a failing strip club in New Orleans and say that I'm at Ozymandias's pleasure palace, I want everyone to laugh and get depressed."

He paused for a moment and stared at Charles. Laugh and get depressed. Get depressed and laugh. What else was there to do?

"Why is that too much to ask? I don't want slaves; I don't even need servants. By the end of this year, I will have to sell my monster of an estate for taxes, and I'll do it gladly — the state can have it! My great-great-grandfather built that place to house the Nashes for a thousand years. How could he have known that some cards and ponies would get in the way of our fortune? I don't even care! I don't begrudge the material loss of my birthright, but I don't think a life of intellectual riches is too much to ask of the world! I give the world thoughtful observations and considered theses, and it gives me back a dozen Kardashians. You know what's going to happen to my library when I sell it? Nothing. Flat nothing. It will probably go to some interior designer who will tell her client how authentic it is, but I'll be damned if a single one of the books are cracked open by their video-game-playing fucktard children!"

Charles looked sideways at Nash. The key right now was to say something, but not too much of something. Enough for his friend to know that he heard him, but not enough to open up the vast floodgates of their twin losses. If the breaking down began, it might never end.

二十八

New Orleans, LA

SOMETHING HAD HAPPENED. Ever since the cake was served, his father and Uncle Nash had been talking, talking, talking at each other nonstop, but now, suddenly, they weren't. Andrew could see the two of them through the window, sitting in the empty room, staring past each other. Merrily and Glenn's friends had all headed down to the bonfire by the creek; Grace was out there with them.

That silence was weird. It scared Andrew a little. The two of them looked tired. Two worn-out men, deliberately quiet. Sad. They looked sad. When had his dad gotten so gray? Andrew wondered what they were not talking about. Actually, he didn't have to wonder, because he knew — what else could it be? If getting money had once been the thing that occupied all of his father's thoughts, losing it must be even more engrossing.

It smelled piney out here on the porch. Beyond it, everything was vast and dark. He heard a faint splash and a yell from the creek, voices that bounced off of the unseen rocks on the other side.

And then Dorrie was standing next to him.

Her sharp, bony fingers gripped his arm. She leaned in, close. He had drifted apart from the rest of the guests to get away from her, but now he didn't half mind that she'd searched him out.

"You're a beautiful thing," she said, grabbing him tight.

"Um, you're kind of freaking me out." But even as he said it, Andrew knew that he liked her intensity. No one at school was like that. Especially not girls. She had these crazy blue diamond eyes with light eyelashes that were a very pale pink and amazing masses of goldish red hair like some sort of fairy queen.

"Do you think I'll hurt you?"

Andrew laughed and flexed the arm under her fingers. "Never."

"Never," she repeated.

And then they were in her car together, headed towards the city. Dorrie drove a long, sleek Jaguar from the '80s, still in good enough shape that it suggested the smell of fresh leather. Andrew's father hadn't said a word when he interrupted and said that he was leaving with someone else, just looked at him with eyes so strange and open that he grabbed Dorrie's hand and rushed out the door.

"You're a really good driver," said Andrew, nervous, as she shifted gears and veered into the oncoming lane to pass a slow big rig.

"Are you unaccustomed to women who can drive?"

"No! Women can do anything! I just don't usually see girls drive stick." Dorrie turned and raised an eyebrow at him. Andrew shrugged. "I don't," he insisted. "*I* don't even drive stick."

"And you're a *man*."

Was that sarcasm? Andrew found that it was always best to ignore sarcasm. It was much easier to defuse that way instead of taking it on directly.

"So where are we going?"

"You said you were a comedian, right?"

"Yeah."

"How funny are you?"

"I'm funny! I don't mean to brag or anything, but I'm pretty fucking funny." Just outside the blurred edges came the thought of Barbra watching him bomb in Austin, but he pushed it down.

"Good."

"So where are we going?"

"You'll like it."

Too much bourbon. Who knew that wedding punch was so strong? It had tasted like kid birthdays, like Kool-Aid and 7-Up and rainbow sherbet, but those Nash cousins kept tipping their flasks into Andrew's cup, and when they let up, Dorrie had procured a bottle from somewhere. Really, just too much bourbon.

Andrew wasn't sure what happened during the rest of the car ride, if he didn't speak a word or if he couldn't shut up. He tried to kiss Dorrie at a stoplight but only managed to put his hand in her lap before the light turned green. The streets outside felt dark, dark, dark, and everywhere there remained the detritus of Hurricane Katrina. Monster piles of broken-down buildings that were still empty three years on, bracketed by tipsy telephone poles. The whole world felt abandoned. Andrew remembered Kanye's rant on the telecast, that whole "Bush doesn't care about black people" thing. He was probably right. Andrew didn't realize that his head was nodding towards the cool windowpane until Dorrie patted his knee.

"Ready?"

He sat up and looked around. She had parked in an alleyway behind a set of row houses. On their left was a trash bin piled high with plastic bags. On their right was a Maybach.

"Are you selling me into slavery?"

"Something like that."

Sometimes, life is like a movie. Andrew had always believed that. And now, spread out all around him, it was turning out to be true. He was caught somewhere between the gangsters at the Feast of San Gennaro in *Mean Streets* and the bikers tripping through the Mardi Gras streets in *Easy Rider*. It was awesome.

New Orleans. N'awlins. Wasn't that how they said it? N'awlins. That's what Dorrie's friends kept saying to him in their velvet voices. She would introduce him with words that were swallowed up in the din of acid jazz and clinking glasses, introduce him to tall glittering figures he could barely see, to older women whose dyed-blonde curls and spackled makeup glared out of the crowd, to boys with pouty lips who were gay in a way that made him uncomfortable, boys who held themselves so that they were sexy like girls, without putting on eyelashes or a dress. Each one of them would lean towards him and whisper, "How are you finding N'awlins?" And he'd say something back, too loud, that would make them nod politely and turn their attention back to Dorrie, a star in the murky firmament. He'd read that somewhere, and it was true. That's what she was. This whole place was a murky firmament, a haze that swallowed up all the other stars besides her.

Actually, no, it was a cabaret. A cabaret! There were real cabarets in the world, and they were *sexy*. Andrew hadn't realized that some places could be sexier than others. Nothing made sense here, including all of the rules he had made for himself. After the smiles and the whispers and more shouting and more drinks, they all sat down on folding chairs and shushed each other, and a beautiful man wearing an enormous ball gown made entirely of brown paper — the kind that delis used to wrap sandwiches — swept into the room, his brown-paper train trailing down the aisle, and Andrew decided that it was the most amazing thing he had ever seen. And then the lights went up on the stage, and he realized that *that* was actually the most amazing thing he'd ever seen. Someone had made curtains out of giant swaths of the same paper, manipulated so that they hung in folds and swayed like real curtains. A riot of brown-paper flowers and foliage grew across them, curling and spreading out across the stage.

The man in the ball gown sang a sad ballad in a bad French accent as powder rose up from his wig and swirled around in the spotlight. A girl covered in whipped cream came out pushing an ice cream cart and did a burlesque number where she wiped off the whipped cream with Popsicles that she handed out to the audience. Andrew got a grape one, which he crunched down in three bites.

"I like to bite," he whispered to Dorrie.

"Your tongue is purple," she whispered back.

A white man in blackface and a black man in paleface did a very serious, very silent magic act together, facing each other instead of the audience and mirroring each other's tricks. A woman dressed like a champagne bottle — if a champagne bottle was also a man who was going to be presented to Louis XIV in court — tap-danced. An old cabaret star who had once had a top-ten disco album shook her sagging breasts at the audience, and they clapped and cheered with such genuine appreciation that Andrew started to think that maybe he had misunderstood what it meant to be hot.

With one last shimmy, she walked out into the audience, breasts bare, ripped metallic tights pulled up to her navel, sweat dripping down her face, and stopped in front of Andrew and Dorrie. Dorrie shook her head and smiled. The woman nodded and extended her hand. And then Dorrie was onstage singing a duet. She had a high, sweet voice that made Andrew want to cry. It was just their two voices, no instruments, not a sound from the audience. They sang some old southern folk tune that felt like it belonged a million miles away from this midnight circus in the middle of this ruined town, or like it was born right there. Maybe he was being enchanted, like George Clooney was by the river sirens in *O Brother, Where Art Thou?* Maybe Dorrie was some New World Circe. Did Odysseus have sex with Circe? But then who was the other woman? A guardian, maybe. A shapeshifter, a changeling, a temptress whose charms were inexplicable, undeniable. Andrew looked down at the drink in his hand. *Was that absinthe?*

"And now, a comic interlude from my young companion." Andrew looked up, surprised. The song was over. Everyone had clapped and clapped and so had he. Now Dorrie stared straight at him. "It's a rite of passage, Andrew. You have to get up onstage your first time here."

Oh. Okay. Like *Rocky Horror* or something. Okay, okay, okay. His notes for the new stuff were still in his pocket, and people he was sure he hadn't met were shouting his name. He didn't have the right props for the finale, but he'd think of something in the moment. He was about to climb up onto the stage but then thought that he'd better get his drink, so he ran back to his seat and scooped it up and held it high, which brought another cheer. There. The crowd was on his side already, and there was no douche emcee like there was in Austin — these people weren't clueless Texans, they were artists, and maybe he was, too.

The stage was a long rectangle of old boards put together by someone with a lot of nails and not much building skill. Andrew stood on a board that creaked under his feet and looked for Dorrie in the direction of their seats, but it was hard to make out any single person in the glimmer of the crowd. He looked down at his notes. Was his handwriting always that bad?

Energy brings energy, Andrew reminded himself.

He had gone skydiving once, trying to prove to himself that he could fall out of the sky without dying. Ten thousand feet in the sky, legs dangling off the side of the plane into nothingness, the instructor strapped to him said, "You decide when we jump. When you're ready, just lean forward."

Andrew leaned forward.

"Most comedians are miserable bastards. They didn't get enough attention as kids, either because they were annoying or because they had shitty parents. Probably both. Me? Well, I'm the opposite. I'm almost *too* well-adjusted. I was athletic — All-American in track. Girls like me." Someone in the audience whistled. "No, I mean it, they really, really like me. And, worst of all, my family's rich — or, at least, they were when I was growing up. My dad hugs me, and not in the bad way. All I want is some shit to get upset about so that I can be a legit comedian already!"

He peered out into the dark. *Were people laughing?*

Was the stage moving?

No matter. The show must go on. It must go on!

"I considered doing a whole act about how good I have it, but then I figured that would never work. So instead, I went with the obvious . . ."

Pause, he told himself. *Give it a moment. Make the audience invest in your act.* He spread his arms out.

"Yep, I'm Asian."

Andrew opened his eyes.

He was still drunk. Seriously, that must have been absinthe. How did he get back to the hotel? This bed was so nice. This was probably the best hotel they'd stayed at so far. It must be the next morning. He'd never been drunk for so long. Where was everybody else? Did Gracie know he was drunk? He smiled and felt the corners of his face tugging up. Then he frowned, just to even it out. He rolled over onto his side.

"Hello." Dorrie. His heart jumped. What was Dorrie doing here? She was wearing a men's pajama top, silky and maroon. Her eyes were olive now. How did it feel to be made of so many colors? Copper and olive and blue and pink and cream, like a box of crayons. Like a tropical bird.

"Cool pj's."

"Thank you."

"So . . ."

She laughed. "Do you remember anything?"

"I remember you. But how did we end up back in my room?"

She laughed again. "You think this is your hotel room? No, darling, this is *my* room. My house, actually." She switched on the bedside light.

Andrew looked around him. Solid. That's how the room felt. Like every piece of furniture had been in here for a thousand years and was just settling down for a thousand more. "Oh yeah, of course."

"You don't remember anything, do you?"

Andrew shook his head and gave her what he hoped was a charming grin. "I think I'm still wasted."

She reached over and scrunched her fingers into his hair. "Oh Andrew, what am I going to do with you?" It was coy, flirtatious, softer than she had ever sounded. Ever since last night, at least. They hadn't kissed yet, he realized. They were in bed together, and they hadn't even made out yet. His breath didn't taste too bad. He must not have been passed out long enough to get totally dehydrated. Andrew shifted up and pulled her in.

In a second, she was on top of him, pinning him into the down pillows. Her hair curtained his face and her tongue darted out, tiny, pink, sharp, to lick the tip of his nose. Andrew laughed. She had seemed so mysterious the night before, sophisticated and ungettable, but here she was, a girl like every other girl. How old was she anyway? He would try not to ask. Instead, he rolled over, taking her with him, and pulled her hair away from her face. And then they were kissing, every point on their bodies lined up with one another, hands pressed together, even, which was kind of weird, but Andrew kind of liked it, just like everything else with Dorrie. They broke apart.

"You're all flushed," said Andrew. Her face was rosy, and even her chest looked red in the V of her pajama top. Her chest. Feeling brave, he slid a hand up the inside of her shirt, up her warm, bare skin, and found her nipple, hard already. She raised an eyebrow at him.

"Do you remember falling off the stage?" *Oh.* Now he did remember, almost. Could he have done that? Andrew dropped his hand and leaned back.

"Oh god. Okay. Tell me what happened."

She smiled. "It was quick. Not painless, but quick. You did about a minute, and then you spread out your arms and said something about being Asian and then you just toppled right off the stage." She traced a finger down his arm. "You were *out*. I thought that you were going to end up in the ER."

Andrew felt around his head. There. There was a tender spot, but the pain still lay somewhere under the haze of the alcohol. The embarrassment, on the other hand, was acutely present.

"I'm so sorry. God. What is *wrong* with me?" The new stuff. Those were the notes he had on him. *Oh god.* "So I talked about how awesome I am, and then I ate it onstage? I'm glad I don't remember. I can pretend it never happened."

"Oh, it happened." She grinned. He hadn't seen her grin like that yet, every little tooth exposed. He grinned back at her. Embarrassed, but happy that something he'd done had made her smile like that even though he'd looked idiotic. They held each other's gaze and something pinged between them. She saw him. She really did. And then she climbed on top of him again. "It definitely happened." She leaned down and they kissed and it was like she was everywhere, touching him, kissing him, teasing him. She stopped. "You need another drink. To wash the shame away."

"What time is it?"

"Does it matter?"

He shrugged. *Not really.*

She swung off the bed and left the room. Andrew tried again to remember the night before. *Had it really been that bad?* That was two bombs in a row — what if only his friends thought he was funny? The worry mixed with his brief glow of connection, scrambling it.

A moment later she was back, carrying a Lucite tray balanced with two cut-crystal glasses and a decanter of something brown.

"Was it really terrible?"

She handed him a drink. "Moderately terrible. But you did make everyone laugh. They thought it was part of the act."

Andrew tossed back the bourbon. "Do southerners really love this, or is it just one of those traditional things that no one really enjoys?"

"When your daddy makes it, you'd better love it."

He looked at his freshened glass. "Someone made this?"

"Someone makes everything, little rich boy."

"What? Don't — no, I know that. I grew up in factories." Or grew up hearing his dad talk about factories, anyway. Close enough. "Besides, you're rich, too. Look at this place."

She slung back a drink. "Used to be. I couldn't keep it up. Now I have this room, a studio, and a little maid's kitchen, and half the time the rest of the grand estate is overrun with school groups and tourists. I have to hide out in my own house."

"Man, that feels like the kind of thing that happens to families in Jane Austen novels," said Andrew.

"It sort of is. I'll show you the pamphlet sometime. It'll make you laugh." She splashed some more amber liquid into each of their glasses. "But let's not talk about that. Look what I do have."

Another grin. She held out a set of handcuffs.

"What?!"

"What's the point of having a four-poster if you can't have some fun with it?"

"You do know where the key is for those, right?" asked Andrew.

She nodded and then bent down to kiss him, the bourbon making both of their mouths slick and cool. God, he loved kissing.

"Just a little fun," she whispered, as she stretched his arms up and locked the handcuffs in place. Andrew pulled, testing them. They must be looped around one of the bedposts.

"You did that pretty expertly."

"A girl has to have some skills in this big, bad world."

She wasn't a girl anymore. That was for sure.

Andrew assessed her as she pushed his shirt up and stuck her tongue in his belly button. She must be thirty-five at least. An older woman. Sexy.

Dorrie paused. "Look at you, you're totally hairless."

"Not totally. But, yeah, no happy trail."

She leaned in again, kissing him on his neck, grazing his ears and jaw.

"I want to touch you," he said.

"You shouldn't even be able to see me. Here." And then she was pulling her shirt over her head, and Andrew caught just a glimpse of her smooth pink skin and pale, pale nipples — he had never seen nipples so small and pale, and they sent a shiver of lust through him — before she wrapped the shirt around his face like a blindfold, crisscrossing the arms around his head and tying them across his forehead. Andrew breathed in. The shirt was warm and smelled faintly of some musk-heavy perfume.

"Wait a minute," said Dorrie. He sensed her rise up and leave the room, and he felt a shot of panic.

"Where are you going?" he called after her.

It was a long minute before she responded. "I'm back. You're not too attached to this shirt, are you?"

It was a limited-edition A Bathing Ape T-shirt he'd stalked on eBay for weeks and finally won for $182. "Nah."

"Good." He felt something cold and hard slide against his stomach, and panicked again. A gun? Was this all some plot to kill him and sell his organs to a drug cartel? And then he heard a snip and the cold line traveled up his chest.

"You're *cutting* my shirt off?"

"It's better that way. Then I can do this." She threw open his ruined shirt and pressed her bare body against his.

"Mmm, okay, that is better." He lifted his hips slightly, looking for some part of her to connect with. She met him, and for a long, exquisite moment they moved against each other until she broke free and began unbuttoning his pants. Andrew had been expecting this moment, wanting it, but now that it was here, he wasn't sure how he felt.

Oh. Wait. Now here he was inside her warm, wet mouth. Andrew's resolve slid out from under him and was replaced by an out-of-body buzz. Why did people bother meditating? They should just have orgasms instead.

A long, perfect minute, and then Dorrie stopped. Andrew groaned.

"I don't want you getting too excited yet." He felt her shifting on the bed. She must be taking off her underwear.

"Wait, I have to tell you something."

"What's wrong?"

It was too soon. It didn't make sense. It should have been Emma, maybe. But he could feel Dorrie breathing over him, waiting for him to speak.

"Nothing, that was amazing. Seriously. I wish it was still happening. But, um, I don't want to be presumptuous, but . . ." *Oh god.* This was ridiculous. He was cold now, pantless and with his T-shirt cut open, his shoulder was starting to hurt, and who knew what she was doing on the other side of the blindfold.

"But what?" She sounded amused.

"I don't . . . I don't really . . ." He'd explained it to at least a dozen girls, but this time the words wouldn't come out right. In a rush, he said, "I just can't have sex with someone unless I'm in love with them."

"Can't, or won't?"

"Well, won't, I guess."

Her hand enclosed him, and Andrew's body rushed to betray itself.

"Won't you?" He felt her next to his ear. "I almost do love you," she whispered, slowly moving her hand up and down. He knew she didn't mean it entirely, but he still felt faintly aglow. She was entrancing. Even now, even like this, helpless and flat on his back, blind to everything, he still felt the force of her odd allure.

He froze. Why not? Really, why not?

It was true what they said about older women. They knew what they were doing. One moment it was Dorrie's hand gliding down his dick, the next it was her mouth and then back again, a constant, seamless exchange that managed to be both steady and ever changing, always some insane new swirl of the tongue or unexpected, perfect point of pressure. Pleasure. Pressure. None of his girlfriends' ministrations had ever felt like this; Andrew floated for an uncountable number of minutes in a sexual dreamworld where he was content, almost, to just let his excitement build and plateau and build and plateau, over and over again, until he felt like he had never been so turned on in his life as he was at this moment, with Dorrie like some creature slithering over him, a million appendages and orifices all focused only on him. And then it all felt different, warm, so warm, and soft and sweet and hot and impossible, and Andrew started thrusting upwards wildly, trying to reach something, somewhere, somehow.

No. Oh no.

Wait.

He must be inside her right now.

Years of determined denial willed him to stop, to still his hips, but she kept on moving on top of him.

Her slim legs were stronger than he ever would have guessed and she clung on, locking him in place, grinding deeper against him, driving her palms into his armpits, biting the side of his neck until her saliva drooled down onto his shoulder and he felt himself release inside of her, an explosion of white light behind his eyes and a slow, silent ebb.

Later, when she'd unlocked the handcuffs and untied her shirt and they both lay naked in the gray morning light, Dorrie had turned to him, something like apology in her eyes.

"Do you want to love me?" she asked.

And he'd nodded and fallen asleep.

二十九

New Orleans, LA

WHY WAS THE SCREEN on her phone always dirty? Grace pulled up her sleeve and wiped off the smudges, then went straight to her own site, Style + Grace. Everything around her smelled like grilled cheese sandwiches and french fries. She looked down at her screen again. It had already acquired a sheen of grease, but at least the feed was finally loading.

Response to her Whataburger post was strong, even though it kind of felt like a lazy image to her — just a shadowy shot of her painted toes against the green glow of the motel pool, the Whataburger roof in the distance. Still, fifty-three comments! The last one was from SmileSteez: *Name of polish! Must know ASAP LOL!* The polish was from her dad's failed line. Quickly, she responded: *Sorry, it's a limited edish! A gurl's gotta keep some secrets!*

Grace looked down at her breakfast. A half-eaten western omelet and a pile of french fries, ketchup squirted over everything. They were sitting in a diner in Uptown that Uncle Nash said they had to go to. If the Fountain Coffee Room in the Beverly Hills Hotel — her absolute favorite place to go as a kid — had a vile evil twin, this place would be it. The Camellia Grill sign outside was a cheesy hot-pink neon, which was especially weird because the building looked like a church, and then inside it was pink walls and green stools, the same pink and green of the Fountain's perfect palm wallpaper. If she was going to run away to a place, like the kids who hid out in the Met, that's where she would have gone. She loved the takeout that came in pink and white striped boxes, she loved the platters of tiny silver-dollar pancakes, she even loved the old people who ate truly weird combinations of things, like a hamburger patty with a scoop of cottage cheese.

As soon as Saina got her driver's license, the three of them went there by themselves all the time, sat three in a row, and watched the hotel workers in their pink shirts and the ladies who went to the spa in their pink robes climb up and down the staircase that spiraled past the glass wall. The line cooks all had stars cut out of the tops of their tall paper chef's hats. When they stood at the griddle making perfect mounds of hash browns, the overhead lights cast star-shaped patterns that swirled and danced on the sides of their white caps. Saina and Andrew had convinced her as a little kid that it was magic, and she still kind of believed that it was, as much as anything else in the world was magic.

"You done with that, hon?"

Grace looked up at the waitress. She seemed so nice. Why did she have to work here, instead of at a magic place in Beverly Hills? Life was so unfair. She nodded, and her half-eaten plate was whisked away, but the adults were all still eating and arguing over something boring, her father waving a piece of bacon in the air, taking bites of it as he talked.

Time to text Andrew again.

We've been here for an hour already. Where are u?

He replied immediately.

On way.

Andrew. She was still mad at him, but having him here was better than being alone with Dad and Babs. Grace peeled open another creamer and poured it into her coffee. It was almost white now, like a toasted marshmallow. As she waited for an earlier Style + Grace post to load, she listened to Uncle Nash, who liked to talk even more than her father did.

"But we must admit that Taiwan has done just fine without China's intervention," he said. "You know that Taiwan's per capita income is higher than Portugal's, Saudi Arabia's, and Liechtenstein's and exactly twice as high as China—"

"Higher than new China," her father broke in, "but that because it has many people from old China. Many people who run away from Communist, who know that study is important and money is important, who all too smart to work in fields!"

"So you think the Taiwanese people had no impact on the Taiwan Miracle? Surely you have to at least admire their lack of violence. Cambodia and Vietnam were in similar circumstances after World War II, and look at what happened there."

"Can't compare. Cambodia and Vietnam, whole different people. Wild. Not cultured. The Taiwanese people all just Chinese anyways."

"Charles! You can't just call them Chinese when it's convenient for you and then denigrate them when it's not! Barbra, back me up here."

Barbra took a bite of her pancake before replying. "I say if you try to make the case that the good economy only is because of *da lu ren,* then you have also to say that it is because of *ri ben ren.*"

Uncle Nash laughed. "What about that, Charles? Are you willing to admit that it was the Japanese occupation that primed Taiwan for economic success?"

"Nonsense! What the Japanese do? They build a lot of Japanese-style houses, okay, not so bad —"

"Hi, guys."

Everyone looked up. "Andrew! Finally!" said Grace, relieved. Except that he was wearing some ugly button-down shirt with little harps printed on it or something.

"Have you eaten yet? Sit down, sit down, order food." Her father pulled him towards an empty stool as Uncle Nash shoved a menu at him.

"Why are you wearing that shirt?" Grace asked.

"Oh, just changing up my style a little bit. I decided to go southern gentleman."

"Shut up! No, really."

He shot her a look. "Gracie, give it up. I'm just wearing it. It's just a shirt, don't worry about it."

"I thought I cared about you not looking ridiculous, but I guess I won't."

"No fighting! We all together again, almost whole family. Andrew, did you spend night with that ugly woman?"

Andrew flinched. "Dad, she's beautiful."

"Who are you guys even talking about? That lady with the red hair?"

"Dorrie," said Andrew.

Protective. That's how he sounded. Which was totally weird, but kind of understandable coming from Andrew. Andrew, who got to go off with some older lady without any questioning from Dad. It was so unfair — if she'd wanted to spend the night with one of those cute boys from the wedding, it would have been a federal case. "Isn't she kind of old?"

"No! Why does age matter?"

Their father put a hand on Andrew's shoulder. "No worry. Andrew not going to marry her or something. Not so serious, just fun."

"Well, actually . . ."

All four of them waited, wondering what he was going to say. God, Andrew really did look stupid in that shirt. Was it a girl's shirt? Was he going to marry that lady?

"Actually, I think I'm going to stay here for a while. With Dorrie."

"What? You'd leave me alone?" asked Grace.

He looked down at the counter. "I'm sorry, I just, I think I might be —"

Their father stood over him, protesting. "No, no, no. Is this because of what you say last night? Now you think that you are in love? So you have sex, so what? It is okay!" He looked over at Grace. "Not okay for you. Different for boy."

And Babs, too. "Andrew! Don't be so stubborn. Don't throw away your life on an old woman just because she sleep with you!"

Even Uncle Nash joined in. "I've known Dorrie since she was a girl, Andrew, and she's not the person you think she is. You should stay with your family."

They talked at him, and Andrew protested, and Grace registered it all, but she couldn't say anything. It was like there was a drumbeat in her head, except that each beat was a pulse of blood that just said, *Gone. Gone. Gone.* She'd never see him again. She was thrown in school and now she was yanked out of school and whatever adults wanted just happened. Nobody cared and she was alone and Saina never even answered the phone. She was going to be an adult soon and then could do whatever she wanted without any of them.

The talking turned to shouting, but finally Andrew ended it by just walking out the door, with the adults following him, without even saying goodbye to her. Without even seeing her. It didn't matter. He was gone anyway. There was Dorrie, sitting in an old sports car with the frizziest hair Grace had ever seen, not looking at her father or Babs or Uncle Nash as Andrew got in the front seat. Uncle Nash ran around to the driver's side of the car and yelled, but Dorrie, who was supposed to be his niece or second cousin or something, smiled and stared straight ahead and zoomed off like the Snow Queen.

The three old people just stood there in the sun, and Andrew was gone. Useless. Everyone was useless. Suddenly, Grace just wanted to go to *sleep*. Forget taking up arms against a sea of troubles — what was wrong with just lying down and going to invisible sleep?

三十

Helios, NY

LOVE SAVES YOU. That's the thing no one told Saina. Or maybe they'd tried, and she'd been too preoccupied with learning that an unconventional life was the only option to hear it. Maybe that's what crazy Republicans meant when they talked about liberal brainwashing and ivory-tower schools that created unrealistic expectations.

Because this was what she'd been taught: To choose marriage and babies over a glamorous career as an artist would be an unthinkable failure. Love was supposed to be a by-product of a life well lived, not the goal.

And this is what she'd realized: Everything she'd been taught was wrong.

Sometimes, Saina blamed her mother. It wasn't just that May Lee had died so suddenly and ridiculously, it was that she'd lived that way, too. Even as a child, Saina had felt that there was something wrong in the way that her mother's mood had shifted based solely on her father's attentions. In second grade, when the class was learning how to tell time, Saina remembered a worksheet that asked you to write down what your parents did all day. Her Father chart was jammed with entries.

6 a.m. to 7 a.m. — He plays tennis.
7 a.m. to 8 a.m. — He talks on the phone.
8 a.m. — He leaves for work.
8 a.m. to 7 p.m. — He makes makeup at his factory.
7 p.m. — He comes home.
7 p.m. to 10 p.m. — He plays with me and we all eat.

Her Mother chart barely had two.

6 a.m. to 11 a.m. — Sleeping.
11 a.m. to 7 p.m. — Shopping. Wait for Daddy.

She hadn't realized that other people's mothers had hobbies and charities and jobs. That they didn't just wait, inert, for their husbands to come home and bring them back to life.

Love saves you, as long as there's a you to be saved.

Saina tilted her head so that it rested against the rough pillow of Leo's hair and closed her eyes to the sun. They were sitting back to back on a long bench out behind Graham's restaurant, sharing the *New York Times* and mugs of tea, waiting for their friend to finish lunch service so that he could join them on an afternoon hike through the dells to an abandoned farmhouse that Saina had heard about.

"You know, this relationship has really been hard on poor Gabo," said Leo, knocking his head against hers. "He ended up doing all of the basil yesterday."

"Leo, why are you a farmer?"

"Why?"

"Yeah, I mean I know it was your job in high school, but did you just love growing things?"

He moved his head rhythmically against hers as he considered. "I do like growing things, but that's not it. I'm interested in systems. Did you know that plants can recognize each other and will share resources with other plants in the same family? Plants are networked the way our brains are networked." Saina smiled at his excitement. "And I liked the challenge of creating a system to work with that system, and to profit from it. And I like being outdoors." She could feel his low tenor buzzing through her chest.

"Talk some more. I like the way it feels."

"Like we're sharing a voice box?"

She laughed. "Like you're talking inside of me. Can you feel me? Or is my voice too high?"

"Talk again."

"You're so dreamy," she squeaked. "Hee hee hee!"

He laughed a low, booming laugh that reverberated in her ribs and lungs, and made her crack up in response.

The restaurant door swung open. "Hey, gigglers!"

Saina wiped a tear from her eye and Leo beckoned Graham — still in his dirty chef's whites — over. "Here, let's see what happens with a threesome."

"I thought you'd never ask!" He ran over, ginger beard bouncing, tripping a bit on his rubber shoes. "What game are we playing?"

Saina and Leo scooched sideways and made a space for Graham. "Okay," she said, "lean against us and see if we can both feel you talking."

"My ass is going to edge you guys off this thing," he said, turning and sitting. As he did, they all felt a buzz. "I'm magic! Is it like static electricity?"

"Actually, that's my phone." Thinking it was Grace again, Saina moved to shut off the buzzing when she saw the number. "Sorry, guys." She jumped up and answered as Graham called after her: "I thought we were a threesome! What's so secret that you don't want us to echo it?" In that split second, she also registered Leo's worried turn towards her. He thought it was Grayson, of course. He thought that she was still susceptible. That would have to wait.

"Hello?"

"Can I speak to Saina, please?"

"This is."

"Saina, it's Bryan Leffert. I'm sorry it took us some time to get back to you."

"That's okay."

A week ago, once it became clear that the bankruptcy wasn't just some dramatic misinterpretation of her father's, Saina had called her accountant and asked him about the situation. She'd thought of it as more of a precaution — the money was hers, she could give it to her family, everything would be fine.

"Look, I'm just going to get straight to it. We weren't sure whether this was going to happen, so we didn't want to worry you needlessly, but it looks like First Federal is attempting to place what is essentially a lien against your trust."

Except that now it wasn't.

"I don't understand. I thought that once I passed twenty-five that was it. That it was just mine."

"That's not quite the case. Because of a little creative accounting, your father's business was shielding the interest on your accounts from the IRS, which now leaves them susceptible to being treated like they're part of his assets."

Saina remembered, suddenly, the day Ama told her that her mother was dead. A cold, sunny February afternoon. Slamming the door of her friend Hilly's mom's car, looking up and seeing Ama in the driveway, and knowing that something was over.

"So what happens now?"

"It may be that nothing will change. We essentially have to wait and see. If, after all of your father's assets are sold, nothing remains owing, you'll be able to hold on to everything in your accounts."

She'd stood there, close enough to Hilly's mom's car that she couldn't drive off, and thought about getting back in. They had invited her out for dinner. They were going to get Hunan Palace, and she could pretend that she changed her mind and was in the mood for gloppy kung pao chicken after all, but in the end, she'd stepped away, Hilly's mom had zoomed off, and Ama had reached out and picked her up, even though she was taller and no matter how hard Ama squeezed and lifted, Saina's Keds still swept the driveway.

"So I can't draw from it now?"

"I'm afraid not."

Two minutes ago she was sitting on a bench with her boyfriend and his best friend, and nothing in the world was wrong. Nothing in her world, at least. She looked over at them. Leo was listening to Graham, who was doing an imitation of Sloppy-Joe Man, one of his favorite daily customers who ran a goat farm and never ate a vegetable.

. . .

"Saina?"

"Yes? Sorry, it's just a lot to take in."

"I know. It, well, it gets a little worse."

"What do you mean?"

"Your investment account is tied up with your trust, so all of those assets are frozen as well. But look, we're going to do everything we can to make sure that everything that you brought in is treated separately."

By the time she finished the conversation, Leo and Graham were looking up at her, quiet. She put the phone back in her pocket as Leo stood and gripped her arms.

"What's wrong?" he asked.

Sometimes Saina wished that she had more friends with trust funds. It would just make things easier. Life wouldn't be as hard to explain. She could complain about losing millions of dollars she'd never earned in the first place without feeling like she didn't deserve to be upset about it.

"Nothing, it's okay, let's go."

He held on to her. "Hey. Tell me."

"You're going to think it's crazy."

"I'm okay with crazy."

"It wasn't Grayson or anything."

"I know that. I'm not worried about that."

And she saw that he wasn't. She was wrong. He had more faith in her sureness than she did. He was just worried because she was worried. It was a novel thing. A nice thing. A good thing.

"It was my accountant." She glanced over at Graham.

"Is this a private couple talk?"

"No. It's just, stuff . . . that I don't know if I want to be unprivate about." She had seen people change around her when they found out the selling price of her work or the contents of her bank account. She had seen Grayson change, and in her starry-eyed lust she had just decided that it was him, falling more in love with her. It felt like that sometimes — people would get brighter, louder, quicker to laugh, and more eager — as if the very existence of those dollars were an electric conduit.

Saina shrugged. What did it matter? The money was all gone anyway. She was sure of it. She should be devastated, but instead she just felt numb.

She looked at Leo. "You know how my dad's going through the bankruptcy?" He nodded. She turned to Graham. "Did Leo tell you?"

Graham swatted the air in front of him. "No way. You think this guy would ever tell me about anything that you might want to keep to yourself? Unh-unh. He's like a vault."

"Well, basically, it turns out that my accounts are still completely tied up with my dad's company, so everything's frozen right now. And I might lose it all." Saying it out loud made her heart bottom out a bit.

"So, give us a little context here," said Graham. "Just how shitty is this? If my accounts were frozen, it would probably be a good thing because then they'd have to stop charging me for dropping under two thousand dollars."

"It's a little more than that."

They waited.

"More like a few million."

Graham fell off the seat. Leo let go of her arms.

"You ate here when you were a millionaire and you never demanded my best bottle? Not once? What's the point of rich friends if they don't buy out your wine list?"

Underneath Graham's antic tirade, Leo said, "You never told me that."

"I sort of told you."

Leo shook his head.

"I told you about my dad, and how the business went under, and how he was losing the house."

"But you didn't tell me about you."

"I guess I just thought that you assumed."

"That you had a trust fund?"

"Well, yeah."

"What did you mean by accounts, plural?"

"I had a career, Leo. Have. I *have* a career. I did well."

"I knew that. I guess I just didn't think about the money part —"

"How did you think I bought the house?"

"It's upstate New York. I just figured that a down payment out here was like rent in New York."

"I don't have a mortgage."

"Whoa." That was Graham again. "Okay, that's probably like the most baller thing you can say as an adult. From now on, my goal in life is going to be to say that someday. Mortgage? I don't got no fucking *mortgage!*"

Saina laughed and turned back to Leo. "Are you mad?"

His hands returned finally, one spanning her waist, the other back on her arm. She felt instantly warmed and leaned against him. This was what she'd missed, what had made her seek out Leo as soon as Grayson had packed up his pile of T-shirts: Their shared physical shorthand, the way they responded perfectly to each other's bodily cues so that they knew when to entwine and when to separate without a word of discussion.

"No, Saina. No." He kissed her, inhaling slowly as his lips pressed against her cheek. "I'm just surprised. And I like us to tell each other things."

Saina turned to face him, pressing her body against his. "I know, but this was a hard thing to tell. I guess, in a way, it's easier to say it to you now that the money's all gone." *Gone.* The word echoed in her head and she repeated it. "Gone." It echoed again, making her feel hollow inside, her brain tumbling down her throat and pounding against her heart, as if the money were the only thing that had filled her up and kept everything in its proper place.

"Hey, you don't know that, right? You said *might.*"

"It's just . . . nothing's worth as much anymore, but the loan is still for the same amount, you know? So they're going to sell off the house where I grew up and pretty much everything in it, and all of the factories and stock, but I don't think that will cover the original loan, and that's when the bank will go after what I have. Not this house, I don't think, because the title's under my name, but everything that's still tied to my dad in name, probably." She leaned closer to Leo, pressing her forehead into his chest.

"What's your dad going to do?"

"Oh god. He has this crazy plan where he thinks that he's going to roll up to the old village in China and somehow be able to reclaim the land that *his* father lost."

"Wait," said Graham, "are you a princess or something? Or, like, the Last Empress? Who just has land to reclaim?"

"And what would he do with it?" asked Leo.

"Become a farmer? You can give him tips. I don't know. I don't think he's thought that far. To be honest, I think he's lost his mind a little bit." She paused, picturing them. Generations of Wangs that had things, and then three that lost things. "It's just old family land. I don't even know if it's real. He says it is, but he's never even been back to China."

"Why not?"

Why not? Saina wasn't really sure. When he was living in Taiwan, travel between the two places was restricted, but America had lifted its ban before he'd immigrated. "He probably didn't want to go unless he could own the whole country."

"But he's coming here now?" asked Graham.

"Yep. Plus my stepmother and my brother and sister. They stopped off at my uncle Nash's house in New Orleans, but I think they'll be here the day after tomorrow."

Graham nudged Leo. "Ready to meet the in-laws?"

Leo looked at her. "Are they ready to meet me?"

"I think so. They'll just be glad that you're not, well, that you're not Grayson."

"See," said Graham, "one step up already!"

Saina looked at them and for a moment she was bitterly, intensely jealous. Life was so weightless for some people. She wanted to call her father right now and tell him not to come. Just wash her hands of the Wangs altogether, never mind that family was family and she should be glad that she was going to give hers a home. A homeland.

Should she even tell her father about this latest setback? He was probably counting on her reserves to finance the pursuit of the land in China, but what was that going to get them? Leo was right, what could her citified father possibly do with it? Even if he got it, which seemed impossible, it would probably be farmland out in the middle of nowhere. Saina tried to picture him out there, far from the modern towers of Beijing or Shanghai, demanding that some poor peasant boy make his cappuccino bone-dry, asking villagers if there was a better restaurant in town, realizing that he couldn't gossip about the man next to him in Chinese—

which sometimes seemed to be his and Barbra's sole pastime — because everyone around him would *be* Chinese.

Her father, sweating through a custom-tailored suit, armed with a bespoke hoe, trying to raise ghosts on that long-lost land.

The price of a single plane ticket to China could probably buy a few acres out here in Helios, thought Saina, looking out at the empty fields behind the restaurant. "At some point every old family's home had to be a new home."

Graham shook his head. "My family's never had an old home. Sharecropper's cabins to boarding houses to rented rooms to me, here, living the dream. And look at Leo — just a little orphan boy."

Saina smiled at them vaguely. How many generations would it take the Wangs to feel like upstate New York was their ancestral seat? One generation? Maybe two at the most? Saina thought about how a child, a son or daughter of hers, might romanticize their upbringing, spinning a narrative out of the way their people started out in the Old East and continued here in the New.

Who were the Native Americans, really, but a band of Chinese people who had set their sights east and walked for millennia?

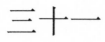

Opelika, AL

2,493 Miles

AMERICA WASN'T DONE with Charles Wang. He gave her his best ideas and basest impulses — the most vital parts of a man — and in return she snatched away his son. Andrew didn't leave; he was stolen. By a smug porcelain statue with an inkwell for a heart who only wanted to feed off of his youth and beauty. Charles cursed every tenth of a mile that ticked over on the odometer, each click placing another impassable length between the remaining Wangs and their only son.

No. *His* only son. And only his son. Without May Lee in the world, Andrew belonged only to him. Barbra had no grounds to lay any claim. Charles's own parents were dead, dropping away, one after the other, soon after he arrived in America. All that remained of them was the shard of bone in his suitcase. May Lee's father was long gone but her forgetful mother still languished in some San Gabriel Valley nursing home that would not be receiving any more monthly checks signed by Charles Wang. May Lee's worthless, passive siblings would have to figure out a way to pay for it now.

What was the point of having children? All they did was leave you. He'd left his parents. May Lee had tossed money at hers and fled. Barbra had slipped away from hers without even telling them that she was going. At the very moment when children might emerge from the uselessness of adolescence and finally take on some of the burden of being alive, that

was when they blithely severed themselves at the root with one cruel, un-
thinking cut. *Little assholes.*

He left too soon. He left and let that woman have his son. Of all the
things that he had lost, this was the very worst.

The air-conditioning broke down somewhere between Biloxi and Mo-
bile. There was a smell, like every frozen thing in the world had just died,
and then nothing. No matter how many times they toggled the air on and
off, nothing stirred in the bowels of the car.

Despite the heat, Barbra kept her window closed, the scarf still wedged
between the glass and the frame. She might choose to melt rather than
sacrifice the pallor that she thought was aristocratic, but he and Grace
had rolled down the rest of the windows.

By the time he pulled into Opelika, all three of them were sweating, shirts soaked through. A quartet of Obama posters — the one that
looked like a piece of Communist propaganda — peeled in the window
of a boutique while a McCain poster was taped to the door of a neighboring furnace-supply store. This place looked like the model for Main
Street, U.S.A., each store an orderly two stories with shingled façades and
colored awnings. As he slowed to the town's speed limit, Charles flipped
through the radio dial until he landed on a talk station.

A nasal twang rang through the speakers. "Well, there are people in my
town, I'm not saying who they are, but *they* know who they are, and I'm
not saying I'm one of them, not that I'd say it if I *were* one of them, but
sure, there are people here who wouldn't vote for a man because of his
skin color, sure. Not me, I treat every man the same, white, black, or purple, but there's a lot of narrow minds."

And then the interviewer. "A Gallup poll of Alabama residents shows
that most respondents would consider voting for a black president but
didn't think that others in their state would do the same."

Grace's head popped up between the front seats. "I have to pee."

The first words from her mouth since they'd left New Orleans without
Andrew. Charles patted his daughter's head.

"I think we almost there, okay? You go at the store."

"How do you even know that they'll be there?" she asked.

He didn't. And, if he was being honest with himself, he wasn't even sure that they'd be able to pay him immediately, and he wasn't quite sure what to do if they couldn't.

"No worrying, Gracie. *Ren je, hao?*"

Ignoring her harrumphs of protest, Charles turned up the sound.

"And now we turn it over to Money Mike who's in Auburn where the Tigers are getting ready to take on the LSU Tigers this weekend. Mike, who will win the battle of the big cats?"

Grace's arm appeared to the left of his head, pointing. "There! It's there! I can't wait for you to park — just let me out!" He slowed the car down and his daughter jumped out the back, slamming the door with so much force that the whole rig shuddered.

"We meet at the store, Gracie!" he shouted out the window, but she didn't turn back or respond.

Parking in Opelika was easy. The streets were half empty and Charles felt a sense of accomplishment as he pulled the wagon, shocks creaking, into place along the curb, cutting the wheel at exactly the right moment so that the U-Haul in back would line up easily. It took only a few long, focused minutes now, instead of the cursing, sweating, quarter of an hour that docking the giant metal fishtail used to take.

He turned to Barbra. "Will you come in?"

She shook her head.

Charles was glad. It seemed less pathetic, somehow, if they just saw him and Grace. He could pretend that they were in the middle of a carefree, father-daughter cross-country jaunt and had decided on a whim to make a personal delivery. There. Life wasn't so bad after all. Smooth down the shirt. Fix the collar. Adjust the pants. Tidy the hair. Too bad men couldn't wear makeup — he could probably use a little lip gloss and rouge, a touch of blue liner to make the whites of his eyes whiter.

Half a minute later Charles was pushing open the weathered wood door of the Magnolia General Store. He could see Grace inside, talking to El-lie Yates, who still looked exactly as he'd remembered her from the plane — tiny and golden.

"Yes. Totally. That's what I want to do." Grace nodded at Ellie enthusi-astically as the two of them looked at something on the computer.

For a minute, Charles wanted to turn around and leave. Dump the trailer full of lotions and balms into a river somewhere so that he wouldn't have to break in on Grace's small happy moment. But there was no land in China without the money to find it and, most likely, to bribe some corrupt Communist official into handing it over, so he pressed forward.

"I have a special delivery!"

Ellie turned. "Mr. Wang!" As he crossed the room to embrace her, he noticed Grace clicking something shut on the screen.

"Mr. Wang, your daughter here was just showing me her style blog — she's got herself some serious taste."

Grace smiled.

"Ah, I think *you* have serious taste," said Charles, looking around the shop. It was expertly done, at once the kind of general store that might have existed in an old American mill town a hundred years ago and a modern art gallery. Every gardening implement looked like a finely wrought weapon, the jars of penny candy were piles of gems, the few articles of clothing equally appropriate for a field hand or a gallery owner. "Everything is even better than you describe!"

Ellie beamed; Charles beamed back. Grace, caught up in the goodwill, opened her blog back up. "Here, Dad, do you want to see it?"

Charles nodded. This was a rare gift, he knew. Grace made space for him in front of the screen and handed him the mouse. He peered down. At first glance, it appeared to be a web page made entirely of pictures of Grace in different outfits. Subsequent glances confirmed it. Grace in her dorm room. Grace lying on a bench. Grace in the woods. Grace in an empty swimming pool. Even though she was all covered up, it felt vaguely pornographic. The whole thing made Charles uncomfortable. His daughter and Ellie were chatting, something about shooting a picture here at the store, but he could feel Grace watching him.

"Very pretty pictures," he said, finally. "Very creative. Nice name, Style and Grace."

"Don't lie. Just say you hate it."

"No, no, no! I don't hate anything you do! Daddy just don't understand blog — it is new thing for me!"

"Well, look." She reached over and typed "makeup" into the search bar. "I did a tutorial with, you know, your stuff."

Charles watched, surprised, as a photo of the Failure's whole line slowly revealed itself on the screen. It was a lovely shot. As good as, or better than, the professional product shots they'd used. He scrolled through the post. There was Grace, putting on the eyeliner that was fine and true, swiping on the richly hued lipstick, atop a caption that read, "OMG Loves It!" Charles wanted to cry. Instead, he patted her hand, and said, "Good girl, Gracie," and then turned to Ellie. "Speaking of makeup, we have special delivery!"

Grace rolled her eyes. "Dad, you made that joke already!"

But she came outside with Charles and Ellie, and smiled as Ellie exclaimed over the pile of boxes stacked in the U-Haul.

"We bring these all the way from California for you — I tell Gracie that the personal is the most important for business."

"Well, I just think that is so sweet, I really do. Trip is going to flip when he sees all this — he built a special shelf and rigged up lighting and everything." Ellie tore into a box right there on the street, using her keys to rip apart the packing tape and scattering the Styrofoam shells out onto the street. Inside, row upon gleaming row of boxes made of the palest, blush-colored paper stock, MAGNOLIA GENERAL STORE printed in gold using a typeface that Ellie herself had designed. She pulled one out reverently.

"I can't believe we did it. Mr. Wang —"

He broke in. "No, no Mr. Wang, please call me Charles."

She smiled. "Charles, we never would have thought this big if it hadn't been for you. Thank you." She held the box up to her nose. "Oh it smells good!"

His heart swelled. It was his factory and his ingenuity, his powers of persuasion, that allowed this southern girl to dream of more than a lovely store in a dying town.

And then they all saw it. Oil had soaked through the bottom of the box, mottling its perfect blush. "Uh oh," said Ellie, joking, nervous. She opened it up and pulled out a glass jar of bath scrub. The label was beautiful. The crystals twinkled in the sun. And the whole thing was covered with a slick, sick sheen. Ellie wiped her hand on the leg of her jeans and looked up at him.

America was ruining everything. Ruining it with her embarrassing heat, with the sticky swelter between her fat white legs. They opened box after box, and each one was the same — a brief, optimistic moment when the contents shimmered in neat, packaged rows, and then the inevitable crash of disappointment as the leaky interiors made themselves known.

The old-towel smell of his own sweat mixed with the sweet magnolia perfume made Charles nauseous. His heart hammered inside his chest with an alarming insistence. It would be incredibly embarrassing to die right now; Grace would never forgive him for it. His head buzzed. He couldn't look at Ellie. With each failed box, the numbers ticked higher in his mind, the tally of money he'd never be able to claim.

"I'm so sorry," said Charles, finally.

The two of them sat on the back of the U-Haul surrounded by a spent pile of cardboard. Styrofoam peanuts swirled along the street. Grace had retreated to the backseat of the car with an excuse about the sun.

"Of course I will refund your deposit."

She nodded. Of course. She would expect nothing less from the accomplished, wealthy businessman in the bespoke suit she and her husband had met sitting in first class, the man who had name-dropped a list of his clients and been so generous about their ambition.

Ellie got up.

"Or maybe we try again? And you can just, you know, ship everything the way you normally do? September in Alabama is hot as hell — it must have been a surprise coming from L.A."

Charles jumped up onto the sidewalk next to her, and before he could stop himself, the words piled out of his mouth.

"There is no try again. When we meet, I have very successful business. Now it is gone. It didn't have to be, but it is. Not my fault, but all my fault. You are young. You don't know the things that can happen in a life."

Ellie's eyes opened wide. "I had no idea, Mr. Wang! Are you, is your family alright?" She looked over at the car where Grace and Barbra were sitting. Charles could see her taking in the age of the car, making some allowance, perhaps, for the fact that it was at least still a Mercedes; scanning the backseat, which was completely covered with Grace's torn-out magazine pages, making it look like a set for some puppet minstrel show. Bird shit was splattered on the roof, and dead bugs were smeared across the windshield. He cringed as his daughter rummaged through an open suitcase. Was that underwear hanging out the side? The Wangs were less than a week out of Bel-Air and already they looked like they'd come from a trailer park.

"We are always alright! We just think of this as a vacation. Look, I will write you a check for your deposit now."

Charles pulled the business checkbook out of his pocket. In some small way, he must have known that this might happen. As he signed his name, he thought about a line from an old gangster movie he remembered seeing as a teenager in Taiwan. "His mouth keeps writing checks that his fists can't cash." No one's fists were going to be able to cash this check because the account was locked, no matter how many gangsters wanted to threaten it.

She accepted the check and folded it in half without looking at the amount. In fact, the bright and lovely Ellie was so well-bred that she helped pack the boxes back into the U-Haul and sent them on their way with a bag of spiced nuts made by a local baker and a giant hug for Grace.

"You all come back whenever you like, alright? I do mean that. And take care of each other on the road." Charles tossed back a fistful of nuts, marveling at their cardamom scent and meaty crunch. Mouth full, he nodded at Ellie, chewing at attention as she walked back to the store.

As soon as she was out of sight, Charles shoved another few nuts in his mouth and knelt down next to the hitch. He was jiggling it, trying to figure out how to undo the thing without tools or assistance when Barbra stuck her head out of the car.

"What are you doing?"

He looked up at her.

She had gotten tiny. Somewhere between California and Alabama, Barbra had lost the fullness that she carried and become skeletal.

"Don't worry," he said.

"You are going to just leave this here? Throw away more money?"

Charles shrugged. "Doesn't matter. By now nobody pay that card. I go return it, they ask for money. I never return, they never find." He felt almost giddy until he looked up and met Barbra's eyes. Contempt. The way that she'd looked at the boys who worked in the kitchen under her father. Yes, he remembered her from the beginning, had admired her naked teenage determination even though he liked to tease her and say that he barely knew who she was when she arrived in America so soon after May Lee's crash.

"Why didn't you know?"

"Know what?" Even though, of course, he knew what.

"That all their things would ruin! *Wo men lai je me yuan, you she me yong?*"

Charles turned his head away, trying to shield himself from her anger.

"Okay," he said. "Okay, okay, okay. *Bu yao zai shuo le.*" He hoisted himself up and walked the long way around to the front seat. Tonight, after dark, he would pull up to the back of a Walmart or a McDonald's and throw away these boxes full of wasted effort, and then the next morning, before Barbra and Grace woke up, he would drive to the closest U-Haul office, fifteen miles outside of Opelika, and return this trailer, feign surprise when the card on record didn't go through, and pay with two of the hundred small-faced Benjamin Franklins that were stacked in a manila envelope in the bottom of his suitcase. But he wouldn't tell Barbra that yet. She shouldn't think that her anger could make him do things.

Charles thought about that meager emergency stash he had stowed away so many years ago, back when ten thousand dollars seemed like an impressive sum to have on hand. Now it had to get them to Saina's house and then wing him all the way to China. But once it did, once he got there, he'd fix everything.

三十二

Atlanta, GA

2,594 Miles

GRACE MADE small noises from the other bed. They could be snores or sighs. Since Barbra had left Taiwan, she hadn't spent a single night sleeping in the same room with anyone other than Charles. She didn't know how to decipher anyone's noises of sleep but his. Until now, of course.

She could hear the clatter of silverware on ceramic outside, the smell of cheap bacon and sweet buns, the wail of an angry infant — all unmistakable signs of a free breakfast buffet, which every fat family in this motel would be lined up for. Barbra thought about the way that the pulpy, from-concentrate orange juice always glugged out of big plastic jars at the far ends of those buffet lines and felt vaguely nauseous.

Was it true that she had married Charles for his money?

Yes.

And he knew it.

In fact, she was fairly certain that he'd loved her for it.

The question, then, was obvious. Without the money, did she still love him?

In the months before news of May Lee's death had filtered back to Charles's old friends in Taiwan, Barbra had been working in a stationery shop downtown. Every day she wore a pink smock and shuffled notebooks into orderly piles while her boss, dirty old Lao, devised reasons to send her up the storeroom ladder. He would watch her climb through his smudged glasses and she would fume inside — it was unfair that she got all the burdens of being a woman with none of the benefits of beauty. Every evening at five o'clock, she would turn down his dinner invitation and head back to the cook's quarters at the university, where she was still living with her parents.

Dinner was always an assortment of reheated odds and ends from the university kitchen — the gritty last bowl of a bone broth; a splattering of tofu about to turn, the stink of spoilage masked by a coat of garlicky spice; dozens of overboiled dumplings, their pale skin split, their insides spilling out. After eating, Barbra and her mother would push the table and chairs against the wall and swab the floor clean before pulling out their flowered bedrolls and spreading them on either end of the room. Then it was an idle evening hour in the courtyard with a score of children underfoot, her parents chatting with the other university employees as she leafed through movie magazines and waved away the scent of the mosquito coil.

On Friday nights, when she received an envelope with her week's pay, always less than she thought it might be, she would meet up with friends and walk through the crowded streets, stopping sometimes to buy a cone of roasted peanuts or watch the noodle man kneading and pulling at a mass of dough until it became a cascade of slippery threads that he snipped into a boiling vat of soup. There would be a purse, maybe, that she wanted to buy, or a scarf, and then three weeks of envelopes would be gone in a single sweep.

It was a life, but Barbra could see no end to it. Even if she saved every yuan she earned, it would never accumulate so that it became a sturdy pile upon which a person might stand.

It felt like she would always be sleeping in the same room as her parents, listening as the walls thundered with her father's snores, rubbing her mother's back and helping her take the rollers out of her hair. Her two sisters had escaped into unhappy marriages years ago, one in New Zealand and the other in Singapore, and rarely wrote. There was no money to call. Barbra had tried to do the same, but her own marriage had been even unhappier. It had been three long years during which she remembered anew each morning that there was nothing lonelier than spending your days with a man you did not respect. In the end, she'd left carrying her five best dresses in a cardboard box under her arm and moved back in with her uncomplaining parents.

So when she heard about May Lee's strange fate, it felt like a summons, like an escape. Barbra knew exactly what she had to do.

She opened the cupboard above the heater and took out the small steel lockbox that lived there. It was powder coated in an army green and felt warm and vaguely alive in her hands. She dug its key out of the drawer where it always rattled around with their jumbled collection of chopsticks and spoons — her parents were so trusting! — and popped open the lid.

Even now, she remembered her dismay at how little there was inside that box. Both her mother and father worked, all day, every day. She worked. The three of them lived in a single room, which her parents saw as a vast improvement on the hovels in which they were born, and yet their accumulated life savings weren't enough to fill a box the size of a brick of radish cake. She could grab up all the money — the loose New Taiwan dollar bills and a few pointless coins — in one try, so she did. She'd taken it, all of it, then locked and replaced the now-cold box, slipped the key under the biggest wooden spatula, and run out to the China Airlines office she passed twice a day on her way to and from the stationery shop. Together with her last week of pay and a loan begged from old Lao by actually kneeling on the ground in front of him and bowing three times at his feet, Barbra had purchased a ticket and, three days later, taken leave of her parents with nothing more than a note.

Months later, after she'd done what she came to America to do, Barbra had wired fifty times the money back to her parents, along with another note saying that they should invite a table full of friends to a banquet in celebration of her marriage. They didn't respond. She tried again and again, seven attempts in all, until she received an undersize envelope addressed only to Mrs. Wang that contained a scrap of paper on which was written *"Wo mei yo nu er."* I have no daughter.

That was that, then.

In the end, nobody but a clerk at city hall had ever congratulated her and Charles on their nuptials. No banquets had been thrown, no special qipao made, no pieces of motherly advice given.

Not much later, Tie Shan, the university's head groundskeeper and their longtime neighbor, wrote to say that both of her parents had died, one right after the other, of swift and merciless cancers — her mother of the lung, her father, somewhat embarrassingly, of the breast. When Barbra got the letter, she had a terrible thought. It was right that she took the money. Better. Her parents would have died anyway. Even if their metal box had remained inviolate, they would not have lived long enough to touch the savings inside. If Barbra had allowed some misplaced morality to keep her in Taiwan, her parents would have died just in time for Charles to marry someone else. And even if they had lived, they wouldn't have possessed the imagination to spend their savings on anything beyond a trip to their own parents' graves.

Spending money was easy. Being a rich man's wife was easy. From the moment she'd walked into Charles's Bel-Air house, so recently emptied of May Lee, Barbra felt like she was finally where she belonged. Even though she'd never had much exposure to the moneyed classes of Taiwan, she knew instinctively how to behave among the rich.

The key, Barbra decided, was to be unbothered by the opinions of others and be always certain that your own choices were correct. Of course, it was a mental state that required some degree of material support. A new Hermès belt. A diamond-studded Cartier watch. These nonnegotiable luxuries were like armor that only retained its efficacy if it was repolished every season.

Barbra had been raised in a world of prized possessions. Small, inconsequential treasures given outsize significance. Her own mother possessed what Barbra now realized was a sample-size bottle of Chanel No. 5, gifted by an employer. For a decade, it sat on the only windowsill in their shared single room, the scent inside turned from age, spritzed by her mother only on special occasions. Next door, the two little Fong girls had a yellow shoebox where they kept their only doll, a broken thing with two dresses. They would change those dresses reverently, once in the morning and once at night, and lay the doll back in its sunny coffin with as much care as a surgeon doing a heart transplant. Little Xu Mei, who worked in the university president's office, had a single pearl-headed pin that she wore on the lapel of every shirt and dress. Barbra had been passing by the office when the pin broke loose and the pearl rolled into some unseen crack, never to be found again. She still remembered the tears and the consolation, the way that Xu Mei never stopped searching for that one tiny pearl.

The Communists had it all wrong. It wasn't the rich who were imprisoned by their possessions, it was the poor.

The sheets at this motel weren't as bad as some of the others in the places they'd stayed at. They were faded and nearly threadbare, but at least they'd started out 100 percent cotton, with none of that cheap nylon burr that had made it hard to sleep so many other nights. Grace still hadn't stirred, but Barbra couldn't tell if she was asleep or not. Petulant little Grace had been barely two months old when her mother died. There was a time, at the very beginning, when Barbra still might have been able to make the baby feel like her own child, but she'd felt no natural swelling of maternal instinct at the sight of the swaddled infant in Ama's arms. And, too, Charles had proven to be a surprisingly enthusiastic father, who bounced and clicked and cooed over his motherless daughter whenever he was home.

Barbra wondered, not for the first time, if May Lee had also married Charles for his money. Had she taken as easily to luxury as Barbra? She had certainly known how to shop. Barbra didn't think that May Lee had been the sort of model who received gifts from designers, yet her clothes, put away for Saina and Grace, had colonized nearly an entire room of the house.

During Barbra's first month in America, when Charles thought that she was just visiting for adventure, a last fling before settling down with her imagined fiancé in Taiwan, she had called him *gege,* big brother, and never mentioned May Lee. But once her fiancé had been dispatched — with the aid of a concocted revelation — and she'd moved into Charles's arms, Barbra employed a series of deft questions to help her draw an outline of May Lee's family history.

There was little about it that seemed auspicious. It was a mongrel history, muddied by generations spent in America. On one side there was a great-grandfather who came to California to perform coolie labor on the railroads, on the other there was a great-grandmother who was imported as a brothel girl, though May Lee's family swore that she'd never actually turned a trick because she'd already been pregnant by the time she arrived in America, where she sought refuge with a group of understanding Jehovah's Witnesses and become a proselytizer instead. The only family member May Lee had been ashamed of, according to Charles, was her own grandfather, who, upon his death, was revealed as a Japanese man passing as Chinese in order to avoid the internment camps.

Somehow they'd all managed to find other Chinese people to marry and have children with — the Chinatowns of San Francisco and Los Angeles were filled with families that had tenuous ties to May Lee's.

These older Chinese people born in America were very disorienting. May Lee's mother had visited the children soon after she and Charles married — a large, lumpen woman with a bowl cut, dressed in a hideous wool suit, who nonetheless spoke English with a lilting perfection that made Barbra feel like her own Chanel jacket was far too pink.

May Lee and America overlapped.

Mei Li and Mei Guo.

Beauty and Beautiful Country.

Dead, May Lee was everywhere. Dead, she became the entire country. It wasn't fair! Barbra turned over so she could open her eyes without looking at Grace. It just wasn't fair. The children used to say that about everything — Grace still did sometimes. Nothing was fair.

The Wangs were fools, thought Barbra. They had everything, and they understood nothing. Charles was the kind of person who had never in his blessed life thought about where the shit went after he flushed the toilet. It was his privilege to empty his bowels in clean white ceramic bowls, and it was the burden of the world to wash it away.

None of the Wangs appreciated anything. Saina and Grace would never appreciate the pure, thrumming pleasure of carrying a tasteful yet outrageously expensive purse. They had never lived a life without such privileges. The nod of recognition that such a purse elicited from a few equally solvent others was an unimpeachable sort of currency, not subject to market fluctuations or whims of fashion. The thick, buttery leather and polished gold clasp were enough to lend substance to her being, the purse became an axis around which the whole chaotic world would spin. Wealth, Barbra knew, should belong to those who understood its power.

Charles thought of himself as a self-made man. He was stupid enough to think that he'd come to America with nothing — "Just a list of urea in my pocket," he liked to say — and wrested a fortune from this country through his own brilliance. Barbra had once heard an American saying: "He was born on third and thought he hit a triple." Baseball was popular in Taiwan and she'd known immediately what it meant. *She* was the one who had started with two strikes against her and, with nothing more than her own determination, had made it all the way back to home base.

Barbra sat up in bed, furious.

She was the one who had made something out of nothing. *She* was the one who'd upended generations of poverty in one move. So what if she'd done it with a lucky marriage? Would it be worth any more if she'd won Charles's hand in a game of poker? Empires rose and fell on luck, and her own was worth as much as any monarch's.

As for Charles, one stroke of ill fortune and he was broken, turned into a demented old man fantasizing about some forgotten family land that was probably not much to begin with. Barbra looked over at Grace, still asleep. *A useless lump. Like all the Wangs.*

When the Failure first launched, Charles had surprised her with the full line, eight shades of foundation, thirty-two lipsticks, sixteen eye shadows, all laid out beautifully in her bathroom. Secretly, she'd been a little sad about putting away her Guerlain powder and Dior mascara, but she'd used his products and he'd praised their beauty on her unbeautiful face. After the Failure became the Failure, after he'd made his announcement, she'd gone into her bathroom and found that they were all already gone, swept into an awkward heap in the Lucite trash can next to her vanity. It was such a peevish act, like a child tossing away a broken toy.

That's it, thought Barbra. *Now, finally, that was it.* She was going to leave all of them, Charles, Saina, Andrew, and Grace. They were all going to give up, but she wasn't. She'd made one life on her own, and she could do it again! After all, there was so much she could do now — the world was a whole different place than it had been when she came over to America. She could marry someone else, or she could move back to Taiwan and make her own fortune! That's what people were doing there now, making fortunes on things like a sandwich cart or a barrette store. Or, better yet, she'd go back to Los Angeles and inform all of their acquaintances that she was actually a feng shui expert. That, in fact, she came from a long line of feng shui gurus. If Saina could sell ridiculous art projects to museum curators, who should presumably know better, then why couldn't she convince a few rich white people that five thousand years of Chinese wisdom could bring them health and prosperity? Feng shui was easy enough to fake. A few tosses of the joss sticks, a compass printed with Chinese characters, a shirt with an embroidered dragon — maybe something from that old Vivienne Tam collection — and she was as good as a guru.

Barbra threw aside her sheet and slid out of bed. The thing was to do everything before Grace woke up, before Charles returned. Her leaving should be presented as a fait accompli rather than a matter up for debate. She tiptoed over to the closet and pulled out her packed suitcase. Rather than risk waking Grace up with the sound of the zippers, she changed into yesterday's clothes, still hanging on the back of a chair, and piled her pajamas on top of the leather case.

She edged around Grace's bed and closed the bathroom door behind her softly. Yes. This was the thing to do. The best thing. The only thing. Charles didn't deserve to have her stay. In a calm, cold rage, Barbra pulled the face wash out of her cosmetics bag and squirted some into her hand, dabbed dots of it on her forehead, cheeks, chin, then worked it into a bubbly lather before splashing her face with water again. An angry swipe of the rough towel that hung from the rack — Orange! Even this ugly motel should know better than to buy orange towels! — that she tempered with softer pats, mindful of the collagen she must try to preserve. Automatically, she reached for the heavy green jar of face cream and unscrewed it, enjoying, despite her anger, the cool weight of the lid in her hand. She looked at herself in the mirror as she dipped a finger into the thick white lotion and tapped it gently under each eye, impatient as she waited for it to soak into her skin. Her skin looked sallow and dull in the unflattering light, but she knew that as soon as she smoothed on a coat of foundation her face would glow as much as it could for a forty-nine-year-old woman — fifty, she was fifty now — who had spent the last sixteen years in a city that worshipped the sun. After that, the thinnest trace of eyeliner, just enough to make her eyes a little less round, then a few coats of mascara and a quick brush of her eyebrows, tweezer ready to eradicate any errant hairs. Last would come the lipstick, a holdover from the Failure that she had snuck out of the trash can — after all, a woman couldn't change her lipstick color based on the state of her husband's business ventures. And that would be it. Her face.

Every morning she did this, every single day of her life.

And every night, every single night of her life, she washed it all off. Only to put it all back on again the next morning.

She could do it with her eyes closed. She could do it while she planned the best way to leave her husband.

It was all so ephemeral. And this was what Charles had dedicated his life to. Makeup. It was enough to make her weep. She had thought, often, about the fact that he had chosen her unbeautiful self to be his wife. Of course, she'd made up for it by figuring out how to look expensive, which, in her estimation, was much more of an accomplishment. Never mind the charms with which you were born, what mattered most was your willingness to put in the effort.

Oh, Charles. At their best, they had talked to each other endlessly, never running out of opinions and observations about the alien world around them. *Where had that man gone?*

Barbra uncapped her lipstick, feeling reassured by the familiar red of it. She turned the bottom of the tube and concentrated as the tip emerged. Already she could smell the rose-scented perfume embedded in that creamy stick; it got stronger as she lifted it towards her face and carefully traced the thin lines of her mouth, bringing herself into focus.

And then just like that, with a smack of her own red lips, Charles reclaimed his place. Barbra cursed. She had given her heart to Charles Wang, and no matter what, she couldn't take it back.

三十三

I-85 North

SHE WAS SO TIRED. And hot. Hot enough to melt, they used to say, and now it was true. Whoever thought the California sun was relentless never wheeled through miles of Texas desert, nothing but giant cacti on either side, nowhere a shady stretch or a wayward sprinkler. All around was sand, just sand, a few degrees away from melting into glass. And they had never rolled out of that desert, astonished at their continued existence, only to find themselves in the unforgiving humidity of the American South.

Nobody even pretended to love her anymore.

Andrew was gone, his seat empty. Where did he go? Why didn't he come back? Why had they left without him? No one spoke of it, just poured gas into her belly and pointed her east, so that she had no choice but to leave him behind. Now it was only Grace in the backseat, dirty bare feet scrubbing against the mat like a street urchin's.

She could feel the rust building up behind her wheel wells — invisible now, but if it went untended, the corrosive brown would bloom across the caverns and there would be no stopping it. These were the things that led lesser vehicles to ruin. The slow, steady wearing away of a body. Unless you were made of plastic — *that* never withered. It cracked, cheap, and clattered off.

The Barbra still wasn't talking. The Barbra seemed different today. She moved her seat forward, granting Grace an extra half inch of precious space. The scarf was still wedged into her window frame, but the Barbra let it flutter, its soft fabric brushing her hot glass. Strangest of all, the woman leaned ever so slightly, almost unnoticeably, into Charles. Grace didn't even look up. What was the point of Grace? The Barbra leaned and Charles, always ready to be adored, canted his body towards the Barbra, a grateful puppy, tongue lolling in the perfumed breeze. Men! So simple! Withhold a thing and it becomes instantly desirable.

The Barbra reached one spider arm up and draped it across Charles's shoulders, wedging a hand between his neck and the headrest until the sharp edges of the cursed woman's diamond rings dug into her plush seat and then, without warning, the hand began to undulate, kneading, pressing, prodding, into Charles's neck, and Charles dipped his head forward, fluttering his eyes. It was disgusting. An obscenity. Flesh and blood might be different from metal and glass, but this was a display as brazen as a twenty-four-karat-gold gearshift.

She shuddered.

She swerved.

And, a moment too late, remembering Grace in the backseat, she tried to catch herself. There was no time. The rings kept digging against her soft parts, and the road just slipped out from under her.

A ribbon, loose, spooling away.

She could feel her bolts tighten in their holes and then: *Boom. Crash.* Done.

三十四

High Point, NC

2,911 Miles

A SICKENING SPIN.

Grace looked up, confused.

Spinning backwards. Spinning sideways.

She gripped the door handle.

Infinitely slow.

Her right leg flung itself skyward until it was stopped by the door itself.

Out of time.

Grace slid sideways. Her neck arced back and her head knocked against the seat, ping-ponging weightlessly.

Airborne. Up, above the gravel on the shoulder, nose down and rear up.

Her face was knocked against the window and her eyes were open. She seemed to be upside down. It was green outside. It sounded like they were underwater. It felt as if she were a necklace in a gift box all padded with cotton. Why would she think something like that? She was so weird sometimes.

A crunch, a scream, a bright, shrill shattering of glass.

And then everything slammed back to earth and sped up faster, faster, faster, and Grace was bracing her feet against the seat in front of her even though it was above her now, and an arm, her own arm, was flung violently in front of her face, luckily shielding her eyes against a hailstorm of glass shards, and she was waiting, every nerve in her body lit up, waiting for the spinning to end, because it had to end; accidents always ended, no matter how bad they were.

Mom, she thought, said, screamed. "Mom!"

Stillness.

Then, "Grace! Gracie!"

For a too-brief angels-and-rainbows-and-unicorns sort of second, she thought that maybe it really was her mother, watching over her, or that maybe she was dead now, and there actually was an afterlife. But, of course, it was her father.

"Bu yao hai pa! Baba gen ni yi qi!"

"Me, too. I'm here."

三十五

Helios, NY

SAINA BREATHED IN, nervous. Leo's truck windows were rolled down, and a recent bout of summer rain made everything smell like warm asphalt; the grass and trees were green in that vibrant way that happened only in the East Coast gloom. They sped by, a verdant mass, as Leo gunned past a vintage truck. This would be her first public appearance since she'd holed up in the Catskills, and Saina wanted to do it as much as she didn't.

"Don't think of it as being in hiding," said Leo. "Think of it as a hiatus. Now you're ready to get back in the ring."

"How did you know?"

"Because I know you, Saina. And I know that you're not going to stay up here and perfect your house forever. And these Bard kids, they're gonna love you."

She felt warm. Seen. And a little bit indignant.

"Hey, Saina."

"Yeah?"

"How come you never talk about your mom?"

"What? Why bring this up now?"

"I've been thinking about it. And you don't let me in, always." He smiled a big flash of a smile at her. "Sometimes I have to stage an emotional sneak attack."

Saina looked out the window. "You know, when I first moved up here, this lady at the hardware store told me that I shouldn't even *think* about planting until the leaves on the trees were as big as squirrel's ears."

"Why don't you talk about her? And that's true, by the way."

"Isn't that just so country? Sometimes people are exactly who you secretly hope they'll be."

Leo took his hand off the gearshift and placed it on her knee.

"Do you think about her? You must. I don't have a single memory of my mother, my birth mother. All I have is a picture, and I still think about her all the time."

"There's a picture?"

"Yeah, it was some Little Orphan Annie shit. A picture of her holding me as a baby. Or, you know, a picture of some black lady holding a fat little kid."

"All the time?"

"Huh?"

"You still think about her all the time?"

"Oh. Yeah. I guess that's something I've never talked about."

"See? Do you still have the picture?"

He shook his head.

"What happened to it?"

Leo cursed as the car in front of them hit the brakes.

"I don't really know. That house was chaos — no one could keep anything. Every time I saved up a bunch of coins in a jar, someone would break into it and say they needed twenty bucks for a phone bill or something."

"You think the picture of your mom got sold down the river?"

"Pretty much."

There wasn't usually any traffic on this route. Unless there was a thunderstorm. Then the Volvos and Subarus piled up in hatchbacked bunches and every stand of trees looked like it could be home to the Headless Horseman. But today was clear after the recent rain, and the glut of vehicles on the county road made no sense.

"You really don't remember anything about her?"

"No, stop. You don't get to distract me with questions about mine. I asked you."

Saina tried. "It's true, I *don't* talk about her a lot. I don't know. There's not a lot to say." She searched for something. "A friend of mine, she lost her mom at around the same time, when she was thirteen. She said the only true thing I've ever heard anyone say about their mom dying. We were . . . I don't know, it's weird. I think we were laughing about something. We were trying to joke about it, because that's what nobody else ever does, right? And then she looked up at me, and said, 'That bitch just keeps on dying.'"

Leo laughed, a low, sardonic guff of it. "Mine, too. Fucking bitches."

Saina leaned over the gearshift and brushed her cheek against his shoulder, soft as a cat. Sometimes she forgot that Leo was an orphan. It was enough to make her cry. Or to make her want to have babies with him so that he'd have someone of his own, a little somebody who might have his big, sweet eyes, his crooked hairline, his easy smile. Leo had grown up looking only like himself, while Saina didn't just have a father who gestured and stood exactly like she did and memories of a mother and two infuriating, adorable siblings, she had a whole giant country, a billion potential family members to love and loathe and claim as her own because the Wang bloodlines were traceable backwards and forwards, if she cared to search them out. She nudged her head into his armpit, digging it against his soft plaid shirt, and said: "Come in."

He kissed the top of her head and they sat like that, quiet, idling at a red light, until Saina raised her eyebrows and Leo grinned in recognition and swerved down a side street just a few blocks from the warehouse where Bard's final MFA show would be held. Without speaking, they opened their doors and, half a second later, collided in the backseat.

"Can people see us?" asked Leo.

"Who cares?"

"The guy who could be mistaken for a rapist cares."

Saina swung one leg over him and ran her hands across his shoulders. "I think the consensual nature of our union is pretty clear." She tugged on his belt buckle.

"Do you remember the first time we kissed?"

She nodded, still struggling with his buckle. "At your place." Why did guys always belt themselves in so tightly? This must be what it was like to have no curves.

"Hey! I'm trying to be romantic here!" he said.

He swiped a knuckle over her lips and she caught it lightly between her teeth. Released it. "I'm just trying to get some. Boys are so sentimental."

"Oh yeah?" In one practiced move, he'd opened his jeans and thumbed her underwear aside.

"Yeah." She smiled down at him, feeling her lids flutter shut as he positioned her hips, the zipper of his jeans digging against her ass until they moved into each other.

One of the things Saina liked most about sex was that it made her *feel* sexy. As if she could see herself through the soft blur of a Vaseline-smeared lens, back arched, boudoir hair a fetching mess. A vintage *Playboy* version of sex. Smut with a smile.

She tried to pull him down onto the seat, but he shook his head. "Stay like this," he said, out of breath. "Just in case."

"Cops?"

"Five-o."

"Oh, you're tough now?" she teased.

He nodded and bounced her in his lap. "Do you think it'll always be like this?"

"In the backseat of a car? Probably."

"Illicit and open to misinterpretations."

"Exactly." They kissed, lips parted a little too wide in their haste to finish the deed, to cap the moment.

She could always tell when Leo was close. He made his surprised face and nudged at her so that she knew to slide up and snatch a crumpled T-shirt from the floor of the cab, positioning it under him just in time.

They rested against each other for a minute, and then she said, "What if you didn't have to pull out?"

"You want to go on the Pill?"

"No, no — I mean, you know, what if we gave one of these little guys a chance?"

"Are you . . . do you mean that? Are you serious?"

Saina thought for a minute. "We'd make some cute babies."

He nodded, wary. Lifted her over his lap and sat her down next to him. Patted down the skirt of her dress so that it fell correctly. Zipped up his jeans. Buckled himself into them. Draped a heavy arm around her, and said, "We'd better go — you're going to be late."

•   •   •

Leo was right, but that didn't make it any better. By the time they'd parked closer to the red warehouse and made their way towards the crowd, the ceremony had already begun. As they got closer, the weight of Leo's non-response started to grow, pulling her off-kilter, sinking the buzz she might have drawn from the waiting crowd, but also dulling her fear.

Someone Saina vaguely recognized was talking now, a woman in black-framed glasses, a fake mustache, and an asymmetrical haircut — a decade of Williamsburg trends distilled. The speaker tugged at the mustache and talked in metered verse about it being some sort of symbol of fidelity to the self, to the artist within. As she ended her allotted minute-long speech, she ripped it off and screamed, and the students all screamed with her. Internally, Saina rolled her eyes.

This wasn't like going back to her world, exactly. It was more of a purgatory. A series of simulacrums, promises being held out to these students of the lives that could be theirs. She saw now that she was here as an emissary from one of those lives, though not quite the same one as the woman with the fake 'stache, thank god. Her name was next on the program, so Saina stepped into place in front of the mic. Saina looked out at the audience. They were backlit, too. The warehouse had been transformed into a gallery for the end of the year show and light spilled out the open doors, casting all of their faces in shadow. It was still easy to pick out the parents. Even in repose, they hovered, nervous. The students were also nervous, but in a different sort of way. They tried harder to hide it, behind giant scarves and aggressively mismatched articles of clothing. They downed their wine steadily and draped themselves over one another, facing forward and paying attention to the speakers even as they stroked and scratched and pawed one another like genderless clumps of grown-up kittens, emanating an unfocused heat.

All these graduates had somehow paid around $100,000 to Become Artists. An extravagant ticket price that some people were brave enough or stupid enough to avoid. Would it work out for any of them? Would they get to be the people that they wanted to be? Out of Saina's class of twenty-six at Columbia, only a few were still making art in any serious way. It had only been seven years since graduation, but most of them were working as graphic designers or teachers. But maybe, for some of them, that was alright. Not everybody wanted a big life.

Behind her, someone coughed conspicuously.

Saina looked down at her cards, but everything written on them seemed blurry and useless.

Everyone in the audience looked up at her.

She looked out at them.

They kept on staring.

The depilated speaker stared, too, sympathetically.

The professors flanking the cheese table stared, less sympathetically.

Was the clock already ticking?

These poor kids who were, some of them, older than she was, but probably on the whole quite a bit poorer. Their parents were starting to look uncomfortable. This wasn't what they had paid for. Saina wondered how many of the students recognized her. If she didn't say a word, if she just stood up there for sixty full seconds without making a single sound, would there be reports of it on the Internet the next morning?

She remembered lifting a slat of the blind in her gallerist's second-floor office as angry women on Twenty-sixth Street picketed her *Look/Look* show. That moment had felt like this.

Grayson leaving her the first time, but not the second.

Her father's everything-is-gone phone call.

That bleak blank minute after she first entered her house in Helios.

All those moments where the bottom of the world drops away and we're left untethered, a cosmonaut lost in oxygenless space.

Behind her, the emcee didn't try to hide his panic. "Fifteen seconds, Saina, *fifteen seconds!*" he hissed.

Well. She might as well say something. "You don't need a whole speech or a performance from me. All I'm going to tell you is that if you're going to be artists, then you have to ask yourselves, do you rebuild the world or do you destroy it? That is the question."

She paused until she realized that she had more to say. "It's okay. There is no right answer. The world's agnostic. It's happy either way. What matters is that you ask yourself the question. That's it. Ask the question. Actually, no. That's not it. Figure out your own question. Figure out your own question and ask it."

She stopped, a little out of breath. Was Leo just scared of babies? Maybe thinking about having children was different if you were an orphan. What had she even said just now? Or maybe it was because they'd really only been together for a few months, and she'd already abandoned him once for Grayson, and, really, who knew what was going to happen? Oh yeah. Rebuild the world, destroy it.

"Okay," she said to the uncertain crowd. "Yep, that's it."

Inside the gallery, no one was talking to her. Even Leo was deep in conversation with someone else, a parent, judging by the polo shirt and pleated khakis. Someone was now serving pie to everyone on cracked china saucers. Somehow, this was their thesis project. Saina hated pie.

Her phone buzzed in the pocket of her jacket. It was Grace again. She had already called five times tonight, no doubt with some complaint about how weird Barbra was or how their dad kept trying to buy her ice cream sundaes like she was a little girl. Saina sent the call to voicemail again. Why couldn't Gracie just text like a normal teenager?

At the far end of the gallery, a woman in her thirties with a pink bob stood behind a life-size papier-mâché version of Lucy's advice stand from the *Peanuts* comic strip, busily slicing oranges and limes under a sign that read PROUST AND PIMM'S 5 CENTS. Saina watched as she dumped the pile of citrus into a giant pitcher, poured in a few liters of soda water, and unscrewed a bottle of Pimm's. Proust was, of course, represented by the pile of buttery madeleines her classmates were snatching off a platter as she shouted, "Five cents, guys, it's a practical exchange!"

Saina had seen projects like this in New York — hospitality art, she and her friends called it. The ButterBeen Collective, who talked their way into a pop-up sit-in at the New Museum, which just involved teaching knitting and serving cookies, or the Shum twins, who offered "residencies" to donut shops at their gallery in Chelsea. How many times did people have to prove that anything could be art before we could finally admit that very little was actually art?

Theoretically, Saina understood it. Art was engagement, art was simplicity, art was an outgrowth of its time, and they were living in a moment in which service jobs were the fastest growing sector of the economy, so it made sense that artists would want to examine the actions that made up those jobs. They were in a period of new domesticity, where women had begun caring about making their homes perfect again — as far as she was from being a suburban housewife, Saina knew that she couldn't deny her similarity to these women — and this was a valid way to critique the shift.

But, really, she couldn't get over the fact that this was as far as their ambitions reached. It all seemed so needlessly ladylike. "'I've made a very, very large meal, enough for multitudes, and I'd like you all to eat it with me! My creation satisfies your hunger.'"

"Do you want a bite?" Leo held out a fallen slice, a hunk of crust soaking in a puddle of blueberry ooze, topped with a miniature plastic fork. *Plastic.* This room had none of what she missed about her former existence. The openings full of wild things corralled into white-walled bunkers and set loose amid armies of perfectly polished stemware, row after row of wineglasses and champagne flutes that chimed against each other delicately, a rarefied twinkle that underscored every conversation. She missed the way the women dressed themselves like pieces of art — their clothes complex and not sexually attractive in an expected way, yet in the rewritten visual code of that world, all of those bubble dresses and harem pants and complicated muumuus became more desirable than some cinched-waist-boobs-out look.

In this blazing bright room full of hopeful graduates, she felt deflated. Saina shook her head at the pie. Leo shrugged and forked it up himself.

"Why are you even eating that? It's gross."

"I'm hungry. We got here too late for the cheese and stuff."

They'd never had a fight before. Leo had never been *annoying* before. She watched as his lips, glistening with a sheen of sugary blue syrup, mashed against themselves, chewing up the art pie. An hour and a half ago, those lips had been on her nipple.

"Why'd you get so weird?"

He stopped chewing and looked at her. "When?"

"You know, in the car."

"Let's not talk about that now."

"Why not? Who cares about these people?"

"I thought you did."

"Well, I don't."

They looked at each other, not speaking.

"Look," said Saina, "I know we just got back together. It's not that I'm dying to have a baby right now, okay? Don't worry."

"That's not it. I —"

"Are you worried about Grayson? Because that's over, you know. I'm here with *you*, not him."

"No, Saina, listen —"

"Hi, Saina Wang?" Winged eyeliner, tangled black hair, flowered baby-doll dress, and Doc Martens. Despite herself, Saina liked her.

"Hi." Saina offered a hand. The girl took it and squeezed it.

"Thanks, but I actually want to see your other hand."

She felt Leo suppress a laugh next to her. "What do you mean?"

"The ring! Sorry, I'm such a dork. *Vogue*'s like my bible. I read that story? The one about your engagement ring? I'm obsessed. Can I see it?"

Saina fluttered her empty left hand. "Sorry. It's kind of like the way you're never supposed to knit a guy a sweater or get your girlfriend's name tattooed on your arm. Never let *Vogue* do a story on your ring. We're not engaged anymore."

"No! Are you serious? No! But you guys were, like, royalty. Was he a dick? Do we hate him?"

"It's fine. Really."

It was strange to think of herself as someone who might be speculated about, but back in college she had been just as breathless over the details of her professors' lives, of the lives of the already successful artists who had graduated just a few years before, thinking mistakenly that knowing was the same as belonging.

They turned away from the girl's disappointed face and ran straight into Saina's friend Gharev, the program head who had invited her to speak. He wedged himself between the two of them and clasped Saina in a hug. He pulled back, hands gripping her shoulders, and shook her enthusiastically. "Brilliant! You were brilliant! Amazing time play. Empathetic anxiety! The anxiety of influence! Oh, you had me sweating bullets!" He paused to pluck a plastic glass of half-drunk wine from a table nearby. Saina was pretty sure it wasn't his. Swirling it, he sipped. "This wine is shit! Next time I see you, you'll come to my place in Red Hook, I'll pour you something good. I just got a case of Zin from one of those bonkers new biody-namic vineyards where they have to bury a ram's horn at midnight — you know Zin's back, right? It's amazing. Smooth. Like velvet! Like tits! Velvet tits!"

"Who is this guy? I love this guy!" Leo clapped Gharev on the shoulder of his sleek black jacket, laughing. "Look at him. He's like a CIA operative."

"Oh my god." Saina dropped her voice. "Gharev. Are you rolling?" His pupils were huge and he still hadn't let go of her arm.

Gharev grinned. "Just high on life, baby, high on life." Across the room, a student beckoned him. As he started moving, he shouted back at them. "We did get some real coffee, though." He waved vaguely towards a side room, where two bearded men in bow ties and heavy canvas aprons were pouring slow streams of steaming water through glass funnels balanced on a wooden board. "It's amazing! It has a nose!"

Saina and Leo looked at each other, laughing.

"It has a nose!" she said, tweaking his.

Leo swirled an imaginary glass of wine, lifting it up and sucking air through his teeth. "Ah, complex. There's a brashness, but under that do I detect a hint of . . . wistfulness? Yes, a supple wistfulness with notes of cay-enne and joy. And Band-Aids."

"Oh, I love it when they say that things taste like Band-Aids."

"And dirt. Though, to be fair, a lot of things do taste like dirt, in a pretty good way."

"You're such a farmer," she said, smiling at him. "I'm still mad at you, though. But we can talk about it later."

He brought her hand up to his lips and kissed it once, twice, three times.

She downed the last inch of her mediocre wine. *Whee!* She was a little bit drunk.

The problem with her, with her friends, was that there was nothing really *serious* to worry about. No war. No famine. The world might be filled with catastrophes, but none were poised to intrude in their lucky lives. The concerns of her father's generation were so much more vital. More global. Saina and her friends might travel the world, but no one lived or died on what they did — having an art gallery in Berlin was not the same as fighting an army of Communists.

Worrying, Saina realized, was a luxury in itself. The luxury of purpose.

A life predicated on survival might have been a better life in so many ways. Who cared about artistic fulfillment when your main concern was finding enough food to eat? And, Saina was positive, she would have excelled at finding enough food to eat, no matter what the environment. The hallmarks of twenty-first-century success, at least in her world, were all so abstract. Be a *Simpsons* character! Give a TED talk! Option your life story!

Each time she thought she'd achieved it, the center slipped away and some other gorgeous abstraction became the only thing to want.

三十六

New Orleans, LA

WHEN THEY drove off from the diner leaving his father and Barbra and Nash standing there in the street, Andrew was all exhilaration, which lasted as long as it took to turn the corner. Faced with an empty street, he felt confused again, ragged and unsure. Next to him, Dorrie's lips curled up in a long, slow smile. He couldn't see her eyes behind her dark sunglasses, but he knew that she was looking at the road, and not at him.

"So what are we going to do now?" he asked. "Am I just going to live with you?"

Dorrie lifted an arm to wave at some tourists in a passing streetcar who had lifted their cell phones to photograph her car, her hair whipping around her face. Finally, finally, she turned and looked at him through her opaque lenses. "Let's not think about that," she said, smiling again.

And so he hadn't. For a while, it wasn't hard. Being with Dorrie meant always being in motion. Forty-eight hours sped by like a joyous montage from some romantic comedy that he wanted to watch as much as the next girl.

Dorrie, leading him by the hand into a tiny cobblestoned courtyard set with battered turquoise tables and cane chairs. Dorrie, tearing apart the long baguette in front of them, slathering each piece with soft pale-yellow butter and feeding it to him, kissing his lips as he chewed. Dorrie, insisting that he drink his coffee black, then finally relenting and pouring in a long ribbon of cream and then adding two, three, four rough cubes of sugar, letting him feed her a spoonful of the crunchy,

bittersweet dregs at the bottom. Him, following her out of the courtyard, eyes full with the delicious view of her bare thighs patterned from
the woven seat.

Him, leaning back after having sex for the third time ever, head sinking in her plush pillows, thrilled that he'd gotten to watch her back
arch and eyes flutter closed. Her, picking up an abandoned goblet of
wine and taking a sip, leaning over to dribble a blood-red stream from
her mouth into his. Them, again.

Dorrie, slipping past the concierge at Hotel Monteleone with a
wink, taking a twenty-dollar bill out of Andrew's wallet and handing it
to the attendant who brought them a pile of towels. Dorrie, napping in
the shade by the side of the rooftop pool, a smile on her face, not even
waking up when her arm dropped off the green chaise and her long,
thin fingers touched the concrete. Him, listening as she breathed, wondering if maybe this was the beginning of things.

Him, standing on the balcony of a double-gallery house holding
something in a martini glass, leaning down so that Dorrie could whisper into his ear. The Democratic nominee speaking on the slice of big
screen visible through the window, his right arm a metronome. Dorrie, turning and laughing, red-rimmed lips wide open, as the host of
the party tugged an Obama T-shirt over his suit. Everyone, getting
drunker. Him, sitting alone on the couch, surrounded by party debris,
reaching up and letting Dorrie pull him out of the house and into the
night.

And then the shiny pop soundtrack screeched to a halt. Andrew
opened his eyes. Oh, it was bright. The world was too bright. And hot.
He kicked off the blanket and groaned, rolling towards Dorrie.

"Good morning."

She looked at him. She was sitting in bed with a platter of fruit and a
newspaper. Freckled fingers picked up a section of kiwi and put it in her
mouth.

"You just passed out last night. That wasn't very nice, was it? Doesn't
make a woman feel very desirable."

Andrew closed his eyes again. Groaned. Rolled back over. Why was
this happening?

"I'm sorry, I'm sorry."

He heard the clatter of a plate on the side table and then a second later Dorrie was straddling him, her tiny nipples pushing against her ribbed wifebeater, the rest of her in a pair of little-boy underwear. On the bureau behind her, Andrew could see framed photos. There were a few of Dorrie and a nearly identical brother — he was ten years gone, dead of an overdose — and one old-fashioned wedding photo. The rest were all Dorrie in a bandanna and T-shirt surrounded by black and brown children with huge white grins, all of them framed by concrete huts and actual grass shacks.

She cocked her head, still looking at him.

"You're beautiful," he said.

"No, I'm not. But I am extremely sexy."

Andrew laughed. Shook his head.

"No, you are, you *are!* You're gorgeous."

She reached over and picked up a strawberry. Pulled the top off. Flicked it at him and popped the berry in her own mouth. Andrew scooped up the wet blob of fruit and put it on the nightstand.

Dorrie reached over again and picked up a banana.

"You're not hungover at all?"

She shook her head. He tried again.

"Do you think Barack Obama has a chance? Could he really win? That would be pretty amazing, right?"

Dorrie nodded and peeled the banana in three swift strokes, dropping the skin on his chest. Suddenly, he was scared. There was a queasy undercurrent of not-rightness to the whole thing that swelled up like a hot air balloon inside of him.

She held the pale fruit aloft like a dagger, squeezing so that its flesh oozed out between her fingers and sent a low, nauseous perfume into the room.

"Honey, I just want to jam this down your throat," she said, sweetly.

Her other hand was on his shoulder, holding herself steady, holding him down.

"Dorrie?"

"Mm-hm?"

"Why did you like me? At the wedding? What made you like me?"

Disdain. Anger. Fear? She was hard to read.

Andrew laughed, uncomfortable. "I mean, besides my devastating good looks."

She lowered the banana slowly. Dropped it and smeared the mush of it on her bedspread.

"That's gross."

Dorrie's eyes weren't olive anymore. Now they were blue. An icy blue so pale that it made her look almost blind. Why wasn't she saying anything?

"Seriously, why?"

Still nothing.

Andrew tried again. "I know why I liked you."

"Oh yeah?"

"Yeah. You're different. I mean, I know that sounds kind of shallow, but it's true. You're . . ." How could he tell her that she was not the kind of girl he ever would have met at college? There probably weren't even any *guys* like her at college. You were supposed to see the world when you were young, right? Well, Dorrie was definitely the world. She was an adventure. Did girls like it when they were called adventures? He wasn't sure.

"I'm what?"

The photos in their frames behind her caught his eye again. "I wouldn't have guessed that you were such a do-gooder."

She glanced back. Shrugged. "It was a phase. I'm a lot more utilitarian now."

"What does that mean?"

"Have you studied Malthusian theory yet?"

"No."

"It's okay, you don't need to. It's brutal and misinformed. But on a much lesser level, I kind of believe in it now. If your village needs a white person to come in and teach you how to dig a well, maybe you don't deserve to last another generation."

"So why all the pictures?"

"I'm a sucker for cute kids."

Andrew shook his head. "I have to warn you, I'm not very good with snark."

He laughed encouragingly, but she didn't respond. Oh god, why had he said that? That was so stupid. What was snark, anyway?

And then, in a half second, no warning at all, she stuck her banana-glopped fingers in his mouth and flopped down on top of him, nestling her head in next to his ear.

"Do you like it?"

Well, he didn't *not* like it. Andrew sucked dutifully, moving his tongue along the tips of her fingers. Dorrie wriggled on top of him, grinding her hips into his.

"Wait," said Andrew, struggling to push her off. "You didn't answer my question."

She sat up again.

"Seriously, why?"

Andrew didn't even know why he kept asking. He usually just let stuff like that go, but if she couldn't tell him, well, if she couldn't tell him, then she couldn't possibly be in love with him, right?

"Dorrie?"

Nothing.

"Well?"

Nothing.

"This isn't really good for my self-esteem here. Nothing?"

Nothing.

Until "Turn over and I'll show you."

"What? What's that supposed to mean?"

She bared her teeth at him, and then, tender, soft, she reached over and tucked a strand of hair behind his ear, brushing his cheek with her knuckles as she drew her hand away.

"I don't like this anymore." He didn't even know that those words were going to come out of him, but once he said them, they were truer than anything else he could have said.

"Aww, honey, what do you mean? We're having fun here."

"No." Andrew shrugged her off. She was so light, actually. There was so little to her. "I'm not having fun. I thought you —"

"You thought I *loved* you?"

"Yes!" No. No, he hadn't. He never thought it, but in trying to convince himself that it wasn't necessary, he'd hoped it, and that was almost as true.

"Oh come on, you're young, but you're not a baby. You can't possibly think that love works like that. You wanted to fuck and I gave you an excuse."

"No!" Andrew flung his legs off the bed and then stood up. "I didn't! I mean, I did, but not like that! I explained it!"

He had to leave. What was he doing here with this stranger? He started picking up his clothes and shoving them back in his duffel.

"Andrew! You don't have to go."

"I'm not handcuffed anymore, so . . ."

There. He could be sarcastic, too. Or ironic. Or whatever.

He continued packing up, going to the bathroom to retrieve his toothbrush and moisturizer, unplugging the cord of his cell phone and winding it up carefully before he looked in her direction. Sitting there on the bed, eyes wide, skin luminescent, she was perfection. He could put down his bag and just stay. She'd love him eventually.

"You're really leaving?"

"Unless . . ."

If she just said one nice thing, just made one gesture towards him, just showed him *something,* he would stay.

"No means no, Andrew."

He and his giant duffel barely fit through the warren of narrow hallways in Dorrie's house. Which entryway had she used? Each door he tried was nailed shut in order to keep tourists from stumbling into her quarters. Finally, one of them gave way and he shoved through it, falling into a quartet of ladies in red hats and crazy purple dresses huddled over one of the pamphlets that talked about Dorrie's family and how they made their money and beautified the city.

"What! Who are you? What's this?" said the smallest one.

"Sorry, sorry sorry." He checked to make sure no one was injured and then took off down the hallway. He could still hear them as he ran. "We should make sure he's not a thief! Oh dear, could he be a thief? Perhaps we ought to chase him! Chase him? Lilly wants to chase a boy! Or maybe someone's chasing him! Oh, ladies, make sure you all have your purses."

By the time he made his way down the circular staircase, they were all gathered at the top, peering down at him.

"I didn't take anything!" he shouted back up. They looked so worried in their ridiculous hats that he laughed. "It's okay! Have a good tour!"

The curved doors were propped open, and the Louisiana sky outside was a bright blue. Andrew started running down the long driveway of Dorrie's estate, but halfway through, a little out of breath, he stopped. The ladies were wrong. He wasn't running from anything. Dorrie wasn't going to chase him. And he wasn't running to anything either.

God, had she really said, "No means no?" Andrew wondered if she'd meant to make a joke. Maybe? It was too bad, really, that she'd never gotten to see him really deliver a set. They'd spent almost three days together without doing much of anything. He hadn't even done any writing since Austin, and according to Jerry Seinfeld, you were supposed to write material every single day. Andrew tried to. Or, at least, he tried to try to. He'd heard somewhere that you needed to have half an hour of material before you could be considered a real comic. Right now he had the seven minutes he'd done at school, and the seven that didn't go over so great in Austin, and another seven that he was ready to try out, and seven more that he should have been working on all along.

This driveway was endless. It was some grand, plantation shit. Could you make plantation jokes? Should he? It was easy to joke about offensive Asian things, but taking on slavery seemed a little advanced.

Andrew thought of the first time that Emma had come up to his room. She'd looked at the posters on his wall and, straight to Richard Pryor's face, said, "Stand-up comedy is just so *annoying,* isn't it?" That had been hard to shake, but later it made him think. What if he took every single thing that was annoying about people trying to be funny and worked it into one giant, hairy superball of a joke? Not comedy clichés, just normal people stuff. He'd left those notes stuffed into the side pocket of the car, but he still remembered most of it.

1: Hey, Carl?
2: That's my name, don't wear it out.
1: Can I borrow a pen?
2: That'll be a hundred bucks.

1: Ha ha, thanks. Do you spell your name with a *C* or a *K*?

2: I could tell you, but I'd have to kill you.

1: That'd be kind of drastic, don't you think? You'd probably get
   sent away.

2: Don't drop the soap, amiright? Huh? Huh?

Total gold. It was kind of hard to be two characters, but the routine worked better that way. The key was to keep it going until it was almost not funny anymore, and then it would be incredibly funny. Andrew headed back towards the city as he ran through other possibilities in his head. He's smoking crack! Make that sound again! Oh, you don't know the price? It must be free!

Oh, it would be horrible and irritating and brilliant. It wasn't the sort of thing that his dad would be into, but Andrew's friends would probably love it. Maybe he should start shooting videos of himself doing stand-up and put it on YouTube. Who needed a girlfriend when he had this, the trying and the promise?

In his luckiest childhood moments, Andrew had been able to make his mother laugh. It wasn't something she did on her own. When his father came home early enough for dinner, she'd always start the meal off serving him awkward, hopeful heaps of food, then lapse into a quick silence that Andrew feared more than anything else as a little kid. Her nervousness thrummed out at him and underlined his own fear that even this semblance of closeness would be broken. Sometimes, though, he could make them all laugh — his mother, his father, and teenage Saina, too — laugh until the tension between his parents popped loose and they could just be together like he wanted.

Being homeless was really boring. That was probably why homeless people spent all the money they panhandled on cheap highs — how else would they get through the days? When you had a home, hours passed magically, spent on just being. Sitting on your couch. Straightening things on your coffee table. Stroking your luxurious piles of toilet paper like a basket of soft little kittens. Adrift like this, Andrew found himself vacillating between an unimportant A and a nonsensical B for useless swaths of time that felt like forever but turned out to be minutes: Walk to the St. Louis

Cemetery so that he could see the Superdome on the way, or spend $1.25 on the bus so that he would get there in time for the free tour of the voo-doo queen's grave? Trust the guy sitting next to him at the coffee shop or lug his giant duffel into the bathroom? Eat now or wait until later, so that he would have something to do at the twenty-four-hour diner where he was planning to spend the night?

He hadn't really slept since leaving Dorrie's house. Last night he'd tried to make it through the uncertain time between midnight and sunrise at a weird twenty-four-hour bar with a Laundromat in back, but he'd fallen asleep against one of the dryers and woken up to his beer spilled across the floor and a shiny black boot tapping his cheek. Back on the menacing, jasmine-scented streets, Andrew tried to talk himself into sleeping tucked into a corner somewhere, but in the end, he'd stumbled across the Café du Monde, where all the waiters surprised him by being Asian, and waited out the night eating beignets very, very slowly — beignets that he thought were not quite as good as the ones at Downtown Disney's Jazz Café — a shot of fear running through him every time he saw a flash of red hair.

Time was endless, yet it also slipped away without borders or edges. It was hard to remember what day of the week it was when the ground under your feet was constantly shifting. America usually felt like iPhones and pizza and swimming pools to Andrew. L.A. was America. New sneak-ers. Sunshine. Pot and blue balls. Phoenix was America. Sprinklers and blow jobs and riding shotgun. Vegas was America, all of it. But if there were monsters and magic anywhere in this country, they would be here in New Orleans. New Orleans was an ancient doppelgänger city that grew in some other America that never really existed. Dorrie belonged here. He didn't. He didn't, but he was going to stay until tomorrow anyway be-cause yesterday he'd picked up a free paper and found a listing for an open mic. Right now he was holding out for Wednesday at eight thirty p.m., when he could finally sign up and do the material that had knocked him off the stage at that midnight cabaret. Once that was done, he'd decide what to do next.

Andrew knew it was probably kind of offensive to think of himself as homeless. He could stay with Nash, but he didn't want to because then

Dorrie would know where he was. He could ask Saina for money. He could ask Fred or Tak or even Mac McSpaley, any one of those guys would probably PayPal him a hundred bucks. But he wasn't ready to do that yet, so all he had right now was what was left of the $250 he'd gotten from poor Mac for his TV. Not bad, but not really enough for hotels. If this was an '80s movie or an episode of a Nickelodeon show, there would be a $5,000 prize for the open mic and he'd win it with a comedy routine instead of a song and it would be magically enough to buy everything back for his dad. Why couldn't life have clearer trajectories?

He'd win it anyway. Even without a prize, he'd win it.

Church bells, always in the distance, rang out again as they had done every hour that he'd been in this city. A gust of heat and sugar and fried dough hit him as he leaned his head into the donut shop.

"Sorry! Um, can you tell me which way is downriver?" The woman behind the counter stared at him. Blinked. Tapped the glass with her long silver nails.

What the fuck? The donuts in here were purple. All of them. Row upon delicious row of purple-glazed confections glistening behind glass. Andrew stepped in.

"Also, can I just say that this is some excellent donut styling? All the cool donuts are wearing purple this season."

She extended a talon and pushed up her glasses. "Where you trying to get to again?"

"Just any stop on the 39 line. Someone gave me directions, but he walked away before I realized that I didn't understand them at all."

"You are downriver already. You're in Bywater, so you'll want to take the 88 past the bend to the 39."

"Man, what do you guys have against north, south, east, west?"

She adjusted a donut that was imperceptibly out of place.

"Okay, well, thank you. That was really helpful. And I really do like your place." He held the woman's gaze, eyes smiling, until his emotional sonar picked up a reciprocal ping from her. There. If he was the one writing definitions, that's what he would call love. It was just hard to keep up that same feeling with someone once you got to know them.

"Oh, and one of the donuts, please."

"That'll be ninety-nine cents."

He nudged himself into her gaze again as she passed back a penny and a donut, and this time she was already open. People, Andrew knew, just wanted to be seen. And, though he felt like an asshole if he thought about it too much, he was pretty sure that people liked being seen by him. It was almost like a public service. The thought made him cringe as much as it made him puff up virtuously, but it was true — he did it because every interaction could have some sort of meaning, because he liked the moments of connection, but also because freshman year of college he and his roommate, Fred, were walking out of Quiznos, and Fred said, "Every time, man!"

"What?"

"You're, like, a flirt, but with everyone!"

"What do you mean? There weren't even any girls in there."

"No, the old dude behind the counter."

"What? What are you saying?"

"I don't know, man. You do this thing. It's like . . . unsexy flirting."

"So you're saying I was trying to mack on a grandpa and not even being smooth about it? Cool. Thanks."

"You know what I mean — you do it with everyone. It's okay, they love it."

And he did know. Up until then, though, Andrew had thought that he was doing it for himself, that he was the only one who needed to be seen. But once Fred pointed it out, he became aware of how much credit he got just for not being terrible. It's not that he was flirting, unless flirting was just about wanting to really *see* someone. People thought that someone like him — good-looking, young, cool clothes — was going to be dismissive, and when he wasn't, when he was just easy and open with them, they glowed. It was a feeling he tried to re-create a hundred times a day, in every interaction. It also calmed him. If he looked at someone and they looked at him and there was a true connection, no matter how brief, then it meant that he didn't need to replay the encounter anxiously afterwards, trying to find where it had all gone wrong.

Shifting his duffel onto his other shoulder, Andrew pulled the donut out of its crinkly white bag and headed in the direction that she'd pointed. Mmm. Why was everyone always going gluten-free when there were donuts in the world? He bit into a greasy edge with thick globs of icing. It was a little disappointing that it didn't taste more purple, but sugar was sugar. One, two, three bites, and done.

Days were confusing when you spent half the night awake. Andrew balanced his bag carefully on the tops of his shoes, one arm still looped through the strap so that it wouldn't touch the gas-station bathroom floor and squeezed his travel-size tube of toothpaste, flattening it to force out the last drib of minty freshness.

It smelled like shit in here. Literal shit. He'd been breathing through his mouth, trying not to think of the little fecal particles he was letting in, but it was really hard to brush your teeth that way. He probably looked like shit, too. The gas station didn't even have a real mirror, just a banged-up sheet of metal screwed into the wall, some inept graffiti keyed onto the surface.

To make the act work, he had to change into a pair of sweats. He pulled his Vans out and placed them on the floor, then set another pair of shoes next to them and carefully laid his bag across all four sneakers. Next, he slipped out of his shoes and stepped on top of them in his socks, balancing on first one foot and then the other as he eased his jeans off. Folded them. Tucked them into his bag. Then, bunching up the legs of the sweats so that they wouldn't puddle onto the floor, he poked his toes through each leg and pulled them up.

Pushing through the fluorescent-lit single aisle of the gas station's convenience store and out into the damp night, he still felt hazy, disconnected from himself. He'd spent the loose hours of the afternoon sitting in back of an olive green streetcar, riding the line from terminus to terminus and back again, watching as the sky turned a misty dark blue before he finally hopped off. Now Andrew crossed the street, walking past a dry cleaner and a couple of small houses. The green awning of the bar was covered with beer names — Bass, Carlsberg, Harp — and a couple of guys stood under it smoking. On the other side of the street, a power plant hummed. He felt like a greaseball, dirty and unshowered, dragging along a bag that was too big and too expensive-looking for this place.

After signing up, he still had half an hour to kill. He should have been excited, sitting there in that wood-paneled bar, a whiskey and Coke in

front of him, waiting to go onstage. Instead, he was lonely. The thirty
long minutes felt like a weight. One extended sip through that skinny
red straw and his drink was gone. All the guys around him — and it was
mostly guys — they looked like people he might be friends with except
they wore really lame T-shirts and they weren't actually his friends.

Maybe this was depression. Tak took Prozac and went to a therapist.
They'd talked about it once. Andrew rolled his eyes at himself. Was two
days of being homeless really all it took to knock him off-kilter? He ordered another drink.

By the time the emcee finally called his name, drawling it out so that
it seemed to go on forever, an endless lazy *a* sound, Andrew had already
toggled his mental state back and forth between boredom and anxiety
and anticipation at least half a dozen times. He'd practiced the last minute of this set over and over in front of the full-length mirror in his dorm,
so even the uncertainty of working with props wasn't enough to keep him
nervous and keyed up. But he was a professional. He'd leave it all on the
stage.

"Yo, is that you?" the guy next to him asked.

"Yep."

"Good luck, man." Andrew checked his pocket to make sure everything was in place, downed the last of his drink, and ran up the narrow
room just as the emcee ribbed him. "Ain't nothing funny about taking
your time, alright!"

Andrew catapulted himself onstage and shook the emcee's hand before
turning around to look out at the room. LSU frat boys, townies, and tourists. He spread his arms out.

"So, I'm Asian. Mm-hm. Yeah."

There were a couple cheers as he turned his head right and left, showing his profile.

"Yep. One hundred percent Asian. I know you want to know what
kind. Because people always say they can't tell the difference between
Asians, right? And that goes all ways. Like, you can't tell the difference
between particular Asians, and you also can't tell the difference between
different types of Asians. You *know* right now you're all thinking, *Is he
kimchee and born-again Christian, or is he sushi and octopus porn?*"

He leaned in and whispered, "*Oh, or is he that guy I used to work with?*

That real quiet one in the IT department with the Hello Kitty license plate frame?" Straightened up. "Except you don't say any of it out loud because you *know* that thinking all Asians look alike is one of those stereotypes that's supposed to be super offensive, right?"

He was starting to feel like himself again. This was different from the club in Texas, where Barbra had seen him bomb. These people were laughing. Who could say why? He saw a guy shush his girlfriend when she leaned over to whisper something. *Yes.* He pumped a mental fist and then stepped a little to the left, turned, and said, in a John-Wayne-as-frat-boy voice that sailed out of him, booming and false, "So, hey, bro, you Korean or you Chinese?"

Stepped back to the right, turned, mimed a super-offended, border-line effeminate gasp and immediately hated himself for it. Still, he pivoted forward to face the audience. "I'll tell you a secret . . . we can't tell the difference either." He pointed to an Asian guy in the crowd who luckily hadn't moved since Andrew had first spotted him. "You, you could be a real cool-looking Chinese guy or a real dorky Japanese guy. I mean, I really can't tell. 'Cause, dudes, honestly, we do all kind of look alike." Thank god that got almost as big of a laugh as he'd thought it would, which buoyed him, making him talk even more expansively. "Oh, by the way, I'm Chinese, so just think, like, dumplings and human rights abuses."

"But you know who else I can't tell the difference between? White people." He glanced at a few of the white people in the audience, half hoping that they would look upset. "I mean, first of all, British, Irish, Scottish? Uh, whatevs. Who knows. Oh, and British people, yeah, you don't look all that different from Germans. Sorry, dudes, y'all both white. Oh, and you all-American white Republicans? Um, yeah. Your average Texan and your average Frenchman? You both wear high-waisted pants and have butter-based diets. Not that different. Sorry, haters. But let's talk about the particular, because you guys are all sitting there thinking, *Oh no, unh-unh, no way, we might be all 'American' but I do not look like this loser on my left, and I definitely don't look like that mouth-breathing scab in front of me.*" Air quotes. What the fuck was wrong with him?

Crowd work. Crowd work. A good stand-up does good crowd work. Andrew held out a hand towards a white guy with a Nirvana T-shirt and light brown hair that hung to his shoulders. "You, grunge boy, nodding

down there. That's what you think, right? Weeeell . . . the only difference
I see is that you've got a Nirvana shirt on, and that equally brown-haired
guy next to you has a Pearl Jam shirt, so you're probably a little cooler."
Okay, that didn't make much sense, but the important thing was to try.
And out in the audience, someone shouted back, gratifyingly, "Cobain
rules!"

"By the way, white people, that's how we tell the males in your species
apart — by hair color. It's kind of like with cats or horses, you know? 'Oh,
Dave? Yeah, he's okay, he's just a tabby, dime a dozen. Eh, kind of a sloppy
drunk . . . Brian? Yeah, yeah, that guy's cool, he's a palomino. Real nice
coat. Shiny. Yo, a little tip: Try to get him on your team when you're playing Trivial Pursuit. Man, that guy knows *everything* about the '80s. Dec-
lan? Oh, he's real weird, but kind of beautiful, not in a gay way or anything, man. It's just, he's a tortoiseshell, and he's got these white paws and
these yellow eyes that just look through you, man, like he *knows* something . . .'"

People were laughing, but he felt the false note in his voice and tried to
center it, to take away the performance aspect of it.

"But you know what I think? You know what I really think? Alright,
join hands everybody, join hands, this is a real kumbaya moment. Guess
what? We *all* all look alike. Every single one of us."

It was still there, a hamminess that had come out of nowhere. Here
he was, swaying theatrically, kumbayaing all over the place. Maybe it was
because he hadn't really eaten anything besides donuts before drinking
those whiskey and Cokes, and these lights were bringing out his claustro-
phobia. Flashing forward to the rest of his act, Andrew felt a sudden emp-
tiness. It wasn't that different from what he'd said already. It was all Asian
shit, and it wasn't even his best stuff. What was he doing here anyway?

He looked out at the crowd, their faces turned towards him, waiting,
and said, without thinking, "Hey. Have you guys ever had everything in
your life change? Like, just everything? Maybe? Anybody?" He waited,
hoping that someone would respond. What the hell was he going to say?

Just say everything.

Everything?

Sure. Why not? He'd never see these people again. Everything.

"Like, whatever you think you are just flips the script and you're left reaching around like an idiot, trying to grab at something familiar, because all you want is some . . . I don't know . . . some certainty?" A couple of guys in the front row were nodding. Heartened, he went on.

"You know, you're like, 'Oh, my father's not the man I thought he was, but . . . at least I still love Cool Ranch Doritos!' Or 'My girlfriend just dumped me because I didn't want to give it up to her, but, hey, I still drive a sick car!' Or 'Oh shit, my sick car just got repossessed but at least I've still got all my college buds.' Or, you know, 'Oh hey, I've been yanked out of college and my family's bankrupt and I'm in the middle of a crazy cross-country road trip in my dead mom's car because my dad might be delusional and my sister might be a whore and who the fuck knows about my crazy little stepmother and believe it or not I was a virgin up until two days ago and I just lost it to, like, a thirty-five-year-old who I told myself I was in love with but that's over and I'm stranded in the weird-ass city and how the fuck is this my life now but, oh yeah, I can still, like, recite the Gettysburg Address so I guess I'm still me, right?'

"Yeah, here's how the Gettysburg Address goes: Four score and seven years ago our forefathers said good fucking luck."

Andrew breathed. *Oh shit.* This was why people loved being onstage. It wasn't the applause; it was the honesty. He'd always thought of himself as an honest person, but he saw now that he wasn't, entirely.

A girl in the audience dressed in a horrible purple pantsuit whooped — she whooped for him! — and he thought of the woman in the donut shop, of her nails and her donut icing and of their connection. It was almost easier to open up to people he'd never see again. He plunged ahead.

"But here's the thing. Here's the shit of it. Here's the bottom-down deep truth of it. I think maybe none of that matters. Like, not the Cool Ranch Doritos part, and not the losing my car part, and not even the losing my virginity part." Even as he said it, he knew that wasn't quite true.

"Well, shit. Okay. The virginity part matters. As much I tried to front like it was cool and I didn't care because it wasn't like no one wanted to sleep with me, I really do feel kind of relieved now. Even though it didn't happen the way I thought it would — and really, what does in life? — at least it *happened* and I can move on and stop being so self-conscious about it all." An absurd thought struck him. "Yo, I can start flying Virgin again! I've been avoiding them for years, even though they're clearly the best airline, because I just couldn't face the thought of anyone seeing me standing under that Virgin sign." That actually was true. "And drinking virgin daiquiris. I weep when I think of all the frosty blended drinks I've denied myself." And so was that. Andrew almost couldn't believe these things were actually making people laugh. "Oh man, you know what? I can finally watch *The Virgin Suicides*! That matters, right? Right? I didn't even want to read the book!" A table of awkwardly matched friends just offstage all laughed uproariously at that, and Andrew felt a surge of love for them, and then for everyone in the bar, and then outward until he wanted to wrap his arms around the entire city of New Orleans. "Okay, seriously though, losing my virginity matters to me, but I think maybe the only thing that really matters, like in a 'the universe and everything in it' kind of way, is the connection you make with another person, whatever your relationship is with them.

"So, me and you here. You know, me up here and all hundred of you down there. Alright, eighty. Seventy-five. Whatever. Yeah, all forty of you, I see you. I SEE YOU. I. Fucking. See. You. Do you see me? Because I see every single one of you even if you're hiding behind the lardass in front of you. And that's all we want, right? Just that? I SEE you. I feel you. I know you. And now that I'm done with being a virgin I'd fuck every single one of you if I could and it would be tender and it would be beautiful. Yeah. That's right. I'm not ashamed. That's what I said. I would fuck you with my heart, and it would be tender, and it would be beautiful."

The words had just rolled out, unstoppable, and he meant every one of them. Now the clock over the DJ booth was flashing down at him. It was showing negative numbers, giant and red, counting him further and further into debt to these people who had given him their attention, and so he smiled and raised the microphone — because what else was there left to say? — and the emcee came back onstage, clapping, clapping, clapping for him.

三十七

High Point, NC

THE COPS DROVE weird cars here. Or maybe they weren't weird; maybe they were exactly what North Carolina cops should be driving. Cars for muscleheads, silver gray, with a black racing stripe, the kind of thing that would zoom in front of you as soon as the light turned green, a douche like Johnny Delahari at the wheel. The cops themselves, though, seemed pretty much just like cops in L.A. and Santa Barbara. Tough but not tough, standing around with their walkie-talkies going off and not really doing anything. God, all they'd done since getting there was block off a lane of traffic with their dick cars and set up a ring of those flame sticks. Grace held her breath for a second. Smoke, sharp and sulfurous, crept up her nostrils, itching the inside of her brain and casting shadows on the wreck of their poor car.

Their poor, poor car.

Its nose was bashed in, its windshield was shattered, and all four of its tires had exploded, making it look like it was sinking into the asphalt. It had rotated around completely so that its nose was pointing at oncoming traffic. She could see her collapsed suitcase through the half-open back door.

Grace felt dazed. Maybe they'd all crawled out of that car seconds ago, maybe it had been hours. Maybe they'd been waiting on the side of the highway forever, and they'd never do anything else with their lives. When everything had finally stopped spinning, Grace pulled on the door handle and it swung open, too easy. Surprised, escape the only thing in her mind, she'd fallen right out on the side of the highway, a pile of battered limbs.

The world ended, and then it didn't.

Now her elbow oozed blood, and she had a scratch on her face that she was pretty sure she'd made with her own torn fingernail. Her father held an ice pack against his blackening eye, and his shirt was ripped along the back. Barbra had it the worst — the paramedics had cleaned and bandaged a long, ugly cut along her shoulder and a constellation of little scratches across her face and chest.

"Tell me the truth," her father had demanded. "Are we okay? Nothing so bad? Everyone okay?" And they'd finally nodded even though the paramedics had wanted to bring all three of them straight to the hospital. But Grace wouldn't leave without the picture of her mother, her dad wouldn't leave without trying to salvage their luggage, the police wouldn't let them back into the car until they were sure it wasn't going to blow up, and Barbra wouldn't go alone, so they were all just still there in the middle of a middle-of-nowhere highway.

On either side of Grace, several feet apart, Barbra and her father leaned against the highway divider, not talking. Grace stretched her bare legs out in front of her. They were still shaking and would probably bruise and look trashy, but she didn't even care. She pulled them in again, laying her head on her knees.

After the paramedics had checked them out and treated all of their scrapes and wounds, they had gathered in a huddle away from the police, laughing over something. After a while, one of the paramedics walked towards her. As he got closer, he shook out the rough woolen blanket that he was carrying in his hands and draped it over her shoulders without even asking if she wanted it. He massaged across her neck with cold, sneaky fingers as he arranged the blanket, murmuring, "It's okay, you're safe, you're going to be okay," over and over, quiet and low. Grace wondered vaguely if her father was watching and what he might think.

Even though she knew it was gross, the attention had felt almost reassuring until he'd pulled back, and said, "So, where are you from?"

"L.A.," she'd answered, knowing what was coming next.

"No, but where are you *from* from?"

She'd stared, her mind still half caught in the accident itself, not quite believing that it was over.

"Like, are you Japanese or Chinese? Definitely not Vietnamese."

Maybe, thought Grace, her mind underwater, *they needed to know for some reason. Maybe there was a census for accidents. A study on who was the worst driver.*

"*Konichiwa? Ni hao ma?*"

She shook her head.

He crouched down, thrusting his head into her space. "You're just a little doll, aren't you? You know, my brother's married to a Korean lady. They have flatter faces, Koreans. I don't think you guys are Korean. Maybe your mom though," he said, head tilting towards Barbra.

"She's not my mom."

He smirked. "See, I knew you guys weren't Korean!" Her dad wasn't even paying attention. Maybe he didn't realize what was happening. He was a guy, but that didn't mean that he knew the way guys could be. "I can always tell. It's a talent."

Sometimes in these situations the only way to get out was to play dumber than dumb. She shook her head and shrugged. "We're from L.A." And then she dropped her head onto her knees, grateful for the coziness of the blanket despite its source. Five seconds. Ten. He stayed crouching, close enough that she could hear his breath wheeze in through his nostrils. What was wrong with this guy? Was he so desperate to get it on with an Asian girl that he didn't care that she'd just gotten in the most insane car accident that she'd ever seen? Actually, why wasn't he celebrating the fact that their survival was basically a miracle?

Grace peeked through her bangs. "Okay," she said. "I'm tired now."

Another five seconds until finally he huffed and pushed himself up. "You're welcome for the blanket," he said, sarcastic. Grace shrugged to herself. *Whatever.* It wasn't like she'd ever see him again. Anyway, he was the asshole first, not her.

When it felt like he was far away enough, she raised her head again. It was hard to stop looking at the wreck. All her life, that car, her mom's old car, had been parked in their garage, pretty and powder blue, driven only by Ama. It used to look totally old-fashioned to Grace, but lately it had started to seem cool and vintage. But now here it was, smashed up and done.

Oh my god. Smashed up and done. That could have been them. Death with no choice. Smeared across southern blacktop. *Dead, dead, dead.*

How were they not dead?

They weren't dead.

They weren't dead and they didn't want to be!

She felt tired and exhilarated all at once. A bright fizz ran through her, a soda-pop high. She thrust her arms up, dropping the blanket behind her, and then let herself plop down on top of it. *Phew.* The stars weren't out yet, but the sky glowed a fading rose gold and the ground was dewy and cold. The sorry grass that covered the median pricked her legs, but it was kind of a miracle that it managed to grow at all, surrounded by six speeding lanes of freeway, choked by gas fumes and battered by empty soda cans and Krystal burger bags.

She looked up at her father. No one looked that attractive from below; that's why short people should never be allowed to be photographers. His head was tilted back so that she could see up his nose and his eyes were closed. He was getting older. His chin wobbled and new patches of gray hair glinted in the moonlight. He was old, but he was alive, and in the unflattering angle there was something unashamed about him. He looked almost beautiful there, standing so straight and still. Beautiful in a way that had nothing to do with being pretty, the way Grace knew she was, thank god. Maybe she should start taking pictures of adults instead of kids. In English class this year they had to memorize a poem, a Tennyson poem about a king. She liked memorizing things. She whispered it to herself now. *Though we are not now that strength which in old days moved earth and heaven, that which we are, we are; one equal temper of heroic hearts, made weak by time and fate, but strong in . . . something . . . um . . . To strive, to seek, to find, and not to yield.*

Was she going crazy? Did the crash make her crazy?

Everyone got old. It seemed impossible, but she would get old. If she didn't die first. Her mother would never get old; she would be forever the beautiful thirty-two-year-old with the dimple, about to step into a helicopter. Her father probably never thought that he would get old, but he did.

He'd gotten old, but he wasn't dead. And neither was she.

I almost died I almost died I almost died we almost died we almost died we almost died we almost died we almost died.

No other life could be as sweet and complete as this one. Not in the whole wide beautiful world.

The whole wide world. She whispered the words, letting them roll slowly through her lips. The world was wholer and more wide than she'd ever understood. Even broken, it was whole. The starry sky above was vast and perfect, each bright pinprick a brave echo of light. If they were on the side of the freeway in L.A., there wouldn't be any stars like this to look up to.

The whole wide world was so beautiful that she could hardly stand it.

Grace could feel tears pooling in her eyes, rising up even though she was lying down. A liquid puddle of them, balancing on the curve of her eye, blurring her vision so that even the streetlights looked like stars. What if everything was beautiful? It made as much sense that this would be true as it did that it wouldn't. Really, what if everything *was* beautiful? That could be a whole philosophy. Maybe she could be a guru. She'd wear amazing white silk gowns and complicated braids with gold chains woven in them, and people would feel blessed just being around her. The tears spilled down her cheeks now, drop piling on drop, and she felt like she might never need to blink again, that her eyes would just always be hydrated because she'd never stop crying.

It had happened before, the crying. When Grace was nine, their dog Lady died. Lady was actually a boy, a scrappy thing, gray, with four neat white paws and wiry hair that always looked matted no matter how much she brushed it. He died, and for a whole day afterwards, Grace had been numb. So numb, in fact, that she was almost blind, like the world had stopped existing. The next morning, getting out of bed, she'd stepped on Lady's favorite fire-hydrant-shaped chew toy, slipped, and banged her knee hard enough to bring tears to her eyes.

Once they came, they didn't go away, and she'd sobbed for nearly two weeks, running into the bathroom at school, crawling into Andrew's bed at night and snuggling against her brother the way Lady had snuggled against her. She'd felt perpetually wrung dry in those weeks, miserable and lonely, unable to believe that Lady had really died and sure that she could have saved him if only she'd known that the problem was real, that not eating was a serious thing for a dog.

She'd looked up once, in the midst of one of those crying jags, to find her father standing over her, looking distraught.

"Please, Gracie, please. *Bao bei. Bu yao ne me shang xing la. Ku go le.*"

Barbra had appeared in the doorway, shaking her head. "She love too hard for a girl. Too, too hard."

Barbra had said that, and she was wrong. So wrong that she couldn't be any wronger. Loving too hard was the only option. Grace was glad that she'd loved Lady too hard. And Greg Inouye. The boy who got her sent away. They didn't talk anymore, but she still loved him, and she probably always would. She would never forget the first time they'd spoken. They went to some of the same parties, but he was a grade above her and spent most of those nights in a tight circle with his friends, passing a joint around. Still, they'd smiled at each other once or twice. Then one day she was standing in line at the sandwich station, a tray in her hands, wearing her mother's cashmere sweater. She'd pushed the sleeves up but they'd drooped down again, the right one about to puddle into her salad. And Greg Inouye had walked up to her and rolled each one up, gently and deliberately. "There," he'd said, with a smile.

She should call him. If they ever got off this highway, she would call him.

Her father and Barbra were holding hands now, looking at each other over Grace's head. Did they love each other too hard? Something panged in Grace's heart and she scrambled up, leaving the blanket on the ground. How long had it been since she and Barbra had really talked to each other? Grace charged at her now, wrapping her stepmother in a hug, holding on until Barbra squeezed back. And then her father gathered them both up.

"*Wei she me?*"

"I just needed to. Why don't we hug more often?"

Grace buried her face in Barbra's neck, feeling the tendons move as she nodded. "We should," said Barbra. "We should."

They finally let go and Grace saw that the paramedic was staring at them. Even though it was gross because he was totally unattractive and probably kind of had a fetish and she was only sixteen, despite all those things maybe he just wanted to find a way to talk to a girl and that was the only way he knew how. Of course, it might have been better if he'd asked if she was hurt, or scared, or where they were headed, but in the end, he'd done the only thing he knew how to do; he'd reached his hand out and tried to make a connection, and even though she didn't want to come anywhere near touching that hand, even that was beautiful.

三十八

US 29 North

BEEP.

"You have one voicemail, sent at 10:42 a.m."

Hi, Greg. I know this is, like, really crazy out of nowheresville, but I just think it's dumb that we don't talk anymore and so I wanted to call and say hi. I just think . . . I just think that we should still *know* each other, you know? Okay. It's Grace, by the way. Oh, um, I might not have this number for much longer, so I'll call you again, or just email me. Okay. Bye.

Beep.

"First voicemail, sent at 10:43 a.m."

So, I just wanted to say that I'm sorry I was so mad, Andrew, and that I didn't even say goodbye. If you really love her, then that's really important, even if Daddy hates it. (Pause.) And, Andrew, don't freak out, but we crashed the car. We're all okay, me and Dad and Babs, but Mom's car is kind of totaled. But, well, I guess I'll talk to you soon. I miss you. I hope you're having fun in New Orleans.

Beep.

"Voicemail, sent at 10:45 a.m."

Hi, Saina. I know this is the millionth time I'm calling, but I'm not flipping out anymore. I'm okay now. Sorry about all those other messages. I guess I just really wanted to talk to you. I still do, but maybe you're never even going to pick up, and that's okay, too. I guess we'll see you eventually. So, I've been wondering about something. Do you think that Mom knows what's happening in our lives? Like, do you think she watches us? She might, right? That would be a nice thing. Um, also. Saina. There is something you do need to know. We're going to be a little slower than we thought because we got into a car accident, but don't worry, we're all fine, no one's hurt, and we'll be there soon. Or, not that soon, but we'll be there. I . . . love you.

Facebook message:

To: Kathy Berroa
From: Grace Wang
   Hi, Kathy — Thank you very much for being a nice host while we were in Twentynine Palms. I hope that Nico and Naia are doing well. I've realized that I do not have a phone number for Ama, and I am hoping that you will let her know that I would like to be in touch with her? I love her. Maybe she can get on Facebook and message me?
Thank you,
Grace

After everything, they'd rented a purple PT Cruiser. It looked like something a hick in a cartoon would drive, with a billiard ball for a gearshift, but it was the only car available at the rental place where the cops took them. When they reached the car, Grace held her hand out for the keys and her father handed them over without even thinking to protest.

   The first thing she'd done was roll the windows all the way down. She didn't want to spend another moment separated from the world around her.

   And then she drove — stopping only for gas and bathroom breaks, not even bothering to plug her phone in when it died. Drove through five states: North Carolina, Virginia, Maryland, Pennsylvania, New York. Her father and stepmother fell asleep around Virginia and passed unseeingly through Maryland, which seemed more like a rumor than a state, oblivious to the butterfly that splattered against their dusty windshield, its gorgeous patterned wings feathering off in opposite directions. They didn't see the rows of crops that unfolded in different triangulating patterns, creating a moiré effect through the tinted windows; the electrical towers that marched across the plains; the antiabortion billboards; the pro-prayer billboards; the shredded plastic bags caught in cow fences. They didn't see the chaotic, swirling flight of swallows as they left their nests under the highway overpass en masse, darkening the sky above their car. She drove for so long that eighty miles per hour started to feel like they were barely moving, like they were just floating along, a leaf in a stream. When she ran into traffic and had to slow down to sixty, it was like being mired in asphalt.

She drove and drove and felt like she was shrinking in her seat, shrinking until she was a tiny thing with fur, paws on the steering wheel, heading straight north. She saw herself on a hand-drawn map, one creature in a world of billions, a tiny light heading slowly north as the world spun below her. Somewhere in Pennsylvania, as the sun set and no moon rose to take its place, Grace knew with a calm certainty that her life was going to ripple ever outward until it encompassed the entire world.

三十九

Helios, NY

3,561 Miles

SAINA HAD JUST given up on flaking the filet of smoked whitefish neatly with a fork and had begun to wiggle her finger under its cold flesh, working along the delicate spine, when she heard a car horn blaring in the driveway. She dropped the fish, half torn, into a bowl that already held a pile of capers, chopped egg, and finely diced onion, and ran for the door. Halfway there, briny hands up in the air so that they wouldn't drip, she stopped and turned back, guilty. Leo was still in the kitchen, searching her cupboards for the rye crackers that he liked. For a minute, she'd forgotten him entirely.

From outside, car doors slammed, and a second later Grace was banging on the front door.

Saina looked at her boyfriend. "Are you ready?"

"You know what? I'm actually a little nervous."

She felt a flash of love for him — why do people's vulnerabilities stab at our hearts? — but before she could say anything, Grace was in the front hall, shouting Saina's name.

"You go have a family hello first," he said. "I'll open a bottle of something." So she turned again and ran, and found that she couldn't wait to throw her still-damp hands around her little sister.

They hugged, and then they hugged again. And then her father came in and slung an arm across her shoulders and surprised her by resting his cheek against hers, sighing. "It was a long trip. America is very wide." Barbra, next to him, held his hand. Her left wrist was bandaged and a thin red scar snaked up her arm. She looked sweet and forlorn, and Saina gave in to the urge to embrace her, too.

"Oh, look at you guys! You're all banged up! Dad, let me see your eye."

He waved her off. "No problem! I have ice pack. Don't worry."

"Are you guys really okay?"

Charles, Barbra, and Grace crowded close to each other in the vestibule. They all nodded. "We are alive, so we are okay," said her father.

She eyed them, skeptical. "Well, you must be so tired. Here, let's leave the bags, Leo and I will get them later."

As she shuffled them into the living room, Grace went back outside and returned with a flat cardboard envelope. "This was on the porch. Is it important?" Saina took it and, her attention on the meeting to come, peeled off the scored strip that zipped the whole thing shut. As soon as she lifted the flap, she realized what it was.

Coming in from the kitchen, Leo set down a tray with wineglasses and a bottle of bubbly rosé, then crossed the room with his hand extended, as if he'd met her father a thousand times before.

Still, she cringed. There was something about introducing a new boyfriend to her family that always felt rude, like she was putting her sex life on display. Greetings safely executed, Leo passed out glasses and poured them each a gorgeous, generous pink swig of wine, delighting Grace by not even hesitating over her glass.

"To you guys making it here," Saina said, and waited until everyone had clinked glasses with everyone else — twenty clinks, she calculated nervously — and taken a sip before she let herself pull out the magazine.

It wasn't a cover. It was never going to be a cover story; Billy must have written it on the train back to New York for him to turn it around so quickly. In the end, it was one in a portfolio of failures — Eliot Spitzer was the cover, and she was one of four other profiles, two thousand words running alongside the more flamboyant failure — something else that Billy probably knew before he smoked her out. She felt a faint, arrogant bit of disappointment at that before flipping to the paper-clipped page. A folded piece of notepaper was attached.

Grace crowded in, reading the headline over her shoulder. "Oh my god, what? Is this about you? 'The Search for Saina Wang.' Whoa, that is so cool!"

"Who need to search? I find you. You are right here!" Her father grabbed her arm and then patted her on the head.

"Are you going to read it?" asked Barbra.

For a moment, she considered putting the magazine back in the envelope and tossing it in the recycling bin.

Impossible. Who were those people who insisted that they never read any reviews? It seemed preposterous. "Here, Grace. You read it to us."

"Wait, aren't you excited about this?"

"I guess we'll see."

Grace nodded back, not looking at her. "Okay, if you're sure." She started to read.

THE SEARCH FOR SAINA WANG

Schadenfreude? Gesundheit! Billy Al-Alani on the psychology behind a New York 'It' girl's fall from grace.

It is sometime around April when I first realize that Saina Wang is gone. I try her cell and get sent straight to voicemail.

"It's Saina. Leave a message."

She sounds warm, but distant. Trademark Saina. I leave a message, but she never calls back.

I go to Dan Colen and Dash Snow's Deitch Projects show, sure that she'll be there with Minni Mung or Peonia Vazquez-D'Amico, part of the tight group of artists and fashion folk that she has surrounded herself with since arriving in New York City to earn a BFA at Columbia. There are plenty of girls with dark hair and long legs crowding the gallery, circulating under the wine-and-pee spitballs, but Saina is not among them.

Saina stared at a bruise on her knee, listening as Billy described in detail his strange, obsessive quest. He made her into some sort of Great Hipster Mystery, hitting up any party or opening where she might be, asking her friends to reveal her whereabouts, staking out her studio, finding out, somehow, that she'd taken a $400,000 hit when she sold her loft, stalking her gallerist until, of course, Billy found Grayson and got him drunk.

Her sister looked up from the magazine. "Do you really want me to keep reading this? It's terrible! Do you think this is how Jennifer Aniston feels?"

They all laughed painfully. Even Barbra. Leo squeezed her hand.

"Yeah," said Saina. "Keep going." The next part was less of a surprise. A dramatized overview of the controversy surrounding her last show, complete with a snarky rereading of the catalog copy, where he called her show "a posthumous beauty contest for victims of war." He wasn't entirely wrong, but she still didn't understand why she'd had to bear the collective anger when it was the photojournalists and the editors who had created those images in the first place.

Grace read on.

We love artists because of the lives they lead. They give us raw id, captured in a frame. In many ways, the art world is best at celebrating the controlled, masterful hand or the wild, impetuous heart. Saina's work, though, is the cynical, observant head, calculating and precise.

"Wait," said Saina, "do you all think that?" They all looked at one another, her family, and she suddenly realized that they probably wanted to rest after their long drive. They had to be tired and hungry and in no mood to hear a takedown of her, of the first failure that led to every other failure. "Never mind, you don't have to answer that. Gracie, let's just finish it. There's not a lot more left, is there?"

Grace looked up at her, worried. "Well . . . it's that old Page Six item. I'm just going to skip it, okay?"

Saina nodded, but it didn't really matter. She could still recite it word for word, down to the pun that stabbed her in the heart each time she thought about it. *Just asking . . . Which socialite artist might find that the uproar over her latest show is nothing compared to the uproar that her fiancé is causing between the sheets with a rival heiress whose name must "ring" a bell?*

"Okay, I'll read this part instead," said Grace.

Perhaps now is the time to say that every successful artist is the product of mythmaking, and that I, more than anyone else, may have been guilty of constructing the myth of Saina Wang.

Leo wrapped an arm around her. "Who *is* this guy?"

I made my own myth, thought Saina. *I did.* She could see her sister's eyes scanning ahead. Grace looked up at her, worried, and put down the magazine. "Well, um, that's about it," she said.

Leo wrapped his fingers around her wrist lightly. "Is it me, or did that article just say a whole lot of nothing?"

"*Dwei le! Luo shuo!* Why that reporter not mind his own business?"

"Yeah, Mr. Wang!"

Barbra laughed, and it was a genuine laugh. Sitting here around Saina's Bertoia table, surrounded by the glistening white walls of her dining room, they felt like a family, Leo included. She'd been selfish, hadn't she? Returning one out of every five of Grace's phone calls, leaving her father, never allowing Barbra to be anything approaching a mother. She owed them these things. In the end, all we had were the people to whom we were beholden.

Later, as Barbra napped upstairs and Leo and Grace brought in the rest of their luggage, Saina found her father looking at the titles on her bookshelf.

"*Ni yao bu yao xian shuei yi ge jiao?*" she asked.

"*Bu lei.*"

But he did look tired. He hadn't even said anything about Leo being black. She was relieved, but it also worried her — he seemed less present in the world somehow.

It had been more than six months since she'd seen him, and so much had changed. When he'd left New York, she'd been engaged, and her gallerist was playing potential collectors off one another, trying to land her pieces in the right hands so that her future work would rise in value. And now who was she? The subject of one public drubbing after another, and at the hands of someone like Billy Al-Alani, who wasn't even a real critic, who was just a gossip.

"Baba . . ." But she couldn't formulate the sentence in Chinese. Her knowledge of the language only extended to daily necessities and small affections. She realized suddenly that this was the first time she'd been alone with her father in more than a year. He picked up a small horned skull resting on her bookshelf.

"Your pet?"

"It's just for decoration."

"Why?"

"I liked it."

He shrugged and put it back on its side, the horns listing over the edge of the shelf. "Have you talk to Didi?"

"Not since *ni men* left New Orleans. *Ta jen de yao* live there *ma*? Grace *gen wo shuo.*"

"*Ta fa fong le.*"

"Maybe he's really in love with her."

"Daddy just want everyone to be all together."

"Oh yeah, I know." Instead of meeting her gaze, he stared at the titles on the shelf then took a handkerchief out of his pocket to wipe a nonexistent layer of dust from their spines.

"Baba . . . I'm sorry."

He looked startled. "*Wei she me?*"

"Because of the article. And the other article. You . . . you must be embarrassed. I didn't know that was going to happen. And then Grayson and, Baba, he had a baby with that other girl, and even that was in a stupid newspaper."

He tucked the handkerchief back in his pocket, deliberately. "What is there to be embarrassed about? I have a daughter who makes a very interesting life, so interesting that everybody want to know what she is doing. Embarrassing for them, that their lives are so boring! Not for you. Not for me."

"Really?"

"Yes. Really. Mucho really! *Zwei* really *de.*"

"Okay, then."

"*Dou shi* okay *de.*"

"All of it?"

"Yes."

"But . . . really?"

He looked at her, nodding.

"Thank you, Baba."

"*Bu yao xie.*"

. . .

That night in bed, Saina picked up the magazine. She pictured her friends — and worse, all those people who thought that knowing her work meant knowing her — reading this article and felt an unsettling hatred towards Billy. She didn't want to let that in with her family here, with the three travelers so strangely buoyant and solicitous of one another. Better to let them think that she was unaffected by it. And maybe she was. Maybe she was even pleased. Now that the dreaded thing had happened, it turned out that it was only one of many dreaded things, and perhaps not even that. She unfolded the note that came with the magazine, knowing it was from Billy.

On it, he'd written *Call it a comeback?*

Without thinking about it much, Saina took out her phone and texted a response. *I've been gone for years.*

四十

Helios, NY

CLOUDS. FAT AND PUFFY. A roller-coaster highway that looped through the air. She and Charles, in the backseat of a driverless car, speeding from side to side as she yelled and tried to climb into the front seat, reaching for the brakes with her foot. Every time she got close, she'd look down and realize that her foot was a tiny, bound hoof stuffed inside a beautiful embroidered slipper, royal blue, just a toe's length too short to stop the car. Charles wasn't helping because he was on the phone, a big, bright-yellow cordless phone, talking in a language she couldn't understand. Barbra knew that if she could just reach the brake Charles would put the phone down and take her in his arms. Even now he had one hand on her bottom, cupping it, making sure that she didn't fall out the window.

Barbra woke up, eyes still closed, and Charles *was* on the phone, whispering in Mandarin.

"How can that be? *How can that be?*"

She lay very still, listening.

"But why would they let him?"

Sensing that he was sitting in the far corner of the room, facing away from her, Barbra opened her eyes.

"So he is there now? Right now?"

Charles sat in a shaft of light, like a nightmare in a children's book.

"No, don't contact him. Don't give him time to run away. I will go. Have you found a number? Does he live in the old house still?"

He took a small notebook out of his pocket and wrote something in it, then stopped abruptly.

"He did? That fool!" A brief pause, and then he said, "It is not your place to tell me what I should do," almost spitting in the receiver. After putting the phone down on his lap, he sat, suspended. Barbra didn't move either; she wasn't yet ready to invest in the reality of this moment. If only she could go back to the dream and find her way to the brake, bound foot or not.

Charles stood up and unzipped one of his suitcases, digging in the side pocket. He pulled out some things she couldn't see and zippered them into a pouch that she'd gotten for him at Louis Vuitton for his birthday four years ago. There was no indication that he knew she was awake. Barbra was about to whisper to him when he picked up a clean pair of boxers and headed to the shower.

A photograph of Charles's mother. A plastic Ziploc bag, with ten stacks of twenty-dollar bills. His father's factory identification card. A sheaf of thin, crinkled papers, handwritten, imprinted all over with fading red marks from official chops. A white jade chop, one of the biggest ones she'd ever seen, in the shape of a mountain with just Charles's surname carved into the base. A piece of something that looked like bone. A worn leather wallet with Charles's National Taiwan University identification card and, hiding behind it, her own fresh-faced high school identification card, which she hadn't seen since she'd lost it in the university cafeteria where her father worked, where she'd first laid eyes on Wang Da Qian more than thirty years ago.

Just then, the blow dryer in the hall bathroom switched off, and a moment later Charles walked in to see the contents of his valise spread out over their bed. Barbra held up her young face.

"How much land do you think you can claim with this?" she asked, teasing.

He laughed, too, and sat down next to her. "All of it."

"Hmm."

Charles folded her into his arms, leaning the still-warms tufts of his hair — baby soft now and snowier every day — against her forehead. She inhaled his clean-laundry and fresh-earth smells, so familiar and good. Inside, Barbra felt loose, liquid. She leaned back and his arms locked, supporting her. As you grew older, there were fewer thrills in life but, despite everything that was happening all around, discovering that her lost ID had been in Charles's possession all these decades was undoubtedly one of them.

"Did you really have this? For such a long time?"

He grinned in a way she hadn't seen since before everything went bad.

"You dropped it one day. I pick it up to give back to you, but then I decide that I want to save it so that I can talk to you in the future."

"But you never did."

"I came to America."

"But you said you hardly remembered me!"

"I remember all the important parts."

He moved closer to her and placed the back of his hand against her cheek. She turned her head and caught his fingers in a kiss. They both closed their eyes and sat like that, almost but not entirely together. Barbra breathed in with her husband's every exhale; he breathed out with her every inhale. It was quiet in Saina's house, no helicopters or police sirens to cut through the stillness. She took hold of his hand and kissed the fingers again, altogether and then separately. He moved closer. They weren't so old. Not yet. The familiar desire still rose within her as he let everything else fall away and focused, slack jawed, on her alone.

When was the last time they had been together like this, both of them completely present and desiring? They fell back together on the bed, but before she could pull off her nightgown, Charles stopped.

"You think I am very foolish for wanting to go."

"Not foolish. No. But is it necessary for it to happen right now? We just got here. Wait a few days. Rest." For a moment she felt desperate that he stay; they'd only just found each other again. "If you buy a ticket right now with that cash, they might think you're a terrorist."

"I cannot wait any more. I've waited already for fifty-six years. My children are starting to think that they need to take care of me. If I wait longer, they will be mushing my food and taking away my beer."

Barbra didn't want to, but she understood.

"Do you want to come as well?" Charles asked.

She considered for a moment, knowing what she had to say. "If you want me to come, I will go. But I think you don't. I think you want to go by yourself."

The moonlight was spreading. Now the shadow of the diamond windowpane angled over the bed. Charles looked at her in that silvery glow and slowly, slowly, pushed his finger up inside the fluttery sleeve of her nightgown and hooked the collar, tugging it off her shoulder.

四十一

Helios, NY

EACH STAIR leading up to the third floor made its own sort of creak. Saina didn't know them as well as she knew the second-floor stairs yet; those she ran up in a pattern of leaps and side steps, appreciating anew the narrow Uzbek carpet that she'd installed as a runner and congratulating herself when she reached the top without a sound. Not that it mattered when she was living in this house alone.

When she had come to Helios six months ago, Saina told herself that she bought this big place because it just made more sense. After a decade of accepting the distorted reality of three-million-dollar third-floor walkups in TriBeCa and SoHo, the idea that she might possess a hundred-year-old house with four bedrooms on twenty-one acres for a fraction of that price was not something that she could bypass. After all, she could redo this place and resell it — instead of making art, she could bring old farmhouses back to life. Or she could invite other people — writers and composers and scientists, even — to do residencies here, hire a good cook, and have intelligent, ebullient dinners at long tables in the garden that would lead to cross-disciplinary collaborations and long marriages. Or she could just restore this bucolic dream and keep it when she moved back to the city to reassume her rightful place.

Really, though, Saina bought an oversize property because she had to. A grand project meant that this was a pivot rather than a retreat, even if anyone who bothered to look could see the lie of that.

Or maybe she was psychic. A new home for the Wangs. Had she known when she was buying it that there were exactly enough rooms for her family? She had not! And yet now here they were.

Saina eased open the door to what had become Grace's room. It was a three-quarter-size door and you had to duck as you entered, but the eaves shot up in the middle, giving it the feel of a rustic temple. Her little sister had all of the windows flung open, and a smattering of maple leaves dotted the coverlet, blown in from the ancient tree that stretched up and over the house. In half a second, Saina ran across the room and leapt on Grace, a warm, sleeping bundle.

"Gooooood morning, good morning, it's time to greet the day!" she sang, wrapping her arms around Grace and squeezing her.

In response, Grace groaned and smiled, eyes still closed. "I can't hear you. I'm asleep."

"This little light of mine, I'm gonna let it shiiiiiine!"

"Oh my god, why are you singing church songs to me?"

"It's gospel, Gracie! Plus, Bruce Springsteen covered it."

"Even worse!"

Saina flopped over and burrowed under the covers, resting her head next to her sister's. "These really are nice sheets. I guess they were worth it."

"Wait, are you worried about money, too?"

Should she tell her? Better not to. "Not yet. But no matter what, a few hundred dollars for some cotton that you put on your bed is ridiculous."

"I guess." Grace snuggled in. "Saina?"

"Hmm?"

"I like your new boyfriend."

She laughed. "Thank you. He was good with Dad, right?"

"And Babs. So . . . do *you* like him?"

"You mean do I *like him* like him?"

"Mm-hm."

"Yeah, of course."

"So . . . does that mean you guys have had sex?"

"Grace! Why are you asking me that?"

"Just tell me! Have you? Actually, you don't have to say it. I know you have. Did he stay over last night?"

"No. You saw him leave. Remember, we said good night to him together?"

"Yeah, but I thought you might have snuck him in after we all went to sleep."

"Like summer camp? No, I'm too grown-up to do that now."

"You're not a grown-up, you're a puppy!"

"Oh god, I forgot. You're right."

Saina yipped and whined obligingly, taking the sleeve of Grace's T-shirt between her teeth and growling.

"No! No! Stop! You're not a puppy! You're a pterodactyl!"

"Don't those not exist anymore?"

"Um, yeah. They're extinct."

"No, I mean wasn't there some sort of grand dinosaur renaming? I don't think the brontosaurus is an official dinosaur anymore either."

"That's impossible, because you're a pterodactyl and you're right here next to me."

"Oh yeah! Phew! It's so sad when species are permanently wiped out!" Fanning out her arms and smacking Grace in the face, Saina let out her best prehistoric shriek.

"Ow! No wonder we killed all of you!"

"You mean you're a meteor?"

"*Bam!* Hellfire! Damnation! Destruction! Earth is over!"

"Do you want some pancakes?"

"Yes! Acts of God love pancakes." Abruptly, Grace's tone shifted. "Hey, Saina? Are you sad that Mom never met any of your boyfriends?"

"Well, I'm definitely not sad that she never met Grayson."

"Yeah, but maybe if she had, she would have known that he wasn't a good guy and you never would have ended up getting engaged to him."

Saina sat up and noticed the old photograph tacked onto the wall eye level with the pillow. It was their mother on the tarmac in Las Vegas, stepping into the helicopter that would ferry her to her death. Strange that their father would have had this roll of film developed, a set of reminders of the last trip he took with his wife and of his own outrageous fortune. "Why do you think that?"

"Well, she was our mom! She would have known you so well, better, even, than any of us know you, and she would have met him and known instinctively that he wasn't right. And she would have given you good advice."

"Mom wasn't really the advice-giving type."

Grace flipped over. "I hate it when you say stuff like that! I don't believe you."

Frustrated, Saina said, "Grace, you didn't ever know her." As soon as she did, she hated herself for it. "I'm sorry. I'm sorry, I'm sorry. I know you wish so much that you did know her. I'm sorry you never got to, Gracie." She nuzzled in close to her sister, who didn't respond, didn't move. "I'm going to go make you pancakes, okay?"

Saina started the pancake batter, cracking eggs into a big glass bowl already half full of sweet, grassy-smelling milk. It was satisfying to watch each one splash down and then surface, a saturated yellow in a field of creamy white. After half a dozen, plus a dash of vanilla, she beat them until the whole mixture was the color of fresh butter then stirred in careful handfuls of the dry ingredients.

As Saina mixed, Grace came downstairs and stood, watching her. Finally, she said, "Remember that time when we made Mickey Mouse pancakes?"

"You still remember that? How old were you? Like, seven?"

"It was the summer before you left for college. And then you started a fire, and we had to put it out with baking soda."

"And then Ama came in and yelled at us and you cried and said that you didn't want to eat baking soda."

"I didn't cry!"

"You did. It's okay, you were only seven."

"I was just a baby."

"Want me to make you Mickey Mouse pancakes now, baby?"

Grace picked up a tiny, deeply red strawberry and ate it. Paused. And then said, "Will you?"

Saina poured the batter in a squeeze bottle and then held her hand over the cast-iron pan, waiting for the heat to rise before spearing a pat of butter on a knife and running it over the dark surface of the pan. She let it sizzle for a moment then drizzled in the outline of a face. It was all wrong for Mickey, though. Too round at the bottom and not long enough. But ... Saina added a lopsided pair of glasses on the face, some tufts of hair and two ears, giving it time to brown before flipping it over, then sliding it onto a plate and putting in front of Grace, who was slicing the strawberries now.

"Who does this look like?"

Grace stared at it for a long moment. "Not Mickey."

"No."

"Um ... Anchorman?"

"No! Does he even wear glasses? No, it's someone you know."

"In real life?" Grace considered. Shook her head. And then, "Is it Dad? It is!"

"Yes!"

"I can't eat my father! Patricide!"

"Gastropatrimony."

Grace broke off an ear. "Oh wait, my father's delicious. We should save this for him, he'll be so into it."

"Will you go wake them up?"

Three minutes later, Grace came clattering back down, a fully dressed Barbra trailing behind her.

"Babs won't tell me where Dad is!"

Not even a full day had passed, and Grace had already tossed aside the beatific calm that she'd brought to Helios. Ah, well, she was only sixteen. There would be other epiphanies. "What's going on?"

"I only need to say the thing one time, not two," said Barbra.

"Okay," said Grace. "So what is it? Say it already, where is he?"

"Daddy went to return the car at the airport."

"What? Why'd he go by himself? He should've waited for us to wake up — I could have gone with him. How's he planning to get back? Should we go pick him up now?"

Her stepmother turned towards the window and looked out at the barn Saina was slowly converting into a studio. "He's not coming back. He's going to go to the airport."

"Right. To return the car." Why was Barbra being this obtuse? "And then he's coming back?"

"And to get on an airplane."

Instinctively, Grace and Saina grabbed for each other's arms. "We just got here! Where's he flying to?"

"Zhong guo."

"Are you serious? Why is he going to China? That doesn't make any sense! Why didn't he tell us?"

Saina's heart sank. Had the shock of losing everything made her father crazy? "Is it the land? Does he really think —"

Barbra looked at her, level. "He thinks yes."

"What? What are you guys talking about? What does Dad think?" Grace's whole body was canted towards them, quivering. "I hate it that no one tells me anything! I'm sixteen now. I'm not a baby. Just tell me already!"

Sigh. "Okay, so Dad thinks that he can roll up to China and they'll just give him back all of the land that his family had to turn over to the Communists."

"Well, he's right! I mean, it's not theirs, it's his. Why should they get to keep it?"

"They do not worry about fair," said Barbra. "You don't take over a country by fair."

"But, Grace, you know there's no way that it'll happen, right? As much as Dad might want it to?"

"It could," she insisted. "Why couldn't it? He could make it happen."

Saina turned to Barbra. "He didn't . . . he didn't have a message for us or anything?"

"No messages."

Why had she spent so much time worrying about whether he would be comfortable here? Whether he'd approve? All he did was deposit Barbra and Grace on her doorstep like chattel and then take off without even saying goodbye. Saina slammed her mug down on the marble counter. "Fine. If he wants to call, he'll call. Grace, let's go get you enrolled in school."

· · ·

From: charlesxmwang@gmail.com
To: Wang, Saina; Wang, Andrew; Wang, Grace
September 19, 2008

Hi, darling children 1, 2, 3 —

How are you? I landed in Beijing today. I am sorry there was not a time to say goodbye before I leave. Tomorrow I will travel to our old home, 老家. Do not be worried, be happy. Remember, if you go out in sunshine put on sunscreen, you do not want to be old and wrinkle like me. Ha!

— Daddy

四十二

Beijing, China

10,310 Miles

CHINA WAS his last chance, and Charles Wang was a man who used all of his chances.

What he didn't expect, what surprised him from the moment he got off the thirteen-and-a-half-hour flight and stepped into the enormous glass-and-steel marvel of the new Beijing airport, was the realization that China could have, should have, been his first chance.

China was *his* old country, so despite all he'd seen of the world, part of him had still expected it to be *old*. A larger, more glorious version of the Taiwan he'd left as a young man. Despite everything he knew about the roaring tiger economy, all the photos he'd seen of this whiz-bang new airport — the sixth-largest building in the world! — which was probably run by a cadre of hyperintelligent robots, part of him still thought that he'd land at a provincial airport, long linoleum hallways half in shadow thanks to rows of blown-out fluorescent bulbs, groups of surly porters impressed by the fact that he'd come from America.

How could he have been so wrong? From the moment he deplaned, it was clear that China had leapt past him and the America he'd so naïvely thought was the Wang family's future. Charles knew that the symbols at this airport were almost too easy to see — the red and gold of ancient China made modern, the skylights shaped like dragon scales — but they still worked on him, immediately recalibrating his impression of the China to come. The surprise continued in the cab, where a screen implanted in the seat in front of him blared advertisements for restaurants and beauty creams as the driver, so small that he sat on a pile of phone books, steered them through a glittering city to the nondescript tourist hotel he'd booked on Priceline, of all places. It was Saturday, and the only information that his lawyer had been able to retrieve about the man who presumed to take ownership of his birthright was his place of employment — a midsize travel agency — so for the moment, Charles would allow himself to play tourist in Beijing. Confronted with the drab cell of a room, twenty-five floors aboveground, Charles disregarded the fact that he had barely slept since New Orleans and dropped his satchel on the bed.

After waiting almost ten minutes for the elevator, which seemed only to go up, Charles found a glass-enclosed staircase that ran along the exterior of the hotel. He descended two dozen floors by foot until, nearly at ground level, he reached an elevated walkway connecting the building to one across the street. Eager to get out into the city, he pushed open the heavy glass door and walked into the smoggy heat of late afternoon.

On the street below, a dark brown ox hitched to a wooden cart stood calmly at a seven-way stoplight. The leather braces around its neck were broken and held together with a length of soiled rope; its horns swung up on either side of its head, an ineffectual crown. To the animal's left, there was a gold Lexus, one blacked-out window rolled down. From a floor above, Charles tracked a plume of smoke from the driver's cigarette as it floated up towards the beast and into its giant eye. The ox blinked but didn't move, just switched its muddy tail from side to side as scooters and bicycles — so many bicycles — pooled all around.

Plunging down the last flight of stairs, Charles finally stepped foot on a real Beijing street. He wanted to lose himself in the city. At random, he chose a direction — East. East was best — and began to walk as quickly as he could on leather soles and three airplane meals. A group of schoolchildren in uniform ran ahead of him — little girls in braids, little boys with their downy heads shaved — and crowded into a shop whose walls were lined with clear bins full of snacks. In the grassy median of Wang Fu Jing Street, men lounged around a metal trash can that they'd turned into a makeshift barbecue, flames licking the juicy, dripping skewers of meat. One man turned the kebabs as the others squatted on the ground playing a game of liar's dice. Next to them, a woman peered into the ear of a white-haired grandfather who sat splayed on a stool, his shirt open and belly hanging out. Charles hadn't seen a long-handled ear pick in decades, but now he remembered his aunt and uncle taking those same positions in the shaded courtyard of their Taipei home, digging out each other's ear wax.

Charles's right pants pocket sagged. After going through security, he had taken the jade seal out of his carry-on bag and put it in one pocket, then taken the small piece of bone and tucked it in the other. He curled his fingers around the bone, that last vestige of his father.

Charles had missed seeing his father alive one final time. When he finally made it back to Taiwan, it was only for the funeral and cremation, both of which took place on the day he arrived atop a burial mountain on the outskirts of Taipei. Jet-lagged and weeping, he had bid the other mourners farewell one by one until he was the only one left, waiting as his father's body was reduced to ash. As the dark crept into the empty hall, he sat in a plastic chair cursing himself for having been a neglectful son while the crematorium manager — a menacing joke of a man in a Hawaiian shirt with a perm and a pinky ring — ate a fried pork chop and watched a variety show on his boxy television.

When Charles startled awake, he had slid half off the seat, and the man was nudging him towards a still-warm metal box filled with ash and bone. Next to it lay a pair of silver chopsticks. Charles knew what he had to do. He picked up the chopsticks and reached into the pile, picking up the pieces of bone and placing them in an urn and then pouring the ash on top. When the man turned away, Charles had reached in and pulled out one of the pieces, light as driftwood, slipping it into his pocket. And now here it was again, back in his pocket, back in China.

He walked by the entrance of what looked like an old hutong neighborhood, its narrow alleyways and crumbling stone walls promising a glimpse of his father's dream of a lost China. It turned out to be a warren of small boutiques selling remarkably avant-garde clothing, each occupying a rammed-earth-and-sun-dried-brick building that would have been home to a branch of a family. Lesser relatives of the Wangs might have lived in a place like this three generations ago. Picking up a thin white shirt with one arm sewn across the front like a straitjacket and the other

missing entirely, Charles boggled at the price. Was it really 2,150 yuan?
He calculated quickly. Could this student art project of a shirt possibly
be selling for $350? And here, in this nondescript area of town? Just out-
side, a makeshift noodle stand straddled a narrow alleyway, and the proprietor, a teenager in a dirty apron, stirred a steaming pot of stock as his
minispeakers blared out Britney Spears.

Charles was hungry now. Something deep in his belly growled and
rolled, and he felt empty enough to consume the entire country.

He'd been following the tourist signs to Tiananmen, but as he crossed
a wide plaza, he spotted a giant topiary display three times the size of a
Rose Parade float, a leftover from the recent Olympics. A rose-studded
banner spelled out LANE CRAWFORD: FASHION IN MOTION. Lane
Crawford. The logo made him feel light-headed. It stoked the anger that
had not dissipated since the day he and Barbra had left their beautiful
home.

Six months ago, in the last flat-footed attempt to bring some money
into his coffers, Charles had contacted the luxury retailer, sure that they
would be interested in investing in an American brand formulated for
Asian faces. He'd been to the Hong Kong branch as a teenager and still
remembered marveling over the glamour of the foreign brands as he tried
out every settee and love seat in the tea shop and munched on cream
cakes. But that was then. The Lane Crawford of 2008, in all their shortsighted ignorance, didn't even consider his proposal for a full twenty-four
hours before issuing a categorical no, claiming that they were developing
their own makeup line.

Light-headed now from hunger, he crossed the plaza, shoving past a
pretty girl in a brown uniform passing out packs of tissues with something advertised on them and pulled on the heavy door, wincing as a blast
of cold air smacked him in the face.

Where was it? Where was their own line? Charles stalked into the
makeup area, enraged by its prettiness, breathing in the perfumed department store scent that was the same in Beijing as it was in Cairo or Beverly Hills. There was nothing with the department store's old-fashioned
logo on it, not a pot of blush or a stick of eyeliner. No house brand, but
everywhere there were women with carefully styled hair and expensive
clothes that hung just so on their shoulders. Even the chubby ones were

well dressed, everything tailored so that no rice-pot binges were betrayed by a lumpy sheath.

Hunger and disappointment, rage and a furious sort of envy for the things that were once his and now were not pulsed through Charles. At the end of the cosmetics section, the glowing glass cases of jewelry began. A woman his age stood at one of the counters with an older man who could be her father but was probably her husband. In front of them sat a velvet-lined box with three massive watches that dwarfed even his beloved Audemars Piguet, surrendered along with the rest of his timepieces.

Who were these people who had stayed in China? That gray-haired man strapping on an ostentatious F. P. Journe and asking whether it was waterproof, was he one of the university students who had fallen under the sway of Mao and overrun the Wang family land?

Nearby, an elderly woman watched her friend exclaim as a salesgirl fastened a strand of fat, lustrous pearls around her neck. Those *tai-tais* tittering over baubles, were they the same vicious Little Red Guard schoolgirls who had pulled his elderly aunts out of bed and paraded them through the streets, stringing their arms through a wooden yoke and forcing dunce caps on their snowy heads?

Across the floor, a kid with the tips of his hair bleached an ugly blond rang up a tower of shoeboxes as his manager fussed right and left, fawning over a girl tapping on her cell phone, who barely noticed his ministrations. That slavish manager who now spent his days fitting six-hundred-dollar high heels on privileged young feet might have been one of the toughs in tattered uniforms who had taken his left-behind family heirlooms — the centuries-old book of Wang family genealogy, the scrolls written by Zheng Xie that his father had still missed, quietly and desperately, a decade later — and burned them all to ash.

How had all these peasants transformed themselves?

And why hadn't his family stayed and done the same?

A man in a suit and a silver name tag touched his arm and asked, in a provincial Chinese that sounded slurring and soft, "Is there a problem?" Charles realized that he'd been hunched over, gripping the edge of a glass case full of Smythson notebooks bound in leather, their covers printed with simple slogans: JUMP FOR JOY, GAME ON, TOP SECRET. He had one of his own that said CHAMPION, a just-because gift from Barbra. Objects that mere months ago had seemed casual and, if not necessary, at least deserved, now felt outlandish to Charles. Had she really spent 460 yuan — What was that? Seventy-five dollars! — on a notebook that he had used twice?

Oh, the man was still there, waiting for his response. Charles's sweaty fingertips squeaked on the glass as he shook his head. "No, no. Just looking at these books, so beautiful!" The store official frowned down at his flashing cell phone and moved past Charles, barely pausing to nod.

For a second, he let himself close his eyes. Charles felt faint and a little numb. *Concentrate,* he commanded himself. Concentrate on the smoothness of the countertop, on the soft music that snuck in through the hidden speakers. Stay present. Breathe. He couldn't have a stroke, here, now. He was too close to the land. He had to push through. Charles breathed in deeply, but the guff of perfumes came at him in a nauseating rush and he struggled towards the exit, wondering if he had remembered to take an aspirin that morning.

Instead of stumbling out into the polluted Beijing air, Charles found himself deeper in the shopping center, crowded by people on all sides. A quick, blank blackness, just longer than a blink, fizzed dangerously behind his eyes and he could feel his blood sugar plummet. In the middle of the mall, there was another topiary, this one of baby pandas frolicking on a dragon — when had the Chinese become so obsessed with these tortured lumps of greenery? On the other side of it lay something that looked like a restaurant, its trendy white gloss of a façade reflecting the dragon's unnatural smile. Breathing heavily now, Charles walked, one unsteady foot in front of another, towards the restaurant and peered at the menu perched on a titanium stand. His stomach poked at him, displeased. The restaurant offered a mishmash of international cuisines, food to make foreigners feel at home and local Chinese feel like citizens of the world: spag bol, wasabi french fries, pizzettas topped with sweet corn and octopus.

As much as he'd left Taiwan because it was not China, would never be China, he'd come to China expecting to find the Taiwan of his youth. Home was home, and what he wanted from home was sausages. Charles remembered when he was a skinny boy, the shortest one in his gang of friends. He and Little Fats and Nutsy and Wen-Wen would tear out of school and hit the streets of Taipei running just for the pleasure of propelling their bodies forward, their schoolbags bouncing along behind them. They ran, and they ate. Sometimes it was a crinkled wax-paper packet of chili-pickled radishes, all of them snatching the bright yellow strips out of a single bag. Other times, they bought a quartet of little batter cakes filled with red bean paste, one for each of them.

The best, though, were the sausages, because these were won, not bought. Yes, you could buy them skewered on thin wooden sticks, but you could also gamble for them. There was never a question what Charles and his friends would do. Someone would dig out a fen and they would all crowd around, breathless, as Charles stood on his tiptoes to spin the wheel — and he was always the one who spun, no matter whose pockets funded the venture, because he was the lucky one. Even then, he was the lucky one. He always spun, and he always won, a brace of six thin, crackling sausages, each bite full of a fragrant funk that he'd never tasted anywhere else, all for a single spin. That's what he wanted. The sausages, and the victory.

He turned to the closest person, and said urgently, *"Yie shi."* It was a young man in thick black glasses, who furrowed his brow at Charles.

Desperate now, he repeated himself. *"Qing wen je fu jing you mei you yie shi?"*

The young man took a step back and waved his hands apologetically. "Oh, I don't really speak Chinese, sorry. Um, *bu shuo zhong wen.* No speak."

"Yie shi! Night market! Street food!" shouted Charles at the person who was not a Beijinger after all, but some sort of interloper, dressed like all of Andrew's absurd friends in a pair of jeans far too tight for a man.

"Ah! Okay, you speak English! Tang Hua market is actually right nearby." Whipping out his phone, he pulled up a map as Charles began to sway on his feet. "Here, look. Just out the east entrance and a few blocks down Taipingqiao Road."

The map blurred behind the cracked screen as Charles struggled to remember the red-lined route. "Okay," he nodded. "Okay. Thank you. *Xie-xie.*"

"Are you sure you're okay, Uncle? Maybe you should sit down."

He waved off the concern and headed away from this globalized bustle. Charles Wang didn't need a man-child in girlish pants telling him what he should do!

Twenty minutes later he was seated on a plastic stool, a sagging string of naked lightbulbs dipped dangerously close to his head. In front of him, a split metal bowl with chicken stewed in medicinal herbs on one side and a fiery red fish stew on the other, along with a tin cup of tea. Craning his neck over the bowl so that none of the liquid would splash onto his shirt, he tipped hot spoonfuls of it down his throat.

Moths and mosquitoes fluttered around the bug zapper, too smart to get caught. Two women in flowered dresses sat on stools to his right, their wrists piled with gold bracelets. He'd never liked the platinum trend in America — what was the point of an expensive material that looked exactly like a cheap one? Much better the deep, unmistakable yellow of twenty-four-karat gold. The Chinese and the Indians had it figured out when it came to jewelry.

The Tang Hua night market was sandwiched between two high-rise office buildings, the sizzling from the grills and the hum of the generators competing with the constant chug of the air-conditioning units that lined one wall. Charles motioned to the proprietor, who turned towards him, wiping sweat from his buzz cut with his shirtsleeve as Charles addressed him in Mandarin.

"Boss, anyone around here bet on sausages?"

"Eh? Bet on sausages?"

"Bet! Bet on sausages! When I was a little punk, we used to do it on the streets. There was a stand with a wheel. A spin for a fen. Most of the punters lost, but you could win half a dozen for the price of one!"

"No, nothing like that around here. Bet on lotto, bet on Olympics, bet on who else is betting, but no betting on sausages."

The man turned abruptly, not interested in conversation, and went back to mincing the chilies that were making Charles sweat. He slurped another fiery mouthful and chewed. It was amazing. Food could make a person feel like all was right in the world even if he was sitting in his abandoned country with the last of his dwindling fortune strapped to his chest and a sinking feeling that he would never solve the mystery of his family's lost land.

Last chance, best chance.

The truth was, Charles didn't know — at least not exactly — where the land was. He knew the name of the village, he had photographs of the old family house, and he had pieces of the 1947 surveyor's measurements and a receipt from a tax assessment, but he didn't have an *address*. That was why he'd needed the lawyer. Someone who could make his pile of stories and documents into something tangible. His piss-poor excuse for a lawyer had at least done that, but he'd also dropped an unbelievable story on top of it, which Charles was here to investigate. But before he could do that, he wanted to see his land.

It had been years since Charles had ridden any kind of public transportation. Growing up in Taiwan, he had hung off the sides of buses with his friends, but the train system in China was a different matter altogether. A mass of Beijing residents poured out of the station, engulfing him, though when he turned in the other direction, there seemed to be just as many rushing in. The two opposing tides lapped up against each other, unceasing, merging without incident.

When had the children of China gotten so tall? They towered over him, these little treasures, six feet high and rising. Except for the tiny ones, so skinny that their skin stretched translucent over their toothpick bones; and the broad ones, with their farmboy shoulders and wide, flat faces. Charles felt comforted in this swirl of humanity, in this sea of black hair. If the billion people of China ever chose to march en masse, they would be overwhelming in their similarity and horrific in their differences. There would be so many variations on the theme of human that all typologies would be completely bulldozed. This was why he had never worried himself about how America viewed his children, never bothered himself over unflattering stereotypes and prejudices. What did it matter how a country full of white people saw them when the whole world was theirs?

Out the window, the horror of the postindustrial landscape was obscured by its own waste, a thick brown mist that hung heavy in the sky. The train windows were filmed over with it. Charles peered at the grimy window-sill. Putrid neon gum had hardened in one corner and a fluff of gray down, the vestige of some long-ago disease-ridden bird, mixed with curls of dust. Charles lifted his sleeve from the armrest and moved away from the window. Would it all be like this? Would the longitude and latitude on his deed point towards rows of tenements and factories where children worked for slave wages? A settled town of cheap shops and pasteboard houses that would collapse like they had just months ago in Sichuan after that unimaginable earthquake?

Disappointment crowded in. What would Barbra say if he had come all this way for nothing, for a place that didn't even exist anymore? Charles closed his eyes and sank into his seat, wishing that he had something to place between his head and the dingy white cover that was meant to protect the top of the train seat from the passengers' greasy scalps.

Before he even realized that he was asleep, the train screeched to a stop. What is that strange skill that allows us to doze through an unknown route and wake up at the correct station? He rushed to pick up his jacket and bag, glad to leave the train behind.

At the station, Charles waited for nearly an hour before a suspiciously new taxi finally deigned to pull up. It bumped him over a series of rural roads, the driver speaking at first in some sort of dialect that Charles could barely understand before he switched to a flawless Mandarin. On the outskirts of town, they saw a benighted huddle of mud-and-straw huts, shocking in their crudity. Next to them, children rolled an oil drum in a field, but they paused and looked up as the taxi passed. One small girl on the end waved, and Charles waved back, wishing that he could take her with him and put some new, clean clothes on her. A little girl should have a pretty dress. As they got closer to town, the road smoothed out and the houses began to look less haphazard. Charles looked down at the map. The mountains rose in the distance, just as they did on the map, and the road began to curve in a recognizable way towards a body of water in the distance. This was it. Charles felt sick. He couldn't wait to see it and he didn't want to look at it at all.

Desire, as always, outweighed fear.

An open ditch ran along the side of the road. Charles directed the driver to park next to it. "This is my family's old estate," he explained, proud. "I'm going to have a look at it. Wait here, please, until I return."

Tapping a cigarette out of a packet marked with a warning label and a photo of a shriveled fetus, the driver spit into the ditch. "How do I know you'll come back?"

"I'll leave my bag here with you."

The driver flicked his plastic green lighter and leaned into the flame. "What do I want with your old clothes? I don't even know if you can afford to pay me for waiting."

Charles was offended. His ability to pay for something like a taxi ride had never been called into question. "I can pay. There's no reason to doubt me."

Their eyes met in the rearview mirror, and Charles saw himself the way the other man saw him. Not as the prosperous businessman he so recently was, or as the scion of a landed family that he always would be, but as a foreigner wearing the same clothes he'd worn yesterday and the day before. He wanted to flash what remained of the bills, which he'd changed into yuan at the airport — that, at least, had made them multiply in a satisfying way — but Charles was now keenly aware of being in a deserted stretch of country where the driver might have compatriots without such law-abiding jobs. He left his money pouch strapped securely to his chest and instead opened his wallet to show the smaller stash of money that he'd placed there for incidentals.

The driver nodded, satisfied. "Leave your bag, and give me half now," he said.

The land in China. The landinChina. *ThelandinChina.*

Charles got out of the cab, hopped over the ditch, and walked straight into the field. He had drawn a painstaking outline of the land on Xeroxed pages of a topographical map and now he held them up, trying to get his bearings. In Los Angeles, real estate had never interested Charles. He had made sure to own his factories and his home — useless ambitions, in the end — but he had never been like some of his friends who snapped up sixteenplex apartments in Koreatown and minimalls in Studio City as quickly as they became available. As a result, he'd neglected to develop a talent for estimating acres or square footage at a glance, but if he had translated the old surveyor measurements on the land correctly, his family's holdings stretched out all the way to the mountains up ahead, acres and acres of it. More than hundreds, for sure. Thousands? Tens of thousands? The thought of it dizzied him. To the left and right, at the far edges of his vision, the horizon shimmered and the land seemed infinite. It was like owning all of Bel-Air and most of Westwood, too.

He peered out at the mountain. Was the family house still extant? It was hard to tell. Clusters of crumbling buildings dotted the mountainside and from a distance it was impossible to tell whether they were newer or older. The outline of the mountain ridge, though, felt familiar to Charles. *I know this place,* he thought. It was a comforting thought.

I know this place. This place is mine.

The soft curve of these mountains, interrupted by a tall jagged peak, was a part of his blood and his birthright. His father may not have managed to pass on the land itself, but this knowing was nearly as powerful an inheritance.

Only the land bordering the road appeared to be tilled. Charles kept walking until he reached a verdant open field dotted with tiny white flowers and climbed up a small rise. From there, he could see another rise in front of him, taller and a good bit farther away. Although each minute was costing him as much as that cheating cabbie wanted to charge, now that Charles was here, he had to see every inch that might have once belonged to the Wang family.

He plunged ahead.

The ground under him was damp, patches of mud hidden by the long grasses. One shoe got mired down, staying stubbornly behind when he pulled his foot up, so he took them both off, and his socks as well, and rolled up his pant legs. He marched forward, not minding that the mud was oozing over his feet. When he reached the next patch of dry grass, he wiped them off, liking the feeling of nature on his bare skin. Out of breath, sweat pooling under his armpits, he labored upward, scrunching his toes to get purchase on the slope.

By the time he got to the top, he was light-headed. He leaned over to take a full breath, and when he straightened, everything went white for a moment. Eyes closed, Charles let the blood drain downwards from his head and took several deep breaths. He opened his eyes. Everything was still a pulsing white. *Was this it?* The big stroke that he feared? He blinked. Shook his head. Bit down on his tongue to make sure that he could still feel things. And then he realized that it was the land itself.

Everything glowed. The fields were incandescent. The last of the morning dew caught the rising sun and sparkled, a tiny drop on the tip of each blade of grass, each drop a world in miniature. A slow breeze kicked up, rustling the leaves on the trees with their dark, elegant trunks that stood nearby. Pure beauty had never really moved Charles. He liked drama, he liked mischief, he liked luxury that bred desire.

But this, this was beauty.

Beauty.

Charles sank to his knees, then put his hands on the earth, not caring if the insolent driver saw him. He wanted to kiss the ground, to eat it.

Wiggling his fingers deeper into the dirt, he remembered a discussion he'd had with Nash once, soon after his friend had taken on a senior seminar populated mostly by second-generation Chinese immigrants. Nash had explained his students' complicated relationship to the country their parents had left behind, finally convincing Charles that not everyone saw the world as simply and clearly as he did. For Nash's students, there were many Chinas. There was the China that was against the world, the China that was the Communist government. The China that existed briefly in Taiwan. There was the China that covered things up and the China that was gradually making things free. And as many Chinas as there were, there were that many Charleses as well. Every immigrant is the person he might have been and the person he is, and his homeland is at once the place it would have been to him from the inside and the place it must be to him from the outside.

All of that was academic bullshit.

This, *this* was the only China.

This incandescent land that glowed all around him.

The mud caked on his soles and the flies that buzzed against his bare toes.

The mountains that rose like they did in ink-brush paintings by the old masters, rows of smoky gray ranges getting darker as they retreated. Charles plunged his fingers into the soil and wiggled them back and forth until he'd made a hole. He took out his father's bone, porous and gray, and dropped it in, covering it back up with the displaced earth. This, this must be what he'd meant to do with it all along.

Charles plucked a piece of grass and put it in his mouth, chewing cautiously. It was peppery and green-tasting, and that was China, too. He licked a little mud off the edge of his thumb. It didn't have much of a taste, just a rich, dirty essence. He could have made a meal of those things, could have lived on nothing else for the rest of his life.

This was the New World. He'd gotten it wrong. His father had gotten it wrong. Never mind the Communists, the Japanese, the murderous urchins of the Little Red Guard. This was China, and the Wangs, the great and glorious Wangs, never should have left.

Still half dreaming, Charles made his way to the far end of the stand of trees and unzipped his pants. He pulled out his penis and aimed a stream of urine against one of the tree trunks, then tilted towards another, reveling in the feeling of release. He would piss over every inch of this land, feeling more awake with every second that he continued to splatter the silvery bark. As he turned left, ready to water another tree, he saw a sign at the far edge of the clearing. Who dared lay claim to his land? Cutting the urine abruptly and shaking the end of his penis, Charles tucked himself back in and zipped up his pants.

The sign, when he reached it, was taller than it looked. He craned upwards, but still had to step back a few feet to read it.

APARTMENT CITY
NEXT SPRING: 3,000 LIVING UNITS

四十三

New Orleans, LA

ANDREW SAT in the meager shade outside of the Greyhound station, eating a slice of pepperoni pizza. In the end, he'd let Saina buy him a ticket from New Orleans to Helios, but he'd insisted on taking a bus instead of an easy plane ride. The route wound through Alabama and Georgia before heading up through the Carolinas and stopping at the Port Authority in New York City, where he'd transfer. *Maybe I should just stay there*, thought Andrew. *Maybe if I stay, I'll end up on* Saturday Night Live. He took another bite of pizza and chewed, happy.

四十四

Helios, NY

HELIOS CENTRAL HIGH was a long, two-story structure built of brick-colored blocks at the end of a country road that crested around a hill before it slid straight into the student parking lot.

"I don't like this," said Grace.

"You haven't even been inside yet!"

"Look at the sign. I mean, seriously?"

The sign was hard to miss. It was the tallest thing around for miles, a thick blue pole topped with a glowing billboard that wouldn't have been out of place on Broadway. Framed by lightbulbs that shone even though the sun was at its highest point in the sky, a giant, grinning cartoon lion — his name, apparently, was Growler — leaned up against the first *H* of the school.

Under the mascot, in perfectly placed letters:

HELIOS VS. M'GTVILLE @ 6 P.M.
NEW DRESS CODE TODAY

"You'll be fine," said Saina. "You're not exposing any unnecessary skin."

"I'm aesthetically offended by the whole thing. Football and rah-rah and, like, monster trucks."

Saina laughed. "It won't be that bad. You'll get to be the mysterious new girl. I bet the captain of the football team will think you're cu-ute!"

"*Ugh*. Muscles. Beefy necks. Gross." Grace slumped down in her seat. "Come on, let's just put it off for a day, okay? Just one day. Tomorrow I'll be a happy camper, but not today."

"We're just going to enroll. You don't have to go to any classes today, school's already been in session for hours."

"No . . . just no! Saina, please. Look, I'm a traumatized youth! I've just spent a week in an old car with my father and stepmother! My father got us in a car accident and then he deserted us! I have to sleep in a room with a weird ceiling!" Grace threw herself back against the car door, one arm sweeping dramatically across her forehead.

Saina always enjoyed her sister so much more in the particular than in the abstract. Grace in person was funny and self-aware. Grace on the phone was unrelenting and concerned with the smallest of slights — in between visits, that became the only Grace that she remembered.

Peeking out from under her arm, Grace tried again. "I know what we could do instead."

"What?"

"I haven't posted on my blog in forever. And you have so much cute stuff. Let me style you! And then we can take pictures!"

"Isn't your blog just pictures of you?"

"Yeah, but you can make a guest appearance!"

"You just want an excuse to get into my closet."

"Okay, maybe . . ." Grace batted her eyes. "I bet there's lots of stuff that you don't want anymore. Things that you've outgrown. Things that would be *perfect* on someone just a *leetle* bit younger."

Saina laughed. "That line of argument really shouldn't work, but okay, fine. No pictures of me, though. After that article, I don't need to be on any fashion blog, not even yours. But I'll take pictures of you."

"Really?"

"Yeah." She gunned the engine and made an extravagant U-turn. "You're free! But just until tomorrow."

It only took Grace one quick spin around the closet to pull out a vintage Ossie Clark dress, a pair of old motorcycle boots still caked with dirt, and a burgundy felt hat that she instantly made ten times as appealing by attaching a silver and turquoise petit point necklace around the brim. Saina was impressed with her sister. It was the kind of mishmash that a civilian could never have assembled and worn with any kind of ease, but somehow Gracie layered it on like a crazy bag lady and came out looking like a fantasy of the 1970s — more substantial than an Olsen twin, and more accessible.

Draping her camera around Saina's neck, Grace led them over the neighbor's collapsed wood-post fence to the horse paddock where a sweet old chestnut mare drank from a hay-flecked trough even as it pissed out a powerful stream of urine. Grace waited for the horse to finish and then led it to the west end of the enclosure, where she positioned the horse so that its nose nudged into the frame and placed herself where the setting sun could glint through the crook of her elbow as she reached for her hat, a motion she repeated effortlessly, each time making the gesture look fresh.

"Do you want some more poses?" asked Saina.

"No, that's my thing. One perfect shot each time. No one needs to see me pretending to look delighted with the world in twenty different ways. Also, I already know the quote I'm going to pair it with."

"What?"

"'I am rooted, but I flow.' It's Virginia Woolf."

Was Gracie some kind of stylist savant? And why couldn't that be as worthwhile, in the end, as dragging a brush over canvas or putting a pen to paper?

They got her one perfect shot and then, still feeling indulgent, Saina let Grace dress her for dinner. As soon as they walked into Graham's restaurant, the three of them — Saina, Grace, and Barbra, the Wangs without their center — spotted Leo, who was waiting for them at the bar. Saina felt self-conscious in the tiny skirt that her sister demanded she wear. Sensing her hesitation, Leo held up one smooth palm to give her a high five, but as they connected, a quick sting of skin on skin, he reached out and pinched her earlobe, deftly avoiding her gold ear cuff, then he wrapped his fingers around her palm and pulled her close, kissing her. Their lips were springy against each other, happy to meet.

From that joining on, everything about the evening was fun. Leo was warm and inquisitive; Barbra, wry and observant in a way Saina couldn't remember witnessing; Grace lit up under Leo's attention, describing the potential horrors of the local high school. Graham tucked them in a corner of the restaurant and kept their votives afire and their wineglasses full, bringing them treats from the kitchen that he insisted were mistakes on the part of his incompetent chef and, at the end of the night, dancing Grace across the empty dining room floor as Cat Stevens played.

When they finally left, every star in the sky was out, shining as hard as it could on them, and Grace and Barbra were actually leaning towards each other, giggling about something.

Her sister turned around. "So," she said sweetly, "when are you guys gonna get maaawied?"

"Grace! C'mon. Don't be embarrassing!"

"What's embarrassing? You love Leo! We love Leo!" She swayed a little on her heels. Oops. Someone should have been watching Gracie's glass. "Leo. Leo! Leo, let me tell you, you're so much better than Saina's last boyfriend. He was super-hot, but he was kind of a dick." Grace clapped a hand over her mouth and looked at Barbra. "Sorry! Sorry! It's true, though!"

Saina tensed. Every time Grayson came up — and she tried to make sure it was as rarely as possible — she imagined Leo imagining them together that morning, a postcoital shame that had never quite dissipated.

But Leo let his dimples show and was about to say something as Grace talked over him, drunk. "Also, your babies will be so cute! Mixed babies are the cutest!" She shot Barbra a look, not noticing as Leo winced. "It's true! They are! C'mon, Leo! Don't you want to see what it would look like if you reproduced?" She stopped abruptly and looked down at her shoes. "Oh! I have to tie these."

They were all quiet for a moment, and that was beautiful, too. The night was both liquid and crisp, delicious and dark, the leaves rustled wildly in the trees. And then Leo was tugging her gently by the elbow, leading her away from Barbra and Grace, who had headed towards the car. The silence extended onward, but Saina didn't notice until she realized abruptly that it should terrify her. Finally, Leo said, "Actually, I should probably tell you something. Saina, I do have a child. A daughter."

Time stopped. Space collapsed. Every star shut down. There. There was the catastrophe she'd been waiting for.

"Before you say anything, I know. It's bad I didn't tell you," he said.

"But *why?* Why not? I wouldn't have cared!"

"I don't know! It was stupid! I was scared to! The first real thing you told me about was how your fiancé knocked up this girl and left you, so I didn't really think that I should lead with that piece of information. What was I supposed to say? And then everything was so good, and it's not like I meet a million amazing girls up here."

"So you just wanted to hold on to me because you were worried that no one else would come along?"

"No! No. I wanted to hold on to you because I *fell* for you."

"And how long were you going to keep it a secret?"

"It was never the right time. When we got back together, I was going to tell you, but at first it was . . . it was just so good that I didn't want to mess everything up, and then you were worried about your speech, and then your family was coming, and you were stressed about that. You've had a lot to deal with, and I didn't want to be the guy adding to it."

"So I'm the delicate flower who can't handle anything?"

"No! No. I was trying to be considerate. I was trying to be a gentleman. Okay, I hear myself. I know. It sounds so stupid now."

"Do you see her?"

"My daughter?"

"Of course your daughter!"

A long pause. "Not right now."

Suspicion pulled at her. Why not? What did Leo do? Was this becoming one of those stories where the perfect man turns out to be a murderous imposter?

"Since when?"

He sighed, long and heavy. "Since a few months ago."

"Why not?"

"Her mom and I got in a fight about stupid shit."

"What."

"What?"

"The stupid shit. What was it."

"She and I had started hooking up again and I guess she thought, you know, that since we had a kid together, and we were sleeping together, that it was going to be happy families."

"And then?"

"I met you. That day. At Graham's restaurant."

"And then she wouldn't let you see your *kid?* That's crazy."

"I know! *She's* crazy."

"I hate it when people say their ex-girlfriends are crazy. It's so fucking misogynistic."

"Saina, life is messy, okay? It's not . . . things don't just fall into place for everyone."

"Why are you saying that to me? You think I don't know that? Hello, you were there when we read that article, weren't you?"

"Yeah, but shit happens in your life and it becomes a *story* in a glossy *magazine.* That doesn't happen for other people. Shit happens in my life and it just sucks. Nobody writes an article about it."

"You think that makes it better? No. No. That just makes it all so much worse. It's like living in a tiny village where you know that everyone's talking about you, but it's all of New York City."

"But I *do* live in a tiny village. And the only reason I'm still here is because this is where they live."

"Why don't you have any pictures of her? What's her name? How old is she?"

"I have a million pictures of her!" He took out his phone and swiped at it, scrolling past photos of him and Saina laughing together at a barbecue and astride his tractor. "Her name is Kaya, and she's three." He thrust the glowing rectangle at her.

"Oh. She's really, really cute." Seeing these photos of a chubby little girl who could only be Leo's, Saina felt unaccountably sad. Is this what would happen forever afterwards now? Would every man she met have some sort of secret progeny who would expose him as an asshole? The future felt dead and unthinkable.

"I don't know, Leo. I don't know what to do."

"Don't do anything. Just think about this for a minute, okay?"

"Did you hide pictures of her in your house because of me?"

"No! I don't have pictures of anything in my house!"

It was true. Leo's house was spare and undecorated, a reaction, he said, against the chaos of his childhood. His childhood. How could an abandoned child abandon his own?

"Saina, don't be mad at me just because you feel like you're supposed to be."

"I'm not! That is so condescending—"

"Look, I didn't get mad at you when I was supposed to —"

"You mean when you walked in on us? You did get mad! I tried to apologize and you never texted me back."

"Grayson was living in your house! How understanding did you expect me to be?" He stood facing her for a long minute, and then added, quietly, "And when you told him to leave, what did I do? I just took you back. Just like that."

She didn't know how to respond to that. It was true, but it wasn't fair! He couldn't think it was the same thing.

Grace broke into their silence. "Guys, I'm really sorry, I know you're fighting and personally I think it's really dumb, but —"

"Grace! We're having a serious conversation."

Instead of speaking, Grace handed Saina her phone.

"What are you trying to show me?"

"An email. From Daddy."

Saina focused on the screen.

Do not be worried. I should tell you that I am in the hospital. Many things have happened that are too difficult to explain here. I am okay.

She turned back to Grace. "That's it? That's all he says? What are we supposed to do with that?"

"Saina, what is happening? You're scaring me," said Leo.

Drawing Grace towards the car, Saina closed ranks.

"It's nothing."

"It's clearly something!"

"It's nothing for you to worry about."

"Saina, tell me. Is your dad okay? What's going on?"

She stopped walking and let go of Grace's hand. "It doesn't concern you anymore, Leo. I can't do this again. I don't hate you, okay? I just think it's better if we stop seeing each other."

"*Seeing* each other? We're not *seeing* each other, Saina. We're —"

"We're nothing. I have to go."

She felt Leo falling away from her, a stuffed animal dropped from the claw of one of those games she used to play at Chuck E. Cheese — so much concentration, so many tokens, and no matter what, the prize never made it to the chute, just tumbled away at the very moment she thought it might be secured.

四十五

Beijing, China

MOST OF THE TIME, Andrew didn't think about his father that much. There was hardly ever any reason to. But from the moment he'd gotten that weird email confession from China, the insistent tug of anxiety that Andrew usually directed towards girls centered itself instead on his father. That tugging had kept him awake through the entire flight from Atlanta — where he'd run off the bus, almost forgetting his duffel bag — to Beijing, and now that he'd landed, now that he was actually *in* China, probably about to figure out what was going on with his father, it had only gotten harder to ignore. The only thing he could think of, the only thing that might make him feel better, was fried rice.

It was one of his favorite pastimes, really. Andrew loved consuming platters of fried rice doused in chili oil in giant bites, preferably with an oversize serving spoon. Warm, fluffy bite after warm, fluffy bite, each one piled high with once-frozen peas and carrots, golden bits of scrambled egg, and plump, glistening pieces of shrimp.

Eating like this, he could never get full. There was no point of satiation; there was only the act of bringing spoon to mouth, of taste buds and heat receptors leaping to action to take in each bite, feeling flavor and warmth spread across his tongue and down the back of his throat. The sameness of each bite, the repetition of the spooning and the chewing, helped calm him. It didn't even have to be good fried rice. He was eating out of a take-out box from an airport place that was like a Chinese version of Panda Express — just as terrible and just as delicious — sitting on a bench next to the baggage claim, waiting for his sisters. Hopefully this was the right baggage claim. There were three China Air flights coming into Beijing from New York at around the same time, so Andrew figured he'd start waiting at the earliest one.

With every bite, a few grains dropped off the heaping spoonful as it made its way into his mouth. Andrew started to like the skittering noise they made as they fell back on the Styrofoam shell.

There should be a German word for that sound. That was a good idea; he should remember to work it out — something riffing on all those tiny, leftover-floss-in-the-teeth-type things that there could be German words for. He was going to have to start coming up with some stuff that wasn't so Asian soon. Especially if, well, what if he did stand-up in China? Did that even exist? His doing material about being a minority wouldn't go over that well here. Even the guy emptying the trash was Chinese.

"Andrew!"

With a shout, he was being hugged from both sides and the take-out container slid dangerously down his lap.

"Guys!" He squirmed his arms out of the pile of sisters so that he could embrace them. They smelled like airplane food and other people's perfume, but they also smelled like home.

"*Ew,* Andrew! What are you eating? That looks gross!" Grace couldn't believe that her brother was downing a giant pile of fried rice for his first meal in China. Shouldn't they be having, like, Peking duck or something?

Andrew squeezed her tighter. "It's kind of gross, but I've been eating donuts and beer for the past few days, so it's actually delicious." When they finally let go of each other, he couldn't hold the anxiety down any longer, trying to sound casual as he asked, "So, guys, are we worried?"

Saina pulled back. It had been almost a year since she'd seen both of her siblings at the same time. They looked back at her, anxious, and she remembered the mom feeling that she hated and missed. "About Dad?"

They nodded.

"Yes and no? I'm not sure, you guys really know as much as I do. I only talked to him for a minute before some nurse came in."

"Do you think Dad really got into a fight?" said Grace. "I can't even picture him jogging."

Andrew thought that was kind of unfair. "He plays tennis."

"Yeah, but tennis is more like a country-club activity. He plays tennis and goes on people's boats. That's not *exercise*."

Saina laughed. "I don't think it was a boxing match! He said he was okay, though, but he seemed to want us to come, so who knows." And then, as much as she had been trying not to think about Leo at all, he came back to her mind. *Had he called?* She reached into her bag. "I forgot to turn my phone back on. Maybe Dad called."

Grace was surprised. "You got international calling?"

"It's still on my phone from when I was in Berlin."

"Isn't that expensive?"

The truth was, she didn't really know. It could have been, but all those bills were deducted automatically from her checking account — phone, Internet, cable, car insurance, house insurance, water, gas, electricity, garbage, membership to the gym that had no branches outside of Manhattan, the CSA that she had only picked up twice, and, embarrassingly, phone, Internet, and cable for her long-sold apartment. She'd tried to cancel them, but the customer service person seemed much more determined to keep her than she was to leave. "Well, we still have to be able to communicate somehow, right?" she replied, guilt making her voice sharp. Frugality was a new thing, and none of them knew quite how to handle it.

"It's just kind of weird that you're still acting like we're rich," said Grace, angrily.

"He-ey," Andrew broke in. "So, uh, did I pick the right baggage claim?"

His sisters were silent for a moment, and then Saina relaxed against Andrew. "You're still the sweetest."

"What do you mean?" He knew exactly what she meant, of course, and knew that his sisters would be looking at each other now, smiling. He checked. They were.

"Don't worry," said Grace. "We still love each other."

"Wait! Here's the real question: Where's Barbra?"

"Her passport was expired."

"No!"

"Yeah."

"Oh, poor Babs. So what's she doing now? Is she all alone in your house, Saina?"

Yes, Barbra was alone in her house, with the keys to her rickety Saab and her friend Graham's phone number in case she needed anything. It had been strange leaving someone else in the house that she'd spent the last few months hiding in and obsessing over. When they were saying goodbye, a thought had struck her.

She'd asked Barbra, "Isn't it weird?"

"Zen yang?"

"That you're here. I mean, when you were growing up in Taiwan, would you ever have thought that you'd end up spending time alone in a farmhouse in upstate New York? When I bought the place, they told me it was built in 1902. I bet that first farmer would never have expected that some Asian lady would end up in his house."

Barbra had looked at her for a moment, confused. "But you are also some Asian lady."

Oh god, she remembered thinking. *How could I be so obtuse?* "You're right. I guess it felt . . . different? But you're right. That's dumb. It's the same thing."

Unexpectedly, Barbra had laughed. "Who knows where we end up in a life? Could be anywhere. Even some farmhouse. Some Asian lady."

Her phone dinged. Emails, a voicemail, five texts. She clicked on the texts first.

917-322-XXXX
I'm dying here Saina.

917-322-XXXX
Have you read it yet?

917-322-XXXX
Check your email.

917-322-XXXX
?

917-322-XXXX
Where are you?

Even though she'd deleted his number from her phone, Saina knew with a sick plunk that it was Grayson. That was his pattern. Their pattern. They would argue, and then Saina would turn off her phone and go to yoga or go for a walk or have drinks with friends, and Grayson would thrash around in his studio until he couldn't take it any longer and then she'd turn her phone on to find eight missed texts and twice as many missed calls. Each time it flattered and embarrassed her. She tapped the email icon, waiting for it to load, her breath shorting in her lungs.

What was Saina doing, buried in her phone? Grace poked her. "Did Dad call? Or Leo?"

"No . . ."

"Then what?"

"I don't . . . I'm not really sure. Wait a sec, let me look."

Sometimes when Grace was with her siblings, she wanted to hold on to them, to make sure that they couldn't get away and have lives that didn't involve her. "Well, did he email?"

Andrew turned to her. "Leo! I forgot about the boyfriend. Grace, did you meet him?"

Grace looked at her sister as she spoke. "Yeah. I thought he was so cool. And nice. And easy to talk to. Grayson's better-looking, but Leo's definitely a better person. Uh . . . except that Saina broke up with him."

"What? Why?"

Saina was still buried in her phone, so Grace answered for her. "Because he has a kid."

She'd accidentally clicked on an email from her friend Lotte, inviting her to Montauk for the weekend, and she was still waiting for the email from Grayson to load when Grace's response sank in. It wasn't untrue. She broke up with him because he had a kid. Seriously, was everyone going to have a kid? She looked up at Andrew.

Saina looked so embarrassed that it embarrassed him. "Well, at least you know he's not shooting blanks."

"Yeah, well. It's not really that he has a kid, it's that he never told me about her until Grace somehow got it out of him."

"How is that even possible?"

"I know! It was . . . well, it was a really dumb explanation."

"But how long have you guys been together? A few months, right?"

"Off and on."

"So how could it not have come out? Didn't he see the kid?"

Did she have to answer all of these questions? "No. But supposedly because his ex-girlfriend was mad at him and wouldn't let him see her."

"But he was trying to?"

"I think so, yeah."

"How long was he not allowed?"

"Oh god, Andrew, I don't know." Saina realized, as she did almost every time she saw him, that her brother was in every way a good person.

"Was it just, like, a little while? I'm just trying to figure out if she's the crazy person in this situation."

"I think everyone's the crazy person." Could she read Grayson's email now? Saina looked at Andrew and then Grace.

"What?" asked Grace.

Why not just tell them? They weren't little kids anymore. "It's not from Leo, it's actually an email from Grayson."

Grace surprised herself by feeling jealous. It wasn't that guys didn't like her, but would they ever pine for her the way they did for Saina? She decided right then that that was what she wanted.

"Well, read it," said Andrew.

"I'm just going to read it to myself. Do you guys want to go check and see if our luggage is out yet?"

"It's not. Nothing is," said Grace. "We can see the carousel from here."

But Andrew pulled her up, and they went to go stand next to a trio of nuns in sky-blue habits.

Saina clicked on the email.

My love (because that's what you are):

I'm just going to sit down here and pour it all out on the page. On the electronic page. You are my love Saina. You and no one else.

You're going to think it's crazy but it's the baby that made me realize it. James. He's the best little dude. I love him so hard and fierce that I'm blind with it and he made me realize that I want it all to be that big.

That's what you do to me baby my other baby. I don't know what was wrong with me but I'm pretty sure I had to do this. I got scared of us I guess but I'm not anymore.

I never explained this to you before and maybe it's really fucking stupid to put it in a love letter but I'm a little drunk right now so I'm going to and hope it will help you understand. I did what I did with Sabrina because she's like a symbol of everything a man is supposed to want. I know you're not going to believe that but it's true. I'm me but I'm also still just a kid from a fishing town in Maine and she's the gorgeous blonde with the moneyed old family and from the first second she just admired the shit out of me. Who could resist that combination. I couldn't. From the second we met all she wanted to do was support me and promote me and introduce me to her rich friends who all actually followed through on calling my gallery and I kind of got high on it. And I'm not going to say I'm sorry about it because that wouldn't even matter. If you think about it, it had to happen this way. I had to have that to know that I wanted you. She does everything for me *because* of me and I thought I needed that. Because you don't do that. You do things for yourself and I do things for myself. We're selfish bastards Saina and now I know it's better that way for people like us.

Because we burn up the world together. You can't deny it. I don't talk to anyone the way I talk to you. No one else has ideas like we do. No one else consumes shit the way that we do. We tear each other apart. We crawl up inside each other and die there. It sounds sick but it's amazing. That's the way we love and I miss it.

I won't lie. I love what Sabrina does for me. But I love what you do TO me and WITH me. And now I'm so lonesome without you. Lonesome. Like Johnny Cash. I know you hate similes (See I remember everything about you.) but they just keep coming out because I've never written a letter like this before.

You know I've already deleted this letter ten times? I know I don't have a lot of shots left with you. Hell maybe I don't even have this shot. But I'm going to try.

You're going to ask if I have any plans for us and I don't. But I know that we should be together. Just tell me that you want to be with me and that will be enough for me right now. We'll figure the rest out. Maybe me and you will have a baby. Why not.

Okay now I really am drunk and I'm at least smart enough not to keep writing this. But you'll think about it won't you. I know you met that guy up there but he's not me and Sabrina's not you.

I love you I love you I love you my little pieces. I love you.

G

She felt calm at first, detached, and vaguely interested. But as she scanned, thumbing the screen upwards, her fury grew. Grayson probably wrote this in Sabrina's apartment, huddled in the kitchen in the middle of the night, draining a bottle of whiskey while his *fiancée* breastfed their baby. Saina could see it. Him, with the screen glowing on his face. Her, burping some adorable, chubby creature, worried about his absence but not wanting to say it.

It was gratifying, a little bit, to think that she could take him away from Sabrina. Her ring was probably in their apartment, too, or in Sabrina's workshop. She'd given it back when they'd broken up. Flung it at him and then run to get the complex, faceted box it had come in and thrown that at him, too. Now Saina remembered how it had felt on her finger, how its heaviness had meant that she was loved, that she could stop worrying about that part of her life at least. She missed that constant reminder, even if it had turned out to be a lie.

Andrew looked back at his sister. She was sitting on the bench next to his duffel, staring at the floor in front of her. Grayson was probably trying to win her back, that asshole. He hoped that she didn't fall for it. Saina and Grace hadn't asked him yet about Dorrie, but he'd tell them the truth if they did.

Just then the baggage carousel started up, and pieces of luggage started sliding down the chutes.

"Oh! I see mine! It was the first one out!" Grace dragged him behind her as she chased her bag and then Saina's. As they walked back to the bench, pulling the suitcases behind them, he leaned in to her and whispered, pointing at the man putting a new plastic bag in the metal bin, "Have you ever seen a Chinese janitor before?"

"I've never even seen so many Chinese *people* before," she whispered back. But it was true. She'd never seen a Chinese janitor or a security guard or even a Chinese boy band like the one that had been on the plane with them.

Saina stood up as they approached. "Okay, so I'm thinking that we just go straight to the hospital, right? It's almost midnight, so it doesn't really make sense to find a hotel and stuff. Let's just go there and maybe they'll let us into his room, or if not, there'll probably be a waiting room or something."

"Wait, you're not just going to slip by us! What did Grayson want?" asked Grace.

How could she even begin to explain it? "I don't think I'm going to respond to him."

"But what did he say?"

"It was . . . a weird love letter. I don't know. I don't really want to talk about it now. It's so late, and I just want us to get to the hospital, okay?" She slipped her arm through Grace's and pulled her in closer. "Are you hungry? Should we get something before we go?"

Grace dropped her arm. "No, I'm fine," she said, moving forward to catch up with Andrew.

Once they made their way through customs, minus an apple that Grace had in her bag, they spotted a gangly young woman in a black necktie and a driver's cap holding up a sign that said SAINA WANG. A girl! That was a surprise. Andrew was impressed. As they walked towards her, he asked Saina, "How did you know how to hire a driver in China?"

"The assistant at the gallery did it."

"Are you Miss Wang?"

"Yes. *Wo men yie ke yi shuo zhong wen.*"

"Oh no. It good. For me. To practice. English," said the driver, who stuck a hand out for them each to shake. "I am Bing Bing."

"I'm Saina. This is Andrew and Grace."

"Did. You all. Have. Good flight. From America?" She picked out her words carefully. Things were going to take a lot longer if they were going to let Bing Bing practice her English, but Saina didn't have the heart to embarrass her by insisting on a switch to Chinese.

"Someday I go. To America. I like Michael Jordan! And *Titanic*! Very good."

Andrew laughed. "Yeah! You like basketball?" He mimed a shot. "Three-pointer?"

"Yes! I like slam dunk!"

Finally, Grace smiled, too. "Me, too. It's the best thing about basketball."

Before they could stop her, Bing Bing had stacked their suitcases on top of each other on her cart and wrestled the bags off each of their shoulders. Even at the helm of the loaded cart, she stalked ahead of them, stopping every few minutes to let them catch up.

四十六

Gaofu, China

ON THE FAR WALL of the waiting area there was a poster of hospital rules and regulations topped with a symbol of a sleeping man, eyes closed and dreaming of a moon. A giant red circle with a slash through it surrounded the illustration. The message was clear. No sleeping allowed. And, according to the rest of the symbols, no eating, no drinking, and no cell phones either. Yet the chairs below the poster were full of people dozing off, care packages of food on their laps and half-empty cans of tea on the floor below them.

Bing Bing had offered to recline the seats in her snub-nosed minivan so that they could sleep in the hospital parking lot, but now that they'd come all the way across the globe it seemed important to close the last few feet of distance between themselves and their father.

Andrew stood in front of the vending machine considering the unfamiliar coins in his hand, change from his airport fried rice. Saina was talking to someone at the nurse's station as Grace staked out a row of seats for them. He looked at the clock, 1:34 a.m. In New Orleans it was still yesterday. He dropped a coin into the slot and waited for the can of chrysanthemum tea to roll to the right and clunk down the chute. Holding the hot can carefully between two fingertips, he popped the tab, releasing a hiss of steam.

After they'd drunk up the tea, holding the cans against their faces as comfort against the swampy chill of the waiting room, Grace curled up in one of Andrew's sweatshirts and fell asleep with her feet dangling over the armrest.

Saina and Andrew whispered to each other.

"Is she going to go to school in your town?" he asked.

"I think so. But we haven't even gotten her registered yet."

"She could just take the GED."

"She has all of senior year left!" said Saina.

"I doubt Grace cares."

"About senior year?"

"Yeah."

"You loved high school."

"So did you."

Had she? "No, I loved having a driver's license and hanging out with my friends."

"Same thing." Andrew looked at his sleeping sister. "Poor Gracie. Too bad she had to go to boarding school."

"I tried to get Dad to send me to boarding school. I had this East Coast fantasy — boys who played lacrosse, long talks about J. D. Salinger, hot cocoa in dorm rooms, that kind of thing."

"I didn't know that!"

"You were a little kid."

"What happened?"

Saina nudged one leg under Andrew's. "Mom died. And then I felt bad about wanting to leave."

He was quiet for a minute. "I hope Dad's okay."

"I think he is."

"I hope so."

"Hey, so what happened in New Orleans anyways? Why'd you end up ditching them? Grace said that you fell in love. Did you really?"

"Yep. An older woman."

"Andrew!"

"*Shh* . . . hospital voice!"

"Okay, sorry! How much older?"

"Mmm . . . kind of a lot older."

"Fifty? Sixty? Was she a sexy octogenarian?"

"No! Like, thirty, maybe."

"Ancient!"

"Sorry, sorry, *you're* not old, but she —"

"I'm kidding! That is a lot older than you. Was it, um . . ." Saina realized that she had never discussed sex with either of her siblings.

"Actually, she was probably more like thirty-five."

"Probably?"

"Probably definitely."

"Were you . . . uh, was it . . ."

Andrew wanted to giggle. "Are you trying to ask me if we did it?"

"Well, I know you once said that you were waiting to fall in love when,
well, remember? We had that talk."

"Yeah, let's not do that again."

"Okay! Okay. Well, whatever happened, are you alright? Do you feel
okay about everything?"

Without permission, a tear forced its way out of his eye. And then another and another. But he nodded.

"What? What's happening? I don't get it. Are you okay? Are you sad
that you left her there? Did she break your heart or something? Are you
going to go back there?"

More tears. "Whisper!"

"Sorry!"

"I'm . . . yeah." How could he even explain it to her? He wiped his right
eye, then his left. "I'm not going to go back there, probably."

"Okay . . ."

He looked at his sister. Her eyes were a lighter brown than anyone else's
in their family, and now the glow from a wall sconce shone through them,
making them look almost golden. He couldn't say it. "Don't worry, Saina.
It just wasn't what I expected, but I'm fine. Let's go to sleep now."

"Okay, but if you ever want to discuss, we can. Even if I am your sister."

"Okay."

Saina kissed his shoulder and matched her breathing to his as he closed
his eyes and slowly dropped off to sleep.

Three hours later, Saina was still up. It must be almost dawn now, but her
circadian clock was out of sync and the weird metallic tang that perme-

ated the waiting room was difficult to ignore. She'd read Grayson's email over and over again until the words had lost their meaning; her ex-fiancé and her now ex-boyfriend chased each other around and around in her head.

She got up slowly, trying not to wake anyone up. An old woman slept to her left, head tucked into her neck, her forehead remarkably unlined under a yellowish white bob. Saina had seen her come in close to three a.m., balancing a set of bamboo baskets topped with a pointed lid. Saina knew that there were steamed buns in there. She could smell their sweet yeastiness and the distinct wood-pulp whiff of the heated baskets. The thought of offering a few yuan for one was tempting, but these must have been made especially for a patient, someone very dear to this granny, who was willing to forgo a night of sleep and possibly a day's wages to make a long journey.

Maybe her father was up, too, somewhere in this hospital. She had gotten nowhere with the nurse on duty, who refused to even look up a patient outside of visiting hours. Saina had tried to circumvent her by calling the number her father had dictated, but it rang right at the desk, and the nurse had picked it up triumphantly, saying in English, "Hey-lo!" Now the woman was finally facing away, engrossed in a Korean drama on the tiny block of a television that sat at her station.

Regrets were the easiest things to remember. She wished that she had never told Leo that Grayson always tried to make her be the big spoon. It was true, but it felt like a terrible thing to say about another man. Her former fiancé had always wanted to be the one who was hugged and protected. "We burn up the world together." That was true, too. At their best, they were incandescent. Electrified by each other. In a room filled with friends and former lovers and people they should probably know, no one else had ever mattered but her and him.

Keeping an eye on the nurse's back, Saina opened a door with another KEEP OUT sign and slipped into a long hallway. She'd kept vigil in a hospital once before, for a daredevil friend who'd been in a drunken motorcycle accident in Manhattan, but that time dozens of nurses had stalked the corridors, following patients in wheelchairs with IVs on rollers. It was different here, an hour outside of Beijing. Almost no staff. A crowd of waiting visitors. As Chinese as she felt in Helios or even Manhattan, the hospital in China was a foreign land. Her flats squeaked on the cheap linoleum floors, and she held her breath as something rattled in the distance. When nothing appeared around the corner, she let her breath out slowly. Yoga breath. *Phew. Safe.*

At the first set of double doors, Saina paused and looked inside the window. *What the hell?* The fluorescent lights blazed, and the patients lay in long, pathetic rows, as if they were in an army ward. Each one seemed to have a leg slung up on a pulley or a bandaged stump resting over their blanket. It was horrifying. Was her father in one of these wards? Alone in a crowd of Chinese people? He'd said only that he'd gotten into a fight and that they were both in the hospital. Were his injuries worse than she thought? She looked at the men — and they were all men — in the narrow room, relieved when she couldn't find her father's face.

They really did look like casualties. Was China fighting some clandestine war in its hinterlands? A true conflict in Tibet? Or another suppression of artists and scholars?

Saina knew that her grandparents had fled the Japanese. There were stories of narrow escapes, of running down a road in soft-soled shoes, a Japanese fighter plane strafing the ground. Somehow, Saina had always pictured it in hazy, romantic tones, as if a pair of torn stockings had been the only casualty. And then one day she'd been online, searching for photos for her *Look/Look* project, feeling slightly ill as she scanned groupings of refugees for a pretty face. She'd started out on the familiar news sites — the *New York Times, Newsweek,* the BBC. One click had led to another, and gradually she found herself moving through sites full of conspiracy theory and invective, with the photos themselves getting more and more graphic, whole slide shows preceded by flashing titles: THE ISH THEY DON'T WANT YOU TO SEE! or NSFW GRAPHIC.

Before that, it had never occurred to Saina that the photos of war she saw in the paper, the long rows of patients with bandaged stumps like the men before her, the dead bodies in ditches, that those were still censored for the coddled public who would — wouldn't they? — rise up and demand peace forever if they saw what war really looked like. If they had seen photographs like the ones that crowded into her browser, image after image of men turned into carcasses, butchers' piles of meat and organs made grotesque by a human hand or head, they could never arm their children and send them overseas to fight other people's children.

Her grandparents' escape could not have been some daring, madcap jaunt. The gunfire, in her childhood imagination, had always pinged ineffectually on either side of the golden path, the stupid Japanese never coming close to her daring grandparents. But, of course, that couldn't be true. It must have hit people, destroyed them, burst open their bodies, and left them twisted and wrecked all over the road. Her grandmother, in her soft-soled shoes, must have run past children with their limbs blown in half, their bloody bones cracked so that the marrow was exposed like joints of lamb, their small bodies sniffed at by mad-eyed dogs.

"They see too much," her father had said once, when she was doing a report for history class and asked him whether his own parents had ever talked about the war. "They see too much so they have to close their hearts tight. Can't get them open again."

She didn't understand that fear. If she was lucky, she never would.

Saina turned down another corridor. A ward full of babies. New life. Little creatures who hadn't yet seen the things we could do to one another.

Saina looked at her cell phone. Another text.

917-322-XXXX
Please.

She turned off her phone.

After another ten minutes of wandering around the hospital, light-headed and unsure of herself, down another hallway and then another, she peeked inside a door that had been left ajar and she saw her father. He was asleep. Peacefully, blissfully asleep. The heart-rate monitor attached to him hopped encouragingly. There was an IV drip that worried her, and the black eye he got in the car accident had bloomed, but otherwise he looked decent.

An accordion screen stretched across the middle of the room, blocking off the windows. Whoever was on the other side had the window and the privacy, something that Saina couldn't imagine her father allowing. What had happened to him? She wanted to sneak in and read his medical charts, but they would be in Chinese, and though she could make her way well enough when trying to speak the language, she really could only read numbers and a handful of words.

Instead, she slid to the floor outside his door and finally, finally, fell asleep.

"Xing lai! Xiao meimei xing lai! Zao an, xiao meimei! Hel-lo! Rise and shi-ine!"

Ugh. Grace's neck was twisted and sore, and her legs were numb from hanging over the armrest all night.

"Wa! Xiao meimei xing lai le!"

Oh. That noise was being directed at her. A man wearing a red baseball cap popped into view. He peered down at her with a giant smile that stretched from one sparsely whiskered cheek to the other.

"Xing lai! Xing lai! Lai kan baba!"

His teeth were yellowed and uneven, and tiny bits of spittle flung themselves onto his lips as he talked way too close to her face. Why was this man telling her to wake up?

"Ni shi shei?" asked Grace.

"Ha ha ha!" He cocked his hat up and looked around the room, searching for someone to confirm that this was, indeed, the funniest thing he'd ever heard. *"Wo shi shei?"*

"Andrew! Wake up!" She kicked at him.

Her brother startled and opened his eyes. "What's happening?"

"I don't know. Who is this guy? He keeps telling me to wake up and go see Dad."

"Maybe he's a relative?"

The man stood there patiently, still smiling at them. *"Lai! Lai kan baba!"*

Grace whispered, "Do you think he's . . . you know."

"Slow?"

"Yeah."

"I don't know."

"Wang xiao hai, shi de ma? Wo shi shushu!"

"I mean, he seems to know us, right? He just called himself our uncle." He turned to the man. *"Hao, shushu.* Uh ... *qing deng yi xia."* Andrew started gathering their stuff. "Wait, where's Saina? Her stuff's gone."

"Oh god, who knows. You realize that at this point I'm the only family member who *hasn't* disappeared?" said Grace, a little angry.

"Maybe she's with Dad already," said Andrew.

It would be just like Saina to sneak up to see their father while she and Andrew were asleep. They followed the man past the deserted nurse's station and into an elevator. When the elevator doors slid open, there was Saina, asleep on the floor.

Grace was startled. "Saina! What's happening?"

Saina opened her eyes as if she had just been waiting there for them, half sprawled out on the floor. "What time is it? This is Dad's room."

Andrew shrugged. "Morning time?"

The man who had gotten off the elevator with her siblings immediately squatted down next to Saina, delighted. *"Ah! Wang Jiejie! Ne me piao li-ang! Lai lai lai, bu yao zuo zai di shang!"* He put out a hand to help her up and, not wanting to be rude, she took it, nearly colliding into him as they both stood. The man kept hold of her hand and began shaking it. *"Ni hao, ni hao, wo shi shushu!"*

Uncle? What was this man talking about? Ignoring him, Saina pushed open the door.

Grace and Andrew stopped in the doorway, shocked. Their father was in a hospital gown printed with, of all things, tiny little *ducks*. He had an IV drip in his arm and wires attached to his chest. His face looked strange. Saina hadn't noticed it when he was asleep, but awake, something seemed off, like he'd gotten Botox accidentally or something.

Their father's eyes fluttered open, and instead of looking at them, he fixed on the man who had brought them to the room. "Wha! Andrew! Grace! Saina! Why are you talking to him? No! Tell him go away! *Ni bu yao gen wo de xiao hai zi shuo hua!"* Charles shouted, his attempts to make a shooing motion hampered by the wires webbed in front of him.

Meanwhile, the stranger who seemed to know them had disappeared behind the accordion divider and was murmuring to an unseen patient on the other side.

"Daddy! Are you okay?" Grace hugged her father carefully as he patted her hair, and then he stretched his arms out for Saina and Andrew.

"All my children!" he said, hugging them each in turn. "All my children in a general hospital!" Charles had known for sure that Grace and Saina would come, but there was a chance that the thieving woman would keep his son in her grasp. He should never have doubted Andrew. A white woman, no matter how alluring, could never be equal to the Wangs.

"Oh, Dad," said Saina, "that might be the worst joke you've ever come up with." She sat down on the bed and held on to his hand. "Are you okay? What happened? Who is that guy in the red hat?"

"Where's Barbra? She is not coming?"

"She's coming. She just has to wait until Monday so that she can get her passport renewed — they wouldn't do it over the weekend."

"And your tickets? Not *tai guei*?" asked Charles.

Even now, it was strange to hear their father speak of money as something that might be lacking, as something to be careful of. "Nope. Grace stowed away in my luggage."

"Ha!" laughed Charles. "Gracie so small and so cute, she can be a stowaway anywhere!"

"Actually, we ended up doing it all on my frequent flier miles, so it was fine. And the gallery helped me expedite our visas," said Saina.

"Okay, okay. Andrew you leave that woman? Good boy. Almost everybody here now. Wang *jia* all together."

Andrew was standing at the foot of the bed. He could just barely see the back of the crazy guy's jacket as he moved around the adjoining space. "Dad, what's going on? Are you hurt?"

"I feel okay now."

Just then the man peered out from behind the divider, his cap askew, and addressed their father. "*Wang Gege! Lai tan tan hua la. Bu yao niang zi la.*"

"*Wo men mei you hua lai tan.*"

From behind the divider, they could hear another voice, arguing, and the man ducked back in.

"Dad, who *is* that creep?"

"Oh. It so long story, Gracie. Like *Lord of the Ring*. So long. Daddy just happy to see you all."

Saina examined her father. As much as she wanted to understand what was happening, he did look tired and worryingly pale, his skin slack against the parade of ducklings on his gown. "Do you need to rest? We can talk to the doctor. Or do you want some breakfast? Do they have *jou*?" He loved rice porridge. Even as a child, Saina had known that it was one of the only things her mother did that made him happy. When he came downstairs to a tableful of dark, rubbery thousand-year eggs, dried pork, and stinky cubes of chili-flecked tofu, a pot of thick rice porridge still bubbling on the stove, those were the only mornings he would sit down and eat with his wife instead of rushing off with a Pop-Tart or turning away a plate of scrambled eggs completely untouched.

Still in her father's arms, Grace pulled back. Saina couldn't possibly be suggesting that they all leave now and go check into a hotel somewhere, that they let their father continue to tell them nothing. Rebellion coursed through her, forcing her words out. "No! I don't care if you need to rest! And I don't care that you're in the hospital! You came and took me out of school and drove me all the way across country and dumped me at Saina's house and took off without explaining anything to me and now you're in a *hospital* in *China*? If you don't tell me, I'm going to get back in the car with Bing Bing and I'm going to make her drive me to the airport and I'm just going to go back home to L.A. and live on the *streets*."

Grace was being a little dramatic about it, but Andrew agreed. Now that they were, improbably, in this hospital room halfway across the world, the time for unspoken things seemed to be past.

When the three of them were together, they always acted a little bolder. Charles looked at his children. Grace, Andrew, Saina. Saina, Andrew, Grace. The three sides of his triangle. He could feel a pressure building in his bladder. Could Andrew help him to the bathroom? They all stared at him, waiting. The pressure continued to build and he felt panicked until he realized that he was attached to a catheter. Release. Relief.

"Oh, *hai zi,* very long story."

"Daddy, *please.*"

"You sit down here again," he said, patting the space Grace had just vacated. For once, she was agreeable and nestled herself in. "You know about World War II."

"Of course!"

"World War II, China also fighting the Japanese, and there are Communists —"

"Dad! We don't need a history lesson! Why are you in the hospital? Why are you even in China?"

"Everything a history lesson. Your life part of a history lesson. Meimei, listen. Okay. Wang family have so much land, *hao duo, hao duo di.* Your grandfather grow up, he manage land with his father, then there is war and many, many people die, but your family mostly are still alive. Wang *jia,* we support Chiang Kai-shek, Nationalist government, and soon they have to fight Communist, too. Communist worse than Japanese. Communist fight their own people, kill their own people, they hate *xue wen,* hate knowledge, culture. Chiang Kai-shek have to flee to Taiwan, many people go with him. Your grandma and grandpa go with him."

"What about our grandpa's father? What happened to him?"

"Killed. Some family *bei* kill, some family go to Taiwan, some family stay and become Communist." He pointed to the divider. "*Ta men* stay."

Andrew looked up. "Wait, so that guy really is our uncle? Like, a real uncle?"

"No," said Charles, dismissive. "Maybe like a cousin. But very far away. Not really Wang family. But listen, for a long time after the Communists take over, we don't know what happen in China. Everything closed. No communications. I grow up in Taiwan; I come to America. And then China open up and we find out everything so sad. I don't even tell you; nobody talk about it."

"What was it?"

"*Tai tsan ren le.* My aunties, they stay in *lao jia,* and when Communists come, they are dragged out in the street. You know *xiao hong wei bing?*"

"*Yes,* Dad. Little Red Guard, we know."

"Okay, *xiao hong wei bing* very scary, they abuse aunties, put them in parade, everybody hit and punch. They spit."

"That *happened?* To our relatives?"

"Everything happen."

A terrible thought made its way into Grace's head. "If you grew up in China, would you have been one of them? Would you have been a Little Red Guard?"

"Probably. Later on, no choice. Everyone have to be Communist. Okay, so you know I think maybe we can get back the land, all of Wang *jia de di*. There are some story, sometime, I hear of people who can live again in their old family house, or who can have some of land again, so I hire a lawyer to look, to see who own the land now. And lawyer contact the local council —"

"What's that?"

"China so big, even government can't be everywhere. So every town and district have a local council, still Communist, and now they control many thing. So the local council say there is an owner, and the owner is me!"

All three of his children lifted their heads at once and brightened. It broke Charles's heart to look at them, but he tried to laugh.

"Oh," said Saina, "it wasn't really you, right?"

"No. Not really me. I find out that it is him!" Charles pointed towards the divider so fiercely that one of the wires monitoring his vital signs, whatever those might be, came loose. He suctioned it back onto his chest.

When the email came, Saina thought that her father had slipped and fallen on an unfamiliar street or gotten into another car accident, but this was shaping up to be a very different story.

"Him? The weird guy in the red hat?"

"No, that is his son. *Him* is lying down because Daddy beat him up." They started to question him again, but he silenced them. "Listen. Okay, so I start thinking about the land in China because I know that last year China pass a law, pass in October, saying it okay for some private ownership."

"So whoever else is behind that curtain, he bought it?"

"No! He steal it and then he lose it. Listen, listen, so my father, your grandfather, have a friend, since they are very small boys —"

"And he's the guy behind the curtain?"

"No, no, quiet! I already tell you, this is a very long story. So my father have a very old friend, from Guang family, from when they were young. Very old friend. Good friend. The Wang family go to Taiwan, but his friend stay in China, and Communist send him to camp. But very hard camp, a work camp, not a fun camp like Camp Hess Kramer that you go to."

"Dad! You remember that?"

"Of course. You all so excited to go. So Guang was send to camp for fifteen years, and when he is in camp, he is force to change his mind and become Communist. And finally they let him go, and then he come back to same place where he grow up, and now they make him head of the local council because he is a good Communist. So then worst part happen. *Zwei bu ying gai de.*" Charles had been almost enjoying telling this tale, but the closer he got to the pivotal moment, the less he could pretend to himself that this was just a bit of old-world gossip. To have everything slip away, to have someone step into his story and disrupt it so completely, it was too much. He had weathered too much. *"Gong fei! Tsao ni ma de!"* he shouted. The old curses felt good, so much more satisfying than an insipid *fuck.*

"Qu si!" was lobbed back over the wall.

"Did you hear what he say? Andrew, you go in there and tell him he can't talk like that."

"Dad! I'm not going to go bully some guy who's in a hospital bed," said Andrew.

Grace jumped in. "I'll do it!"

Andrew huffed. "Just ignore him and tell us what happened already."

"No, no, no, Gracie. You stay. Okay, I tell you. So hear some story, sometimes, about family going back to old house, or maybe share land with *yi qian gen di de ren,* uh, with old peasant, old employee. So Daddy hire a lawyer to see if maybe I can do same thing. But we find out instead that he"— Charles pointed again, violently, at the divider wall —"pretend to be me. And everybody believe."

"What? What do you mean?"

"He *pretend* to be *me!* Me. He fool Guang, my father's friend, and make him think that he is me!" When Charles had first understood the full extent of his treacherous cousin's misdeeds, he'd thought that there would turn out to be some honorable explanation. It was not implausible to hope that the cousin was holding the property in Charles's name, so that he, the eldest son of the eldest son, could return and assume proper ownership. But as they'd spoken in the dingy, cigarette-smoke-filled office of the travel agency where his cousin, Wu Jong Fei — not even a Wang! — was employed, Charles had felt his anger expand and take shape in his chest until it had become a sentient thing that willed itself into shape with feathers and claws, a ripping, tearing beast no longer under his control. It wasn't just the betrayal. It was the man himself, who had stolen Charles's past and his future, who sat there in a thin, cheap shirt and didn't even attempt to conceal his misdeeds. He'd confessed it all without shame, and now Charles opened his mouth and spewed out the truth.

"Okay, I tell you the worst part. So he trick my father's friend and he pretend to be me. But why do you think he does this? Because he have some big plan for land? No! *This* is the very worst part. It is because he love to go gamble.

"Go gamble like doing drug to him. Every weekend he go with travel group to Macao, some special gambling group to go bet. Bet, bet, bet. All day long bet. He lose all his own money, so he need to go find more money. He look everywhere, *xiao zang lang,* like little cockroach, and then he get scared. So scared. He owe so much money that he don't know what will happen.

"The main person who give him gambling stake is big house builder, and so Wu Jong Fei he think, Okay, what do builder need most? Builder need land! So as soon as he hear about the law that pass last year that say that some private ownership of land is okay, he go to *lao* Guang and he show a newspaper article about my business to pretend that he have money, that he will build school, build good house, bring job to people in the town. *Lao* Guang believe him, because *lao* Guang will believe me. But instead he just give land to developer so he can have no debt and more money to gamble and now they build a whole ugly apartment city over Wang *jia de* land. *Wo men wan le. Mei le.*"

The force of their father's sorrow and anger flattened the Wang children. They listened to him rage, sinking farther into his pillows with every bitter word.

"It make you so angry," said Charles. "Angry to death."

A shard of fear pricked at Grace. "Not to *death,* Dad. But really, really angry."

And then the imposter, the man who ruined their father's hopes and dreams, the gambler and pretender, appeared on their side of the wall in a wheelchair, his foot propped up in a cast and his son, the crazy guy in the red hat, pushing him. The imposter was somewhere around their father's age, with a remarkably similar pair of aviator-style reading glasses. He looked straight at Grace and smiled.

"Xiao meimei hao piao liang."

Grace looked at her sister, and then at her brother and father. They were all frozen by the strangeness of the situation. What was wrong with that man? He'd stolen all of their land and then ridden out here on a wheelchair to say that she was pretty? Sometimes Grace hated being a girl.

Her father closed his eyes.

Andrew looked at the two unfamiliar men who had somehow become so entrenched in their family story. "Uh, *shushu, ni ying gai zou le.*" But the man didn't leave. He continued to look at Grace, and then at Saina, and then finally turned his milky eyes towards Andrew. *"Wang Da Qian shen le san ge hao hai zi. Ta yi jiao ni men jiou lai."*

Was this man jealous that he only had one child, and their father had three?

"Hao le ba," said the weird man, who Andrew realized was actually not much older than Saina. "O-kay, o-kay," he added, looking at them. A nurse with a clipboard came into the room and handed the man in the wheelchair a sheaf of papers and a pen. Without a glance, he passed the forms to his son and continued to stare at the three of them.

They waited there, all six of them, until the last of the forms was filled out.

"Should we say goodbye?" Grace whispered to Andrew.

"No!" said their father, opening his eyes. "He does not deserve you to talk to him."

Andrew was torn. The man was in a wheelchair, but he was like Professor X or something, just sitting there like a boss when he was the one who had messed everything up to begin with. Andrew felt like he should finish what his father had started and break the man's other leg, but instead he allowed them to wheel out of the room, that other father and that other son.

四十七

Helios, NY

BARBRA COULD HEAR their voices from the vestibule of the restaurant where a lonely pair of green rain boots sat under a battered painting of sailboats.

"There's nothing wrong with calling."

"But what do I say? I don't really have another explanation." It was Leo.

"I don't think you need to explain. I just think you need to tell her that you're invested in the relationship."

"Gay men are very smart about girls," said Barbra, peeking her head into the main dining room. "Leo, you should listen to your friend."

"Oh, I'm not gay," said Graham.

"He's just a hipster," said Leo.

What was a hipster? The term was vaguely familiar to her, buried somewhere between *beatnik* and *hippie,* but it wasn't important now. She pulled out the keys to Saina's house and placed them on the bar. "Here, Graham. Saina said I should leave these for you, and you would go water her garden."

"Oh yeah, okay. So are you off to China now? Did your passport get renewed?"

"Yes, I'm going to pick it up, and then I will fly to China." What was it that Saina had said? How strange it was that she'd ended up here, in a farmhouse in upstate New York? "You know, I never thought I would go there."

"Aren't you from there?"

"No, no, I grew up in Taiwan. Very different." She studied the restaurateur, who didn't seem at all offended that she'd thought he was a homo-sexual. "Why didn't *you* tell Saina?"

He blushed suddenly and raised his hands. "You gotta choose some loyalties in life, I guess." That was true, though she'd never thought that it was the sort of truth this ready-to-laugh young man would know. "Anyways," he said, "I think intent matters with lies, and I knew Leo wasn't trying to screw her over, he was just trying to keep it real."

"A lie does not sound very real."

"Yeah, okay, well, he was just trying not to get dumped."

Barbra had seen young people in L.A. with tattoos like this, their whole body covered like Saina's notebooks in high school, but she'd never had the chance to speak to one of them before. She tapped his forearm. "Is this pig your friend?"

Graham looked down and laughed. "They're all my friends," he said, pointing at the row of dancing vegetables on his other arm and the knife that loomed above them.

Saina's boyfriend had built a tiny bridge out of the discarded straw wrappers on the table, twisting them together until they had enough integrity to stand. "Leo," said Barbra, "I know what you should do."

He looked up. "What?"

"Go with me."

"What?"

"Yes."

"To China?"

"Why not? I've done the same thing."

"You mean if you were in this situation?"

"No, no, I already did the same thing. I came to America when Saina's mother died. I heard about it, and I knew I wanted to marry Charles, so I came. If I don't come, I don't have my life."

He looked lost. "I don't know, this really isn't the same thing, is it? She was . . . she was so *done* with me."

Barbra glanced down at her watch. If this boy couldn't recognize that you had to grab at life, there was nothing she could do about it. "Okay." She shrugged. "Then you stay here. But I think at least you should try."

"I don't know if I can intrude right now. It feels like a family thing."

She looked him straight in the eye. He wasn't as alluring as Grayson

— he didn't have that elusive thing that would make a girl disregard any failing — but he seemed like the kind of man that Charles would want his daughter to be with, someone kind and joyous, even if he was black. "A family thing. And you want to be like her family."

"Maybe you're right."

"I have a taxi outside."

"I might see you there."

He wasn't going to come, she knew. The people of the world could be divided into two groups: those who used all of their chances, and those who stood still through opportunity after opportunity, waiting for a moment that would never be perfect.

四十八

Gaofu, China

"GYM. NAS. TIC," said Bing Bing, returning to the car. "Like O. Lym. Pic."

They had been stopped on the wrong side of a blockade for ten minutes before she decided to get out and investigate. "There. Is. A show. Happening. Right. Now. It will take. A long. Time. For us. To go past. It." She passed back a crinkly plastic bag of candied winter melon, and they each took a stick of the pale-green sweet even though they were headed to a dinner of some sort.

A few years out of college, a friend of Saina's got a job teaching English in a small prefecture in Northern Japan. Her arrival had triggered an avalanche of invitations to official dinners and gatherings — she'd even been invited to a wedding. Other friends had told her about visits to their homelands and how they were always crowded with command performances, the immigrants expected to show up whenever they were summoned. And now here they were, going to some sort of a family dinner with family they had never met.

Andrew leaned his head against the window. He had always been aware, vaguely, that there were relatives in China, though he didn't know their ages and couldn't keep track of their names. If he'd known that he was going to meet them, he would have packed a little more carefully.

After the imposter and his son had left, the three of them spent the rest of the afternoon napping in turns on the vacated bed while nurses came in and out with pills and charts. Whoever woke up was immediately dealt into a never-ending game of hearts that their father, despite his grogginess, was winning.

Even though he had gotten into a fight, it wasn't a punch that put their father in the hospital. He insisted that the other man had barely managed to touch him. He swore that he'd been standing when the imposter's coworker had called the ambulance, but when the ambulance left, he'd somehow found himself on it, regaining consciousness on a gurney next to his sworn enemy. It turned out that he'd had a stroke, and when Saina spoke to the doctors, they said that he'd been having small strokes for months and that he needed to rest before he could be sent back to America.

They had tried to be angry that he never mentioned any health issues, but he'd refused to respond to their scolding, so instead they all rested together and had long, elliptical conversations with no beginning or end and watched the sun rise and fall over the elementary school next door, still deserted for summer vacation. Andrew thought that he'd finally tell his family about what happened with Dorrie, but no one asked. Instead, they'd dealt hand after hand and talked about lost nuclear warheads, their score sheet growing longer as they considered various claims on the New World — everyone knew that Columbus wasn't the first, but maybe Leif Eriksson wasn't either. It could have been an Irish monk named St. Brendan, and now there was a Chinese map that had emerged, a map Columbus might have used to navigate the globe. It could prove that the Chinese really were the first to explore every corner of the globe, or it could show that they'd gotten the world all wrong, leading that idiot Columbus to mistake his destination completely.

Charles talked about the land. How vast it was, and how green. He tried to explain what it had felt like before he knew anything, when, for a brief and glorious moment, the land belonged to him again. He showed them the old land deeds and explained the map; he pointed to the spots where their grandfather had laid his seal, and then he asked Grace to get his jacket from the closet, and he pulled out the jade chop, matching the underside to its imprint on the deed. None of them had ever seen it before, this relic from another life, and none of them would ever forget it. It was a block of carved jade as big as a pepper grinder; the top had a house on a mountain with soft sloping sides and a jagged peak and the bottom was slashed with their last name: 王.

Through it all, they listened as their father's heart propelled the jump-roping line, sending out a rhythmic *beep, ba-beep, beep, ba-beep, beep*.

And then it was almost evening, and their father declared, completely out of nowhere, that it was time for them to get ready because they had to represent him at a big dinner. "Listen, don't worry about eating, but don't eat any dehydrated mushroom, okay? Things from Chinese factories no good. So many chemical. Make sure you only eat fresh one!"

So now here they were, still in their grubby travel clothes, on their way to dinner with relatives that they'd never met. In the jangle of this unfamiliar homeland, with her father lying in a hospital bed, Grace felt raw and open again, the way she had right after the accident. She wanted to get back to that without anything horrible happening. She wanted to be a transparent eyeball like that Emerson poem, bright and full and receptive to everything.

"Gan bei! Da jia gan bei!" A man with an old-fashioned pompadour aimed a small porcelain teacup full of spirits down Andrew's throat and then clapped him on the back as he coughed. He'd had an infinite number of shots forced upon him since they'd walked through the bustling restaurant into this aggressively air-conditioned private banquet room. Now he and Grace were seated together, and Saina was sitting all the way across the room at another table full of red-faced men in business suits. *This was probably what it was like to be a celebrity,* Andrew thought, as the room swayed around him.

"I think I have to go to the bathroom," he whispered to Grace.

When Andrew rose, a doughy young man around his own age immediately popped up and followed him out. Silently, he pointed down a hallway to the bathrooms, and when Andrew emerged, he was waiting there with a warm towel, which he urged into Andrew's hands. There was an awkward moment when Andrew stood there with the used towel, but luckily a waiter swooped by just then and lobbed it onto his tray of dirty dishes.

"That was bananas," said Grace, when Andrew slid back into his seat.

"It was like you had a servant. I thought they were all supposed to be Communists."

"Dude waited outside the bathroom while I peed. It was *so* bananas. Wait, are Communists really not into servants? Someone must have driven Mao around."

"You're the one who's in college — you should know."

"Oh, yeah, well, I just wear a Che Guevara T-shirt. It doesn't mean that I know anything about actual Communists."

Someone dinged on a glass, and a man at the table next to theirs rose as waiters came in with yet another course.

Andrew leaned over. "Let's bet. Do you think he's going to lead with how hardworking and decent the farmers or fishermen or whatever are, or do you think he's going to go with how he's pioneering an untapped commodities market?"

"Neither. I think it's going to be more of a, like, 'I'm so flattered you're all here to taste the humble foods of my region,'" said Grace. Could she find something beautiful about these men who seemed so obsessed with the things they could grow or kill? She would try.

"I don't know, that guy doesn't look too humble to me."

It had gradually dawned on Andrew and Grace that this wasn't some sort of family reunion after all — in fact, it seemed to be a banquet for the local agricultural bureau, which was headed up by some distant relative of theirs who had caught wind of their father's arrival and insisted that his children represent him at this dinner. At least that meant their Chinese family wasn't made up entirely of middle-aged guys in business suits with big shoulder pads, and it made a little more sense that their father had called out as they'd left his hospital room: "You take Daddy's place, you are the Papa Wang!"

Across the hall, Grace laughed as Andrew whispered something to her. It looked to Saina like they'd both stopped eating somewhere around the seventh course, which turned out to be a platter full of stewed chicken testicles. Their plates were piled with tidbits from all the subsequent dishes, which their tablemates insisted on serving them — the overflow was ignored, somehow, by the servers who whisked in with a score of new plates between every course, picking up the old ones and depositing them on a waiting tray. By the time the meal reached its halfway point, the tablecloth beneath Saina was smeared with the remains of a dozen courses that she'd dutifully consumed, but the plate in front of her was once again brand-new.

The unrelenting backslapping and good cheer in the room made it hard to concentrate on the man next to her as he bragged about his daughter, who was a brilliant pianist and wanted to go to Juilliard, and maybe Saina, whom he'd heard was an artist of some renown, might be able to make the necessary introductions? She should come to his house and listen to his daughter play for herself! And when she was there, maybe she could make them a painting, ha ha ha, that they would hang in their offices? She could paint all the beautiful things that this land produced! And maybe she knew people in America, she must know so many people in America since she was such an accomplished and respected young woman, maybe she knew someone in America who would want to open up a new market for sea urchin or small turtles, such delicacies, if only they were aware! Or did she instead have things that she could sell? Real estate in America was so cheap now, they'd all heard, and maybe she knew a reputable real estate agent, someone who wouldn't cheat him — Not a Jew, ha ha ha, or maybe a Jew was better! Ha ha ha — who would point him towards a good investment property because he knew somebody who had tripled his cash on a condo in Las Vegas in just nine months!

These men wanted to consume everything. By the time they'd reached the fourteenth course, turtle soup, Saina wouldn't have been shocked if they'd seasoned her with a dash of white pepper and eaten her. These men didn't pluck politely from the small dishes set out before them — they picked up those dishes and shoveled the contents into their mouths, never able to get enough in a single bite. They gulped up each other's talk in the same way, loud and eager, quick to rage and quicker to laugh. They wanted to dig into the ground and pull out all the roots, trawl the seas and scoop up anything formed of flesh, search the forests and the fields, and snatch creatures out of their burrows and knock birds down from their perches so that they could be plucked and skinned and seasoned and diced and trussed and steamed and broiled and roasted and stir-fried and served up at banquets designed to demonstrate the abundance of the land and their dominance over it.

Bizz-buzz. Bizz-buzz. Bizz-buzz. It took several rings before Saina realized that the odd noise breaking through the hum of Communist bonhomie was her own phone, which had somehow acquired a foreign accent. Heart slamming against her chest, she pulled it out, looked at the caller ID, and without letting herself think, stabbed at the green button.

"Hold on," she said into the receiver, as she rose and walked double-time along the perimeter of the room, thankful that enough rounds of toasts had been drunk that her hosts were more focused on each other than on the Wangs. Dodging a waiter carrying yet another bottle of *gao liang,* she slipped out the door and leaned against a wall papered in a pink moiré.

"Hi."

On the other side, Leo was silent.

"Um, hello?"

"Saina. Saina! I can't believe you picked up. I rehearsed a message, but I didn't really think about what to say if you actually picked up."

"Well, you'd better say something."

"Hi."

"Hi."

"Tell me about your dad first. Is he okay? Did he tell you what was going on?"

"Yeah — it's too long to get into right now. He seems a little wrecked, but physically, at least, I think he's okay. Or he'll be okay."

"Oh, that's a relief. I'm glad. I'm really glad. Saina . . . "

"Yes?"

"I want to make this right with you."

"I . . . how?"

For a long minute, Leo was silent.

"You know, that first day we met, at Graham's place, initially I thought you were just some pretty girl."

She laughed. "This is a weird way to apologize to someone."

"Listen, okay, and then we hung out there that whole afternoon, and after a while, you just, you started to feel so *familiar* to me. So often you meet people and they're just cartoons. They might be entertaining or attractive, they might even be brilliant, but they don't feel fully *human*. And that's the only way I can explain it. From the very beginning, you just felt familiar. Like home."

Waiters in colored vests whizzed past, balancing trays crowded with heavy white platters. A lobster, shell cracked open, meat chopped and sautéed, then reassembled so that it waved two crimson claws in the air; a mound of some fowl shingled with carrot slices carved like feathers; a parade of beasts she'd never dreamed of consuming. The whole menagerie of them now swam uneasily in her stomach.

She felt a soft, damp spot in her heart begin to open up. "Oh Leo. I know."

"Like we were both people trying to figure out how to really *be* in the world."

"Yeah. Yeah. We are that. We are people like that."

"We're the same kind of animal."

They were quiet for a moment, and then Leo asked, "Do you think you're going to come back to Helios?"

"Well, I kind of live there now."

"Do you . . . well . . . what if we lived together?"

"Oh. What? No. I don't know if that's a very good idea." *Was Leo actually crazy?*

"Look, I know what I did was a real betrayal, and I am really, deeply sorry. And I, Saina, I'm not just sorry to you, I'm also sorry to Kaya, you know. She deserves so much more than that. It was wrong of me not to hold her out as the most important thing. Look, I'm a beginner soul still. I get a lot of stuff wrong, but I care about getting it right. With you."

Saina closed her eyes and knocked her head back against the wall. She could hear the sizzle and clang of the kitchen, the cooks shouting at each other as they sped through the dinner service, could smell the garlic and oil coming together.

A heat traveled through her hand from the back of her phone, probably irradiating her bones.

She sensed the desperation in his voice, and it scared her.

"Leo, I feel like I should break up with you, but I don't want to."

"Then don't! Baby, that's crazy. Don't. Just come back, and I'll show you how much I mean it, okay? I can ... oh, I want to. I'll show you." They were quiet for a moment. "Is it ... are you offended that I said that we should live together instead of asking you to marry me?"

"No! No. No, no, no. That's not what I want right now. Everything's crazy with my family, I have to figure out if I even have a career anymore. I just don't know if I want to be that for anybody. I don't want to have the kind of insane relationship where you would not see your daughter because of me."

"Saina! Is that what you think?"

"That's what I'm scared of."

"No. I can't stress that enough. It is amazing how much I would do for you, considering how briefly we've known each other, but you are not the reason why I haven't seen her. I would never do that. You're the reason I haven't talked about her, at least to you, but I haven't seen her because Leah really is a difficult person."

"Leah and Leo?"

"I know."

"I don't understand why you didn't just tell me."

"Honestly, Saina, I don't get it either. It's all I've been thinking about and I don't have any answers yet. Fear, probably. I didn't want to lose either of you. I still don't."

"I didn't realize that I came across as some horrible person who would refuse to date a man with a child."

"Not everyone wants to be a stepmother. But, listen, it wasn't just that. Okay, this ... god, I'm embarrassed to even say this."

"What?"

"I think part of me didn't want to come across as that guy, you know?"

"What guy?"

"Saina."

"What?"

"You know, that guy. The black guy who's a deadbeat dad. With a baby mama in every town."

"Are you serious? Why would I even think that? You're an organic farmer!"

"Okay, that's not the only thing. I think I was also afraid, and to be honest, I still am, afraid —"

"Of what?"

"That you'll convince me to sue for visitation or something and I'll lose her forever. Leah's family is in Quebec. If I piss her off, she could take Kaya up there and hide out from me."

"You could have explained that to me!"

"I know."

"Leo, you are so good, and so generous, and so caring, but I think that sometimes you don't want to let anyone else be those things." She waited. She listened to him breath and think. She willed herself not to speak in the long silence that followed, but in the end, she broke down. "Hey, so is your daughter the reason why you shut down when we were in the car before the Bard graduation thing?"

"You noticed that? Of course you did. Yeah. It didn't seem like the best time to bring it up."

"But you wanted to."

"I did."

"I thought you were just freaked-out that I talked about babies."

"Oh no, no. I wasn't. I wasn't even thinking about that."

"Do you know what I was thinking about?"

"Hmm?"

"How you lost your birth mom's picture. How you didn't know what your family looked like. And that if you had a baby, maybe you would."

"Oh, Saina. Come home, will you?"

"Is Helios home?"

"No, but I am."

"Leo."

"I am. And you are."

She was quiet until it felt like she'd been quiet for too long, and then, "Okay."

"Yeah?"
"Yeah."

After Saina hung up the phone, she stood in the hallway for a moment with her eyes closed. It was comforting being in the midst of such a din, becoming invisible in a way she realized she never had in America.

Had she just un-broken-up with Leo? She had. She had. It meant that she would meet Kaya and accept that someone else had already done the good work of anchoring him in the world. *Was that okay?* It would have to be, at least for now.

Without even realizing it, Saina was smiling to herself. If she walked back into the banquet room now, Andrew and Grace would definitely know that something had happened. Stalling, she scanned her emails. There was a new message from Xio, the curator who had written to her months before, asking her to propose a project for the new Beijing Biennial.

Dear,Saina,

How are you?I know we already try,to inquire if you are interested?Although I do not hear you back,now I try for second time,because,we have a confirmed artist from Israel who have many visa problems,so he cannot participate any more.Perhaps I askasecond time and have a better reply?I hope so!We think this is a verygood opportunity.This is not nonsense just to promote friendship,to give opportunity for banquet.It isofficial Biennial.We work with top museum in many country: Dubai,Russia,Portugal,Uruguay,and more.

Addendum:Please excuse my poor English!My assistant is not here today so I write for myself!

Hope stabbed at her. She hit reply and wrote:

Xio —

So lovely to hear from you again, and big apologies for not getting back to you much sooner! Believe it or not, I am actually in China right now, not far from Beijing, and would love to set up a time to meet and discuss possibilities! Are you free this week?

Send.

And then, without letting herself think about it, she pulled up Grayson's email and hit reply. Typing quickly, she wrote:

I can't love you anymore.

Send.

Saina was still standing in the hallway, knowing that she had stayed away long enough to be noticed, when Bing Bing grabbed her hand.

"It. Is. Time to. Go. The hos. Pital. Call. They. Say to. Come. Now."

四十九

THEY WERE running blind through the long hospital corridors, past the ward of wounded, past the newborn babes, Bing Bing bringing up the rear carrying, of all things, a thermos printed with an image of Barney the dinosaur. It was nighttime again. In each of their three hearts was pure panic. Pulses stampeding, they approached the door to their father's room just as a doctor was walking out. He looked up at them, weary.

"You're Mr. Wang's children?" he asked, in Mandarin.

They nodded. "What's happening?" asked Saina.

"He had another small stroke. We've stabilized him and we're monitoring his vitals. We've given him some medication so he may be —"

Grace cut in. "But what does that mean?"

Andrew looked through the window into his father's room. His stepmother had arrived. She was lying on top of the covers, her body folded around his father's, their hands entwined, the tips of her stockinged feet touching his, a pair of dumplings wound in hospital sheets. They looked beautiful like that, his shrinking parents, lying nose to nose. A sudden fear raced through him, and he pulled Grace by the arm. "Let's talk to the doctor later, come on," he urged.

Their father and Barbra both looked up. "Ah, Andrew will know. Who is the Viking?"

"Dad, what are you talking about?"

"He is very confused," said Barbra, clutching his hand tighter, her eyes not leaving his face. "He was okay, but now he keeps asking about the Viking."

Andrew knelt by the side of the bed. "Dad, do you mean Leif Eriksson?"

Charles beamed. "Yes! Very smart boy. Always very smart, very good. But everybody wrong, they are not the ones who discover America. Not Vikings. Not Christopher Columbus. He discover nothing!"

"Okay, Dad." What was happening? It was like his father was drunk.

"Je chuang je me ne me chou? Shei gei wo mai yi ge chou de chwang?"

"Hou le la," soothed Barbra.

"Dad. Baba." Grace crouched uncertainly at the foot of the bed. She wanted to crawl onto the mattress, but there wasn't any more room.

"Grace, Meimei." Charles looked at his daughter. "You are very smart, too. You know that love too much is okay. That is the best thing in life. Love too much." Charles looked up as Saina came into the room. "Jiejie!" There was something he had to tell her; there were things he had to make sure all of his children knew. "Sai-*na*. My beauty. Oh yes." *No. That wasn't it.* The words weren't traveling correctly between his heart and his head.

"I should get the doctor back," said Saina. The five of them fit into such a small space. She squeezed in closer. "Should I?"

No one answered.

"Dad, you're acting kind of weird. Is it the medication? Do you feel okay?" asked Andrew.

There it was. It wasn't advice; it was gratitude. "Thank you for giving me a good life," said Charles, to his children, to his wife whom he had known since she was almost a child. "A beautiful life." It was becoming harder to focus, and even as his body lay calmly on the bed, his mind skipped frantically above, trying to keep its grasp on the moment. He looked at them, each one of them, locking eyes, and felt a sudden panic. "Daddy doesn't want to die. Life is too much fun! Always new thing in life!"

Barbra looked at him, tortured. Grace wailed and Andrew put his arms around them all, pleading with his father, "Don't die. Don't die. Just don't! Don't do it." Saina got up and ran into the hallway, calling out for the doctor.

Something serious was happening. She was so scared, his daughter.

He had always wondered what would happen after death, and now he would find out. What if death was just a perpetual state of dying? A never-ending fall into a blank forever?

The children. Saina, Andrew, Grace. His wife. Barbra. Their lives unfurled in all directions, skipping out from his hospital bed like pebbles across a lake, all magic and light, bouncing from water to air and back again as he sank under the cold, cold surface. Cold in here. Too many blankets. He must say something to them. Why had they put him in such an ugly bed?

There were other things that he knew. The Indians were just a tribe of early Chinese people who took a long walk across the Bering Land Bridge and ended up in a New World. The true Americans were Chinese! It was too bad it had taken him so long to remember that.

Charles struggled to hold on to the receding world, to the knowledge that his loves, the four of them, were all around.

Love burned bright white in him.

A glow, aglow.

The world began to slip from his grasp.

Earthquakes. Floods. Infidelity. Betrayal. Failure. The fields burn and the next harvest is assured. The world destroys itself and we rebuild it. The destroying is as important as the rebuilding. There can be as much joy in the destruction as the rebirth.

Three. He had three children, blue, green, yellow, each one a pulsing thing.

A glow, aglow.

He had Barbra, another heart outside his own heart. Red.

A glow, aglow.

They still lived. They leaned in over him now and pressed their bodies against his, warm living things. They talked, but he couldn't hear their words, couldn't understand what there was to say even though he remembered, still, that words were important to alive people.

His heart was in his skull now. Somehow the hospital had switched the two organs, so that his brain pulsed in his chest and his heart beamed in his head, controlling everything, sending signals out to the rest of his earthbound self. All his life his heart had been trying to get up there, to take its true place at the top of his body, and now it was to have only the briefest of reigns.

The only logical solution was just to do everything while you were alive. He had done so much. Yes! He had discovered an entire land. Yes!

America was his. Yes! The whole green land! Yes! China had always been his, and now he had America, too!

The heart thought and the head beat. *Boom, boom!* Yes, yes!

Charles Wang feels something brush against his face.

Something hard and bright.

The same brightness that started in his heart and traveled down to his brain. He's about to let it overtake him when he thinks the best thought again: He has discovered an entire land! He can knock down the world and discover it anew!

Charles's eyes fly open and he sees his children and his love, the entire spectrum of light, arrayed in front of him. They peer down at him and he sees nothing but love love love in their eyes, love that pings out to the heart in his head. Their eyes widen and all his infinite selves are contained within those glistening dark globes.

A doctor in a white coat appears now behind them.

Now, he has to speak now, before there are machines and medicines that put everything back in its place. He has to rebuild himself before the doctor does it for him.

His thoughts are lucid, but it is a struggle to form the words and force them out. They push against each other, each word a fat and slippery thing, until only the important ones remain. And then, finally, the three words he most wants to say wriggle their way through the net and land at the feet of his waiting family.

As Grace and Barbra weep and Andrew clutches his hand and Saina gestures at the doctor to hurry, he smiles at them and watches their faces bloom with relief. He smiles again and pings back their love as hard as he can while also focusing on speaking the truth that he has known for so long, the truth that will make the whole world theirs.

"Daddy discovered America!"

He leans back, triumphant, exhausted. Later, they will learn how to rule the New World but for now, this is enough. This is everything.

Acknowledgments

THANK YOU . . .

To Marc Gerald, for seeing the future from the very first page.

To Sasha Raskin for sending the Wangs abroad with such aplomb; Kim Koba and Jaime Chu for keeping them brilliantly on track; and Juliet Mushens for saying the words that won me over.

To Helen Atsma, for being such a perfect combination of wise, insightful, funny, understanding, and very, very cool and for making this a much better book. And also to Taryn Roeder, Liz Anderson, and Lori Glazer for your PR and marketing genius; David Hough, for your kind attention; Larry Cooper, for taking this to the finish line; and Naomi Gibbs for all your help along the way. But, really, to everyone at HMH — especially Lauren Wein and Bruce Nichols — for your love of the Wangs.

To Jennifer Lambert and Juliet Annan, for your early enthusiasm, your editing expertise, and for bringing the Wangs to Canada and the UK.

To my first, best readers: Krystal Chang, Keshni Kashyap, Bill Langworthy, Lauren Rubin, Lauren Strasnick, and Margaret Wappler for pointing out my crucial mistakes in the most helpful of ways. I never would have found my way home without the six of you. And also to Akira Bryson, Christy Nichols, Steph Cha, Eric Lin, Charles Yu, and Amanda Yates Garcia for reading later versions and answering my many questions. I am really lucky to be surrounded by so many fellow writers and artists, who do such good and true work.

To my many friends who always believed — with little proof or evidence — that I was working on something worthwhile, for your buoying presence.

To Dave Makharadze for helping me figure out how to bankrupt the

Wangs; to my workshop at Squaw Valley in 2010 — especially stalwart leader Geoff Shandler — for being the first to get behind Charles Wang; to the fine people of Writ Large Press for ninety days of insanity and, along with Binders, giving these pages their first stage; to Elizabeth Chandler, for giving me a place to land; and to Jack Erdie for the spark.

To Margaret, again, for so many long days and nights eating bad sandwiches over laptops. There's just no way I would have written all these pages without you working right across the table. We finished our books!

To my sister, Krystal, for sharing a love of the food parts of books and a very singular childhood.

And always and most of all to my parents, endlessly loving and supportive, who didn't just come to America for opportunity — they came for adventure, and they found it.

Additional Thanks

I wish that I'd kept a log of all my book-related Google searches. In some alternate literary universe, the countless online words that I read on everything from the life of Madame Louis Lévêque — a celebrated French writer once engaged to Antoine de Saint-Exupéry and now memorialized in the breed of roses that line the Wangs' Bel-Air driveway — to the destruction of the hutongs in Beijing would become a kind of navigable undercurrent to this book. A sincere thank-you to the many people who contribute to our virtual store of knowledge — the Internet is not just cat videos!

I owe more specific gratitude to the work of John Lanchester, Felix Salmon, and Matt Taibbi, journalists who covered the madness of 2008 with great intelligence, clarity, and depth. Felix Salmon's February 2009 *Wired* cover, "Recipe for Disaster: The Formula That Killed Wall Street," was instrumental in helping me understand the role of David X. Li and the Gaussian copula. The version of the formula Professor Kalchefsky writes on the board comes from this article, but differs from the exact formula used by Wall Street.

The lines that Charles thinks about in chapter 十五 — "Companies fail the way Ernest Hemingway wrote about going broke. Gradually, and then suddenly" — come from a May 2002 *Fortune* story by Ram Charan and Jerry Useem, "Why Companies Fail." That line seemed perfect and true when I read it in the long wake of the first dot-com bubble and bust, and I've remembered it ever since.

Finally, the horoscope that opens chapter 二 is from an actual horoscope by Holiday Mathis that ran in the *Los Angeles Times* on July 13, 2007. It was, of course, originally written for my sign.